AMY MYERS was born in Kent, where she still lives, although she has now ventured to the far side of the Medway. For many years a director of a London publishing company, she is now a full-time writer. Married to an American, she lived for some years in Paris, where, surrounded by food, she first dreamed up her Victorian chef detective Auguste Didier. Currently she is writing her contemporary crime series starring Jack Colby, car detective, and in between his adventures continuing her Marsh & Daughter series and her Victorian chimnney sweep Tom Wasp novels.

By Amy Myers

Summer's End

AMY MYERS

Allison & Busby Limited
12 Fitzroy Mews
London W1T 6DW
allisonandbusby.com

Hardback and paperback editions published in Great Britain as *The Last Summer* in 1996 under the pseudonym ALICE CARR. This paperback edition published by Allison & Busby in 2015.

A CIP catalogue record for this book is available from the British Library.

10 9 8 7 6 5 4 3 2 1

ISBN 978-0-7490-1916-7

Typeset in 10.55/15.55 pt Sabon by Allison & Busby Ltd.

The paper used for this Allison & Busby publication has been produced from trees that have been legally sourced from well-managed and credibly certified forests.

Printed and bound by
CPI Group (UK) Ltd, Croydon, CR0 4YY

For Audrey with gratitude and love

Prologue

'*Tom, Tom*, the Piper's son . . .'

The Austin's engine chugged rather than sang as it tackled the shallow incline past Tillow Hill, a cloud of dust billowing behind to mark its passage. Always the son, never the daughter, Tilly thought bitterly.

'Stole the pig and away she run . . .'

Run? She'd *marched* out. Families should shelter, not judge, surely? There'd been no haven for wounded chicks at *her* home, though – not unless she betrayed everything she believed in. Yet what, ironically, was she doing now? Why, motoring straight towards another family, her brother Laurence's. Life at the Rectory was different, however, Ashden was different, and they sang to her a siren song.

'Over the hills and far away . . .' In the mildness of the Sussex air, it would be all too easy to abandon the fight, and let England drowse on. But she couldn't, and someday

7

soon she would be forced to leave even Ashden.

As the Austin motored over the brow of the hill, she glimpsed Lovel's Mill and now the first tentative leaves of Gowks Wood, the cuckoos' wood. It was early April and Ashden's children would be listening eagerly for the sound of the first cuckoo, just as Laurence's brood used to when they were younger. Caroline her favourite, Isabel, Felicia, Phoebe and nephew George. Well, my pretty darlings, here comes your cuckoo! Tilly laughed, but soon stopped, for it hurt to do so, and, besides, there was no humour left in her.

She turned the wheel of the tourer to round the bend, and the wind caught her face, attacking even the secure moorings of her black toque, and assailing her dustcoat. It exhilarated her. Something was thudding as loud as the engine, her heart perhaps, if she still had one. Then the wind was breeze, and before her was the rose-red warmth of Ashden.

From Stumbly Bottom, wild daffodils and primroses sang of spring, trumpeting her arrival, but the woman did not need trumpets. Already, perhaps, she had been over-daring, by choosing to drive here by motor car. Call it her gesture, her snook at disapproving Society. Ashden, she thought with a touch of impatience, could call it anything it dashed well chose. She had promised her brother to abide by Ashden's rules while she was here, both in the Rectory and in the village, and that meant slipping back into the role she had filled at home – no, not home any more, at Dover: dutiful, all fires damped down, and waiting.

Such had been the pace of events in her life recently, however, that it was nearly two years since her last visit to

Ashden, and the village unfolded itself in one panoramic swoop as memory's clutch released its hold. Bankside, rising from the Withyham road to red-brick cottages, the ugly Village Institute, the proudly white Norville Arms, and beyond it Nanny Oates' cottage. She must go to see Nanny tomorrow; she'd be expected of course, Tilly realised with pleasure. Over to the left was St Nicholas, Laurence's church, and beyond it the village high street. Wasn't that a new sign? Teas! Who for, she wondered. Outside boys were playing, spilling all over the roadway. Marbles? Of course, in readiness for the great Marble Day of Good Friday in a few days' time. A girl was bowling a hoop, pinafore skirts flying. Wryly, Tilly noted that she, who believed so fiercely that England needed change, was already being seduced by a scene that was yesterday, today – and, if she knew Ashden, had every intention of being tomorrow.

People were looking up. Surely now, in 1914, motor cars were not so unusual even on this remote Sussex road? Motor cars were the future, however, even Ashden must see that. She was glad that in a spirit of bravado she had kept the top down, for this, the Austin's first outing since its winter lay-up.

Taking a deep breath, she gripped the wheel to turn in to the familiar driveway. Who would come racing out to greet her? Anyone? She gave a defiant toot on the hooter as she swept around the garden, its grass still sheltering the countless daffodils and tiny blue scillas that dotted it in clumps under the trees.

Somewhere a dog barked, her tyres crunched on the gravel, still muddy from the March rain. Loving mud they called it in Sussex, because it held so fast to you. Like Sussex itself in the mind and in the heart. Somewhere a door slammed, girls' voices were raised in laughter, sounds distanced by her own memories. She had driven over the hills and far away, and now 'far away' was *here*.

The smell of the rich earth brought out by the spring sun caught her with a rush of emotion for the timeless England she both loved and resented. The late afternoon sun mellowed the red brick of the rambling Rectory, and the front door was opening.

Chapter One

The Rectory shook itself awake. Outside the red bricks were already brightening in the early morning light. Inside, still dark, the house waited expectantly as the first feet clattered down the servants' stairs. Soon the shutters would be flung open, letting the new day into the Rectory's cheerfully cluttered rooms. In the kitchen a print-gowned backside swayed vigorously as its owner attacked the kitchen range with black-lead, and another was soon at work in the dining room with cinder pail, black-lead, broom, and tea leaves to strew on the carpet for easier sweeping. Any moment now the descent of a superior being would herald the turning of the key in the clock of the Rectory's daily life: the cook–housekeeper Mrs Dibble was never late.

Upstairs in her small room on the second floor Agnes Pilbeam yawned. It was six o'clock and it was her privilege as parlour maid to enjoy another thirty minutes in bed. She was no longer a mere housemaid like that dratted Harriet, but almost old Dribble Dibble's equal. Any moment now, Mrs Dibble would, she guessed, be strutting round 'her' kitchen, superintending Myrtle, the new tweeny, like a sergeant-major as she prepared breakfast for the servants and later for the family. She debated whether the moral advantage of keeping even with Mrs D. by forgoing her precious lie-in was worth it, and decided it wasn't – especially on Easter Day. High up in her small room on the second floor, she felt as far away from grates and bed-making as the birds singing their spring song in the waving branches of the tall larch tree outside her window. They must think a good day lay ahead – and they were right. It was her half day off.

'Water, Miss Pilbeam.'

The raucous shout was unnecessary. The thump outside the door would have told her that Myrtle had plonked down her jug of hot water. Agnes sighed, forced to contemplate the tasks ahead before she met her Jamie this afternoon. Dribble Dibble was all too adept at nabbing the tweeny during the times when she should properly be assigned to house cleaning. Not if Agnes Pilbeam had anything to do with it she wouldn't. With sudden resolution she swung her feet to the floor on to the old Wilton carpet – it was threadbare, but nevertheless *carpet,* which was more than Rosie Trott got at the Manor. That reminded her what was unusual about today. Those Swinford-Brownes were coming to luncheon, instead of the Squire. Yet the Hunney family *always* came to the Rectory on Easter Day. She supposed it would not affect her, except in so far as everything that went on in the

Rectory mattered to her; it almost intoxicated her, in fact, and had right from the moment she'd nervously asked Mrs Lilley what her wages might be.

'Tuppence a week and jam every other day,' had been the alarming answer. It had been Miss Caroline who had explained it was just a joke, a quotation from some book, and the wages were sixteen pounds a year. Then she'd lent her the book, not even asking if she could read. From then on, she felt part of the family. She never let it show, but within herself, she laughed when they laughed, grieved when they grieved and stomped around bad-humouredly when there was stormy weather. And that was inevitable from time to time, what with the Rector and Mrs Lilley, the four girls, young Master George, and now Miss Tilly, the Rector's sister, come to stay.

Often Agnes played silent umpire when these thunderclouds appeared: 'Miss Isabel, you're being downright bossy'; 'Miss Caroline, don't you let your ma leave everything to you'; 'Miss Felicia, stand up for yourself'; 'Miss Phoebe, remember you're a young lady now'; 'Mr George, don't you cheek your father'; and above all, 'Mrs Lilley, don't let them get away with it!' – by them she meant old Dibble, Percy Dibble, and that Harriet (Agnes's own thorn in the flesh), as well as Mrs Lilley's family.

Or did Mrs Lilley let them get away with it? Agnes reconsidered this as she hopped on one foot struggling with a recalcitrant black stocking. Now she came to think of it, no one did get away with much in the Rectory. For all Mrs L. never seemed to get involved in quarrels, either in her family or in the servants' hall (and what a silly name that was for the converted apple storeroom allotted to them at the back of the house, comfy though it was), everything usually turned out the way Mrs Lilley wanted. Luck, Agnes supposed vaguely.

The Rectory was large; even with seven family, plus six live-in staff (if you could call poor Fred Dibble staff), they rattled around like old peas in a pod. Somehow, however, the only time it *seemed* large was when the girls and Master George went to Dover once a year to visit the Reverend's mother, the Countess of Buckford. Then she missed the laughs, the cries of horror or disgust, the constant noise. To Agnes, the only child of elderly parents, coming to the Rectory (even though that had meant only a half mile walk down Silly Lane from the cottage she'd lived in with her parents) was like being thrust into a pen at market, deafened by moo's and baa's. She wasn't sure she liked it at first, but once she got used to it, it made her feel safe. And *that* made her think of Jamie again – his warm arms round her and the way it made her feel.

'Agnes Pilbeam, you should be ashamed of yourself,' she informed her reflection in the oval mirror, before slipping her blue print gown over her head, automatically tugging at those dratted garment shields. No afternoon black for her today, she rejoiced. She'd be wearing her Sunday best, her new pink linen costume with a wrap-over skirt, not to mention underneath. Daringly she was going to wear the nainsook camisole and knickers she'd bought in Weekes' in Tunbridge Wells. Her mother would be shocked; if she had her way her daughter would be in cotton bloomers and neck-to-knee whalebone for the rest of her life. But times were changing – because of Jamie Thorn. She'd never let him see how she felt about him, of course; that wouldn't be proper. Any more than she'd let the family see how much being at the Rectory meant to her. It was better that way. She remembered hearing years ago: 'The Royal Sussex is going away, leaving the girls in the family way.' What did it mean, she asked her mother, only to receive the sharp reply, 'It means keeping yourself to yourself, gal.'

So she had.

Talking of families, she remembered she'd promised to clean Miss Caroline's blue felt hat, the one messed by the jackdaw last week. Miss Caroline had joked that the feather must have annoyed the bird on behalf of his fellows, and made her smile. Strictly speaking, it was Harriet's job as housemaid, but Agnes was known to have a way with stains. Anyway, it was always a pleasure to do something for Miss Caroline. Secretly, she was her favourite – perhaps it was because of her brown curls, and her quick, light way of moving, so different to Agnes's own dull straight lumps of hair, and deliberate steps. She twisted the offending locks up into the usual bun, glad she'd given them a rosemary rinse when she washed them. Jamie seemed to like her hair, she couldn't think why. She'd do that old hat straight away to be ready for church. For her, Miss Caroline was the centre of the Rectory whirlpool, and if a mix of lime and pearl-ash could help her, then Agnes was only too willing to dab it on.

'Caroline!'

The door of her room crashed open, and defensively Caroline burrowed down under the bedclothes. Pointless, of course, since if Isabel had a crisis she would rampage through the household until it was solved. Why pick on her first, though, on Easter Day of all times? She peered out cautiously to see Isabel posed behind her bedroom door, a Second Mrs Tanqueray, tragedy writ large on her face. Unfortunately her fair curls and English rose complexion, plus her carelessly tied dressing gown revealing dancing corset, bodice and pink tango knickers, made this a difficult role to sustain.

'Despair!' Isabel continued.

'Don't tell me,' Caroline muttered. 'You've torn a button off your glove.'

'Worse. Truly. I've lost my silver buckle.'

'But that was Grandma Overton's.' In her shock Caroline sat bolt upright.

'I know. Isn't it a nuisance?' Isabel sighed. 'But you do see I simply must have a special buckle. Could I borrow the jet?'

'Why *must* you?'

'I simply must, that's all. I want to look my best. You do see?' She opened grey-blue eyes earnestly.

'Just because the Swinford-Brownes are coming to luncheon, I suppose?' Caroline came back to the heart of the grievance. It was Easter Day, and for some unknown reason for luncheon this year the Hunneys had been superseded by the ghastly Swinford-Brownes.

The Rectory living was in the gift of Sir John Hunney as lord of Ashden Manor, although neighbouring parishes were held direct in the Diocese of Chichester, so surely this meant that close links should be maintained between the two houses? Caroline had always thought of Ashden

Manor as a second home, since she and Isabel had shared a governess with the three children of the Manor, Reginald, Daniel and Eleanor. Felicia, Phoebe and George, being younger, had been drawn into the family by a kind of osmosis.

So why was everything to be different today? George was furious because Reggie and Daniel provided a rare ration of menfolk among the monstrous regiment of women he lived with and Felicia upset because she, as Caroline, liked tradition. Only Phoebe was not too perturbed, probably because she could poke fun at some new victims, her sister thought indulgently.

Caroline realised that Isabel was getting her own way as usual over the jet, but, if she refused to produce it, the large eyes would fill with unshed tears and Isabel would depart in silent bravery to tell Mother all about it. As usual, her sense of proportion came to her aid.

'All right. But be *careful*.' Despite her porcelain looks, Isabel was renowned for her clumsiness, and jet was fragile.

Isabel jumped up and planted a kiss on her sister's forehead. 'You're a dear. I knew you would.' She skipped over to the dressing table, yanked open the lid of the wooden jewellery box (Caroline's own remembrance of Grandma Overton) and extracted her prize.

Caroline watched her sister prance out. Only Isabel, she thought in amusement, would have bothered to tack lace all the way round cheap cotton knickers. There were four years between herself and Isabel since sister Millicent, born in 1890, had died of diphtheria at a year old. Once upon a time she had looked up to her pretty, talented elder sister in blind adoration. At sixteen Isabel had gone to Paris to finishing school, paid for by Grandmother, Father's dragon of a mother, the Dowager Countess of Buckford. After her return, Caroline had seen her with a new detachment, and adoration had tempered into affectionate tolerance. Somehow for all Isabel's looks and charm she was still unwed at twenty-five, and Caroline suspected the fact terrified her. Isabel, of all of them, found the constant lack of money at the Rectory hardest to treat as a challenge, as Mother encouraged them to do.

She decided she could no longer ignore the rapidly cooling water Myrtle had brought in twenty minutes ago, and reluctantly put foot to floor.

The Rectory boasted two bathrooms, one for themselves and one for the servants, but seven of them, let alone any guests, all expecting to wash at the same time led to strike action by both ancient boiler and boiler guardian, Percy Dibble. Since Father's timetable necessarily governed the Rectory, he had precedence, with Mother coming second, and, then, of course, came Isabel. Somehow no one ever challenged her right.

'Blackbird has spoken'. Caroline thrust up the sash in her everyday ritual. Below her lay the Rectory gardens and beyond several farms, and beyond them the Forest of Ashdown, that mysterious and enchanted 'other place', almost all that was left of the great prehistoric forest of Anderida which had once covered three counties and even now cast its spell of the past on those who stood still to receive it. 'My sermon today is life,' Caroline solemnly informed the world. 'He that hath ears to hear let him hear.' A blackbird in the larch tree apparently didn't, because he promptly flew away with a loud cry of alarm, followed by annoyed clucks. This was her life, these green lawns, this village, this church, this house, and every day she reminded herself how much she loved it, in case, she supposed, something changed. As it might do. Perhaps there was still time to be an intrepid lady traveller, another Lady Hester Stanhope or Isabella Bird; maybe she'd travel the desert like Gertrude Bell and write a book as good as *The Desert and the Sown.*

Now the water really was cold. Ugh! She hurried over her ablutions, impatient now for the day to get going as she struggled into corset and stockings. She had already put on her new straight-skirted costume when she remembered she was going for a walk with Reggie Hunney this afternoon. *Some* consolation for the coming disaster of luncheon. Still, she couldn't wear her blue walking skirt for church and anyway she'd forgotten to ask Harriet to clean the bottom from last week's mud splashes. She thought enviously of the frightful Patricia Swinford-Browne and her daring appearance in old-fashioned bloomers on her bicycle. A brief appearance, for Patricia's mother had all but fainted. All the same, trousers, or at least divided skirts, were entirely sensible forms of dress. She regarded herself critically in the mirror, thankful that for once her wayward hair had condescended to be swept up reasonably neatly and to remain there shackled firmly with pins. Perhaps the day wouldn't be so bad after all. She raced down the stairs to family prayers and breakfast. Dear Aunt Tilly, still not recovered from the nose and throat problems that had brought her here a few days to convalesce, would be deputising for Father and Mother who were still at early Easter Celebration. Tilly was next in seniority, but it was hardly fair on her, Caroline thought. There was something a little odd about this visit, for her aunt was very vague about how long she intended to stay. She could not, Caroline wondered, by any chance have quarrelled with Grandmother? No, surely not; she was far too quiet and unassuming to quarrel with anybody.

Caroline was a little late in arriving at prayers and the Dibbles, Agnes, Harriet and Myrtle were already sitting in their row. So was eighteen-year-old Felicia who was the most quietly organised of them all, as well as bidding fair to becoming the most startlingly beautiful with her dark hair and deep brown eyes. Amazingly, Isabel was already here, and Phoebe and George were sauntering up behind her with the lackadaisical privileges of youth at sixteen and fifteen respectively.

'Beastly shame,' glowered George.

'What is?' his elder sister enquired. George's dislikes varied from day to day.

'Ever-so, ever-so Edith and What-a-good-fellow-am-I William coming to lunch, of course.'

Caroline laughed at her brother's apt characterisation of the Swinford-Brownes. Emboldened, George continued: 'Not to mention Pasty Patricia and Rainbow Robert.'

'Rainbow?'

'Have you seen his spotted waistcoats? And his stocks. *Striped*! I ask you.' George spoke with the lordly disgust of a youngster for his elders. Not much elder, though. Robert must be twenty-six by now, Caroline guessed, without much interest, as she took her place for prayer.

'Hast delivered us from the power of our enemy,' Tilly was intoning, as Caroline brought herself back with a start to 'Boot parade', so dubbed from time immemorial because of the row of undersides of servants' boots in front of her. She was hungry, and breakfast, awaiting them in chafing dishes on the sideboard, smelled good. After prayers, George would bear in the traditional Easter eggs, painted with caricatures – his own work. Caroline began to feel happy again, for life in the Rectory tended to be regulated not by months, or even by seasons, but by the Church calendar, which chimed out the high points, like the hours on Mother's beloved French Cupid clock: Advent, ding dong, 'Lo He comes with clouds descending', help wash and pick over the fruit for the Christmas puddings; Christmas Even, ding dong, decorate the church with greenery, holly, mistletoe, and rosemary, Solemn Evensong; Christmas, ding dong, 'Born this happy morning', carols, candles, goose, presents, love and laughter; Epiphany, ding dong, 'Brightest and best of the sons of the morning', blessing the orchards or apple howling (according to whether you used the old religion's terms or the new, Father had explained); Candlemas, 'Let there be light', Septuagesima, sing the *Benedicite;* Lent; Passiontide; Holy Week, and now Easter, which meant that the huge stove in the Rectory entrance hall would stop spreading its warm glow until Michaelmas.

Soon summer and autumn would tumble over themselves with activity. Church Helpers' Supper, the Sunday school treat, fêtes at Rectory and Manor, and Harvest Supper were but a few of them. The village had its own seasons; hoops, tops, marbles, Ladyday and Michaelmas, for instance, when the farm labourers got bonuses and bought their new boots for the year from old Sammy Farthing. In August the hop-pickers swarmed down from London, in autumn the stonebreakers arrived to break up the huge piles of flints for road-mending. The Rectory too had its immutable timetable: 'Dibbles day', for a massive spring-cleaning when carpets were pounded and cleaned with vinegar and water, monkey soap made for the coming year, clothes put away with moth balls; lavender day, when the church altar cupboard drawers received their new season's bunches to keep insects away from the purificators and napkins – Caroline's favourite job as a child; and there were bottling days, wine-making days, chutney and preserving days, all *sorts* of days, each with its own special flavour.

The more she fretted for new fields to conquer, the more important the measured clock of the Rectory year seemed. And she still could not understand why today it had to be changed.

Elizabeth Lilley closed the heavy front door behind her. The chill of waiting in the porch for the sake of avoiding any more questions about luncheon today was worth it. By the time she and Laurence had returned for breakfast, the family had departed save for George, still munching his ravenous way through toast and marmalade. Her genuinely enthusiastic reception of the egg he had painted for her, complete with caricature of Grandmother Buckford (which she had hastily whipped away before Laurence could see it) had temporarily banished his opposition to the advent of

22

the Swinford-Brownes for luncheon, just as she had hoped. Much the best way to avoid dispute. The cloudy morning was dithering between declaring itself spring and retreating back to the uncertainties of March. She felt rather the same herself: in a few moments she must walk to the church with Laurence thus declaring herself a symbol. To be within the walls of the Rectory with her family would be her preference.

'Skulking, Elizabeth?'

Tilly had found her out, and come to join her in the porch. Elizabeth liked Tilly though they had little in common and treated each other with caution. One of the few things they did share, however, was a lack of interest in fashion, Tilly because she thought it of no importance, though her tall spare figure and innate grace made her always look smart and stylish, Elizabeth because her striking good looks and mature figure needed little pampering; she wore what colours and styles she chose, not what fashion houses and magazines dictated.

'Listening to the cuckoo, Tilly.'

You've got at least one inside, Tilly thought to herself, but did not speak aloud. This Mother Hen had no sense of humour where her chicks were concerned. 'The bluebells will be out soon,' she commented brightly.

Elizabeth did laugh at this. 'All right. Skulking. Hatted and gloved to go on parade three quarters of an hour early for once.'

'I'm honoured.' Laurence Lilley, carrying stole and chasuble over his arm, came to join his wife. When Laurence saw Tilly as well, he raised his eyebrows even higher. 'I am doubly honoured. Why so early?'

23

Elizabeth brushed this aside. 'Have you talked to Isabel again, Laurence?'

He pulled a face. 'No chance. I had to return to the vestry and don my Solomon's mantle to settle a dispute between Mrs Mabel Thorn and Mrs Lettice as to which fair linen cloth should be laid for the Eucharist. It left no time for family discussions. You must have noticed Mrs Lettice had laid her grandmother's cloth, elegantly trimmed with lace and far too Roman for Mrs Thorn. She insisted on its being changed for this service.'

'Isn't that the sacristan's job?' Elizabeth asked mildly. She hadn't noticed, of course. She had been carried away with the music and majesty of Easter.

'Poor old Bertram has only held the position since Lady Day, Elizabeth, and Mrs Lettice is of Mutter stock. If I set him to resolve a quarrel between a Mutter and a Thorn, he'll faint into the grave Job Fisher has just finished digging.'

'Laurence!' Elizabeth was still capable of being taken aback when her husband joked on 'church ground'. To her, the division between the formality of Church and the rumbustious informality of home was absolute.

'Come, Elizabeth. We are adults. I meant no disrespect.' He paused. 'And Isabel, too, is an adult, you must remember. She makes her own choice.'

It was Tilly who built the bridge. 'They're all sensible children, Elizabeth, thanks to you both. They know what they want.'

'But are they right?' Elizabeth's anxiety gripped her with a painful intensity, though no sign of it appeared on her placid face. Four daughters, one son, all her babies. No, that was not all, for there had been her darling Millicent, and the gap her baby left was as real to her as the five living children: Isabel, the butterfly that blindly fluttered where it chose; Caroline, the bird that longed to fly, save in her heart of hearts; Felicia, who wanted only to stay close in the nest; Phoebe the ugly duckling – no, that was wrong, for Phoebe was not ugly, though the future might be easier if she were; and George, the colt that would one day soon become a thoroughbred like his father. *Did* they all know what they wanted? It is a wise mother who knows her own child, the saying went. Was *she* wise? *Did* she know them? Probably not, but she was a peaceful haven from stormy seas. Today even Elizabeth could see the prospect of troubled waters.

'Caroline, may I walk to church with you?'

Caroline glanced up from her struggles to stab her hatpin into the newly cleaned hat as she sensed the restrained excitement in Felicia's voice. Her sister was fidgeting on the threshold of the room, her heavy hair carefully swept up under the rose velvet hat. Felicia was gifted with her hands, she had long sensitive fingers, which Caroline envied, as if she expressed through them, whether making a hat, a cake or drawing a wild flower, the inner feelings she kept so firmly to herself. Her other sisters tended to take little notice of her. Isabel was somewhat scornful, sixteen-year-old Phoebe wary, for although closer in age they had nothing in common. Caroline felt fiercely protective towards her, especially since the fiasco of the finishing school. Pushed into it by Grandmother, she had been so unhappy that Father had taken her away after only six months. Yet sometimes Caroline felt Felicia might have a strong inner core that would sustain her however rough the waters.

'I have to tackle Mrs Dibble first. Mother's orders.'

'I'll come with you.'

'Where's Isabel?' Caroline was slightly surprised. Usually Felicia avoided any possibility of conflict with Mrs Dibble, whom she found intimidating.

'She had a headache. Father excused her.'

'She was well enough half an hour ago.'

Mrs Margaret Dibble, together with her husband Percy, odd-job man, gardener, boilerman and sometime driver, dominated the small servants' hall. Since the departure of Nanny Oates her position had been undisputed. The Dibbles' younger son Fred (their two older children, a boy and a girl, had married and moved away) was also nominally one of the staff, but no one talked a great deal about Fred. At nineteen, he affably wandered his way through a life bounded by the Rectory, for he could not cope with the world outside.

When Caroline saw the cook–housekeepers of her friends' homes, she wondered how Mrs Dibble had escaped the mould. The comfortable plump bodies that stomped heavily round her friends' kitchens bore no relation to Mrs Dibble. She was small and quick, with lithe movements, and she bustled rather than clonked across the floor. Her eyes were like a robin's; she watched, and then she hopped. Mrs Dibble was all-seeing, all-doing, the grand vizier to her mother's sultan.

Caroline and Felicia found her up to her wrists in pastry mix, singing in her surprisingly deep, lusty voice: 'Once

he died, our souls to save; Where thy victory, O grave?'
Mrs Dibble saw it as her duty to uphold the Rectory's
spiritual values at all times, and believed her cooking was
only possible with the Lord's blessing. She and Mother did
not always see eye to eye as a result, and Caroline found
herself a frequent but unwilling go-between when there
were awkward tasks to perform. As now.

'As we have guests,' she began brightly, 'we wondered
whether you still had time to make your lovely pond
pudding, Mrs Dibble. They—'

Mrs Dibble slowly extracted her hands from her basin,
rolled up the mix and slapped it on the marble slab. 'That's
Palm Sunday, not Easter, Miss Caroline. Easter's apple and
primrose pie, as you well know.'

'Yes, but—'

'I daren't, Miss Caroline.' Mrs Dibble relented into
humanity. 'Thirteen for dinner. It'll be unaccountably bad,
that I can tell you.' Her religion was a pastry mix in itself,
Caroline thought, old and new mixed with a dash of Dibble.

'I thought you always told us the sun danced for joy on
Easter morning?' Felicia ventured.

'That I did, and see it's cloudy already. Praise the Lord,'
Mrs Dibble added and picked up the rolling pin, having
won the argument. Caroline stole one of the precious new
mint shoots to chew and retreated in defeat. 'I'll do you
a Bible cake,' was thrown after her as a peace offering.
Caroline's heart sank. She hated figs, a prominent feature
of the recipe.

'Nahum, III, 12,' Mrs Dibble shouted, as if reading her
mind. "If they be shaken they shall even fall into the mouth

of the eater.' And raisins is up to tuppence a pound.'

Caroline ran, before the first book of Samuel reached her too. George was in the choir so, thanks to Isabel's headache, only three of them and Aunt Tilly took their decorous places at Elizabeth Lilley's side in the front pew. How could Isabel bear to miss it, Caroline wondered. After the solemn darkness of Passiontide and Good Friday services, Easter Day was a happy service. She enjoyed the changing liturgical colours, from Passiontide to Palm Sunday's violet, to white on Maundy Thursday, then black, and now glorious white again for Easter Day, and so on through the year. And she enjoyed watching Ashden dressed up for the occasion, for whatever motive, from Mr Roffey, the sweep, and his wife in their Sunday best to Mrs Swinford-Browne in her ghastly new hat. *That* must be new. The black ostrich feather was far too stiff and ostentatious to be anything else. The Swinford-Brownes were chapel-goers normally, so this rare visit must be because of the Rectory luncheon. Caroline's heart sank again at the prospect, but she firmly dragged it up again. They should *not* ruin her day.

Private pews had been abolished at St Nicholas's fifteen years ago, despite the loss of their revenue to her father, albeit a small one. Mysteriously, however, there still seemed to be a Hunney private boxed pew, and even a Norville pew, just as there were Hunney and Norville chapels. The Norville pew was rarely occupied for the Misses Norville were recluses and over ninety. Risking her mother's disapproval, she twisted round to see if the Hunneys were all here – which immediately brought back her sense of grievance over luncheon once more.

Caroline knew Sir John enjoyed the company of his enlarged family at the Rectory, though Lady Hunney behaved more as if it were her social duty to those less fortunate than herself. Poor Lady Hunney, she thought. Her problem was that as leader of village society everyone was her inferior, and the charm that had made her the toast of London society while her husband was still able to pursue his army career had curdled when the death of his father brought him back to Ashden.

Caroline caught Reggie winking at her, while apparently staring straight ahead with a solemn face. Lady Hunney smiled at her with honeyed sweetness. 'Beware the jaws that bite, the claws that catch.' Caroline thought, gracefully inclining her head to the Jabberwock, before grinning at Eleanor. Eleanor was wearing her new royal blue costume which they had chosen at Debenham & Freebody's, and it suited Eleanor's pleasant looks better than the usual nondescript shades she wore. No doubt Caroline was getting the blame for this radical move. Only Lady Hunney was permitted the height of fashion, having long dismissed nineteen-year-old Eleanor (Caroline suspected) as a non-runner in the social race.

'Christ the Lord is risen again . . .' She sang out in happiness as the hymn began.

The Easter Service is glory, all glory . . . Mrs Thorn got her way over the altar linen – no lace. That meant sometime in the future Mrs Lettice must be appeased . . . What would the future hold for her sisters, and George? Would they marry? Would she marry?

'Alleluia!'

Caroline quickly offered an apology to God. How could she take Communion with such secular thoughts on her mind?

Elizabeth rather liked Edith Swinford-Browne, or perhaps it would be more truthful to say she felt sympathetic towards her. She knew Edith was feeling out of her depth in the Rectory drawing room. The high puffed coiffure, the over-ornate Magyar sleeves, and the inappropriate velvet bag all testified to her ordeal. It wasn't at all like The Towers in Station Road into which she and her husband William had moved five years ago; William was the biggest landowner in the parish, rivalling even Sir John Hunney of Ashden Manor, and he set out to ensure that the village knew of and benefited from his enormous wealth. All except the Rector. Elizabeth was quite convinced, despite her husband's refusal to discuss the issue, that Swinford-Browne deliberately undervalued his yields for the purposes of the tithe rent charge, on which the Rector depended for his income. He was a self-made man, as he proclaimed modestly, a phrase which had caused much mirth in the Lilley household.

However, the Rectory, not the Manor, was the key to village approval, and Edith knew if she could but grasp the intangible thread that led to this, she need fret no more. Yet here she looked lost, as if she was longing for the moment when the gentlemen – William, Robert and the Rector – would emerge from their little talk to rescue her. Not that she was shy. Far from it. But she obviously liked to know where she stood, and here she did not.

Elizabeth watched her, pityingly.

Poor Edith would see only that the Berlin-worked tapestry on the chairs was well-worn, the piano long past its prime, the rosewood what-not battered, the souvenirs from Worthing and Brighton cheap and chipped, the frames of photographs and sketches crammed together, and the books left lying on tables and chairs, instead of being placed decorously back on their library shelves.

Edith was obviously searching for a comment. She found one.

'It's the servant problem, isn't it?'

Elizabeth agreed with her warmly, as sympathy oozed from her guest's voice. 'Indeed it is.' Then, unable to resist temptation, she added: 'I should be quite distraught if any of our efficient servants left, now I have fully trained them.' She felt she was being unfair to Edith, who had done nothing to deserve such a put-down, even if she would never recognise it as such.

'I wonder,' Edith asked brightly, 'if you would care to join my Committee for the Relief of Fallen Women, Mrs Lilley? We meet at the Pump Room in Tunbridge Wells.'

'I regret not.' Elizabeth gave her slow, warm smile. 'I never join committees. It sets such a bad example.'

Edith stared at her nonplussed, as Elizabeth knew she would be. 'Oh, quite,' she said weakly.

Elizabeth was the daughter of a Kentish hop farmer. What extra money there was at the Rectory had come from her, not Laurence, for all that he was a son of the Earl of Buckford. He had only the money from his living, a sum of £490 a year, greatly diminished over the last thirty years owing to the general agricultural depression, and always at the mercy of late payers and deliberate avoidance, sometimes to Elizabeth's fury, by those who so officiously carried out Church duties. It was love, not money, however, that had brought about her marriage to Laurence. She knew Ashden found her puzzling as a Rector's wife, for she did not move among the cottagers unless the need was great. Her parish was the Rectory, her parishioners her family, and through her ministry her husband and her children prospered. Why waste time on a thousand essentially useless missions?

With relief, she heard Agnes beat the gong inside; it seemed a fanfare of release – until she remembered what was to come.

Thank goodness Reggie arrived promptly at the Rectory. Luncheon had been a nightmare. Caroline was aware she had not behaved well, though better than Phoebe and George, who had giggled together whenever Mother's eye was not on them, aided and abetted by the frightful Patricia Swinford-Browne, who was not above mocking her own mother, Caroline noticed. The tradition of eating the first lamb of the year at Easter persisted in the Rectory despite the fact that modern farming meant they could enjoy it in January if they wished. Now that treat had been spoiled, and so had that of the primrose pie. How could one *enjoy* such delights while having to entertain Robert Swinford-Browne, who was sitting next to her? He was tall, good-looking in a vapid kind of way and, to her at least, as interesting as a tailor's dummy. She liked him, but she found him hard to talk to, since he seemed to have no purpose or interests in life – save tennis, of course. She had obligingly raised the subject of Anthony Wilding and his prospects at Wimbledon, about which she knew little, and he, unfortunately, knew a great deal. 'He's like Brookes, he can play from any position on court. Of course, Brookes' horizontal volley.'

And then it had happened.

'Reggie, what do you think?' Caroline could wait no longer. She had hardly taken in a word Reggie had been saying, so full was she of the thunderbolt that had struck at luncheon. They had reached the wicket gate of Crab's meadow and Pook's Way, the track which led to the nearest gate into Ashdown forest, before she could contain herself no longer.

'She's a stunner!'

'Who?' Caroline was thrown.

'Penelope Banning, of course, Caroline, you never listen, that's your trouble. I've been in love with Penelope for three whole months now. Why do you think I've dragged you out today? I need your advice and I'm blowed if I'm going to have the whole of your blessed family chipping in on my romantic life.'

'*Your* romantic life, Reggie,' she replied, nodding to Alf Tilbury as he painfully hobbled down the garden path of Whapples Cottage, 'can wait for once. I have something much more important to tell you. Now *listen*.'

'It's hard to listen when you're stumbling over stones and *your* dog is intent on seeing me come a cropper. What do you think horses were made for? Why wouldn't you ride? Smith needs exercise too, you know.' Smith was his hunter.

'Because shouting at someone on horseback is not

conducive to having a serious conversation. Besides, Poppy isn't mine, she belongs to all of us, and Felicia wanted to ride this afternoon.'

'Mother would have lent you her mare.'

Would she? Caroline doubted it. Lady Hunney's famous charm seemed to have a steel edge where Caroline was concerned. Isabel called her Aunt Maud, but there had never been any suggestion that Caroline should adopt the same informality. It had occurred to Caroline that since she got on well with Reggie, Lady Hunney might fear she had designs upon him, something that would not look well in her social book. The second daughter of the third son of an earl, and an impoverished one at that, was the kind of catch that Lady Hunney would immediately throw back in the sea.

To her annoyance, he continued to talk non-stop of the wonders of this Penelope Banning as they strolled into Five Hundred Acre Wood. The Forest – a misnomer now that much of Ashdown Forest was open heathland – was heaving with signs of spring and the sun had chased away the clouds of the morning. Yet Reggie hardly noticed. Couldn't he feel, as she did, the magic of this place?

'Oh, Reggie, do stop to look.' Caroline was momentarily side-tracked from her impatience at not being able to impart her news.

'What is there to look at? Trees, flowers, birds.' There was all the gloom of the frustrated romantic lover in his voice.

'That's a Dartford warbler,' she said crossly. 'Very rare. What more could you ask?'

'Penelope.'

'Reggie, pretend I am Penelope, and *listen* to me.'

'All right. What is it? You overboiled the jam again?'

'No,' she said scathingly. '*Real* news. Isabel is engaged.'

'What?' He staggered around, clutching his brow. 'My secret hopes blighted.'

'Don't be an idiot, Reggie. It's Robert Swinford-Browne.' The awfulness of it engulfed her again. It had seemed unbelievable at first. Father standing up and making the announcement in his 'parish' voice, so she knew he wasn't happy about it either; then William Swinford-Browne opening bottles of champagne which he'd brought with him. and all the time Isabel, sitting there nakedly displaying not dewy-eyed love, but a kind of triumph – or so it seemed to Caroline. Perhaps that was just the champagne which had made her head swim, and Isabel suddenly seem a stranger.

'By Jove, she kept quiet about that.'

'Exactly what Phoebe said. Perhaps Isabel didn't want it to be known in case we teased her, but if she loves him—'

'Aha. Did I note an 'if'?'

'Oh, Reggie, I can't believe she does. Robert's not like his father, but marry him? It would be like marrying Fred Dibble. I'm not being unkind,' Caroline added hastily.

He glanced at her bright hazel eyes and the light brown hair leaping out as usual from its restraining pins, saw that she was indeed worried, and began to take the matter seriously. 'You're never unkind. But it's not the same. Robert's got his own mind – somewhere. He's a decent chap, is Robert. Handy with a racket, too. And a lot of money.'

Caroline sighed. 'You know Isabel. Once she gets her way, she no longer wants it. I suppose I shouldn't say that either.'

'It's only me, Caroline. You're not being disloyal.'

She looked at him gratefully. 'After she came home from finishing school and got presented at Court, and after that man backed out of marrying her, I think she grew obsessed with marriage.' There had been two men, in fact, one who backed out and one highly unsuitable one (if rich) whom Father had chased off.

'It's always the same with you girls that have got no money,' Reggie said encouragingly. 'Family isn't everything these days.'

'How nice of you to put it so tactfully. Isabel obviously agrees with you, or I can't believe she'd be marrying into the Swinford-Browne family.'

'Perhaps the patter of tiny feet will change her.'

'It wouldn't me.'

'It would most women.'

She fell silent. Did he mean she was not a womanly woman? Not like her mother? She wanted to be like Mother, only there was a restlessness in her that made her suspect she could never be so.

'Look,' he continued, 'even you and Isabel have more choices than me. I didn't ask to be the eldest son, after all. Yet here I am, and as soon as the old man dies, I'm lord of the manor and the Ashden estate whether I like it or not.'

'Don't you want to be?'

'Of course I do. It's an honour to carry on the torch like that, I love the old place, and I love the village. There have been Hunneys at Ashden for over three hundred years. But just once in a while, I feel like cutting loose.'

Caroline had never questioned Reggie's attitude to

36

his heritage before, and now she wondered why. The established order must continue under Reggie. Daniel, his younger brother, would be off travelling the world as soon as he came down this summer from Oxford, but Reggie had had no hope of taking up a full military career after his degree, despite his time in the university officers' training corps, and his periodic visits to something called 'camp'. His father had been called back to Whitehall to assume his formal title of Major-General Sir John Hunney, on the Balkan troubles in 1912 – 'Just an army desk job' was all he said about his duties there. Since then Reggie had had to take his place running the estate. He ran it well. The bailiff was a good man, but Reggie was the one the village turned to. He may be young, but he was a Hunney.

'But I'm a woman. How can you say I have more choices than you?'

'You chose not to go to finishing school. You're helping your father.'

Helping, Caroline wondered? Was what she did now worth those rows, first with her grandmother when she refused to go to the Paris finishing school, for which Lady Buckford was so generously paying. Instead she had remained at St Margaret College in East Grinstead, and then taken up her duties as the Rector's daughter. Just like Reggie. Little by little, she had gained ground in expanding her role, first writing the parish magazine, and then helping her father by copying and making sense of old decaying registers; now she also worked in the Ashden Manor library – Reggie's suggestion – cataloguing and repairing volumes. Interesting, but ultimately stultifying. In return for this, she sometimes took the Rector's wife's traditional place at the Mother's Union, and in organising flower shows and fêtes. Recently she had done some teaching at the village school, which was Church of England controlled. But at times, particularly now in spring, none of this was enough. Much as she loved home and Ashden, she felt her life was straining against a liberty bodice that had grown too small.

Reggie broke into her thoughts. 'I suppose you'll get married some day anyway.'

'Why do you suppose that?' Her step quickened; the criss-cross of beaten paths was taking them across exposed heathland, the bedraggled dead bracken still covering most of the ground, with only a few green shoots struggling through here and there. Ferns were the oldest greenery, Father said, prehistoric, pagan, and here in the middle of the forestland it was easy to believe it. All around them must be hidden some of the thousands of animals that dwelt here, retiring, waiting for the friendliness of night before they emerged. Unknown shapes in the dark. Like the future. Like marriage.

'Women have to.'

'Suppose no one asks me?'

'Oh, come. What about that curate, Oliver, who stomped off to drown his sorrows in Manchester? Or Philip Ryde? He's always making sheep's eyes at you. Don't say you hadn't noticed.'

She had, but was carefully ignoring it. She liked the schoolmaster, but that was all. Marry him? She simply couldn't imagine kissing him. 'I have no intention of marrying Philip Ryde. If it's any of your business,' she

38

added brightly, glad that the path was taking them back into the comforting shady woods full of the familiarity of the known.

'It is,' he said seriously. 'In my position as future lord of the manor, I feel I have to keep an eye on you village girls. It's my *droit de seigneur.*' He yelped with laughter as she attacked him with a dead branch, to the great astonishment of a young couple walking decorously by who quickly averted their eyes.

'That's a fine example to Agnes,' Caroline said ruefully. Agnes was so restrained, she was never quite sure what she was thinking, though her sweetheart always had a twinkle in his eye.

'Your parlour maid, wasn't it? And young Jamie Thorn?'

'It was. Future lord of the manor brained by branch wielded by Rector's daughter, the *Courier* will say. Maybe even the *Church Times.*'

'I won't tell Joe Ifield,' he reassured her. 'No charge will be made to the police.'

'Joe Ifield doesn't know what a charge is. He thinks it's made by a goat. In this case he's right.'

Crashing over the dead bracken to catch her as she tried to escape, Reggie pinioned her arms from behind. 'Apologise.'

'No,' she said suddenly.

Reggie watched her, knowing she was upset, not knowing quite why. 'When's the wedding?' he asked casually.

'The first of August. They wanted it in July, but there's the Rectory fête, Sunday School treat, the flower show *and* my birthday.'

'Good.' Reggie was pleased. 'Daniel will still be here before he goes off on his grand tour. Come up to the Manor after church and meet him. You haven't seen him since Christmas, have you? Bring the whole bunch of lilies if you like. Come to dinner.'

'No. I can't miss supper. The lily bunch will be chewing over events.'

'You can spit them out at the Hunney Pot afterwards, then. If I know the Mater, she'll be dying to hear, though she'll pretend she isn't.'

If only to gloat, Caroline thought crossly.

Sleep was coming hard that night. Unfinished thoughts whirled round her mind like rose petals on a windy summer's day, falling to earth only to be whisked up once more. Isabel engaged – that meant she would leave the Rectory when she married. What would happen here when she did? They all loved the Rectory as home, but Caroline saw it almost as a member of the family with its own character, one who needed to be consulted on such major events as Isabel's marriage.

She knew the old red-brick house was far from beautiful to most people's eyes, but it was to hers. It was a higgledy-piggledy mixture of styles from the medieval to the almost modern, including one wing which was an early Tudor house, serene in its red-brick, mellow glory, and a pretentious tower and porch added last century. The centuries had settled down contentedly together, however, into something that shouted home. Inside the house was a children's paradise and a maids' nightmare. Odd steps linking different levels provided traps for the forgetful; nooks and crannies beckoned everywhere.

Bedrooms . . . Who would have Isabel's bedroom now, the coveted one on the corner? Would she still be the same Isabel after she was incarcerated in The Towers like Rapunzel? Would there be a baby? She'd be Aunt Caroline, if so. The Swinford-Brownes would become part of the family, take part in the games, be present at their table. Her thoughts raced on. Why had Felicia been so quiet this evening at the Manor? She was always subdued, but this evening it had been very noticeable. Only she and Felicia had gone to the Manor, for the others could not be prised away. Daniel, Reggie and Eleanor had made up for it, firing questions like a machine gun at them, but it was nearly always Caroline who answered – even when Lady Hunney was questioner. Her rigidly corseted self-control shimmered within its midnight blue velvet dinner gown, and its high-necked lace fichu displayed the Hunney pearls as a discreet reminder of her qualifications to render what would be overbearing inquisitiveness in others into her proper sphere of concern. Eleanor, bless her, a silent but whole-hearted sympathiser with Caroline's predicament, winked in a most unladylike manner as her mother proclaimed:

'Such a pity Isabel takes nothing with her to the marriage. I presume that is the case?'

'Yes, Lady Hunney.' Nothing but her youth, warm heart and good spirits, she had thought angrily, loyally overlooking her sister's defects.

'A home wedding. At the Rectory, you say?'

'Naturally.' In fact there was no 'naturally' about it. The

Swinford-Brownes had pushed hard for The Towers, and Isabel had visibly wavered.

'How delightful. Provisioned by Fortnum, of course. Their usual pies. They are most reasonably priced, I am told.'

'Provisioned by ourselves, Lady Hunney, as our privilege and pleasure.'

Reggie had given her an approving pat as he and Daniel walked them home afterwards. The sky had been clear and the air still mild. The April evening touched them with the silken hopefulness of spring.

And still she could not sleep. Try as she would, she could not imagine Isabel sharing a bed with Robert. Caroline was fully aware of what this meant, not through any enlightenment from her mother but through the auspices of Patricia Swinford-Browne, who was by no means as repressed and demure as was generally believed – particularly by her own mother.

Isabel and Robert. Yet curiously enough it was not of them she was thinking as at last sleep came, but of Reggie's new brown boots marching over the fresh green shoots aggressively pushing their way to the light in Five Hundred Acre Wood. How silly.

Chapter Two

Even the cows seemed to be looking at Caroline reproachfully as she hurried along the footpath through Manor Farm, waving guiltily to Hilda Sharpe, the farmer's wife, who was coming out of the dairy on Silly Lane for her milk round, bowed under the wooden yoke with its two buckets. She always looked the same, man's cap on head, and cracked black boots on feet under the hitched-up serge skirt. The Sharpes did not welcome passers through, not even the Rector's daughters, because generally it meant they were Manor-bound, and the Sharpes did not see eye to eye with their landlords, the Hunneys. But on a God-given day such as this, which shouted summer rather than late April, much should be forgiven, Caroline told herself.

'I'm glad to hear about Joey,' she called, conscious of seeking favour. The Sharpes' fourteen-year-old son had been rushed to East Grinstead hospital by Dr Marden with suspected scarlet fever, but it had proved a false alarm.

Hilda grunted. 'Danged doctors.' It might or might not be an overture. Certainly the buckets lurched in grumpy agreement. They had almost lost their round thanks to the brief quarantine, and Arthur Sharpe had had a battle with the predatory Sebastian Plum of Grendel's Farm, on the outskirts of Ashden. It had started as a verbal battle, continued as a fight outside the Norville Arms, and ended in a win for the Sharpes after Father had donned his Solomon's cap at 'Rector's Hour'.

The tradesmen's entrance to Ashden Manor had two advantages: it was the nearest to the path across the park; and it greatly reduced the chances of meeting Lady Hunney, whose morning territory, even on a day such as this, extended from her upstairs boudoir to the morning room, with a short tour of inspection of dining and just possibly drawing rooms.

For Caroline, there were two Ashden Manors, the one demanded of its social and economic position as the hub of the village, and a secret Ashden, discovered in her childhood, that a sudden whiff, a jolt of memory, would raise before her like a lost Atlantis.

To enter Ashden as a child and run up its stairs to the day nursery was to enter a land of the story books, where anything might be possible, for the Hunney boys might have turned their domain into Treasure Island or the Scarlet Pimpernel's Revolutionary Paris, or Ruritania. 'Hunneying' she had called it, as talks of derring-do flashed like sabres through the eternity of youth.

A young Reggie, wastepaper basket on his head, poker

in his hand, astride his desk. 'I'm Kitchener at Omdurman.'

'And I'm a whirling dervish,' shrieked Caroline, hurling herself into the fray, as Reggie leapt from his horse, whirling his sword menacingly.

When the Hunneys came to the Rectory, their headquarters was the secret room Caroline had discovered years ago when, investigating a cupboard by the chimney-nook in her room, she had come across a narrow staircase. Here, in the stifling atmosphere, plans were laid and expeditions mounted. The consciousness, even as a child, that there were differences between them, other than those of Hunney and Lilley, gave these conferences an extra thrill, but after Reggie went to Winchester a gulf had gradually opened between them. Now it had narrowed again almost to imperceptibility, thanks to the tennis parties, the rides, the picnics and the dinners that permeated their social year, but Hunneying was relegated only to the echoes evoked by an idly tossed down book of travel, a mountaineering stick, or a postcard from Cannes or Rome.

Proud of his heritage, Sir John had taken pleasure in once showing her the plans of the Tudor house that had stood here – if plans they could be called, for this was before the days of architects. The present white-painted house had replaced it in the eighteenth century. The Hunney family had been granted the manor by Queen Elizabeth I, and had remained here in an unbroken line ever since, as in so many other of the country houses of England. They had come to Ashden as usurpers in village eyes, but a century later were accepted as incumbents, and were now more greatly respected than their predecessors. The Norvilles, Sir John had told her, being Catholics and too outspoken in their political preferences, had been dispossessed. Caroline had felt a traitorous sympathy for them, probably because in the Hunneying dramatisation of the Battle of Ashden Manor, she was always forced to play a Norville, albeit, by special concession, a male.

Two centuries later, a Norville returned to Sussex, perhaps attracted by the forest hunting. He had settled on Tillow Hill to the east of the village, and turned the existing property into a monstrous folly castle merely to annoy the Hunneys by dominating the skyline, higher even than the oaks that had given the hill its name. He had then browbeaten the innkeeper into restoring the family name to the Norville Arms, and endowed a Norville pew in St Nicholas in a change of religion as convenient as the Vicar of Bray's.

The last two Norvilles, sisters, now lived as virtual recluses in the ruined castle, with one retainer almost as ancient as they. A girl from the village so clumsy she could find no other work attended daily. Even she had refused to live in and found her way by the stars each night to her parents' cottage. Caroline had never visited Tillow Castle, and nor had anyone of her acquaintance, save for her father and, on one rare occasion, the doctor. Father would never speak of it, though they were all agog with curiosity. Needless to say, no Hunney ever crossed the Castle threshold, and the pews, to her father's annoyance, had been carefully chosen so that no Norville need lay eyes on a Hunney.

It was the Norville collection on which Caroline was

engaged in the library this Tuesday morning when the door opened, and the impossible happened: Lady Hunney entered, as always immaculately attired, this morning in a straight purple gown with tunic draperies that added regality to her already imperious slender figure. Caroline sometimes tried to reduce the spectre of Lady Hunney to manageable terms by imagining her in bed at night smothered in cold cream and wearing a chin-strap (to preserve that impossibly angular jaw). Reality, however, usually quickly dispelled such momentary relief.

'Good morning, Caroline.'

Sugared sweetness on her lips – so she had been well aware of her presence before she came in, Caroline realised, heart sinking, for she knew every nuance of Lady Hunney's voice. She glanced up with a happy smile.

'I was so much enjoying this volume, but I feared you might miss it,' her ladyship continued.

'It's very good of you to return it.' Caroline took the book, congratulating herself that for once she was giving the right answer. She laid it on the desk without glancing at it, though she was longing to see which of the thousands of tomes here had been so fortunate as to attract Lady Hunney's attention.

Lady Hunney did not leave, once this vital mission had been accomplished. 'Mr and Mrs Swinford-Browne have kindly invited us to dear Isabel's engagement ball. I do hope the arrangements progress well?'

'Thank you, yes.' Caroline proceeded to answer her question, still puzzled as to why Lady Hunney should have bothered to seek her out. 'Mrs Swinford-Browne wished to hire the Pump Room, but it was decided the inconvenience of travel would be a disadvantage.' She was beginning to sound like Lady Hunney herself, Caroline thought crossly. As soon as she saw Lady Hunney's smile, she knew she had somehow played into her hands – as usual.

'Travel,' Lady Hunney murmured. 'Such a problem for you.'

Caroline was nonplussed. The Towers was little more than half a mile from the Rectory, and even in the dark this did not seem a matter of pressing concern.

'How fortunate your aunt is staying with you. She has a motor car, has she not?' Lady Hunney continued.

'Yes, but—'

'Normally Reggie would have been only too delighted to have driven you himself.' There was deep regret in her voice. 'However, he will be escorting his friend Miss Banning, and his new motor vehicle, as you know, ridiculously allows only one passenger.' Caroline was more taken aback at Lady Hunney's desire to impart this information than at its content. 'A delightful person. The daughter of the Viscount Banning, of course.'

Let there be light, and light there was. The Viscount Banning had unexpectedly become heir to a dukedom, so no wonder his daughter had won such high approval from her ladyship. Caroline felt tempted to advise Lady Hunney that any assistance she could render her son in ridding Penelope of her chaperone might reap greater long-term rewards for her than continually expending effort in trying to nobble a non-runner in the Matrimonial Stakes for Reginald Hunney. And non-runner Caroline most certainly was. She elected to refrain from pointing this out in case such levity won her a permanent ban from Ashden Manor, and, fully satisfied with Caroline's silence, her ladyship departed. Not until her task was finished for the day did Caroline pick up the book that had so engrossed her ladyship.

It was *Bicycling Tours in France.*

In high good humour again at the thought of a tightly laced, serge-bloomered Lady Hunney pedalling to Paris, Caroline blithely sailed out by the front entrance, ignoring the disapproval of Parker, the butler, who always managed to imply she was a complete stranger to him. Perhaps like dogs, butlers grew to look like their mistresses?

Late that afternoon, Caroline decided to visit Nanny Oates. Nanny had cared for both Father and Aunt Tilly at Buckford House. She had come to Sussex when Elizabeth was expecting Isabel, and had simply stayed on to wait for the next. After the tragedy of Millicent's death, there was no question of her leaving. Now she had retired to a cottage whose rent was paid by the Rector. She was eighty-three now and, as she put it, not going in for no pancake races no more. Even the chickens she kept behind the cottage were under threat. 'You'll be for the pot, the lot of you, afore long,' she'd heard Nanny threaten them on her last visit, 'especially you, Miss Caroline of Brunswick.' They were all invariably named after the Queens of England – except for Victoria, whom she deemed it disrespectful to consign to a pot, or to claim eggs from. So when Nanny reached Queen Adelaide she started again at Boadicea.

She knocked at the door of the cottage, at the far end of Bankside, and almost simultaneously turned the knob and walked in as she usually did. Nanny had a visitor, but the strange thing was that at her approach both of them instantly fell silent. Even stranger since the visitor was Aunt Tilly.

'Don't tell me you're discussing your dress for next Friday too, Nanny?' Caroline bent down to kiss the upturned button face. Here was a comfortable double chin that saw no need of chin-straps.

'That's right, Miss Caroline,' she agreed. 'Scarlet, 'tis, showing me bosom, and with a hat to match with three white feathers. Being presented to His Majesty, I am.'

Tilly laughed. 'And I'm in white lace with a pale pink underskirt, Nanny, with darling little embroidered rosebuds.' She rose to go. 'I'll leave you to talk to Caroline.'

'Tell the Rector, mind,' Nanny said.

'What about?' asked Caroline. She'd been right. There was something odd going on.

'None of your business, miss. Just jawing the hind leg off a donkey like I usually do.'

'Why don't you tell her, Nanny? You can trust Caroline.'

'She's a young lady, Miss Matilda,' Nanny reminded her charge severely. 'She's unwed.'

'Young ladies grow up, Nanny, and I too am unwed.'

'That's different, Miss Tilda, and you know it.' Nanny's mouth snapped shut. Her decision was made, and Caroline knew she would get no more out of her.

When she returned to the Rectory, none the wiser, she was surprised to find Felicia in her bedroom, and Isabel draped gracefully on the bed looking supremely bored. Caroline's room was the only one that boasted a full-length mirror and Felicia was standing somewhat dolefully before it. This too was surprising since Felicia was the least interested of them all in what she wore, though she was easily the most striking in looks.

'You'll help, won't you, Caroline?' Felicia pleaded. 'Isabel won't take me seriously and I must do something to this.' She glanced disparagingly at her old white satin skirt and blouse.

'I don't know why Felicia's getting so het up about it. It's my dance,' Isabel pointed out unmaliciously.

Seeing the flush on Felicia's face, Caroline quickly intervened. 'We all know you're to be the belle, Isabel, but even bells need clappers.'

'What?' Isabel stared at her, then dismissed, first, this incomprehensible statement, and, secondly, the problem. 'Ask Mrs Hazel to look at it, Felicia. There's still time.'

'We can't afford her, Mother says. Not for all of us.' The village dressmaker lived on Bankside next to old Sammy Farthing the shoemaker, and was occasionally employed on new dresses for the Rectory womenfolk, and frequently on repairs and alterations.

Isabel made no reply, but Caroline knew what that look on her face meant: that Isabel was planning something she was slightly ashamed of. If so there was no use pursuing it, for Isabel kept her own counsel.

'It needs an overskirt adding, Felicia, or ruche this one up and provide a different underskirt. You could have my blue one,' Caroline offered, 'and dye the blouse to match. You could do it, Isabel. You're the handiest with a needle.'

'Me?' Isabel looked astonished. 'I'm far too busy. Get Harriet to do it.'

'It's too big a job for her. She hasn't time.'

'She's only a housemaid. She'll do what you tell her to.'

'You're not a Swinford-Browne yet, Isabel.' Caroline was irritated. 'And this isn't The Towers.'

'Don't I know it,' Isabel yawned.

'Please don't be horrid,' Felicia pleaded.

'Why not? You'll be even more glad to get rid of me.' Isabel slid off the bed. 'I'm quite sure you're already fighting over who's going to have my room.'

Caroline grinned guiltily. 'Discussing, not fighting.'

'Fighting,' Felicia corrected, unusually light-hearted. Normally she left her two older sisters to squabble, and Phoebe to battle with George. 'I'll go and ask Mother what she thinks about the dress.'

There was a brief silence as she left, which Caroline broke: 'Now we'll be in trouble. Are you sure—' She stopped, diffident about what she wanted to ask.

'Go on.' Isabel's voice was studiedly neutral.

'That you'll be happy?'

'I'll be rich. I can't bear this scrimping and saving. Wouldn't you like to be rich, and never have to make home-made perfume again?'

'Not if it meant marrying someone I didn't love.'

Isabel flushed. 'I do love Robert. *Real* love. Not like Phoebe—'

'Phoebe?' Caroline forgot Isabel's dexterity at switching away from unfortunate subjects.

'You'll have to keep an eye on her when I've gone. I think she's crushed on Mr Denis.'

'*What*?' Caroline burst into laughter. 'He's far too

52

sensible.' Christopher Denis was a most earnest young curate whose passions centred on Greek, not girls.

'Perhaps, but Phoebe isn't, and I do have a position to keep up.'

Caroline's mouth twitched. 'What as? The Rector's daughter?'

'As Robert's fiancée. You're very sanctimonious all of a sudden, Caroline.'

'I grew up,' Caroline replied shortly. 'Perhaps you should.'

'I have. I shall be sharing a bed with Robert, after all.'

It was almost, Caroline thought, as if Isabel was determined to drag the subject up. 'Have you thought about that?' she asked tentatively.

'Of course,' Isabel answered lightly. 'There's nothing to it if you shut your eyes.'

'You mean you know already?' Caroline was taken aback.

'Of course not,' Isabel snapped. 'Mother told me, now that I'm going to be married,' she added importantly.

Caroline didn't believe her. Mother wouldn't. Isabel must have discussed it at finishing school. Somehow marriage didn't seem much fun if all you had to do was shut your eyes. But then perhaps marriage was not meant to be fun, merely an almost necessary evil, as Aunt Tilly has once said jokingly to her. It seemed a doleful prospect.

'I'm bored.' Phoebe appeared at her bedroom door the next morning. An open door was understood between them as signalling they were 'at home'. 'You all do nothing but talk dresses, invitations, and dances. Nothing *interesting.*'

Caroline was tempted to suggest she spent some worthwhile time on her appearance. Both cuffs of her blouse were misbuttoned, the garnet brooch at her throat was askew, and the bottom of her skirt suggested, first, that perhaps she hadn't abandoned tree-climbing and second, that communication between herself and a cleaning brush, and/or Myrtle, was non-existent. Although Caroline was conscious of her own imperfections in this respect, Mother's dictum that a lady is known by her shoes, gloves and hat appeared to have fallen completely on deaf ears where Phoebe was concerned. Her attractive plump, rosy looks, like a wild peony coming into bloom, owed nothing to grooming and much to her restless bouncing energy. She was going to have a shock at finishing school in September – or would the shock all be on the school's side?

'What do you classify as interesting?'

Phoebe searched in her repertoire and found nothing she could offer. She shrugged. 'There's something going on between Father and Aunt Tilly in his study. I think he's throwing her out.'

'*What?*'

'She's harmless enough,' Phoebe continued, pleased with Caroline's reaction. 'And she does have a motor car. She took me for a drive. It were unaccountable exciting,' she mimicked.

'Don't mock the servants. You'll do it to their faces one day.'

'Who cares?' Phoebe felt on safe ground where Caroline was concerned, whereas Isabel, being older, was an extension of authority. 'Go and listen, Carrie, do. I dare you.'

'I won't do anything of the sort,' Caroline replied heatedly. 'I don't believe you. And what's all this about you and Mr Denis?'

Phoebe's eyes flickered. 'What about our blessed Saint Christopher?'

'Don't get keen on him, Phoebe,' Caroline said quietly.

'When I get keen on someone,' Phoebe retorted rudely, 'it'll be someone far more exciting than a mere curate.' She swept out, congratulating herself she'd handled that rather well.

Caroline was bound to admit Isabel might be right. Since Phoebe had no interests in Ashden (except the curate?) it was as well she would have Paris to distract her (and control her). She decided to go downstairs – to find Mother, she told herself. She saw Aunt Tilly coming out of Father's study, and was alarmed to see that she did indeed look distressed, her normal composure decidedly shaken.

'Are you all right, Aunt Tilly?' she asked with concern.

Tilly opened her mouth as if to reply, then shook her head, not so much in answer to the question as in reproach at herself. 'Quite, thank you, Caroline.'

'You're not leaving us, are you?' Caroline asked, alarmed that Phoebe might be right. Aunt Tilly, with her quiet dry wit and observer's sharp eye, was a tonic to Rectory life in Caroline's opinion, though her younger siblings failed to agree.

'I'm nearly better. Soon I must go.'

'Not till the wedding, surely? You've got to stay till then.'

'Mother—'

'Can exist very well without you,' Caroline interrupted firmly.

'Grandmother is a tyrant and the more you tolerate her, the worse she will be.'

Tilly's eyes looked unusually moist, and, saying nothing further, she hurried past Caroline and up the staircase, muttering about changing for luncheon, a rare observance on her part.

Caroline hesitated for a moment, then walked into the study, a privilege she alone seemed to have, though there had never been a formal ban on others entering, so far as she knew. They just never did, and she rarely took advantage of her freedom either. 'Father, Aunt Tilly seems upset.'

He was standing by the window looking out across to the shrubs that hid the coach house and stables. He'd chosen this room deliberately so that the view towards the distant forest should not distract him, but today the plan seemed to have failed. His face was grave as he turned to speak to her.

'We disagreed, Caroline. It is of no great consequence.'

'You won't let her leave us, will you?'

He looked surprised and hesitated. 'I may not be able to prevent it.'

'You can't let Grandmother win.'

'If only,' he said wryly, 'it were as simple as that. No, we disagreed partly over a village matter.'

'Nanny Oates?'

'She is involved.' Her father's study and ears were a confessional as private as any to be found in the church, any judgement his alone, and so she was surprised when he continued, 'It will be public soon enough. Am I right in thinking that our parlour maid, Agnes, has an understanding with young Jamie Thorn?'

'Yes, they've been walking out for two or three years, and they'll be married soon, I'm sure of it.'

'I fear not.'

'Why?' Caroline was alarmed. They were all fond of Agnes, and Jamie, younger son of the blacksmith, was well liked.

'Ruth Horner, who as you know is one of the Swinford-Brownes' housemaids, is to have a child.'

'But she's not married,' Caroline said immediately, then awarded herself full marks for stupidity. Of course. That was the greatest shame even now in Ashden, though most young couples caught in such a dilemma marched themselves quickly enough to the altar.

'No. She names young Jamie as the father.'

'But how could he be? He loves Agnes.'

'He denies Ruth's claim, and has refused to marry her. As a consequence the Swinford-Brownes have thrown the girl out.'

'That's cruel and unchristian.'

'That, as you must know, is the way of the world.'

'Chapel-goers,' she said fiercely. The village was divided in its religious attendance, between St Nicholas and the Wesleyan Chapel in Station Road which the Swinford-Brownes attended. 'Typical.'

'And often churchgoers too, Caroline,' he said gravely. 'Nanny Oates has taken her in for the moment; Ruth is an orphan as you know. Nanny's cottage is too small, however, so some place must be found for her save the maternity unit of the Union workhouse, and a dismal future thereafter.'

'What is to be done, Father?'

'Much as I would like to, I cannot unmake an unwanted child, or stop public opprobrium falling on the girl's head. But I can diligently seek the truth, and lead the way to compassion.'

'Surely Mr Swinford-Browne's minister should take the matter up.'

'His purse is too heavy for the Minister to feel eagerness at such a task.'

'That should not weigh in the matter,' Caroline cried fiercely. In inclination she sensed her father often felt as she did, but Ashden's rules could vary from the Church's, and the Church's from his private convictions. The Rector walked a daily tightrope between leadership and respect with the chasms of alienation and compromise on either side.

'Agnes will need our help, Caroline.'

'But you can't mean Jamie must be forced to marry the girl if he does not love her?'

'He should have thought of that when he took advantage of Ruth's innocence.'

'Suppose Ruth is lying?'

'Why should she?' her father asked gently. 'She needs to name the father if she is to obtain a magistrate's order for support for a child born out of wedlock. But she prefers to wed him, naturally. She is not a bad girl, my dear. I will naturally talk to them both at length to be sure of the truth.' He looked tired.

'But why is Aunt Tilly so upset?' Caroline asked.

Laurence Lilley hesitated, choosing his words. 'She fears I may not use my influence strongly enough to force Jamie to marry the girl.'

'She feels for Ruth, then. Is she right about you, Father?'

'Naturally I will not press him if I can establish his innocence *without question*. If there is doubt, then bear in mind that villagers are slow to change. Not so long ago the Ruths of this world would kill themselves, and the village folk would not lift a finger to save her. Not far from here, not long ago, people stood and watched one poor girl drown herself. Nowadays their death would be slower. In towns they go on the streets, in villages they go to the Union workhouse and afterwards they have to live like lepers, scorned by the women and men too – in their own way,' he finished diplomatically. 'I would condemn no one to that life if words from me could change it.'

'And what of Agnes's life, Father?'

'A broken life against a broken heart. Broken hearts sometimes mend, a life broken by social stigma never does. How would you weigh those, Caroline?'

The week before Isabel's engagement ball was entirely given over to the coming occasion. The warm dry weather continued and Caroline imagined Edith Swinford-Browne having put in her order to God for twelve hours of sun per day along with her order to Fortnum & Mason's. She hardly saw Father; he simply came and went on his daily routine of matins, breakfast, church business, luncheon, parish visiting, his 'surgery', Evensong, dinner, reading and bed. Mother gave the impression of gliding over the trials and tribulations of the week, towing her brood of ugly ducklings, one of which was turning into a beautiful swan. Caroline wasn't going to begrudge Isabel these few months of hectic attention before her marriage, though she could not understand quite why the present week should be proving so busy. The catering was very firmly in the darting, claw-like hands of Mrs Swinford-Browne, and the house was being decorated by the Swinford-Brownes (not personally, naturally). The Rectory girls had longed to help, but much to their annoyance had been refused. They had no role, yet the week was a 'twittering one', their father's word for times when anything disturbed the measured order of his life.

They could not even discuss Isabel's own toilette, for her first visit to Mrs Hazel for a new dress for the ball had been followed by her future mother-in-law's swift intervention. She swept Isabel up to Jay's at Oxford Circus in London for their models to be paraded before her and then to Maison Nichol in Bond Street for attention to her hair. Caroline suspected she now knew the meaning of Isabel's sudden silence on the subject of Mrs Hazel. Edith had been egged on by Isabel who now spoke of 'transformations' and 'Nestle's permanent hair waves' with assured nonchalance until they laughed at her, and then had to soothe her wounded feelings. Meanwhile Elizabeth had soothed Mrs Hazel's feelings by assuring her the wedding dress would be hers to make, *and* those of the four bridesmaids (the Rectory girls, together with, naturally, the beloved Patricia).

Caroline was waiting impatiently for word from her

father that she should talk to Agnes. Not that she was looking forward to it, but gossip could sweep through the village like wind rippling through a cornfield, and who knew when Agnes might hear of it – and *what* she would hear?

'What's wrong with you, Agnes Pilbeam?' Margaret Dibble's voice was sharp. 'There's Master George's clean boots still here.' That wasn't like Agnes. The sharpness disguised concern, not, it was true, entirely for the parlour maid, but for the smooth running of the Rectory. Pale faces meant slack work, in her experience.

'Nothing.' Agnes straightened her shoulders and tried to look as if boots were all that concerned her.

Mrs Dibble eyed her. 'Have a cup of tea.'

'No thanks.'

'I said, have a cup of tea.' Mrs Dibble's voice rose with an authority granted under far older rule than those of staff seniority, and Agnes promptly sat down. 'It's that young Jamie Thorn, isn't it? He doing things he oughtn't?'

Inside, Agnes shrank with horror. So Mrs Dibble had heard. The whole village must know then, and her life was in ruins. Jamie had only told her last night, and she hadn't slept a wink, going over and over it again and again. Not a word of truth in it, he swore, not a word. Just lies to get herself a husband. It was Agnes he loved and always had. She wanted to believe him, she *did* believe him, until night brought the niggle: *But he would say that, wouldn't he?* Why would he, day had answered? Marriage faced him, either to Ruth or her. So even if it were true – and it wasn't, it *wasn't* – it must mean he loved *her*, Agnes. Unless he were just playing with her, too, saying he'd marry her, just so as she'd go all daft and let him have his way.

Agnes's fingers trembled as she picked up the cup, but the first sips of tea began to steady her. This was Jamie she was talking of, *Jamie*, who needed her support to see him through. She forced herself to listen.

'You young folks have too much freedom, you do,' Mrs Dibble was saying. 'Tell him to keep his hands to himself.'

'It's a bit late for that.'

'You mean—' Mrs Dibble sat down heavily. This was worse than she'd imagined. 'You're in the family way?'

Too late, Agnes realised that they were at cross-purposes. The gossip, if any, hadn't reached Mrs D. But how long before it did? And anyway, what she was thinking was bad enough.

'No!' She looked shocked. 'I never would. Jamie never would. We just had a bit of an upset, that's all.' She tried hard to smile brightly.

'Men!' Mrs Dibble snorted companionably, feeling somewhat disappointed that the olive branch she had with some effort thrust forward had proved to be unnecessary after all.

The story of the oaks at The Towers had by now entered village folklore. They were already young trees when the house was first built in the middle of the last century, although then its pinnacles, gables, and crenellations soared proudly above them. When the Swinford-Brownes arrived in 1909, the oaks had grown to such a height that William

62

immediately decided to chop them down so that the full glory of The Towers could be appreciated. To a man, the tree-cutters of Ashden, and even of Ashdown Forest, flatly refused to wield an axe, and William's own staff promptly invented mysterious weaknesses of limb that prevented such exertion. The oaks had been planted time out of mind and were sacrosanct. Edith was all for dismissing the mutineers, but William, though equally incensed, knew when he was beaten. He forced himself to chaff his men heartily that if they were to show the same loyalty to him as to the Sussex oaks he would have no complaint.

As Tilly turned the Austin tourer into Station Road, with Caroline at her side and Felicia hunched up in the rear seat, the pinpoints of glowing light from its oil lamps were overpowered by the light from The Towers' driveway; at first it was a dull glare above and through the trees but as they drew nearer The Towers the brilliance of the acetylene flares not merely twinkled but burst through the oaks' dark forms. Edith had been proudly talking of 'my lights' for the past week – 'electricity is so vulgar now . . .' – and, like her own, their effect was somewhat overpowering. Nevertheless Caroline felt a rising excitement, even though something seemed to have gone amiss with Edith's weather order to heaven, for the day though dry was chilly and cloudy.

Coming to The Towers seemed almost like visiting a different village. At one time Ashden station, about a mile from the old village, lay virtually isolated. Now the coal merchants' and the premises of one of the carriers hugged close to it, and houses were springing up to fill the gaps between those erected in the first flush of the prosperity brought by the railway.

Dances were common enough in Ashden, ranging from village hops to full balls at Ashden Manor, with a fashionable fancy-dress ball last August to celebrate Daniel Hunney's twenty-first birthday. Sometimes the Lilleys had informal dancing on the lawns of the Rectory or on the terrace, but the latter wasn't a great success, since cracked, uneven paving stones with tufts of buttercups and thrift growing in the crevices were hardly comparable to a polished ballroom floor, and the dances deemed suitable for rectories rapidly gave way to the Turkey Trot or the Huggie Bear, until the noise brought Father out to make a formal plea for respectability.

Caroline felt modestly pleased with herself tonight. The raspberry coloured silk, which had seen her stalwartly through three seasons, had been cleverly disguised to masquerade as a new gown by the simple means of drawing the skirt up into panniers and providing a new white underskirt, plus – and this was her pride – embroidery in raspberry silks to match the overskirt. That, and a feather discarded from one of the Ashden peacocks, stuck in a bandeau round her head, should do nicely. She smiled at her aunt, hoping perhaps that she would share her sudden enthusiasm for the evening.

'Do you enjoy dances, Aunt Tilly?' she asked curiously.

'No,' was the brief answer. There was silence from the rear seat too.

'Why come then?'

Tilly laughed. 'Because Ashden, Dover and England expect every lady to do her duty.'

'And you don't approve of that?'

'I do in practice. Where else are girls to find husbands? In theory, no.'

Surely, thought Caroline, there must have been a time when Aunt Tilly set out for an evening wondering whom she would meet, and what excitements – or disappointments – the evening might bring forth? 'Girls like me?' she queried.

Tilly thought quickly. She had gone too far already. 'Be thankful for Ashden dances, Caroline. Think of Dover.'

'I almost think,' Caroline observed, glancing up as the Austin pulled up in front of The Towers, 'that I prefer Buckford House.'

'Kindly don't exaggerate,' Tilly said drily, climbing down from the motor car and extinguishing the lamps. As she did so, Caroline noticed a familiar motor car, Reggie's new Perry. She took a deep breath and took first Felicia's, then Aunt Tilly's arm.

'Come on,' she cried cheerfully. 'Let's tango with The Towers.'

When they reached the ballroom, she was amused to see that the tungsten lamps were not in use. For this occasion oil lamps and candlelight were obviously deemed more suitable for flattering complexions. She was forced to admit the ballroom looked spectacular, with so many fresh flowers artfully adorning it that it smelled, from where she stood somewhat above the dancing floor level, more like the summer flower-show tent. A large 'I' and 'R' monogram was picked out in early roses amid a sea of lilies of the valley on the top of a large garlanded maypole at one end of the room, in honour of the date, the first of

May. This afternoon had seen the annual May procession through the village, culminating in a somewhat artificial (in Caroline's opinion) maypole dance by the schoolchildren in their playing field. She'd spent hours coaching the quick and the clumsy through their paces, and organising flower garlands, and was relieved that the children had managed to skip through their paces with no worse disaster than a collision between Annie Mutter and Ernie Thorn (who engineered it).

Trust the Swinford-Brownes to make this a State Occasion. Only the Household Cavalry were missing. In front of them, Caroline saw, were: the entire male staff of The Towers (though true, she couldn't see the gardener) in full dress livery, complete with violet-powdered wigs; an unfamiliar pseudo-patrician face similarly clad to announce them in stentorian tones; in the far distance Father and Mother doing their best to live up to the occasion; Isabel resplendent in blue charmeuse standing with Robert (he *was* handsome at least); and at the head of the line – oh, joy.

'What is it?' she hissed at Tilly.

Her aunt, clad smartly but dully in mole brown velvet, considered the question gravely. 'I rather think it's the new lampshade look.'

Caroline peered at the bright blue taffeta overskirt that stuck stiffly out from where Edith Swinford-Browne's waist must be presumed to lie, and at the mauve tube that linked this area of Edith to her feet. 'I hope someone turns her off soon,' she whispered. By her side to support the lampshade with his impressive tail-coated bulk was William, looking like a plump penguin with aspirations to being a sea lion. Then she sobered, remembering that these two were not the figures of fun of George's beloved caricatures but real people, who had just thrown their housemaid out in cruel circumstances. Moreover, this was the household where, presumably, Isabel would be living, at least at first. Would *she* turn into a Swinford-Browne by nature, as well as name?

She forced herself away from this unwelcome thought and back to the ball. She was surprised to see how many people here were strangers to her. True, most of what might be termed Ashden society was present, even the Minister, and she had to repress a desire to interrogate him then and there on his views of the plight of Ruth Horner. The Reverend Frederick Bowles and his wife had lived in Ashden only slightly longer than the Swinford-Brownes, having moved from somewhere in North Kent. Caroline rather liked him, but both of them seemed to behave like Martha and Moses, the figures in the Rectory weather house that adorned their drawing room windowsill – they popped out anxiously from their home from time to time and scuttled back inside for safety as soon as they could. Caroline decided the strange faces must be brewery staff, or Robert's friends. It underlined the fact that Isabel was entering upon a new and very different life. Then she saw Reggie. Her first impression was that he was dancing with another maypole, but perhaps that was simply the effect of the painfully (literally, it appeared) narrow yellow skirt, and tall sparkling bandeau doing its best to look like a tiara. The Honourable Penelope Banning, she presumed.

She quickly turned away to see what her sisters might be doing, telling herself she must keep an eye on Felicia . . .

Felicia sat close to Aunt Tilly. If Caroline were nowhere to be found then Aunt Tilly was her natural choice, for there was little chance that Tilly would leave her on her own, exposed. She felt her feelings must be written all over her face. If *he* came over to her, she felt she might faint from sheer pleasure. Someone was coming, but it wasn't him. It was the schoolmaster Philip Ryde, for whom she worked two afternoons a week teaching religious instruction. He would ask Aunt Tilly for her permission to request Felicia to dance. She looked in alarm at her aunt, who ignored her plea, or did not see it for what it was. So Mr Ryde asked her to dance, although she knew perfectly well he'd rather be dancing with Caroline. She smiled, rose, and gracefully stepped on to the floor, realising with gratitude that it was a military two-step and she would not need to talk to him for very long.

'You look very charming tonight, Miss Lilley.'

She instantly froze inside. She liked Philip Ryde, but she wished he wouldn't say things like that. It meant nothing, for everyone knew he adored her sister, so she never knew what to reply. She whispered the only thing she could think of.

'Thank you.' Then she was seized and clutched, pushed and pulled, as they marched up and down. Oh, that it were quickly over. Oh, that she were like Phoebe sitting out. Lucky, lucky Phoebe . . .

* * *

Phoebe sat scuffing the toe of her satin shoe crossly, in the happy knowledge that Mother could not see what she was doing under the pink satin dress. In fact, Mother was getting up to dance. A *tango*! That would set Ashden twittering for weeks. The doctor and the Rector's wife doing the tango. Phoebe didn't care as Felicia did about sitting on her own. To her, the women and girls looked like the chattering parrots in London Zoo, and the men like the penguins. Perhaps finishing school was going to be a mistake if it was merely lots and lots of dances, as Felicia had warned her. She had insisted on going there to escape from Ashden, but she could see it was going to be *just* as boring as home. Or, she amended, as boring as it had been till she started to tease Christopher. That at least was fun, especially when he went red and awkward. In some annoyance she saw Dr Cussed, as Father called him, though his name was Cuss, coming towards her. Martin Cuss. The vet was smug, opinionated and talked about animals all the time. Very well, if there was no getting out of it . . . Phoebe smiled welcomingly. 'I'd love to dance.' She jumped up eagerly, gazing innocently into his eyes. 'I remember exactly what you were telling me last time about that dear little litter of newly born pigs, and I wondered afterwards how little pigs get started in their mummy's tummy?' Phoebe thought of no one save herself, not even Isabel, whose evening it was . . .

What was wrong with her, Isabel wondered crossly. It was *her* evening, and she should sparkle like the champagne her father-in-law-to-be was so lavishly splashing around in the supper room. Instead she felt like a glass of champagne that had been left out overnight. It couldn't be anything to do with the way she looked. The blue charmeuse gown she had chosen, and Robert's mother had forced Jay's into making within the week, suited her delightfully, and she knew she was looking her best. It occurred to her that the reason might be that no one was asking her to dance. Of course. No one would until she had danced with Robert, and he seemed more interested in chatting to his friends. She decided to assert herself, left Edith almost in mid-flow on the subject of the redecoration of their rooms to be (a subject on which Isabel had a few as yet unvoiced thoughts), and appeared at Robert's side.

'Darling, I'm longing to dance with you.'

Robert jumped guiltily. He did not greatly enjoy dancing, though he was good at it, but he did enjoy pleasing Isabel and was suddenly conscious of his shortcomings when he saw her dear little pleading face. Fine husband he'd make.

'Happy now, little bird?' He expertly guided her into the waltz.

'Very,' Isabel sighed. Everyone was smiling at them, making way for them, sharing in their happiness.

'You'll be even happier when we get married, you'll see.'

'I want so much to be alone with you.' First step. 'We can go to Paris, can't we?'

The answer was yes, of course; she had never doubted that it would be. She glanced over Robert's shoulder and found herself under the scrutiny of the most impudent pair of eyes she'd ever seen. What's more they were familiar eyes, weren't they? Wasn't it the Swinford-Browne's hop-garden manager, Mr Eliot? She quickly looked the other way. After all, she was engaged to the heir to the whole estate, and he had no business to be looking at her like *that*.

Why was Mr Swinford-Browne rising to his feet, Caroline wondered, since the official announcement of the engagement had been made at the beginning of the evening? She was out of spirits, as well as out of breath from almost continuous dancing, and did not wish to face the fact that she felt peeved at Reggie's complete absorption in Miss Banning. He hadn't even had the courtesy to come over to introduce her. Raspberry silk might not match bright yellow satin for fashion, but it did suit her and she had spent a lot of time on it; it would have been nice if he at least *saw* it. Then she thought how ridiculous she was being. Reggie wouldn't notice if she was wearing strawberry silk or brown sacking. She concentrated fiercely as William, smug as a Toby Jug, began to speak:

'. . . I'm a plain man,' (*so he was, she thought crossly*), 'so a few plain words are all I'm giving you before supper and the rest of the evening. I want you young folks to enjoy yourselves' (*young folks, it made them sound like pixies*). 'We old folks have had our waltzes, now you striplings can suit yourselves. Huggie Bears, Bunny Hops, Ragtime, whatever you like.' He paused for applause and an enthusiastic amount was raised by his brave employees. Ashden, Caroline observed gleefully, was scandalised, its corporate identity shocked to the core at these imported dances which were passports to impropriety.

'And there's something else for you young folk. I'm

71

giving Ashden a present to mark the occasion.'

Caroline waited with mingled curiosity and apprehension. And then he told them –

'Caroline!' Reggie caught her white chiffon sleeve as she returned to the ballroom from supper.

A certain carelessness was the right note, she decided. 'Oh, it's you, Reggie.'

'I want to introduce you to Penelope. Darling,' he drew the maypole forward, 'may I present Miss Caroline Lilley, an old friend of mine. Caroline, Miss Banning.'

Old friend sized up the new. Reggie would be bored in no time, Caroline decided promptly, then thought perhaps she wasn't so sure. There was an amused intelligence in those blue eyes that hadn't been present in her predecessors. Moreover, at close quarters she could see that this maypole had an enviously developed figure. Suddenly the raspberry silk dropped in her estimation.

'You don't look that old, Miss Lilley,' Penelope observed, straight-faced, then grinning.

Caroline found herself smiling back. 'Reggie is known for his charm. I'm delighted to meet you,' she added truthfully. Much better than having Reggie drone on about a faceless love.

'Yes, he—'

Reggie interrupted his beloved. 'Darling, it's the Huggie Bear,' he cried joyfully. 'Enjoy the dance, Caroline.'

He swept Penelope off, and Caroline was left bleakly wondering why she was not rejoicing in Reggie's good fortune. The terrible Penelope seemed rather nice. With

72

reluctance, she pinpointed the reason for her discontent. Reggie usually danced the Huggie Bear with her. They always had fun with their hugs and lumbering rocks to and fro, and they had developed a particularly fine joint growl. Now it appeared she was partnerless. She looked round, suddenly desiring a partner very much indeed.

Philip Ryde, having thankfully returned Felicia to Aunt Tilly for the third time, was rewarded for having done his duty as a pair of dancing brown eyes accosted his.

'*There* you are, Philip. You've been avoiding me. Why haven't I seen you earlier?' This time Caroline forgot all about what her sisters might be doing. Even Phoebe.

The Reverend Christopher Denis, having bravely abandoned the supper room where he was able to indulge in polite and noncommittal conversation with the older members of the parish, was suddenly appalled to find his right arm under siege from the cream-satin-gloved hand of the Rector's daughter, the one he most feared . . .

'Oh, Mr Denis,' she declared sweetly. She smiled at his companions. 'You don't mind if I sweep him away, do you? I have a parish problem to discuss.' Phoebe looked grave.

'Later, perhaps.' His voice was almost a squeak, as he realised he was being propelled towards the gardens.

'Now. About Ruth Horner's baby—' Phoebe was adept at listening at doors.

'Miss Lilley!' Shocked, he could only submit. There was no end to what this frightful child might do. Once outside, however, he felt free to speak his mind.

'I explained, Miss Lilley, that in view of what occurred

in the vestry last week, I felt I should not see you alone again, for your reputation's sake.' And mine, he was thinking desperately.

'Didn't you like kissing me?'

'You're very young, and I'm twenty-eight.'

'I'm nearly seventeen. And,' her voice trembled, 'you do think I'm pretty, don't you?'

She looked so woebegone, he foolishly laid a hand on her arm. It was meant to be a clerical hand of consolation, but was not taken as such.

He found himself imprisoned in her arms, and her lips pressed on to his. Try as he would, he could not but respond, and, as her arms slackened their grip, he felt no immediate urge to break away. Indeed, to the horror of the normally undisturbed core of restraint within him, he was aware of more than his lips responding.

Phoebe set him free. 'That *was* nice,' she observed innocently, and sauntered back into the ballroom well satisfied. Not that she knew exactly what was happening, but, whatever it was, it gave her a sense of power. Each night now she inspected her breasts, greeting them as two symbols of her entry ticket into the adult world. A world that must surely have more fun in it than merely teasing Christopher. She looked around for inspiration, and noticed Felicia was still talking to Aunt Tilly. She didn't understand Felicia. She never had . . .

Daniel Hunney collapsed by his sister Eleanor. 'I need protection,' he told her ruefully. 'Don't desert me.'

'Why not? I might want to dance?' Eleanor replied, 'and

I'm certainly not going to dance with my own brother. Be grateful anyone wants to dance with you. You're not precisely Ranjitsinhji.' The trouble was that he *was,* she thought to herself. His dark hair and eyes and olive complexion would make him look, if not Indian, then almost Italian, had his square jaw, sturdy build and the bulldog determination in his expression not instantly corrected that impression. Daniel had always been too attractive for his own good. *And* too naturally charming. And he didn't care a fig about any of the girls who sighed after him.

'Surely you'd dance with me if it would save me from the clutches of Patricia Swinford-Browne?' he asked in dire tones.

Eleanor laughed. 'Poor Daniel. You're quite capable of looking after yourself, and you know it, especially against a poor girl like Patricia. Don't be unkind. It's not her fault she's unattractive.'

And as predatory as Jonah's whale, he thought. Poor little girl indeed. If only Eleanor knew. Patricia could wreak her terrible will upon Jem Mace himself. He'd met one or two just like Patricia at Oxford, but there they were so heavily guarded that there were few chances of granting their desires, though there was always a way if he really wished to find one. He didn't very often. His view was that there was enough time for that later, but that now there was the whole world before him, and he was going to see it without the complications of a woman in the background. Never had there been a time of so much opportunity.

Hell and Tommy, Felicia was coming over. 'She's hardly

danced at all,' hissed Eleanor. 'Daniel, do be nice to her at least.'

'Nice?' Felicia alarmed him more in a way than the Patricias of this world. She was coming ostensibly to talk to Eleanor, but he knew instinctively that he was the attraction. For all his natural charm, and to his own surprise, Daniel panicked.

'Eleanor.' Felicia's smile was genuine, for she liked her very much. They all did. Although she was the youngest of the Hunneys, Eleanor was easily the most sensible and good-natured, and was frequently not only the arbiter between her two older brothers, but between the Lilley girls as well – not to mention George. Eleanor was about the only girl of whom he ever spoke with full approval. She far outstripped his four sisters.

'I haven't seen you for so long,' Felicia said, apparently lightly. 'Nor you, Daniel. Aren't you dancing tonight?'

'I've promised this one to Eleanor.' Daniel smiled ruefully, sensing the hidden appeal. 'Just my luck to be tied down to a mere sister. She's quite ruthless.'

He deceived no one.

Robert was nonplussed. Staff and even managers of hop farms were servants and didn't stroll up and casually ask for a tango with a gentleman's fiancée. This fellow obviously did not know the rules, and Robert could hardly say no, especially as Isabel was looking at him expectantly. Taken aback, Robert nodded, and consoled himself that he didn't like dancing much anyway, and Isabel deserved everything he could give her, even in trifles like this.

On the floor, Isabel was at last feeling the old excitement returning, even if it had taken this strange man to awaken it. He was an excellent dancer, but not at all in the same way as Robert. Robert steered, guided and performed neatly and correctly. This man seemed to think he was breaking, or rather coaxing, a thoroughbred horse by moulding himself to its form, and her form, she was suddenly aware, was rather too obvious in this narrow gown. It had looked so elegant on the Jay's *mannequin* as Mrs Swinford-Browne called her, that she had suppressed her momentary doubt as to its suitability for the dance floor.

'Your fiancé is a very fortunate man,' he murmured in her ear at one particularly sharp twist of the head.

'So am I. I mean, girl.' It wasn't like her to be flustered.

'His father must be proud of his enterprising son.' She looked at him suspiciously. Surely he could not really think Robert enterprising, yet he seemed perfectly serious. 'And a good lover,' he added.

Her eyes flew wide open. '*What?*'

'I said an excellent brother,' Frank Eliot repeated blandly. 'I had the pleasure of a dance with Miss Patricia earlier.'

Isabel gulped. For a moment she'd thought he'd said something quite outrageous. *Was* Robert a good lover? His kisses. 'He is very fond of her,' she replied shortly, both anxious to get away from those disturbing eyes and aware that the hand in the small of her back was possessively firm.

Caroline glanced idly round as Philip went to fetch her a lemonade. All her sisters seemed happy enough, particularly

Isabel who was throwing herself high-spiritedly into the most odd gyrations with Robert; even Felicia was jigging around. Philip was a dear, really, and she'd had a wonderful evening with him, she told herself. After all, she could always talk William's 'surprise' over with Reggie next week. She saw Aunt Tilly's eye on her, and went to join her. 'Why don't you dance, Aunt Tilly? I saw Dr Marden ask you.'

'Do you know, Caroline, I think I will.'

To Caroline's amazement, Tilly broke all the rules of Ashden by walking boldly up to ask William Swinford-Browne to dance.

'A picture palace!'

Elizabeth shrieked with laughter on the way home, waking George up. He couldn't see what was so funny about it. Old Swinford-Browne's announcement had been the only high point of a mighty dull evening. A cinema in Ashden was heady stuff.

Even Father appeared to think it amusing. 'Do you realise what he's taking on, Elizabeth, if only the man had sense enough to realise it? He insists on putting it on the corner, this one—' He pointed to the junction of Station Road and Bankside.

'There are cottages here, so he can't.'

'If he buys them, he can, and they're not part of the Ashden estate any more, so Sir John can't stop him. You realise whose cottages they are?'

'Of course. Mrs Leggatt in the old ale house and – oh, Laurence, Ebenezer Thorn next door.'

'Yes. And Mrs Leggatt's from a Mutter family. He'd never get them *both* to agree to sell in a million years. I'm afraid his cinema is dead before a brick is laid. I don't think we need to worry about its moral effect on the young.' The famous Mutter–Thorn feud had raged since the eighteenth century, its original cause, a smuggling dispute, long since forgotten. It had subsided into a dormant volcano, but it still bubbled beneath the surface and was liable to erupt at the slightest provocation.

George, fully awake again now, wondered what was so immoral about a cinema. It would put sleepy old Ashden on the map. All sorts of wizard things were happening in the world, and Ashden still lumbered on in its own plodding way. A cinema would open its eyes, teach it there was an outside world. On his visit to Porky's folks' home in Buckinghamshire they'd sneaked off to London and seen *The Musketeers of Pig Alley*. He couldn't see Ashden taking to that; they wouldn't know what a gangster was down here, but the adventures of Pimple, now. Why, even Father would laugh at that. Or *Sixty Years a Queen*. It was *educational*. Besides, if there was a cinema here, the chaps at Skinners might even visit, he thought wistfully, as in the starry night the pony trap drew into the Rectory driveway.

Chapter Three

There was a battle looming. Caroline watched uneasily as Mrs Hazel kneeled on the sheepskin rug beside Isabel, who was pirouetting before the full-length mirror in the fitting room – a grand name for the curtained-off section of the dressmaker's cottage workroom. Her pinbox at her side, Mrs Hazel was ready for business but so, unfortunately, was Isabel. Caroline knew that half-smile, which to the outsider meant that Isabel was her usual charming self, and to her family was a warning that Isabel was about to dig in her heels. Now Caroline realised why her mother had insisted on her accompanying them. Elizabeth liked to have reserve troops at her disposal. Isabel had been moody since last week's ball, which Elizabeth had interpreted, probably correctly, as a sign that her daughter was already regretting her choice of the Rectory for the wedding breakfast.

'Lured by the violet-powdered wigs,' Caroline had

joked, but if they were going to have to endure Isabel's moods until August, it was no joking matter. This first fitting of the wedding dress was going to be a good test.

'You're so clever, Mrs Hazel,' announced Isabel admiringly to her own white silk reflection in the mirror, straining at the tacking stitches yet further as she twisted round to get the full effect. 'But don't you agree with me that the skirt could be just a little narrower, more elegant? Mother always thinks—'

Mrs Hazel removed three pins from their temporary lodging place at the side of her mouth. 'Not for a wedding, Miss Isabel.' She replaced the pins, discussion at an end.

'A full skirt is much more flattering, Isabel.' Elizabeth leafed placidly through Mrs Hazel's pattern book. 'That ball dress was far too restricting. You could hardly dance.'

Caroline stopped her mental applause. Mother did not usually set out to wave red rags in front of bulls. It must be part of her battle plan.

'At least it had elegance. I didn't look like a country bumpkin.' Isabel galloped full tilt into the cavalry.

The pins were removed once more. 'Don't you worry, Miss Isabel. I've been dressing country bumpkins to pass as gentry for thirty years now. I'll see you don't let them Swinford-Brownes down.' There was instant silence, and Mrs Hazel followed up her victory in ominous tones. 'I'll have to let this dart go. The tailor tacks are there, see? Grown you have, since I measured you. Too much of Mrs Dibble's lemon pudding, I'll be bound.'

'Peach, I think,' Elizabeth observed before Isabel could reply.

'Never heard of peach pudding.'

'For the bridesmaids,' Elizabeth amplified.

'Oh, *no.*' Caroline hated peach, or rather peach hated her.

Isabel shot her a vicious look. 'Lovely,' she enthused. 'That's just what I want the bridesmaids to wear.'

A pin found a passing target on Isabel's thigh as Mrs Hazel entered the lists again. 'Blue's best.'

'Green, perhaps,' Elizabeth said.

''Tis an unlucky colour, Mrs Lilley.'

'Not in the Rectory, fortunately. One of the benefits of my husband's calling.'

'That's as may be.'

Caroline's head was beginning to ache. Who said weddings were happy affairs? So far Isabel's had brought nothing but wrangling, albeit in subdued voices in case Father were disturbed. The Rectory seemed to be housing a flock of starlings, squabbling over guest lists, invitation cards, food, and now the Gown. The Gown was the prize morsel at stake, or rather, Gowns. Not the bridesmaids' of course – today was the first time Isabel had mentioned them – but trousseau dresses, suitable for a Paris honeymoon. Caroline's jet buckle had apparently formed an integral part of this trousseau and it had been with considerable effort and some guilt on Caroline's part that it was recalled to its rightful home. How to ensure that she (rarely they) received suitable gifts to fit their home was another of Isabel's favourite topics. This one had greatly surprised Caroline, since she'd thought the happy pair would live in The Towers, but Isabel finally drew breath to announce that the Swinford-Brownes were modernising Hop House for them. Her frequent hints to Robert on the virtues of being 'together' had, just at the right moment, swelled into a head-on appeal for 'their own little nest'.

Hop House had stood empty since Swinford-Browne bought the hop farm five years ago, perhaps because he had considered it too large for any mere manager. Who did this new suggestion spring from, Caroline wondered? Isabel's lazy nature would not make her over-eager to run her own household, but it would give her independence – of a kind – from Edith. It appeared her problem was that she still had to put up with Edith's choice of decoration and furniture.

For Caroline and the Rectory this had proved to have one priceless advantage. It meant that Edith was otherwise occupied and could not add her relatively well-meaning contribution to the subject of food. Elizabeth had striven to keep them apart, but on one disastrous occasion Edith had met Mrs Dibble. Caroline had come into the kitchen just in time for the climax, as Edith demanded grandiosely, 'And, of course, *paupiettes,*' and Mrs Dibble had promptly crossed herself and declared this was a Christian household. 'None of your Roman popery here, not over my dead body, never. 'Halleluia, sing to Jesus.'"

A thunderstorm had broken out then, and it looked as though the same would happen now, both inside and outside, for the sky was dark. Caroline excused herself. Rain would be better than this heavy airlessness, and she might be back at the Rectory before it started. She wasn't. As she skirted the pond and dashed across the road, narrowly avoiding Cyril Mutter's butcher's van, the heavens opened, lightning streaked across the sky, and the thunder that speedily followed it told her the storm was almost overhead. By the time she hurtled in the Rectory door she was soaked, her skirt and underskirts clung to her legs and her straw hat was a wet lump sitting atop dripping hair.

'Oh, miss!' Agnes took one horrified look as she hurried from the drawing room. 'Here, give them to me.' She took the hat and jacket Caroline had ripped off, and eyed the wet skirts. 'You get them wet things off now.' Caroline hesitated; clammy or not, she couldn't let this opportunity pass. Agnes had one of those faces that expressed little, so it was hard to know whether to speak or not. Caroline couldn't remember ever seeing her laugh, and she rarely permitted herself even a smile, at least 'on duty'. She was an attractive girl, though, with her grey eyes, oval-shaped face and shining hair as straight as a yard of pump water, as Ashden would put it.

'Leave them here for a moment, Agnes.' She took the offending garments back and hung them on the stand used for visitors' coats and vestments.

Agnes eyed her warily as Caroline led her back into the drawing room. '*I've* done your walking skirt. That Harriet doesn't know a clothes brush from a broom.'

'I don't know what the Rectory would do without you, Agnes,' Caroline said sincerely. 'You're happy here, aren't you? You'd come to us if you were in trouble?'

A slight stiffening of Agnes's shoulders told Caroline what she wanted to know. 'Of course.' Her voice was suddenly flat.

'Even if it's your private business?'

Agnes looked at her steadily. 'There's no one can do nothing save Jamie, me, that trollop and maybe the Rector. I'm sorry you've been told, miss.'

'This is a small village. I'm afraid most people do know now. I heard talk about it in the stores yesterday.' No point in hiding the fact that the village not only knew, but was rapidly taking sides. She was getting used to the low buzz that would stop as she entered and resume as she left. In the post office yesterday, as children hummed and hawed over important choices between humbugs and bull's-eyes, their mothers had gathered in a consciously self-righteous group to gossip. They spoke of Jamie Thorn, and with disapproval. Unfortunately the disapproval had now spread beyond the Mutters, and into the 'neutral' third of the village. She knew the all-powerful Lettices at the general stores would come down against Jamie Thorn, since Mrs Lettice had been a Mutter, but she was alarmed to find that so had the Wilsons at Lovel's Mill. They were usually neutral, and respected by all. Cyril Wilson was the miller and baker; Elsie, his wife, served in the shop. Gwen, his somewhat eccentric sister, always clad in enormous baggy trousers, bright blue jacket and a man's cap, was the delivery woman. All her life Caroline had listened for the distant tinkle of her bell in winter, followed by the haunting cry 'Hot muffins' floating across the Rectory gardens as she huddled by the fire: 'Come and buy 'em.' That cry seemed to reassure that all was right with the world. If the Wilsons had turned against Jamie, it was a bad day for him. His father, Alfred, had visited Father's surgery yesterday and Caroline had little doubt what it was about. Business had been slacker than usual in the forge, and even slacker in the ironmongery shop next door, which Jamie helped his mother run. In normal times the Mutter–Thorn feud by unspoken agreement never interfered with Ashden trading. That it now appeared to be doing so was ominous indeed.

'Mrs Dibble didn't know,' Agnes cried. 'I only knew myself ten days ago.'

'Ten days is a long time for gossip. But knowing isn't the point, Agnes, it's facing what will happen if Jamie has to marry Ruth.'

'But he hasn't done anything.' The voice rose to a wail.

'You can't *know* that for sure, that's the sadness.'

'Suppose someone came to you, miss, and said the Rector had pinched the poorbox. You'd know he hadn't, wouldn't you?'

Caroline forced herself to play devil's advocate. 'The Rector isn't young and—'

'Jamie loves me,' Agnes interrupted. 'Make no mistake about that. We're going to wed and live in the old gentleman's cottage. 'Tis all arranged. Ebenezer needs someone to look after him, he's got spare rooms and there we are. Why would Jamie do anything to upset that?'

'That's the cottage Mr Swinford-Browne wants for his cinema.' Caroline was suddenly side-tracked.

'What he wants and what he can have are two different things, begging your pardon, miss. That cottage belongs to old Master Thorn and that's where we're going to live.' Agnes's brave words were interrupted by a hiccup. 'She's lying, 'cos she needs a man to wed her.'

'But she's not been seen with anyone who could be the father.'

'No, and not Jamie neither. If he ain't done nothing, why should he be punished the rest of his life?'

The question was unanswerable. But it couldn't rest at that. Village opinion could bring terrible pressures to bear, right or wrong. The divisions were growing more marked; the Mutters stayed in the Norville Arms tap room of an evening, the Thorns in the public bar. It did not bode well. The only thing that could stop the rift spreading would be proof. Jamie could not produce it, so Ruth must be made to, and Caroline must see that she did.

'Something amiss, Harriet?'

It had penetrated even Myrtle's mind that Harriet was looking tediously sour, as if she had some real quarrel with that doorknob she was polishing.

Harriet Mutter was torn between making a mere tweeny her confidante and her need for allies. She never ought to have come here, she ought to have known she'd be walking into a Thorn-bush, as her ma would call it, what with Miss High and Mighty Pilbeam walking out with that Jamie. Her nose had taken a tumble now all right, Harriet thought with satisfaction. It was almost worth Miss P. taking it out on her.

'You're all right, Myrtle. She'd have old Dibble to reckon with, you being shared with the kitchen, but me, she thinks I'm her slave. 'Harriet, do the drawing room fire'.' Her voice rose in protest. 'That's *her* job. And me in my black, too. Look at me, just *look*.'

Myrtle did. Harriet looked her usual skinny but spick and span self. Since Myrtle was built on sturdy lines, with nondescript hair and a round face, she was humble about her own appearance, and kept an envious eye on Harriet's tall, angular form. Not that she was envious of Harriet in any other way. Life, Myrtle considered, was a matter of day to day and presented both treats and disappointments; usually there were more of the former, so Myrtle had nothing to complain of, and was puzzled as to why Harriet was so bad-tempered much of the time. Her looks would be handsome if it weren't for her sulky expression, and she could be a real grizzle-guts. Still, conscience told her that as Harriet was nearest to her in rank, she should take Harriet's side, even though her mother had warned her to keep away from all those Mutters and Thorns.

'That Miss Pilbeam can be a –' Myrtle searched her vocabulary – 'pig.'

'I went to the Rector.' Harriet swept on with her real grievance. Only very rarely did any of them go to the Rector. To Mrs Lilley, yes, but she hadn't been here, and Harriet wasn't going to wait. The Rector after all dispensed justice, he was God of the Rectory, and now he'd let her down by pointing out that Agnes was under a lot of strain, and Harriet should make allowances. *Why* should she? No one ever made allowances for her.

She knew why all right. The Rector was a Thorn at heart. Everyone knew he'd seen Jamie, but there was no sign of that skunk marrying Ruth yet. By doing nothing the Rector was as good as patting him on the back. He should exorcise him or something. A very faint memory of Sunday School came back to her.

'But the Rector's gone over to the Thorns,' she continued darkly. 'Everyone has. That poor girl.' She sniffed loudly.

'Not me, Harriet,' Myrtle assured her quickly, wondering whether she should comfort her by putting her arm round her. She remained stock-still.

'Harriet, you ain't done that silver yet.' Mrs Dibble marched in like she was Police Constable Ifield himself. 'I don't know what you think you're paid for; it's not chatting, that I know.'

Harriet smarted. Telling her off, and in front of Myrtle too! Old Dribble Dibble would pay for this. They'd all pay for it.

Caroline didn't envy her father his job. Every evening he must hold Evensong whether anybody attended or not, and this was followed by Rector's Hour, from which he always came in looking worried and preoccupied. There were few absolutes in human nature, he told her. Few all-good people, fewer all-bad. Every issue had two sides and the weighing of them demanded as fine an adjustment as the iron scales Mrs Dibble used. If Caroline were to help she must see Ruth Horner, she had decided, and made, as her preliminary gambit, an excuse to go to Aunt Tilly's room next morning. The room looked impersonal even taking into account the dullness of morning light and the fact that Aunt Tilly was a visitor, not a resident. Caroline perched on the bed, watching Tilly brushing her hair back into its usual severe coil. She had rather nice hair, and it seemed a pity that like Aunt Tilly herself it was tidied back so severely that it could never boast its glories.

'You never told me whether you enjoyed your dance with Mr Toby Jug at the ball.'

'It was rewarding,' Tilly said decorously.

'Goodness,' observed Caroline. 'How dull.'

'Dull?' repeated Tilly. No, it had not been that, at least . . .

'I hear you've turned poor Ruth Horner out on the street. Don't you have a duty to look after your servants' welfare?'

The jerk of William Swinford-Browne's hot hand on her back was highly satisfying to Tilly. But he merely laughed. 'I pay them well.'

'That's not what I asked.'

'You ladies are too soft-hearted. I have a duty to keep standards. If I keep her on, what kind of example is that to the housemaids of Ashden?'

'A compassionate one. What is she to do? The Relief of Fallen Women Society has turned her away. There is nothing but the workhouse for her.

'Nothing to do with me.'

'Your wife sits on the committee, and you on the Union board.'

The hand scored into her back, the other crunching her hand till it hurt. He was not a man to march away from trouble. 'Are you implying the decision was ours?

'I'm stating facts.'

'Then I'll state a few to you, Miss Lilley. Ashden doesn't want your sort. His hand moved up and down, caressing, threatening. She knew exactly what he meant. 'Any more of this nonsense and Ashden will see you no more. You understand? He relaxed the grip, and drew her closer. 'Good to see the young people enjoying themselves. He raised his voice heartily.

'Provided they don't look to you for help afterwards.'
She raised hers heartily too. The look on his face was worth
the broken promise to Laurence.

Did plain costumes and dull hats necessarily go with
being subservient in a household, as Aunt Tilly was to
Grandmother, Caroline wondered, looking at Tilly's navy
blue skirt and mauve blouse – smart, but oh how plain. She
plucked up her courage to tackle her aunt now. 'Now that
Toby Jug has turned Ruth out, do you think Jamie should
marry her whether he loves her or not?'

'I believe in men observing the same standards of purity
as women, Caroline,' Tilly answered after a moment. 'Why
should all the public censure fall on the woman?'

'But if Jamie is not the father, why should he be forced
by that public censure to marry her on Ruth's word alone?'

Tilly chose her words even more carefully. 'It's becoming
more and more possible for women to run their own lives,
Caroline, but as yet most of us are dependent on men
economically. And Ruth's life depends on economics. How
can she *prove* who the father is? Or live on the five shillings
a week a magistrate would order the father to pay for the
upkeep of his illegitimate child? It takes pressure to bring
feckless men to a sense of their own shame.'

'But Jamie Thorn isn't feckless.'

Tilly ignored this, bent on her own thoughts now. 'We
can own property, more and more women are working.
Some go to university, some are typists, even bank clerks
now. Even the lot of the women in the sweatshops will
improve. Society is a snail, but it will get there in the end.'

'Too late to help Ruth and Agnes.'

'The Ruths and Agneses of this world are in a sense immaterial—' Tilly broke off hastily, seeing Caroline's appalled face. 'Here in Ashden, of course, they are far from immaterial. If something goes amiss here, it slows down the wheel of life until it is mended. Just like my Austin,' she added, to lighten the tone. But Caroline shivered; the temperature had dropped now, and spring no longer blew so gently.

'I have been considering whether or not Jamie *is* the father,' Tilly continued carefully.

'Father asks why else Ruth would have named him.'

'Suppose the real father were disinclined?'

'And that she may have thought Jamie was so gentle he'd give way immediately under pressure?' Caroline was interested. 'Aunt Tilly, surely Ruth needs evidence? Has she any?'

'In Ashden,' Tilly pointed out drily, 'rumours fly without wheels and settle as judgements.'

'I want to talk to Ruth. I'm going now.'

Tilly considered this. Could it help? It could do no harm. 'I'll come. I'll talk to Nanny.'

Nanny greeted them suspiciously; their visits were not usually quite so frequent. 'Ruth?' She looked from one to the other. 'Don't you go upsetting her, Miss Caroline, I'm just getting her trained. Those Swinford-Brownes don't seem to have taught her anything. Fancy putting *linen* sheets on the bed and me with my rheumatism! Mind you, she's never going to make a parlour maid. A general, that's her limit. No interest in their work nowadays, that's the trouble with young gels. She's supposed to have put the pie in,' she banged the hearth with her stick for emphasis, 'half an hour ago and I don't smell nothing yet.'

Thanks to Father's help, an efficient oil-heated Excelsior kitchener stood in the scullery, and the cottage had its own well, which was more than many of these cottages did. Caroline went through to find Ruth. A flat iron was warming on the kitchener, though Nanny's ironing day was always Tuesday. A basket of clean washing waited patiently in a corner next to the copper. The hip bath hung above her head, ready for the ritual Friday night bath tonight. The pie, however, was a long way from ready. A bucket, used for storing dairy foods in the well to keep them cool, stood on the draining board, while Ruth slowly and incompetently peeled apples in the stone sink. The pastry dough on the scrubbed table was apparently left to roll itself. Caroline rolled up her sleeves. Elizabeth was an expert pastry-maker and had insisted on all her daughters being equally proficient, on the grounds that it would stand them in good stead whether they made their lives in palace or pantry. Only with Isabel had she totally failed.

'Morning, miss.' Ruth greeted her guardedly. With her auburn hair and heavy-lidded eyes she would have been handsome if her face had been less sullen and her stance less drooping with resignation. She had always been so and the current crisis had not improved matters. Her waist was noticeably thickening.

'Come to plead on Agnes's behalf, have you?' Ruth continued without malice. She looked pale, and Caroline suddenly felt sorry for the girl. She might dislike her, but Ruth was quite definitely in trouble. In a way Ruth reminded her a little of Phoebe but she had an instinct for self-survival that Phoebe, her sister suspected, lacked. Ruth had, Caroline reminded herself, found her way to Nanny Oates' haven in very little time.

'Come to help get your pie in the oven first.' Caroline set about the dough with the rolling pin.

'You want to know whether it were Jamie or not,' Ruth continued plaintively. 'Why does everyone think I'd make a mistake over Jamie? He courted me, told me Agnes were a dull old stick. No fun, and Jamie likes fun. He took it and now he can pay for it.'

'It seems so out of character. They were planning to marry soon, and to move into Ebenezer Thorn's cottage.'

She saw Ruth's eyes shift suddenly. 'So I heard. Well, now it's going to be Jamie and me. That's where we did our courting,' Ruth added nonchalantly.

'In the cottage?' Caroline was aghast.

'It were January. Hardly likely we'd romp around in the fields, is it? Love don't keep you that warm, miss. Ebenezer pops into the Norville Arms most nights, so Jamie and me slips in the back and no one's the wiser, certainly not the old gentleman. You should have heard Jamie laugh. Ebenezer never uses his parlour and there's nice old sofa there. That cottage will do me nicely, and you can tell Agnes I said so,' she ended up triumphantly.

Caroline got no further, indeed she seemed to have moved backwards, for there was now an explanation as to why no one had seen Ruth and Jamie together. They had only to cross the field behind the almshouses and they could enter the cottage from the rear path. Her lack of progress and the seeming impossibility of Agnes's plight left her deeply uneasy, as she walked back to luncheon leaving Aunt Tilly with Nanny. She just could not see Jamie stealing in to the back of a cottage with a girl he did not love, not just to kiss and cuddle, but to create a baby.

Caroline found herself almost stumbling up the driveway and in at the ever-open door of the Rectory. Within the safety of these walls, with the voices of her sisters coming faintly from the morning room, the smell of lunch, and her mother's laugh as she talked to Mrs Dibble, normality restored itself. This was solid ground, no matter what might lie outside.

Rector's Hour had taken longer than usual this evening, and Caroline suspected Father's last problem had been Aunt Tilly since both looked remarkably flushed when they entered for dinner. From the way Mother looked at them she obviously thought the same. Caroline knew she'd never hear about it, not from her parents, anyway. Sometimes, she decided, there were distinct disadvantages to being young and unmarried. Why did everyone think she had to be protected against the world? She had to live in it, after all, and yet Mother seemed to think anything to do with their minds above household affairs and fairy stories or their bodies below their chins was an unfit subject for discussion. Even their chins had to be protected against spring winds. It had been Nanny's job to initiate them into the mysteries of puberty, but the general messiness of being a woman she had learned about from her schoolfriends, and then in turn herself became an instructress, based on the fine art of theory.

Dinner was always, or nearly always, by common assent a time at which they were encouraged to talk over the day's events. Problems were left for morning or luncheon, as were politics and putting the world to rights, So whatever it was he had been arguing with Tilly about (and that took not much guesswork) Father was making an effort to forget.

'It seems, as we thought, my dear,' Laurence nodded to Elizabeth, 'that the cinema will run into a few problems.'

'What?' Isabel looked up belligerently, obviously prepared to take anything to do with the Swinford-Brownes personally.

'Mr Thorn refuses to move, but Mrs Leggat, being a Mutter, is therefore only too happy to oblige. She claims that ever since her ale house was forced to close nine years ago, she's been living with the smell of stale beer, and she cannot wait to leave.'

'I think Mr Thorn's a nuisance,' declared Isabel. 'It's most generous of Mr Swinford-Browne.'

There was an awkward silence.

'A good deed, if not from a good egg,' George broke in.

'A curate's egg.' Phoebe sniggered, till she saw Caroline's eye on her.

'Can't the cinema be built somewhere else?' Felicia contributed.

'Mr Swinford-Browne has apparently decided upon a central village position. That is the only one available – owing to the pond, the village oak, ourselves, the churchyard and the general stores inconsiderately taking up his other choice positions. However, *where* this cinema goes is immaterial. The more important issue is what it would mean for Ashden.'

'It'll be jolly exciting,' George enthused.

The Rector looked grave. 'For such excitement we have Tunbridge Wells and London. In Ashden we have a community that would be threatened by such an intrusion.'

'We could visit it sometimes, couldn't we, Father?' Felicia asked eagerly.

'I fear not.'

'Whyever not?' George was aghast.

'Pictures are exciting,' cried Phoebe, horrified. They would at least be *something* to look forward to in her visits back from finishing school. Besides darling Christopher, of course.

'And informative,' Caroline put in hopefully, but in vain.

'I fear, Elizabeth,' her father said, 'our community seems already split.'

'Between Mutters and Thorns,' answered Isabel impatiently. 'It always will be.'

'Not that.'

'Between chapel and church?' Tilly asked.

'No. Those rifts are surmountable, but this one is between the older generation and the new, and in that there can never be compromise.'

'It's nice here.' Agnes looked primly around her in the crowded Pantiles teashop in Tunbridge Wells; she looked everywhere but at Jamie.

'But you don't like towns, do you?'

'I'm a farm girl.' She tried to joke.

'You're my girl,' he replied quietly. 'Aren't you?'

Agnes swallowed as she felt tears pricking at the back

of her eyes. To be sitting here with Jamie, hearing his laugh, and him so handsome, with his strong arms and that special twinkle just for her, and the prospect of being kissed on the way home, would have meant heaven only a week or two ago. Now everything had changed, and he was looking at *her* in appeal, reversing their roles and leaving her floundering.

She fastened her attention on the fairy cakes as though they could provide some sort of answer.

'Aren't you?' he repeated.

'Yes.'

'Come on, Aggie, let's get out of here. Let's breathe.' No one knew them here in the big town, not like Ashden where Agnes felt eyes following her everywhere she went now. She didn't care whether they were looking at her in pity, or if they were laughing at her for being a fool, she hated it just the same. She told herself it was worse for Jamie. Seeing him so desperate changed things. She had been a princess with a handsome prince to look after her, but now she was only Agnes Pilbeam with a man she wasn't sure she knew. They walked in silence up to the common where they could be alone.

'You're doubting me, aren't you, Aggie?' Jamie asked sadly at last. 'Just because of that Ruth's lies.'

'It's not that, Jamie—' She turned to him, she couldn't help it, and the prince put his arm in hers to show passers-by they were engaged, and everything was all right again. Then those insidious voices began again. *Did he do this to her?*

Jamie felt her stiffen and took his arm away. 'If you don't believe me, Agnes, who will? I might as well make away with myself.'

'Have done, Jamie,' she replied sharply. 'No talk like that. It's just I remember that evening – you wanted me to – well, like we were already married, and I wouldn't. I wondered if you did it with her because you were cross with me for not – obliging.'

Jamie did not reply. Didn't she realise how difficult it was to respect her like he should? When your head and your heart told you one thing, and the rest of your body was shouting something quite different. Why did he bother? His brother Len never did. He'd been boasting since he was thirteen about the girls he'd had. Disgusting, he'd thought it, until he grew up and found out what it was like.

'You think what you like, Aggie. I thought as we were to be wed you might just about have trusted me, that's all.'

She burst out crying. 'I do, I do, Jamie.'

When there was nobody around, they kissed and made up, but there didn't seem much to say on the train back home, so they didn't say anything.

Laurence Lilley wondered curiously what this summons to Ashden Manor might be for. It was by no means unusual for Sir John to ask him for a discussion at the end of 'Squire's Day'. From Tuesdays to Fridays Sir John worked in London, on some army job he would never define, and Reggie ran the estate. On Mondays, Sir John had decided the Squire himself, not his heir, should be present, for the equivalent of the parson's 'Hour', when parishioners as well as ten ants of his estate might come to seek advice on anything that might be troubling them. Caroline and Eleanor were frequently called on to write letters as a result for the older, illiterate villagers, and occasionally to act as peacemakers over some trivial issue. The Rector dealt with matters of conscience, or with urgent issues that could not wait till Monday, and Sir John dealt with secular matters.

There was an urgency about today's summons to the Manor that puzzled the Rector. Unlike his daughter, he went to the front entrance of Ashden Manor. Lady Hunney, or Maud as she was referred to privately between himself and Elizabeth, was not a figure of awe, but rather to be pitied. He had suffered too much at the hands of his own mother to fear any lesser mortals cast in the same mould. He wondered whether Sir John's summons could be connected with the Ruth Horner affair, which was growing in intensity and urgency. How, if so, could he be involved?

The affair had, from Agnes's point of view, taken a turn for the worse, for he had now spoken to Jamie. He liked the lad, and so the outcome of the talk had distressed him. He wasn't, or so the Rector had thought, born in the same mould as his elder brother, Len, and he could have sworn he was well-intentioned. But even the best of intentions could be forgotten when the flesh took over. Laurence was not so old that he could not remember Elizabeth, the summer evenings, and the agonising wait before they were wed.

Jamie had denied it, of course, and stood up to him – at first. 'Ruth is lying, sir. I never did see her.'

'Her story is very convincing, Jamie. I've talked to her again and she has told me of your meetings in your grandfather's cottage.'

'What?' The boy's face had suddenly gone white.

He'd shut up like a clam, guilt written all over his face.

The Rector had seen that look on too many faces to have any doubt at all. Guilt, caught by the unexpected. So how could Tilly's ridiculous theory be true? He loved his sister, but they were chips off the same block and when they clashed it was Titan against Titan.

The butler showed him into the study where Sir John was waiting for him.

'Thank you for coming, Mr Lilley.' On rare occasions after port and a cigar Christian names would be used, but on occasions such as this formality was a strength, not a distancing factor. Their wives maintained the same formality, but with different reasons, and it was never relaxed despite their long and on the whole peaceable relationship.

The subject was not Jamie Thorn, for which the Rector was thankful, as he sat down in the chair to which the Squire had waved him. Sir John was a shorter man than Laurence, but their faces betrayed characters with much in common: men of firm opinions, and considered judgement. Where Sir John was often content to be silent, however, assessing situations as on a battlefield, the Rector usually pressed forward, using dry humour as a cover to talk his way to the truth. There was kindness in both men, but little humour in Sir John. Moreover, the one considered an incorrectly folded newspaper a sign of disintegrating society; the other could see little relevance between private preferences and public heart.

'Thomas Cooper visited me about his cottage.' Sir John did not believe in lengthy preambles. 'Mr Swinford-Browne has asked him to move into an almshouse. He has refused.'

'The former oast-house worker on the Towers' estate? But he's retired.'

'Precisely. It's a tied cottage, because he used to work for the hop farm. After his son moved out last year, there's no legal reason Swinford-Browne should continue letting it to old Tom. As I gather Swinford-Browne pointed out, it was decent of him to find him room in the almshouses.'

'Church almshouses.' The Rector rubbed the side of his nose absently. 'But there is a vacancy, so no matter.'

'No matter? My dear Mr Lilley, take care. You and Swinford-Browne are shortly to be linked by marriage.'

Sir John was the politician, he the moralist. Of course, Laurence realised belatedly, anything linking Swinford-Browne to the Rectory would be scrutinised by the village for signs of favouritism. 'I could not at the moment see grounds for not granting an almshouse to Cooper, when there is one available. Mrs Hastings died last month.'

'I understand, though I gather Sammy Farthing has his eye on it, but the point of my concern is that Cooper does not want to move.'

'He worked the hop fields and oast-houses for fifty years. It would be a hard man that turned him out for his last ten or so. He must be seventy.'

'Unfortunately that does not count in law.'

'His son was dismissed to make way for Mr Eliot, the new manager.' Laurence thought for a moment. 'I cannot believe Swinford-Browne wishes that small cottage for Eliot. He has some plan.'

The Squire eyed him appreciatively. 'I'll make a politician

of you yet, Mr Lilley. He wishes, I gather, though I have no proof, to move Mrs Leggatt into the cottage – and she is not eligible for an almshouse yet.'

'Of course. The cinema. He needs to buy her cottage. I gather, however, Ebenezer Thorn is refusing to sell his cottage, so Swinford-Browne's efforts may be in vain.'

'He is not a man to give up so easily. I have advised Cooper to go to my lawyer, but I fear he stands little chance, unless there is something in the deeds about the cottage being used only for farm purposes, and even then Cooper himself has no claim.'

'And what is my role?'

Sir John trod carefully. 'My instinct tells me there are murky waters round this episode and, as the stick that stirs them is shortly to be linked to your family, I wished you to be warned, since there is also the question of the new cemetery. Do we have no rights over Tallow Field? It is glebe land.'

'Ah yes, but rented to the Swinford-Browne estate since at least 1850, and while its owner continues to vote against it as a site for the cemetery on the grounds that it would be desecrated by the hop-pickers, I cannot revoke the agreement, since there are no deeds or documentation. It is a 'time out of mind' arrangement, as his solicitors have informed myself and the diocese. I suspect Swinford-Browne has plans for Tallow Field as well as Cooper's cottage. He needs new hoppers' huts.'

'You have no alternative site?'

'None suitable. Swinford-Browne suggested the present cricket ground, but not with any degree of seriousness.'

Sir John managed a smile. Lordsfield, as its name suggested, was on the Manor estate.

'The matter is becoming serious,' the Rector continued. 'If it is not settled soon, we shall be forced to re-use or double up on plots.'

Sir John frowned. 'I don't like the idea of that, if only on more secular grounds. Whose family? Which plot? Every stone is known and dear to someone here. Yet we have a public benefactor for a cinema who stops short of ceding rented land for a burial ground.'

'He thinks of the future, we of our heritage, Sir John. Both have value. Have you visited the cinema?'

'In London, yes, many times. Quite out of place in Ashden. It would be a bad influence. The darkness of the cinema can only encourage a familiarity between the sexes that is already growing fast out of control amongst our youth. What should be a privilege of unchaperoned meetings between a young man and woman is fast being taken as a right, and, moreover, abused, and see where it has got us.'

'Jamie Thorn.' The Rector sighed. It had to come.

'I give you a word of warning, Laurence.' Sir John looked grave. 'I am told there is talk of rough music.'

'That outmoded mob law? It died out years ago, surely.' The Rector was shaken. 'It has not been known in Ashden in my time.'

'Merely talk, Laurence. But it is a sign that feelings run high.'

The Rector walked home, in disquiet both at the machinations of man and at his darker side. None knew more than he that the conquest of reason by passions, whether violent or sexual or both, was ever present in a village, however deep it lay buried. And rough music which turned the victim into a social outcast was one ugly manifestation of it. He slipped into St Nicholas, so that its silent certainty might strengthen him. The seemingly massive problems of today faded into insignificance besides the calm relics of yesterday. He knew and loved everything about this church, like the Rectory itself. Its lancet windows and pointed arches, the mural of St Nicholas with his three purses, whitewashed over by the Puritans and lovingly and with difficulty restored, the magnificent bells, two of which were cast by the early eighteenth-century Sussex itinerant bellfounder John Waylett, the hassocks woven by the Mothers' Union, the disputed altar cloths, the beetle in the beam above him, each carved pew head, the devil's door in the north wall, the three holy initials on the font: IHC, the stone effigies of the Norville and Hunney chapels, and its centre-point, the altar, all mellowed into a whole, and the whole was God. God was here, God was his help, but the decisions were still his.

The Forest was leaping with life. Bracken that had been slimy brown in February and peppered with a few yellowy-green shoots in April was over a foot high and, save on the higher ground, conquering the dead undergrowth with fresh green leaves. Green canopies formed overhead; and branches waved over their path, triumphant in their victory over winter. Gorse and broom flamed yellow on the open ground. Felicia had dragged Caroline out to Five Hundred Acre Wood, determined to show her a spiked rampion, whatever that was.

'*Please* come,' she pleaded. 'I wanted to be sure I wasn't dreaming. It's so rare.'

Caroline capitulated. She needed some air after being closeted in the Hunney library. After the most glorious April she could remember, the weather was bad again; rain might be good for the trees but it was bad for the spirits, so a dry day like today, even though it was cool, when the undergrowth would not brush wet against her skirts and soak through to her stockings and then to her legs, was not something to be passed indoors, especially with Mother and Mrs Dibble cloistered together over menus and budgets, both for the Rectory fête in July and the wedding. The very word 'wedding' was taking over the Rectory, lurking in corners ready to jump out at her. The carrier had three times delivered samples of material on approval for the bridesmaids' dresses, three times returned them to Messrs Weekes and on the fourth delivered them with such a glare that even Mrs Hazel pronounced herself satisfied. Escape would be good, Caroline decided, and anyway it was pleasant to see Felicia so enthusiastic about something, even if it was a wild flower. She had been very quiet for the last two weeks. When she was younger, Caroline had nightmares that Felicia might slip away from them like Beth who won her heart in *Little Women* and then devastatingly died in *Good Wives*. Mother had comforted her by informing her that it was Felicia's emotions that were fragile, not her body, and, anyway, she had every intention of keeping all five of her children with her, since she was far too lazy to do without her little chicks.

'Should you like to be married, Caroline?' Felicia asked,

bending over to inspect the ground closely, Sherlock in search of a clue, Caroline thought, amused.

'And leave you? I should think not.' Caroline decided to go cautiously.

'I should. But I sometimes think I never will be. Do you believe there is only one man for each of us?'

Caroline considered the question gravely. 'How could I answer that unless I line up every man in the world, from Shanghai to Chicago, and study them one by one? Then I'd know, but I'd be too old to marry then. It is a problem.'

Felicia laughed, to Caroline's relief. Their footpath crossed a bridle path, and she heard, then saw, two horsemen, or rather a horseman and horsewoman. 'It's Reggie,' she cried with pleasure, straining her eyes in the sun. 'What on earth is he doing away from the estate on a Tuesday?'

'Who's with him?' Felicia demanded urgently.

Caroline stared at her in amazement, and looked again. 'It's his lady love, Miss Penelope Banning.'

She saw Felicia blush, was puzzled, and then in one flash guessed the reason for it. 'Oh, Felicia,' she said in despair rather than reproach.

'I thought it might be Eleanor with Reggie.'

'No, you thought it might be Daniel.'

'I can't help it.' Felicia sounded agonised as the pair galloped up to them. 'Don't tell anyone, *please*.'

Penelope dismounted, and somewhat reluctantly, Caroline thought, Reggie followed suit.

'Good morning, Miss Lilley.'

Caroline introduced Penelope to Felicia, conscious that

Reggie's beloved was looking very smart in her riding habit and she, Caroline, was looking very unsmart in her old gingham print. 'Breeches,' she commented. 'Not even a divided skirt. Oh, how I envy you.'

Penelope grinned. 'That reminds me. I saw your aunt in London the other day—'

'It can't have been her. She'd have told me if she was going to London.'

'Perhaps not. I thought it was her, though. In Kingsway,' Penelope added, with what seemed to Caroline a faint query in her voice.

'I say, Penelope, do let's move,' Reggie said impatiently. 'You don't mind, do you, Caroline? This is the first blessed time we've thrown off the chaperone.'

Penelope gave a distinct wink to Caroline. 'Literally thrown off. So enthusiastic is Reggie he simply tossed her off her pony into the undergrowth.'

Reggie daringly seized her round the waist, leaving Caroline feeling curiously out of joint at seeing his familiarity with Penelope. 'Come on, young woman. Let me show you how I can throw ladies on.'

Penelope remounted easily, looking even longer-legged in her breeches. Oh, the wonder of it, Caroline thought. If one of his daughters appeared in the Rectory in such garb, Father would faint – or promptly begin an exorcism ceremony.

'She's first-rate, isn't she?' Felicia observed as the couple rode off.

'Who?'

'Miss Banning.'

'Yes. Yes, I suppose she is,' Caroline replied snappily. 'Now for goodness' sake, let's find your blessed rampion.'

Caroline suspected one of the reasons her father so liked Rogationtide was that its traditions still harked back to pre-Christian rituals. He saw no reason that traces of the old religion might not sit comfortably with the new. His fear was that like so many traditions, even the Sussex dialect itself, they were beginning to die out. Not in Ashden, he had resolved, and at first sight it seemed the whole of Ashden must be here for the beating of the parish bounds, Caroline thought, as she pushed her way through the crowds milling in the churchyard at two o'clock on the Sunday afternoon. The reappearance of warm weather obviously helped. She could see Sir John's bailiff doing his best to discipline the milling huddles into some kind of order with the help of Sammy's son, Mr Farthing the churchwarden, and the village band was getting ready for its noisy battle with the choir. Hymns usually gave way to more secular melodies. Last year the whole procession, choir and all, had started off decorously singing 'O God, our Help in Ages Past' and ended up back at the churchyard bawling out 'Goodbye, Dolly Gray'.

Felicia was with Mother and Isabel with Robert, who still luckily appeared to think his lady love could do no wrong, judging by the slightly hangdog look of adoration in his eyes. There was no sign of Phoebe. Caroline could also see something even more ominous. Agnes, her arm defiantly hooked in Jamie's, was surrounded by a crowd composed entirely of Thorns. The Mutters were similarly grouped together. It did not bode well for a Christian festival in which village unity was a dominating factor. She made her way to join her mother and Felicia as the band struck up with something she dimly recognised as 'All Things Bright and Beautiful', and miraculously Ashden turned itself from a disorderly rabble into a well-dragooned column, as they all swarmed down Beggars Lane between Ashden Manor Park and the cricket ground towards the first boundary stone. Not too quickly, however, for Ashden had its own traditions for this festival, one of which was that the church warden, sacristan and curate should race each other to this first marker, at the corner of the far wall of the Ashden Manor estate. Christopher Denis won easily by twenty years, and Phoebe was quickly at his side, Caroline noticed with misgivings.

'I mark this stone—' The parish clerk, Horace J. Trimble, who owned the cycle shop, was so overcome at the importance of his suddenly public role that his voice came out as a squeak and had to be quickly schooled into pomposity.

Then it was round Ashden Manor and south into the outskirts of the Forest. Like its neighbours Hartfield and Withyham, the parish boundaries of Ashden took in a little of the Forest land, and gave a few lucky parishioners the traditional rights of 'estovers', cutting wood for fuel. Then the boundary re-emerged from the Forest to take in Owlers Farm where legend had it that smugglers hid their loot betwixt the south coast and London. It had always seemed a somewhat sinister as well as lonely outpost to Caroline and she was glad when they reached Hodes Meadows, bright with cowslips, the beat of the clerk's stick hitting the stones in turn. The youth of the village for whose benefit this performance was staged, in order – so the theory went – that the parish boundaries might be protected by an oral tradition, were already losing interest in the markers and concerning themselves with more worldly matters, like sweethearts. And not just the villagers!

'Caroline, I've got to talk to you.'

'Why?' Caroline asked, banging the marker stone at the Devil's Bed on the far side of Tillow Hill, supposed to be a prehistoric burial chamber, Father said. At the moment she wished it were Reggie's head.

'She's jilted me, Carrie.'

'Who, *what* are you talking about?'

'Penelope.'

'You mean she wouldn't let you kiss her?'

'Concentrate. I really need you, Caroline. She says she won't marry me. She's decided to devote her life to loftier things, she says.'

'You're quite tall.' The chance to tease him was irresistible.

'Be serious, *please*. You've got to help me get her back.'

'Why?'

'Because I love her.'

'The truth, Reggie.'

He sighed. 'I wish you didn't know me so well. Because I don't like being jilted. And I do love her. I want you to go and tell her what a stout fellow I am. I'll give you her address.'

'Kind of you. But no.'

'Why not?' He looked astounded.

'Because, Reggie dear, you've always fought your own battles. Remember Omdurman?'

'What on earth are you talking about?'

She stared at him, taken aback. 'The games we used to play in the schoolroom. You were always Kitchener, Eleanor your horse and I was a whirling dervish.'

'Was I? I don't remember. Look, about Penelope—'

Her limited patience snapped. 'You're a pompous, inconsiderate ass, Reggie, and she's quite right to jilt you.'

He said nothing, merely looked hurt beyond belief, and waited for the usual contrition from Caroline. It didn't come. 'I do remember, now,' he offered at last.

She tried, but somehow she couldn't meet him. 'We're not children any more.'

'No.'

So Reggie saw it too, that gulf that had unexpectedly opened between them, too wide to cross now. There was a grub crawling up the side of that old stump. At any moment it would get to the top, and meet that ladybird. There were three empty acorn cups lying on it too, and Caroline felt like crying. She wasn't going to, though, not in front of Reggie. Everything had to pass, everything had to change, even friendship. She turned to go back to the path, stubbed her toe, and stumbled on into the sunlight.

'Caroline!'

She took no notice of his cry for it was drowning in the deep shining pool of their childhood.

Whitsun, two weeks later, was usually the crown on Caroline's favourite season, but with the cool dull weather the prospect of the weekend ahead lacked the excitement she always associated with it. It was a time of smoking fires and rattling windows, most un-May-like. She felt restless, dissatisfied with her work and her life. The Rogation Sunday festivities had ended in the brawl her father had feared between Mutters and Thorns, as the Mutters refused point-blank to allow any Thorn across their land (a Mutter owned Robin's Farm, which unfortunately, near the end of the boundary walk, was split between Ashden and Hartfield). They had yielded in the end, with the Rector's intervention, but it had set a public seal on the Jamie Thorn split, and she had seen Agnes in tears twice since. It was stalemate: Jamie refused to wed Ruth; Ruth continued to maintain he was the father. Ostensibly the village remained the same friendly place Caroline had always known, but she found now she was always glad to return home.

The Rectory seemed a charmed world. The gardens were blazing with flowers, the blues and purples of May showing signs of yielding to the pinks and whites of June. The tennis court had already seen more play this season than for some years and even Percy Dibble's grumbling had been reduced to a minimum, since their flying feet greatly reduced the number of times he was obliged to drag out the heavy roller. Yet this did not seem to cheer her in the slightest. Not when the kitchen was full of Mrs Dibble's mutterings on quantities and supplies, and dark prognostications on the likelihood of rain on August the first. Everything apparently depended on St Swithin's Day. The oak had done its best by coming into leaf before the ash tree this year, thus ensuring light rainfall for the summer, but the Saint was apparently the ultimate arbiter. July 15th was going to be a tense day.

Caroline wasn't even looking forward to their annual grand tennis party which was always held in June, partly because she hadn't set eyes on Reggie since the beating of the bounds and, she realised, had no wish to, though she couldn't analyse why. After all, they hadn't really quarrelled, a few words were easily forgotten. It took some time for her to acknowledge it was deeper than that. Could it be she was outgrowing Reggie? It had been all too easy to take him for granted, but just as childhood passed, so usually did childhood's friends. They had different paths to follow – whatever hers was – and sometime they had to reach a crossroads. They'd reached it, that was all. Where her own particular path was going she had not the slightest idea, but it looked an extremely obscure one at the moment.

Everything seemed at odds this year, not only with her and Reggie, but in Ashden with this business of Jamie Thorn and Ruth, which was throwing up a darker side of the village than that which she knew and loved. In the outside world, too, there was trouble, for in Ireland there was talk of Civil War over the provisions of Mr Asquith's Home Rule Bill. Life seemed to be gathering pace and loping out of control, just like their English sheepdog Ahab when he slipped his lead, lured by the mysterious depths of the forest.

The next event to take them by surprise was that Christopher Denis resigned his position, having felt called to a chaplaincy with the armed forces overseas.

'I can't understand why,' Father told them frankly. 'I

thought he was happy here. Not that it's for me to interfere with God's purpose, but I do sometimes wonder if His intentions get a trifle confused in transmission. Christopher is happier with a book than a rifle.'

'Perhaps that's the reason, Laurence,' Tilly suggested. 'Sometimes one feels called to do something one's never dared do before.'

'Like being rude to Grandmother?' Phoebe asked rudely.

'Phoebe!' Retribution was swift. 'Go to your room.'

It wasn't fair. She was in the wrong, but she wasn't a child and Father kept forgetting it. Phoebe burst into tears and dashed out of the room. Elizabeth said nothing. She would never plead with Father in their hearing. Or could it be, Caroline wondered, that she too suspected Phoebe's rudeness was prompted by her dismay at being deprived of Christopher Denis?

The next event marred Whitsun itself, and, though it did not touch them so nearly, was far, far worse. On Whit Saturday Caroline rose early, and ran downstairs to find her father preparing to depart for Matins with a grave face. 'What's wrong?' she asked in alarm. It was clear something terrible had happened.

'The newspaper reports that the *Empress of Ireland* liner has sunk after a collision with a collier in the St Lawrence river. The loss of life is put already at over a thousand. There was a rumour yesterday, but it seemed unbelievable.'

'But how could it happen *again*?' she asked, aghast. 'After the *Titanic*? Were there no lifeboats, no lifebelts, *again*?'

'Plenty. It must have sunk too quickly.' He paused.

'Laurence Irving is lost and his wife also. Both splendid actors. Many women and children lost. You never saw his father act, did you?' he continued absently.

'No.' She had only been thirteen when Henry Irving died.

'Fine, oh, very fine. That *was* acting. Did you know I wanted to be an actor once? And this was his son, some consider he was a greater player than his father, especially in modern pieces. Gone, the senseless waste.'

'What caused the collision?' Her father was more shaken than she had ever seen him, he must be, for he never usually rambled in his speech.

'Fog. However good the ship, however great the technical achievement, nature can always defeat it. In the end, though, man will always cause his own destruction, trusting in his own superiority, not God's. A thousand gone, Caroline, a *thousand*, and in a ship of such a name. These times are out of joint indeed.'

He departed to Matins and, concerned, Caroline waited anxiously for his return, slipping out from the breakfast room when she thought he would be due back. To her surprise he pulled a doorbell on his return, and she ran to open it. It was not her father but the local policeman, Joe Ifield. She stared at him stupidly, her thoughts still on the appalling tragedy she had been reading about in *The Times* during her father's absence.

'It's official, miss.' Nevertheless he took off his helmet, twisting it awkwardly in his hands.

'My father isn't back from Matins.'

Aunt Tilly came up beside her. 'I believe it is me, not the

Rector, you wish to see, is it not, Constable Ifield? You've come to arrest me.'

He stared at her blankly. 'You, miss? Whatever for?'

Tilly reddened as she saw Caroline's amazement. 'Please let's get this over, Constable, before the whole household is privy to the news. I have my suitcase packed ready.'

'You're not a Peeping Tom, are you, miss?' Joe gabbled in astonishment.

'A what?'

'I come to arrest poor young Fred.'

'Fred?' Tilly repeated faintly.

'Fred Dibble, miss. I know he's simple, and don't mean no harm, but I have to arrest him because there's been a complaint. I should've gone to the trades entrance, but I thought it fair to have a word with the Rector first.'

'You'd better come to his study to wait.' Caroline took charge as her aunt seemed incapable of speech. She speedily returned from ushering Joe into Father's study. 'Why should they wish to arrest you, Aunt?' She rushed after Tilly as she tried to escape, determined to get to the bottom of this extraordinary episode.

'It was a joke.'

'It wasn't. Please tell me.' She had a sudden thought. 'Someone mentioned they'd seen you in Kingsway – is it connected with that?'

'I promised your father not to speak of it.'

'You haven't,' Caroline pointed out. 'I've spoken to *you*.'

Tilly sighed. 'I suppose it's no use pretending any more – if it ever was. Before I came here, I did not have quinsy. Your grandmother threw me out for bringing disgrace on the family name.'

'How could you ever do that?' The world wasn't making sense any more. Aunt Tilly, with her dull clothes and reserved manner?

'Easily. I'd been in prison, Caroline, on hunger strike. I had been forcibly fed, and was released under the Cat and Mouse Act.' She forced herself to ignore Caroline's instinctive revulsion, and continued: 'That means, as you probably know, that I can be re-arrested at any time they choose – in practice at any time if I re-offend. I *have* re-offended.'

'You mean, you're one of *them*?' Caroline managed to stutter.

Tilly nodded. 'I'm a militant suffragist. A suffragette, as the newspapers love to call us.'

Chapter Four

Outside Caroline could hear Harriet banging up and down the corridor with the Hoover electrical cleaner Grandmother Buckford had given them at Christmas (to their great surprise). How could everything seem so normal, when self-effacing Aunt Tilly had transformed herself into one of these pillar-box burning, picture-slashing, window-smashing termagants whom she read about in the newspapers almost every day, women who had committed crimes like burning down the Nevill cricket pavilion at Tunbridge Wells, and now were even attacking churches?

Aunt Tilly in *prison*. It was almost funny to think of Grandmother's face. Buckford House's bricks must have begun to crumble in horror at such desecration of its heritage.

Tilly was looking at her in amusement, as though she could sympathise with all the thoughts running through Caroline's mind. She was sitting in the old wicker basket chair by her bedroom window as placidly as Nanny Oates herself. No wonder her room was so impersonal, everything was tidied away as hidden as Tilly's own secrets.

'When did you last visit London?'

'About three weeks ago.' Caroline was taken aback by the unexpectedness of her aunt's question. 'Eleanor and I went to see *Pygmalion,* Mr Shaw's new play, at His Majesty's with Mrs Patrick Campbell and Herbert Beerbohm Tree himself. You must remember, you recommended it. Eleanor was all agog to hear the famous word –' Caroline mouthed it – 'and—'

'Where else did you go?' Tilly cut in.

'Nowhere much.' Caroline was puzzled. 'We went to the matinée, and took luncheon at Debenham & Freebody's.'

'And as you took your cab to the Haymarket, did you spare a thought for the brothels that flourish there just off that fine street; as you emerged from Mr Shaw's enjoyable farrago about one flower girl rescued by a gentleman and transported to the drawing rooms of Mayfair, did you think of the gaudy, desperate women of the street who would soon be gathering to earn their daily bread?'

Caroline flushed. 'I don't understand.'

'Did you see nothing else in that whole vast city? The female slaves in the back rooms of the milliners that serve Mayfair, working from eight in the morning to ten at night for a few shillings a week. The sweatshops of Bethnal Green, and women and children toiling by one dim light at home to make a few pence sewing sacks, or shirts, or making *matches*? Did you hear of the accidents, and those burned to death? Did you see the pimps of Limehouse preying on children and girls for *gentlemen* –' she uttered the word with scorn – 'or shipping them abroad like animals? Did you see the children whose lovers are their own fathers—' Tilly saw the look of shock, or perhaps incomprehension, on Caroline's face. 'That's why,' she continued more quietly, 'I'm a suffragette, matching ugliness with ugliness.'

Caroline swallowed. 'No, I *don't* know about these things. How could I?' She felt she was being unjustly rebuked.

'Perhaps not,' Tilly conceded, 'but now I have pointed the way, Caroline, what will you do about it, that is the question.'

'I have a question, too.' Caroline was not mollified. 'I thought suffragettes wanted the vote. Father says the problem is that as only about sixty per cent of men yet have the vote, which is also injustice, the issues must be linked, or there is no hope of equality.'

'Political shenanigans,' Tilly snorted impatiently. 'We have been hearing such shilly-shallying from one politician after another, one Bill after another, each time gaining a majority in the House and then ignored on the grounds that the majority is insufficient, even when the vote in favour surpassed that against us by over a hundred votes. The enfranchisement of women has been debated nearly *fifty* times in the House of Commons and still nothing. And for the last year, silence too. For years we have been tortured in prison, reviled on the streets, and merely humoured by governments who think we are too foolish to realise we are being hoodwinked. Until we have the vote we will never be able to advance the cause of ending

121

women and children's suffering at the hands of men. And men will fight to the last inch to prevent our having it, for that very reason. *That* is why we must fight fire with fire. That is why I was with Mrs Pankhurst when on Friday last week she was refused a hearing at Buckingham Palace, and borne off struggling from its gates. That is why I approve even of church-burning, Caroline.'

It was a gauntlet, and Caroline recognised it as such, even as she resented it. Her aunt had always been her unquestioning champion – or so she had thought. She could not adjust so quickly to this formidable *volte-face*. 'And your reason is that if women have the vote, they will use it to improve the lot of suffering women and children?'

'All women. Those who suffer physically, and live in appalling conditions, and those who, like you, Caroline, live comfortably enough within the rules but when they seek to expand their horizons are balked at every turn by the laws of men. Not all of us are suffragettes from the same motives, just as not all women suffragists are suffragettes. Many still believe in peaceful means, whereas we believe in an active response. Among us, there are those who believe in the freeing of women from the domination of men because they believe in our superiority as a sex. Some wish the vote as an acknowledgement of equality. Others like myself see the vote as the struggle to continue Josephine Butler's work – to force men to adopt the same standards as women. Purity, as I said to you when discussing Agnes. How can they defend the illogicality of licensing brothels or forcing their women to have examinations for disease, instead of teaching men not to go to brothels? If they would

122

but refrain, their wives and children could be free from infection; to license brothels merely condemns yet more women to the disease.' Tilly saw she had lost Caroline. 'Are you shocked?' she demanded impatiently. 'I had thought you had a mind. Use it.'

'I do,' Caroline flashed back. 'But I do not *know* about these things, so how can I judge?'

'You can find out.' Tilly calmed down. 'I should apologise. You live in Ashden. How could you know?'

'There is nothing wrong in that,' Caroline replied defensively.

'Nor in a chrysalis, hidden from the world, merely protecting its own.'

'But Ashden *does* protect its own,' Caroline protested. This was something on which *she* felt strongly. 'Whenever someone has a problem of whatever sort they can come to my father or to the Squire for help. And you know very well my father is always compassionate if people genuinely cannot pay their tithes, just as Dr Marden is about his bills. And the Squire frequently sends people to his own solicitor and pays the bills for them. We all live together, and help one another.'

'Is the village helping Ruth Horner?'

'Yes,' Caroline hurled at her, upset she should raise this contentious issue once more. 'The Squire's solicitor is advising her on claiming money from Jamie by magistrate's order if he refuses to marry her.'

'My point *exactly*! Money is good, but what of the child? It needs a father. Why not force the man to own up to his responsibilities?'

'Jamie still claims he—'

'I believe he is right and that William Swinford-Browne is the father.'

Caroline felt the jolt of shock physically. Irrelevantly, a part of her was crying that this was Whitsun, one of the special holy days, and that it should be celebrated as it had been for centuries, rejoicing that Our Lord's year was peacefully ticking by. Yet what had happened? A disaster almost as great as the *Titanic,* the discovery that her beloved Aunt Tilly was someone completely different to the woman she thought she knew so well, Fred arrested for being a Peeping Tom, and now *this*.

She grappled with Tilly's casual statement about William Swinford-Browne and all it implied. 'I want to say impossible,' she said at last, 'but you won't let me get away with that. Do *you* have proof, though?'

'As with Jamie Thorn, there is no such thing. I *believe* he is guilty.'

'If so, why does Ruth accuse Jamie?'

'William Swinford-Browne is powerful, rich and married.'

'Then why would she not accuse him publicly? Does she love him?'

Tilly laughed. 'You think in storybook terms. He probably paid her and suggested she accuse Jamie. I put nothing past that man.'

'Why Jamie?'

'Why not? He is a handsome lad.'

There was more to it, there had to be, and Caroline instantly made the connection. 'Of course. It's not

Swinford-Browne's plan, it's Ruth's revenge. The cottage he wants for his cinema is blocked by Ebenezer Thorn. If she marries Jamie, they move into Ebenezer's and there goes the cinema.'

'It would certainly explain Ruth's determination to wed young Master Thorn.' Tilly considered further. 'Do you know, Caroline, I believe you're right. Ruth is the woman scorned.'

'And unfortunately Jamie and Agnes will reap the hell.'

'Not,' Tilly said firmly, 'if I have anything to do with it.'

'I'll have to take him, Rector. Question him.' Joe Ifield perched uncomfortably on the edge of the chair in the Rector's study. He was a frequent visitor here of course, over one problem or another, but this was the first time he'd been here on a mission directly affecting the Rectory. Everyone liked Fred Dibble, though he was 'dinlow', and everyone included Joe Ifield. A policeman's lot, as they sang in that Gilbert and Sullivan opera he and Edith had seen in London, is not a happy one. Edith and he had had a good laugh about that on the way home, but he wasn't laughing now.

'I would prefer you speak to him here. Fred would be terrified to go to your house.'

'It's the station, though. I'll have to take him,' Joe said miserably.

'Who is his accuser?' the Rector asked.

'Miss Harriet Mutter.' Even more miserably.

'Our *housemaid*?' The Rector was horrified. 'Is this offence supposed to have taken place in the *Rectory*?'

'The young lady claims he peers in when she's taking a

bath. She hadn't seen who it was before. This time she did.'

'How does one *peer* in on the second floor? The servants' bathroom is up there, and unless he crawls over the dormer roof and suspends himself upside down, I see no way of peeping in.'

Joe Ifield shifted uncomfortably. 'There's a bath in the old scullery. It's warmer than upstairs, and so the girls take their bath there sometimes.'

'This is the end of May,' the Rector pointed out.

'She says Mrs Dibble will confirm that's where she was.' Joe began to get obstinate, annoyed at having to reveal his case.

'And when did this happen?'

'The last time was Thursday night, Rector. She had the light on, not expecting anyone to be outside, so he could see in easy from the laurel bushes.'

'And this is all your evidence? Suppose he were passing innocently from the kitchen to his workshop?'

'There's more, sir.' In for a penny, in for a pound. 'Seems he's been taking to following her around in the gardens.' He paused. 'And *touching* her.'

The Rector was shaken. All this, invading the boundaries of his own home? Harriet had no reason to lie, yet instinct told him Fred would not do such a thing. He had to bear in mind, however, that Fred might be without the controls that normal lads of his age possessed – whether they used them or not.

'I shall come with Fred, Joe. It seems to me we both have the same problem, you with Fred, myself with Ruth Horner. One person's word. How is justice to be done?'

126

'We do our best, sir. Can't do more than that.'

Our best, thought the Rector. Yes, he tried to do that, but it did not satisfy him.

The village had always had its fights and squabbles, which disturbed its surface for a while but left the basic tempo of life unaffected. Ashden went on. Yet this time Caroline unwillingly faced the fact that the situation was getting serious. One evening Joe Ifield had had to don his helmet and hurry to the Norville Arms, as clashing groups of Mutters and Thorns spilled out of its premises over Bankside, down the hill and perilously near the pond. Meanwhile Agnes still walked around the Rectory with a set face, and Jamie Thorn still refused to marry Ruth Horner. The Squire's solicitors had given their opinion that she needed at least circumstantial evidence that she and Jamie had been sweethearts in order to convince the East Grinstead magistrate. At least her father had managed to get Fred released and returned to the arms of his ashen-faced mother uncharged, for the same reason – lack of evidence. He had talked to Harriet, but what the outcome was Caroline did not know. Harriet remained at the Rectory. Mrs Dibble refused to speak to her. Elizabeth had arranged a compromise whereby Rectory matters would be discussed direct between them, and Mrs Dibble accepted that Harriet might genuinely have been mistaken in her identification. Harriet maintained she was not, though not to Mrs Dibble's face. Felicia became Fred's defender and ostentatiously spent time with him in his shed in the garden where he clumsily carved animals from wood, and tended injured animals and birds. Father asked her not to. Felicia refused. Isabel lectured with the authority of an about-to-be-married elder sister. Felicia still refused. Fred was seen whispering to the bees in the hives by the compost heap, in the old country way of sharing trouble.

The weather did not help. It was chilly and miserable for early June, and fortunately this somewhat distanced the discord from Caroline, since she devoted as much time as she could to reading, taking books about the woman's suffrage movement to her room to devour, to talking to Aunt Tilly, and just thinking over the issue for herself. Always it came back to the same point: she believed in votes for women, she believed in adult suffrage for men, regardless of who they were or what they owned, but she could not be entirely convinced by the militants' approach to suffragism. In their discussions Aunt Tilly too always came back to the same point: 'What will be remembered in a hundred years is not Mrs Fawcett's history of the suffrage movement, nor even Mrs Pankhurst's, but Emily Wilding Davison flinging herself under the King's horse at the Derby.'

But did living in public memory justify such violent means?

Yes, in Tilly's view. Not in Caroline's, and not in Father's. Nevertheless Caroline felt she was being shown a door out of Ashden, and one she should at least open to survey the scene. She decided to ask Tilly if she could come with her to her next rally, so that she could hear the speakers. Tilly agreed instantly, provided, she added drily, she were not re-arrested by then under the Cat and Mouse Act. Of this there was apparently every chance, since, after Mrs

Pankhurst's recent re-arrest outside Buckingham Palace, the Government had decided on tough measures, issuing summons against the main suffragette leaders, raiding their headquarters time and time again, and vainly trying to suppress their newspaper *The Suffragette*. So much for freedom of speech.

I want to leave Ashden, I want to stay . . . The conflict constantly nagged at the back of Caroline's mind, preventing her from throwing herself enthusiastically into the preparations for the annual Rectory tennis match next Saturday, 13th June, even though the sun at last relented and condescended to reappear at intervals two days before. Somehow the sun always *did* shine for the Rectory tennis match, which had thereby acquired a mystique in Ashden circles. The roses, refreshed by their ration of rain, were out in full splendour on the day before the match, as Caroline, tired of the house, sneaked into the garden to read. Who, she asked herself, could be at odds with life surrounded by roses such as these, lazily sprawling over the red-brick walls, bathing the garden in perfume by night and colour by day?

The answer appeared to be: she could. She was forced to admit that the cause of her dissatisfaction might well be the dilemma of her future, but it was exacerbated by the fact that she hadn't seen Reggie since Rogation Sunday several weeks ago now. He was never in the Manor when she went to the library to work and somehow the usual spontaneous visits were failing to happen, though Eleanor popped round frequently enough. Daniel of course was still up at Oxford. Not that she cared about Reggie. It was a relief, she told herself, to do without his perpetual lovelorn wails about his girlfriends, and she was glad of the respite. She could write an advice column for *Peg's Paper* with her experience.

Isabel was up first. That was Caroline's first surprise on this momentous day. Yesterday had been baking time for pies for the buffet supper at the 'dance' this evening, to be held on the uneven stone terrace with a band courtesy of His Master's Voice. Meat loaves shrank in their tins as they cooked to the sound of 'Guide me, oh my Great Redeemer', jellies wobbled to 'Morning has Broken'. Tradesmen scurried in and out to 'Onward Christian Soldiers'. This morning the kitchen ovens were groaning under trays of cheese straws and anchovy paste puffs. Even Percy was much in evidence for he prided himself on holding the key to the cellar – a key all too infrequently called upon for use and guarding far too little, in Caroline's opinion. Today a *real* wine punch would put in an appearance, not concocted from home-made fruit wines which Percy, when in complacent mood, could be prevailed upon to make from the fruits and vegetables painstakingly gathered by the four girls and, for once, an equally enthusiastic George. Mrs Dibble was teetotal, Mr Dibble was not.

Caroline rapidly tired of the charms of contributing to a pile of sandwiches as high as Mont Blanc, and found herself alternating between excitement and rehearsing in her head what her greeting to Reggie could be. Careless indifference might be best. Should she leave it to him to speak first? No, why should she? She didn't *care* where he'd been, after all. He probably had some other poor unfortunate woman drooling at his feet now, or even – it suddenly occurred to her – be hoping to win Penelope back. Penelope had been invited for today before Reggie and she had parted, but an apologetic telephone call, answered by Aunt Tilly, had asked whether she might still come. It was some time before Caroline wondered if it might be Aunt Tilly who was the attraction, rather than Reggie. (He *would* be annoyed.) Penelope had obviously been right about seeing Aunt Tilly in Kingsway for that, Caroline now knew, was where the HQ of the Women's Social and Political Union was, run by Mrs Pankhurst and her daughter Christabel (though the latter operated from Paris to avoid arrest, her aunt had told her).

By luncheon, although promoted to cake-filling, since Felicia had taken her place building Mont Blanc, Caroline was impatient to be free of the kitchens.

'No Master Dabb are you, Miss Caroline?' Mrs Dibble grunted.

Master Dabb was the spectre held over them in their youth, a paragon of Sussex fairies particularly gifted in the kitchen and with household tasks. It was obviously the smug Master Dabb who had unwittingly inspired this suffragette fervour in her, Caroline decided, escaping thankfully. By one-thirty she was dressed in her white linen tennis skirt, and relishing the extra freedom its ankle-length gave her. The sun was blazing out after the cloudy morning and, having crammed on her old straw boater, she ran down to the gardens where Mr Dibble's aggrieved back was pushing the heavy roller back to its home.

At the tennis court Robert and Isabel were already

winding the net up and measuring its height with an unnecessary solemnity. Mr Dibble must have mown the court too, for the fresh scent caught at Caroline's nostrils, a summer's gift rewarding her early arrival. Pounding feet would dissipate it all too soon.

She summoned her sense of social duty and went to greet Patricia Swinford-Browne, sprawled on a rug surveying the scene before her with her usual irritating air of amused superiority. It wasn't as though Patricia had much to be superior about. She was rather clumsy, her red-brown hair was heavy and unmanageable, her face was square and somewhat pugnacious (though Caroline was frequently surprised to see she never lacked partners at dances). She was, more importantly to Caroline's mind, ungracious and self-centred. Caroline was glad when Mrs Dibble arrived to check the china table, and she had an excuse to leave her. Mrs Dibble would be in charge of the grand silver teapot inherited by Elizabeth from her mother – grand because it was large enough to have supplied the Five Thousand and was about as old.

Agnes was coming now – escorting someone through the terrace door. Caroline shaded her eyes, and saw Penelope, stepping as if from *Vogue* in a white tennis dress and dashing soft hat. Aunt Tilly was going to greet her. Then, in the way things happen, everyone seemed to arrive together – everyone, that is, save Janie Marden, the doctor's daughter.

Looking back later, so much later, Caroline wondered whether this day could ever have happened as she remembered it, so poignant was the image of a perfect June day, the distant thud of tennis balls rhythmically thumping away the hours of that last summer. Were they all blind to its precious gift as they scraped and chirped away like grasshoppers in the summer sun? Maybe, and perhaps the only true definition of happiness was that it was untinged with longing for the past or the shadows of an unknown future. Time provided a hazy screen, like the cheesecloth and muslin rounds Mrs Dibble so carefully cut out to protect her bowls in the larder, that no unpleasant thing could mar the perfection of her work. There must have been trifling annoyances: the sun burning even through sun bonnets, the flies that landed in the jam, the perspiration oozing down between her breasts, the low-flying gnats gathering on the terrace to join their dance when the sun had gone down. But these had all been brushed aside by memory. And no wonder, she supposed.

'We *won, we won.' George's yell echoing down the years.*

'*Well played, Felicia.' Daniel's careless godlike praise.*

'*Two-love.' Reggie's triumphant shout. Ah, yes.*

Everyone – that is, save Janie Marden, the doctor's daughter.

'She is unable to be here,' Tilly told Caroline. 'That's what I've come down to tell you.'

'But what are we to do?' asked Caroline in dismay. 'We'll be a lady short.'

'I'll play to make up your numbers.'

'But—'

Tilly laughed. 'I do play, you know.'

133

'It's very good of you, Aunt Tilly.' There was nothing else she could say. They couldn't be one woman short, and Mother had never lifted a tennis racket in her life.

'I hope I draw you.' Reggie gallantly leapt into the breach.

So much for wondering how to greet him. He hadn't come near her until he saw she was busy talking to someone else. On the other hand, he hadn't rushed up to Penelope either, Caroline noticed. He had been talking to Isabel, with whom he'd always got on well. Not as well as with her, of course. Half of her wanted to rush up to him, as she always would have done in the past. Now she felt disinclined to do so, so she took the easy way out by chatting to Philip. Poor Philip wasn't much of a player, because of his limp, but he always gallantly made an effort – in case he wasn't invited again, thus depriving him of the honour of seeing Caroline, Phoebe pointed out scornfully. Caroline remained chatting to him even as her father called them together for the draw for partners. Reggie was standing right by her now, albeit with a casual arm linked in Phoebe's, and she supposed she could not ignore him any longer.

'Oh, it's you, Reggie.' Stupid, how stupid.

'I've been here some while talking to Penelope.'

Liar, she thought, realising with surprise he was bent on annoying her at any cost. Well, he wasn't going to succeed.

Daniel reached into the Rector's proffered panama and took out one of the screws of paper. He looked at it, then up. 'Felicia, you're the unlucky lady who's drawn me,' he announced cheerfully. Unlucky? Felicia said nothing, but inwardly she danced. Christopher Denis, safe in the knowledge that his departure was only weeks away, nevertheless took his piece of paper nervously. Relief shot through him: Miss Hunney. Eleanor mentally shrugged; it could have been worse. Dr Jennings looked even more apprehensive but failed to get relief: Miss Phoebe Lilley. Dr Cuss, with whom he shared a house on Silly Lane, had forewarned him, and he consoled himself that she couldn't ask him embarrassing questions in broad daylight on the court, or could she? Martin Cuss himself was even less fortunate: Miss Swinford-Browne. He hardly knew her, but he'd heard about her; like Dr Jennings he told himself little harm could come of a half-hour one-set match, and as he was a bad player, they'd be knocked out after one round. Or, perhaps, he thought with alarm, he should play *well*, in order to stay in and avoid off-court intimacy.

Caroline's heart seemed to be thumping extraordinarily loudly. Why on earth hadn't she bargained for the fact that she had had a one-in-eight chance of being partnered by Reggie? As Philip picked Penelope, it increased to a one-in-three chance, then one-in-two as Robert picked Isabel (to his mixed delight for, completely overwhelmed by Isabel's beauty as he was, it had not escaped his notice that she was a very poor tennis player). One-in-two chance. suddenly George had never seemed so attractive as a partner. Caroline saw Reggie's hand shoot out, hesitate, and plunge, then she saw it undo the twist of paper and with a dreadful inevitability heard him announce: Caroline. Odd that she registered not Reggie's but George's look of horror as he realised he'd therefore be playing with Aunt Tilly. George was the least fond of all of them of Aunt Tilly, and add to that the shame of being partnered by an old maiden aunt and his cup of chagrin was complete. If only he knew, Caroline thought with some amusement, that he was playing with someone who'd been in prison, it would send his stock up at school for the next year.

Each couple would play a set, and the winners would play each other in the semi-finals. The final would be held after the punch break early in the evening, and the dance would follow that.

Felicia and Daniel drew to play first against Penelope and Philip, and Caroline promptly decided to help Agnes at the tea-table, since Reggie would obviously have his nose pressed to the wire to see his lost love play. Unfortunately Agnes made it clear she could manage perfectly well by herself. For a moment Caroline wondered whether to insist, thinking the girl had refused out of pride, but the thought passed, as she saw Eleanor sitting with Martin Cuss, and went to join them. From the look of adoration Robert was giving to Isabel, gracefully reclining on a pile of cushions, he needed no company either. As she passed, she caught the romantic words 'Hard hook volley' and wondered with whom her sympathies should lie. With neither, she decided cheerfully. Isabel would just have to grow to like tennis.

Penelope's long arms and legs should have made her an excellent player, yet, like Daniel, she was too haphazard in her playing. She attempted too much, and concentrated too little. Perhaps, Caroline thought, listening to the lively banter thrown across the net almost as frequently as return strokes, it was because the Penelopes and Daniels of this world might *like* to win, but had no *need* to. Whereas Felicia . . . she watched the graceful arch of her sister's body and the lightning curve as her racket hurtled down so fast that Penelope did not even see the ball coming.

Daniel looked startled. 'Well played, Felicia.'

Hadn't he ever noticed before how good a player Felicia was, Caroline thought crossly. She was always good, but today she had wings to her feet and a power engine to her elbow. Her dark hair and glowing face as she sped over the court, her linen skirt flaring out, turned her into a modern-day Atalanta, racing to avoid the attentions of Hippomenes. Only Felicia wasn't avoiding anyone.

'She's playing for Daniel,' Eleanor whispered in Caroline's ear. Her heart sank.

'You've noticed?'

'It isn't difficult. It's hopeless, of course. Daniel's set on becoming the next Scott of the Antarctic. Or perhaps the next Livingstone. He doesn't like the cold. Anyway, I'm afraid Ashden doesn't loom large in his aspirations. Or—'

'Felicia,' Caroline finished for her.

'I was going to say marriage. The sooner he leaves the better. I'm surprised he's here today. I thought he'd still be carousing the end of his time in Oxford but, no, he's managed to tear himself away for the weekend. Not, I'm afraid, for Felicia's sake; he needed to see Father about money. I hope once he's gone she'll forget him.'

'Felicia isn't very good at forgetting.'

'Nor Daniel at remembering.'

Caroline was surprised at the unusually disparaging

note in Eleanor's voice. 'Don't you like Daniel?'

'Of course I do. He's my brother, and he's adorable. But those whom both the gods and the world adore, tend to adore themselves rather too much, don't you think?'

Caroline had never heard Eleanor speak so before. Eleanor had always been Eleanor, pleasant, good-humoured and reliable. She lacked the good looks and accomplishments of her brother and, being the youngest, it occurred to Caroline for the first time that she might feel her position keenly. First Aunt Tilly, now Eleanor. She was beginning to think that as a judge of character she was less accomplished than a two-year-old.

Daniel and Felicia won their match six-four, and unsurprisingly Isabel and Robert all too easily won theirs against Phoebe and Peter Jennings. The time had come. She chatted eagerly to Eleanor and Christopher as they walked on to the court, leaving Reggie to walk behind them – rather to Eleanor's puzzlement. She looked at Caroline in inquiry, but she pretended not to notice.

Reggie was a good player and she was mediocre, but nevertheless Caroline was unreasonably annoyed when he said, having won the toss, 'I'll serve first, shall I?' It might technically have been a question, but the fact that he strode straight to the right-hand court made it clear it wasn't. Suddenly she could appreciate all the arguments in favour of becoming a suffragette, she fumed – and missed an easy return.

Reggie said nothing. Usually he'd have yelled: 'Wake up, woman.'

I hope he's sickening for measles, she thought crossly, brushing past him without a word as they changed court.

She pulled herself together, and returned Daniel's service with a volley almost by accident, winning a surprised, 'Not bad,' from his lordship, her partner. She said nothing, but when he netted Eleanor's lob she could not resist: 'Did they teach you that shot in the OTC?' Reggie was always talking of his Oxford Officers' Training Corps experiences (when he wasn't talking about women, that is).

'Yes. Just like you must have learned to serve in an army canteen.'

That was more like it. She began to warm to the game, and they won six-four. She was pleased – until she realised this meant they'd have to play in the semi-finals. Off-court Penelope congratulated her, and from her detailed analysis of their performance Caroline realised she had been observing very closely. Perhaps she was regretting her rejection of Reggie? Perhaps that *was* why she was here today and it was nothing to do with Aunt Tilly. Of course it must be. How could she have been so blind?

'Where are you off to?' Penelope asked, surprised, as Caroline went to walk away, convinced that she was right, and only too pleased to let them get on with it.

'To the croquet lawn.' She said the first thing that came into her head.

'Aren't you going to watch your aunt play? Here.' Penelope patted the rug at her side, and unwillingly Caroline sat down, surprised there was still no sign of Reggie. Anyway, in fairness to poor George, she supposed she should watch his ordeal.

Tilly's first stroke showed George what aunts could be made of, as her serve zinged the ball across the net and past Patricia. This was as well for George was goggling so much he'd have been incapable of movement had Patricia returned the serve.

'Quite a lady, your aunt.' Penelope observed.

'She is indeed.' Caroline proceeded cautiously.

'She said she'll take me to London. You too?'

Caroline stiffened in amazement. 'Are *you* interested?'

'Very. You remember the uproar last week when the debutante livened up her presentation at court by curtseying to the King and crying out, 'Your Majesty, stop forcible feeding'?'

'Of course.' The whole of England knew about it, and mostly deplored the girl's outrageousness.

'She's a good friend of mine, and a very brave soul. They say her mother fainted. I rather like Lady Blomfield, so I sympathise, but we can't have our opinions ruled by our parents, can we?'

'I can't imagine your parents having much success,' Caroline said frankly.

'No. I've been spoiled by my father, because my mother's long dead,' Penelope announced cheerfully. 'My aunt brought my brother James and me up and promptly left us there. James has vanished into the Army and here I am.'

'I'm so sorry.' Caroline tried to imagine life without her own mother, the backbone of the Rectory, and could not. 'Doesn't your father worry, though, and try to marry you off?'

'He wouldn't dare try. I don't see any advantage in marrying at all, save for children, and that's not everyone's burning ambition. I told Reggie so.'

'He was very upset,' Caroline replied, taken aback at this frank exposition.

'Vanity. You'll never make a suffragette if you feel so compassionate towards the enemy.'

'But if women are equal to men, then they must acknowledge men hurt as we do, surely, and we should be as considerate to their feelings as they to ours.'

Penelope grinned. 'Conquer the enemy, *then* show compassion – with your boot on his chest.'

'I can see why you'll make a good suffragette. I wouldn't like to be a policeman unchaining you from the railings.'

Reggie chose this inopportune moment to stroll up self-consciously. 'I brought you ladies some lemonade.'

'Oh, Reggie, how chivalrous,' Penelope squeaked in mock gratitude, winking at Caroline. Reggie noticed and flushed angrily, just as a tennis ball pinged at the wire fence in front of them. So he was still keen on Penelope. Well, Caroline wasn't going to wait to be an unwelcome third at the tea heralded by George's roar from the court 'We won! We won!'

'Oh good, it's you, Reggie. Help Mother take round the cake, would you? I've got to see what's happened to Phoebe . . .' Caroline glanced back as she hurried away and saw him standing looking after her in surprise, lemonade still in his hand.

Phoebe once again found herself bored. After tea she had wandered off. There was no one her own age there, even Patricia had disappeared with Peter Jennings. He was a silly man anyway, and it was all his fault they'd lost their match.

Now she couldn't even vent her boredom on a tennis ball. Anyway it was too hot for tennis. She felt as though she wanted to burst out of these stupid, stupid clothes; even her light girdle felt clammy and uncomfortable on her hot skin.

She decided to take a ride on Poppy; then they might miss her and come looking for her. Even Christopher with luck. Besides, she felt good on a horse, with its moving, rippling body under her. Old Poppy didn't move very fast, she acknowledged, but she was better than nothing.

She came round the corner to the stables and saw there was a man standing there, lighting a cigarette. He looked up and saw her but he didn't put the cigarette out, as he should when a lady approached – particularly as this one was Miss Lilley of the Rectory, and he was only Len Thorn, the blacksmith's elder son. She rather admired his nerve. He straightened up in the stable doorway but didn't move aside to let her pass. His eyes travelled down her tennis skirt and up again, disconcerting her.

'Let me pass, please.' There was an imperious note in her voice which was not feigned. She'd never before noticed how creepy his eyes were, they were almost tawny, set in his swarthy-skinned face. And the way he just stood there! She wasn't going to give way. Why should she?

'Very well, Miss Lilley.' His voice was disconcerting too, a slow Sussex drawl, thick like his lips. She'd have to squeeze past him, because despite his words he still didn't move. She summoned all her courage. She wasn't going to back away in their own stable. She turned sideways to get past him, trying to ignore how close he was.

'There's an entrance fee, miss. A kiss.' He was practically

142

breathing in her face as he made this outrageous statement.

Nor did he ask if she'd pay it, he merely put his hands on her shoulders, drew her closer than she was already and kissed her. She was hardly aware of the lips, only that his hands were now on her bottom and of the odd sensation she had even through her corset. Not just odd, rather frightening, like being on a horse. Only better. But frightening nonetheless.

She tore herself free. 'I'll tell my father,' she stammered. 'I don't want to have a baby.' Everyone knew you had a baby if you kissed someone.

He threw back his head and laughed. 'You won't tell him, Miss Phoebe. You enjoyed it too much.'

She started to run, pursued by his sibilant whisper: 'Come back when you want to, Miss Phoebe. I'll see there ain't no babies.'

She was unusually subdued as she sat with Patricia, watching Caroline and Reggie playing George and Tilly. Lucky, lucky Caroline. She was never in turmoils like this, feeling in turn sick, frightened and excited inside; Caroline was always so calm and sensible . . .

Caroline was painfully aware of Reggie's annoyance as she lost her second service game to George and Tilly. She was aware she was not playing at her best, and 'best' wasn't very good anyway.

'Two-love,' he'd shouted triumphantly when he broke George's service game. Now they were at three-four, and Reggie was looking grim, not triumphant, thanks to her.

He promptly turned into another Anthony Wilding and,

ignoring her presence on the court, completely took it upon himself to cover all return shots. It seemed to annoy him even further that he couldn't get the better of Aunt Tilly's service game, and, sensing Caroline's unworthy satisfaction at this outcome, he won his own service game to love, and smashed George's to smithereens. With a glance that said 'beat that' he reluctantly (or so her smarting pride told her) handed the baton back to his humble partner for her to serve. She lost. The score was five-six, and Reggie was livid. It needed only Tilly's pounding serve to win the semi-final for herself and George.

She didn't dare look at Reggie. To avoid his recriminations she kept away from him as the famous punch was brought out by Percy, his own particular triumph, and felt rather as she had on Easter Day. Another special feast spoiled – only this time she had undoubtedly contributed to the disaster herself. The punch glass felt like the poisoned chalice, and as soon as she decently could she melted away from the gathering to gather her equilibrium in the orchard. She perched on the stile and gloomily surveyed the tiny apples already forming in the trees. Perhaps they could tell her what on earth the matter was with her.

'What on earth's the matter with you, Caroline?' Reggie echoed her own thoughts uncannily, having come right up behind her unheard and put his hands on her shoulders. She jumped like one of the rabbits which were beginning their daily pre-sundown romp in the orchard.

'Nothing.' She climbed down into the orchard, but he leaped over the stile to follow her. Reggie was never one to take a hint.

'There must be. Or with both of us,' he added fairly. 'I can't stand this any more. I'm sorry I was so rotten to you on court.'

'I was worse to you. Anyway, it doesn't *matter*.'

'It does. Why do you treat me like a particularly unnoticeable ghost whenever I come near you?'

'I thought you'd prefer to spend the time with Penelope,' she flung at him, and was instantly ashamed.

'*Penelope*?' He stared at her, then roared with laughter. 'That hop-pole? I must have been mad.' He began to look more cheerful.

'It's not funny,' she shouted.

'Yes it is. If only I could make you understand—'

'We understand each other too well. We've grown out of each other.'

'We never grew in. You don't understand me in the slightest, and I certainly can't make you out. You seem to have turned into a shrew.'

'I have *not*. It's you, it's you. You're stupid, obstinate and—'

'Point proved.'

Something gave, something between a laugh and a strangled sob emerged, something that might have been 'Reggie', something that vanished the ground between them and hurled her into his arms. She might have heard 'Caroline' somewhere beyond the drumming of her chest and the dizziness in her ears. In her *ears*?

'Caroline.' She did hear it this time, but even if there had been an answer, she could not have given it, because his lips were on hers. It was quite, *quite* different from feeling them on her cheek, nor did the arms around her feel like those of the man she'd gaily waltzed with through the years. But it *was* him, here with her in the apple orchard, and his lips, and the feelings they were arousing, were beginning to seem part of her, an inseparable part. As her lips opened, he drew her closer, and a tremor ran through her that seemed entirely answered by her closing her eyes, relaxing and enjoying feeling his hands travelling down behind her, holding her even closer. Then he broke away, and there were two of them again, not one. Was it alarm she saw in his face? Regret?

'Caroline, I think I love you.'

How did little white clouds supply themselves so conveniently to be danced upon?

'I think I love you too.' Why be shy *now*? Why did words never express what you were feeling inside? It sounded as if she were doubtful, but she had no doubt at all.

She stood there, dancing inside, as he threw back his head, cupped his hands round his mouth, and yelled to the heavens: 'I love you.'

'They'll hear you at the match.' She wanted to cry. No she didn't. Laugh? No, she wanted to come out of this paralysis.

'I don't care if they hear me in Timbuctoo. I love *you*!' Reggie swung himself round several tree trunks, peering anxiously through the lower branches of the nearest: 'You haven't vanished, have you?'

'I'm too solid to vanish.' Still, paralysis. Passing time.

'You're like thistledown.' He came at her in a run, swept her up into the air, put her down again, then ran

146

his hands gently down the sides of her body. She felt them burning through the linen. Then, delicately, watching her to see if she'd object, over her breast, until suddenly shy of him she caught his hand. She held it there and at last was sharply aware of everything: a distant shout of victory on the tennis court, a furious shout (Farmer Lake's sheep from Owlers Farm had met a delivery van again in Pook's Way), a pigeon cooing continually at his mate, and that Reggie was no longer a friend. He was her lover.

'You look happy, darling.'

Caroline hugged her bliss to her as she slipped the raspberry silk over her head. Miraculously no one had heard Reggie's shouts, so tonight was their own; tomorrow everyone could know, they had decided.

'I enjoyed the afternoon.' She could hardly keep the grin from her face.

'So did I.' Elizabeth paused curiously, speculated, and left it. 'Your Aunt Tilly provided a surprise, didn't she? George is still going round boasting about *their* success. I wonder why she's kept so quiet about her skills?'

'I suppose because Aunt Tilly is in the habit of keeping dark about everything,' Caroline said lightly.

A pause. 'I understand.' If her mother were annoyed, she did not let it show. 'So now you'll be expecting me to forbid you to have anything to do with those terrible women. But that would be foolish of me. You would rush away and set up house with Tilly.'

Caroline thought this over. 'No, I wouldn't.' Inside she glowed, her mind not on the vote at all.

'I'm glad.' Elizabeth glanced at her. 'I want to keep you here.'

'Unmarried, like Tilly?'

'Good gracious no. I should have said, here in our hearts.'

'Oh!' Caught, Caroline rushed to her mother, and threw her arms around her.

'Would you like this frock buttoned up, darling?' Elizabeth enquired after a moment. 'I seem to be clasping your girdle.' And what was she going to tell Laurence, Elizabeth worried, as Caroline, dutifully dressed as befitted a young woman of not quite twenty-two, bounced out of the room to find Felicia. It was quite clear that Caroline was in love, and there was no doubt at all as to with whom. Perhaps she might wait a little before telling Laurence; something told her there might be extra news to impart.

Felicia was not in her room so Caroline hurried downstairs, afraid by her tardiness she was missing part of 'the treat', which *now* she could enjoy.

The lamps were already lit, although it was still quite light at eight-thirty. How *much* nicer the glow of the oil looked than the harsh glare of The Towers' lighting. The air was still warm, so they could dance on the terrace till midnight if they wanted, until the very last stroke of twelve told them it was Sunday and God's day. Only Felicia was on the terrace as Caroline came out, and she turned a radiant face as her sister approached. 'Isn't it lovely, *lovely*?' she asked fervently.

'You are,' Caroline told her sincerely. Felicia had beauty, everyone agreed that, but Caroline had never seen her look

148

as she did tonight. She was blazing forth in splendour, her dark eyes glowing with fire and her cheeks pink with excitement. No lily maid this, no Lady of Shalott, but a rose indeed.

'I had a wonderful time,' she assured Caroline, the gardens, and a passing cat.

'Do I look all right?' Phoebe bounced out to join her sisters, reassured by their company and by the knowledge that no worse awaited her this evening than the known company of Drs Jennings and Cuss. And Curate Christopher, of course.

Caroline surveyed her toilette. A low-cut pale green gown which didn't suit her in the slightest but which had been a present for her sixteenth birthday, unwillingly made by Mrs Hazel with many disparaging remarks on its suitability for a young lady. Phoebe battled her way through, won it and adored it, as a symbol, Caroline thought. Surely even Phoebe could see it didn't suit her? But naturally all she said was: 'Apart from the pin holding your sash on, yes.'

Phoebe giggled, and Isabel, who sauntered up in her engagement ball gown, looked disapproving. Wisely she did not comment on the reappearance of the green dress.

'Is Robert here yet?' Caroline asked.

Isabel yawned. 'I don't think so. He's coming with his parents.'

'What joy,' Caroline said without thinking.

Isabel pounced. 'What a cat you are. If someone's not called Hunney, they're of no account, are they?'

No, something joyously agreed inside her, then jabbed

her with a stab of doubt as she recalled Lady Hunney, the undoubted and substantial fly in her Zambuk ointment. Zambuk was the cure for everything, the Rectory considered. Insect bites, rashes, sunburn – everything could be charmed away with Zambuk. She feared Lady Hunney could prove the exception to the rule, but Reggie would take care of her, she thought happily.

Inside the house it sounded as though the whole pot of Hunneys had arrived, she realised, clad now in evening attire and complete with Sir John and Lady Hunney. Informal or not, a Rectory event must be blessed by the Squire – rather like the blessing of the crops by the Rector in spring. Anyway, keeping them happy was Father and Mother's concern, not hers. And nor were the Swinford-Brownes her concern. Nothing, no one but Reggie. George, full of importance in his first dinner suit and white tie, was bending over the gramophone putting a new needle in, a task he always treated with as much ceremony and precision as their weekly clock-winder the old moon long-case clock in the Rectory entrance hall. Being considerably less plump than Mr Cyril Wainwright, retired soldier and clockmaker, the effect was not so impressive. 'Alexander's Ragtime Band' blared out, and *here came Reggie*. Daniel and Eleanor too, of course, but she hardly saw them, hardly saw Felicia crossing shyly to greet Daniel.

Suppose it was a dream this afternoon, suppose he laughs and says wasn't that a fine joke, Caroline, suppose I look at him and realise it's only Reggie again. It wasn't, he didn't, she didn't. A glance at him, at the look in his eyes, and she knew it was all right. A wave of happiness engulfed her and kept her in its embrace, with only odd snatches of the evening intruding from the outside.

'Your sister's beautiful,' Penelope nodded towards Felicia.

'She is. She always kept some of it back, as if she was waiting, though.'

'If so, I think she's found it . . .'

Daniel could not take his eyes from Felicia. The girl was beautiful; those eyes, the hair, her perfect skin and, most amazing of all, it was Felicia whom he'd known all his life. He soon got tired of dancing; he wanted to be alone with her. Not that he quite knew why. Curiosity, he supposed.

'It's a beautiful evening,' she said as they walked by the tennis court.

'You make it so. It could not be so presumptuous on its own.' Because the night was warm and she was beautiful, he kissed her, not as he would have done a year ago, as the Rector's daughter, but as he would any woman who intoxicated him. The thought did occur to him that he should not, for he was an honourable man, but he dismissed it. In a few weeks he would be gone; Cupid's darts would not long hurt her, and such beauty as Felicia's deserved to be reverenced. Besides, he was very fond of her.

When he drew back, because her lips were not only tender but too trusting, he picked a rose and presented it to her to break the moment. 'For the queen of beauty,' he said seriously.

She took it in her hands, and held it until he took it from her. 'Here, I'll fix it.' He twisted the thin stem through the lace of her fichu just above her breast, and as his fingers rested on the white skin, he wished just for a fleeting moment that she were not the Rector's daughter.

'Oh, Caroline, take pity on Robert, will you and dance with him? I'm *exhausted*.'

Isabel tottered theatrically past her into the dining room, where the supper was laid out. She managed to revive remarkably quickly, Caroline noticed, obediently offering her own services to Robert. It was the military two-step and two minutes later she saw Isabel dancing with Martin Cuss.

Robert was a dear, Isabel was thinking as she marched up and down, but not *exciting*. She could hardly define this to herself, but she supposed she must mean someone who not only admired you but disturbed you. Like Frank Eliot. She noticed no one had suggested inviting *him* this evening. Not quite socially acceptable, she supposed. What a pity. She bestowed one of her famous smiles on Martin Cuss. 'Isn't this exciting,' she murmured.

Martin Cuss, concentrating every muscle on trying to whirl Isabel round on a paving stone without sending her headlong into the garden, politely agreed.

'You won't ever dance the Huggie Bear with anyone else but me, will you, Reggie?' Caroline collided with his chest and was flung back again, celebrating her release by a hop in the air.

'Never.'

'Will you dance *anything* with anyone else again?'

'On my life. Never.'

'This won't vanish, will it, Reggie?'

152

'The terrace?'

'Idiot.'

'No, it won't.'

And then when he pulled her after him to walk in the gardens, in the 'wilderness' which lay beyond the rhododendron bank, so that they might not be seen, '*You* haven't vanished, have you?'

'No.'

'Then you'll marry me?'

She'd always thought this should be a momentous event, but it wasn't because the answer was so obvious to both of them. 'Yes, of course.' *Then* came the doubt. 'It's not like before – with you, I mean?'

'How can you ask that? All those other women seem like practice rows for the big race. I suppose,' he added with dismay, 'that doesn't sound very romantic.'

'It does if it's true.'

'It is. The odd thing is I didn't need the practice. I just needed to realise that I loved you. I always will.'

'And I you.'

'Then what are you crying for?'

'Because I'm going to marry you.'

They both saw the funny side at the same time, and he held her close. 'You'll never cry again, Caroline. I promise, I promise.'

William Swinford-Browne swung Elizabeth into a lively waltz. He had had a great deal of the Rectory punch, to which he had added his own private supply of brandy, suspecting the alcoholic content of the punch to be low.

He was happy with himself and happy with the world, especially with a fine woman like Elizabeth Lilley in his arms. Not too little either, he thought appreciatively.

'I'm looking forward to our wedding,' he announced, steering Mrs Lilley down to the less public lawns. 'Lucky young people, eh, starting life out together, making their own way. Little youngsters in due course, eh?'

'Yes, indeed. Shall I take that glass from you, Mr Swinford-Browne?'

'You think I'm inebriated, don't you?' He deposited it by the hedge, and wagged what he told himself was a saucy finger at her. 'How could I be, when I'm dancing with a wonderful woman like you?' He put his right arm round her to join the left, which ostensibly had been placed behind her in the interests of the waltz, and she struggled to free herself. She tried in vain since she found her arms firmly held in place by his and to her horror felt his gloved right hand feeling the bottom of the rounded figure he had so much admired. She could not shout, for that would call public attention to her ridiculous position, and had just determined upon drastic measures with her knee when help arrived. Outraged by all men, and Swinford-Browne in particular, Tilly cared nothing for attracting public attention. Indeed she welcomed it. Into a silence as George changed records fell Tilly's strident voice:

'Kindly confine your sexual gropings to your housemaids, Mr Swinford-Browne. As you did with poor Ruth Horner.'

It was a long time before Caroline fell asleep that night. All five of them, even George, had gathered in Isabel's bedroom

154

to commiserate with her tears and howls on the disgrace her drunken aunt had brought on them, and how could she ruin Isabel's life so callously. Then, without Isabel, they had hurried back to Caroline's room to chew over the shocking, exhilarating results of the evening until the candles required no snuffing, and they had to creep back to their own rooms in darkness. Caroline had been in no way sure it had been proper to include George, but George had come all the same.

'I've never seen Father so angry,' Felicia breathed, the stars still in her eyes.

'I think that awful man came off lightly,' declared Caroline. 'Father and Mother will never let the story get round the village.'

'It will, though,' George said confidently and with glee. 'I saw Agnes listening. Anyway, Mother won't mind.' He wasn't, in fact, quite sure what all the fuss was about. Mother was old, and so was Swinford-Browne, and so how could sex come into it? With studied nonchalance he yawned, and wandered back to his own room with a long detour to Mrs Dibble's larder for leftovers en route.

'But the wedding,' Caroline said to her sisters as soon as he'd gone, 'everything's got to be all right for that. Suppose Robert *does* call it off?'

'It would have to be Isabel, not Robert, or she could sue for breach of promise,' Phoebe pointed out gleefully.

A pause, with the same thought in their minds. *Would she mind* if she could have money without Robert? They looked away from each other, self-conscious about their instant reaction.

'I'm ashamed of us all,' declared Caroline, looking round. 'We're a Christian household. We've got to forgive. Or rather Mother has.'

'Perhaps it's Agnes who has to forgive,' had been Felicia's last words.

But this episode vanished from Caroline's mind as she lay in her bed that night, watching the flickering shadows of the candlelight on the ceiling weaving strange, mysterious patterns. What pulsed through her was the memory of her walk back through the garden with Reggie, hand in hand silently like children, and then he said, 'Which is your bedroom, Caroline?'

'That one.' She pointed. 'It hasn't changed since I was about ten. You must remember. You were in it often enough when we were young. Why?'

'I want,' his hand tightened, 'to imagine you there tonight, to imagine what it will be like to sleep beside you and love you. Shall you like that, Caroline?'

Shall you like that, Caroline? His words floated back as the scented night air filled the room. Shall, not should. It would happen. The room did not seem empty now, for she *could* imagine Reggie here, beside her. She snuffed out the candle, but the restlessness her thoughts had created in her kept her awake until she heard the moon clock downstairs strike three.

Chapter Five

What on earth was happening? From being its usual happily humming beehive the Rectory seemed to be preparing to swarm, heaving with bodies seething in every direction. True, Caroline was aware that she was herself one of the heavers, but then she was a happy heaver, and so, all too obviously to Caroline's eye at least, was Felicia. Others, particularly Isabel, were definitely not happy. She had been trailing around like Sarah Bernhardt ever since she got up.

Yesterday afternoon's sunshine had disappeared once more into this morning's close atmosphere and overcast skies, and unlike yesterday the pall seemed reluctant to lift. Caroline had discovered the reason for Janie Marden's absence yesterday. Her aunt, Dr Marden's sister, had been confirmed as lost in the *Empress of Ireland* disaster. There had been a muddle over names, and the Mardens had been in doubt all this time, keeping their anguish to themselves.

Now there was no doubt, and Father had said a prayer for Rachel Smythe. The tragedy of the loss of the liner hit Caroline all the more vividly, now it had touched Ashden, and made her own happiness seem all the more precious.

Her father's pall of preoccupation hadn't lifted either, for she had witnessed the brief encounter between him and Mr Swinford-Browne who had dared march up to him after the service (which he had not attended) and demand to speak to him *now*. He did not even bother to remove his hat in Caroline's presence.

'Tomorrow,' Father had replied in his 'church' voice, the vein standing out in his left temple which meant he was deeply angry, 'would be a more suitable time for secular matters. On Sundays I am amply paid by Our Lord to look after His affairs. I suggest six o'clock.'

Swinford-Browne had seemed about to ignore this suggestion when Elizabeth came to join them, and he promptly, to Caroline's amusement, changed his mind. 'Very well.'

'I suggest today we *both* devote time to contemplating our duty to the Lord,' the Rector continued.

'Good morning to you, Mr Swinford-Browne,' Elizabeth intervened calmly. 'Pray do tell your wife how much I enjoyed my talk with her last evening.'

That had silenced the terrible Toby Jug. He even remembered to tip his hat to Mother before he marched down the path even more angrily than he had marched up it.

Caroline had then been torn between waiting for Reggie, who had said he would speak to Father this morning, and accompanying Mother, as the grim grip of her arm indicated was Elizabeth's wish. Obviously she had noticed

Sarah Bernhardt too. Robert had not been in church, and this was ominous since, although he was Chapel like his parents, he had since his engagement to Isabel faithfully attended St Nicholas.

'Today,' Elizabeth announced, 'we shall discuss the *final* menu and invitations. Then you girls can write them out. There are a mere six weeks left to us. Shall we begin *now*?'

Caroline's heart sank, but casting only one hopeful glance behind her to see whether she could see Reggie approaching Father (he wasn't), she obediently helped shepherd Isabel home and into Mother's boudoir – a grand name for the untidy large room on the first floor. It had been the nursery; now it was full of patterns, sewing machine, half-completed embroideries, recipe books, memories of their childhood and anything else that Mother took it into her head to collect, including a pile of cut-out scraps for a screen that would never be made. The pile had been waiting patiently for as long as Caroline could remember.

As soon as they entered and Mother closed the door, Isabel's (or rather Sarah's) big moment had come. She burst into tears. 'What's the use? The wedding will never happen. And it's all Aunt Tilly's fault. I'll never forgive her, never. Oh, Mother, what shall I do if the Swinford-Brownes call the wedding off?'

'My dear, Robert is twenty-six. How can they forbid him to marry you?'

'They won't pay for Hop House. Or Paris. Or our allowance. Robert hasn't a penny of his own.'

'He could earn some. And I'm sure we can find a cottage for you to rent. Or you can live here.'

'Here?' Isabel lifted her face in horror. *'Here?'*

'Yes, *here*,' retorted Caroline. She saw Mother was hurt, and was furious with Isabel for her tactlessness. Isabel's reasons for marrying Robert were all too transparent now. 'It will be fun to have you both living here.'

'So everything is settled.' Elizabeth hid her wounded feelings.

'Settled?' Isabel repeated dramatically. 'My whole life is ruined and you say it's settled. Robert would never—' She bit off what she was going to say, not so much, Caroline suspected, in loyalty to Robert, but because of the unflattering light it would place her in. 'It would upset him too much to marry in defiance of his parents' wishes,' she finished.

'It has been known,' Elizabeth murmured.

Isabel stared at her impatiently: 'You and Father were different.'

'Were we?'

'It wasn't as if Grandmother Buckford had quarrelled with your family. She just didn't approve of you. That's why she cast Father off without a penny.'

'And a good job too,' Caroline pointed out to deflect her sister from yet more faux pas. 'To think we might have been brought up in Buckford House.' Even as she said it, the word approve struck her with double force. Grandmother Buckford . . . Lady Hunney . . . Reggie said he was going to talk to Father today. Had he come yet? I'm going to marry him, she told herself. He'll be my husband.

Elizabeth remained silent. So easy for Isabel to say those careless words, and so typical. It seemed only yesterday to Elizabeth: the heartache, the agony of wanting to know whether Laurence would choose her or his mother. That woman's rudeness in ignoring her parents, ignoring her, all because Elizabeth, without a title to her name, had had the temerity to love her favourite son. Never mind that the Overtons were respected all over Kent, they weren't gentlefolk like the Lilleys. Gentlefolk? Lady Buckford? A killer whale was gentler than she, and Tilly took after her. Fortunately, like Laurence, Tilly was born with her father's kindness and compassion. The Earl of Buckford had died when Laurence was only fourteen, and his heir, Laurence's eldest brother, a bare twenty-one, and Lady Buckford had had plenty of time to sharpen her killer teeth.

'How many on Mr and Mrs Swinford-Browne's list?' she asked Isabel briskly.

'Ninety-six.'

Ninety-six? Grandmother Overton's teapot was going to be working ten times as hard, Caroline thought. It had only been thirty-two a few weeks ago.

'And yours and Robert's?' Mother continued without a blink.

'Sixty-three.'

'And ours is forty-four. At the moment.' Elizabeth did look dismayed now.

'Two hundred and three in all,' supplied Caroline helpfully.

'Very well. Your wedding breakfast is a wedding tea, Isabel. You can be married at two o'clock instead of at twelve.'

'Oh no, Mother. Not *sandwiches*.' Isabel's cry was pitiful. 'Mrs Swinford-Browne has set her heart on a real wedding breakfast. She does have very important friends.'

'Either her heart or our purse must be broken, Isabel. It is too much.'

'They would pay for it all.'

'No doubt. And they will offer to hold it at The Towers. Do you prefer that? Tell me now, before Caroline writes the invitations.'

It was Caroline's turn to look alarmed. Was Mother expecting her to write *all* of them? It was too bad. Isabel, however, looked set on agreeing to anything provided the wedding went ahead.

The agony of waiting . . . Oh, how Elizabeth remembered. That was what Isabel was going through now, and Elizabeth would be fighting the Swinford-Brownes every inch of the way if they dared to threaten her moody chick.

Reggie *had* come. One look at Father's face had told Caroline so, as he called her into his study just before luncheon. 'You are happy, Caroline?' was his first question.

'Very. You do approve, don't you, Father?' For one terrible moment she thought he might not, that he was going to say no, or 'not altogether' or 'it depends', one of those terribly balanced Rectorial answers. But he didn't. 'Reggie is a good man, a credit to his name; steady and just. He's a worthy heir to Ashden. I know he loves you, Caroline, and therefore I gave him, and now you, my blessing.'

Relief swept through her like the River Rother in spate. If Father had hesitated, it could only have been because he did not wish to lose a second daughter so quickly. They had grown loving of each other's ways in the Rectory and the web they had spun around them would be hard to break, voluntarily or not.

'Reggie is speaking to his parents today, Caroline, so we shall not say anything of this to your sisters or George or Tilly. Naturally your mother must know.'

Caroline was disappointed, having looked forward to a moment of glory at Sunday luncheon, just like Isabel had had on Easter Day, but consoled herself that this way Monday would be a special day too. Anyway, it would be nice to have such a wonderful secret to hug all to herself for a little longer.

When the afternoon came, a squeeze of Mother's hand was enough to tell her she knew. Caroline almost whispered to her that they might discuss buying stores for both weddings and save money, but decided not. Isabel should reign in her temporary glory alone, and her elder sister would certainly notice nothing odd about Caroline this afternoon. Caroline could have nothing of importance in *her* life, could she? Poor Isabel, she'd always be reaching out but never arriving at whatever it was she imagined she wanted.

She and Isabel found their mother in the boudoir after luncheon, armed with Mrs Beeton under one arm, the shadow of Mrs Dibble hanging over her, plus – the sign of a *really* special occasion – not only Grandmother Overton's copy of Mrs de Salis's *Savouries a la Mode* but her very own manuscript recipe book begun when Grannie was a bride in 1853 and continued until only a few months before she died, like the old Queen she so closely resembled, in 1901. Here recipes for puddings, catsups, cakes and wines were mixed up with those for furniture polish, pomatum and pot pourris, which had puzzled Caroline greatly as a child when she fell in love with the word pomatum and waited feverishly for it to appear upon their table.

'Perhaps if we chose cheaper food we could manage,' Caroline suggested doubtfully some time later, enthusiasm for their task rapidly waning. 'We could pretend this is a teetotal household.'

'This is my wedding,' sobbed Isabel tearfully. 'I will not have my guests chewing through Mrs Dibble's meat puddings. I want it to be elegant.'

Caroline recognised a deadlock when she saw it, and took up her accustomed role of problem-solver, ready to hand over to Mother's role of soother. 'Why don't we start a new fashion. Marry at, say, one o'clock, and offer a late light luncheon, or a savoury early tea, and we could have lobster patties not lobster salad, for example,' having glimpsed at what Isabel still had blithely written at the top of her preferred menus, despite all previous warnings.

'I don't want *sandwiches*,' wailed Isabel again. 'Or Grannie Overton's gingerbread cake.'

Elizabeth was racing through Mrs de Salis. 'Shrimp canapes,' she declared with relief at finding a solution. 'Indian eggs.'

'*What* on earth are they?' Isabel demanded.

'Curry flavoured.'

'I don't like curry.'

Caroline gave a despairing glance at Mother, who ignored it and said firmly: 'A few for those that do. And some lobster savoury creams. Lobster set in aspic, cream, tomato juice.'

'It sounds terrible.'

'We'll try it first. I'll ask Mr Barnes' (the travelling fishman with the lugubrious face, known as the Hound of the Baskervilles to the Lilleys) 'to bring me a nice lobster next week.'

'Not in sandwiches, though.'

'Raspberries will still be in season,' Caroline said hastily. One more word about sandwiches and she'd crown Isabel with Mrs Beeton *and* Mrs de Salis.

'Wine jellies,' Elizabeth waxed enthusiastic. 'And Grannie Overton's cream cheesecakes.'

'Not those terrible junkets.'

Caroline happened to love junkets but she refrained from reminding Isabel of this. Lots of lovely things could whisk themselves out of the kitchens at the last moment.

Vegetables proved an even knottier problem. By the time they had calculated the cost of four large Stiltons, three large Cheddars and six pounds of Gorgonzola, then had to recalculate it omitting the Gorgonzola, reducing four and three to three and two respectively, and adding plenty of goats' cheese instead, they were all cross and irritable. The afternoon was punctuated by claps of thunder but remained close, and Caroline's head was aching.

'How much does that all come to, Caroline?' her mother asked. 'You're good at figures.'

Someone, anyone, *Reggie,* rescue me soon, she prayed. She counted the figures and counted again. It came to something different. She re-counted. 'I make it £20 11s 6d,' she announced at last.

'How much?' cried Elizabeth. 'It can't possibly be as much.'

'And that doesn't include the champagne, or any other drink. Champagne will cost between two and four pounds for a dozen bottles.'

'Your Aunt Tilly has kindly offered to pay for that.'

Isabel pounced once more on her grievance. 'So she jolly well should after she's done her best to wreck my marriage.'

Elizabeth did not mention that Tilly's offer had been made solely to prevent the Swinford-Brownes from having any say in the day's affairs and to give Elizabeth an excuse for declining any such offer from them.

'Is Grandmother coming?' Caroline asked curiously.

'Yes. I want her invited,' ordered Isabel.

'Naturally we shall invite your grandmother.' Elizabeth was surprised anyone should need to ask. 'I doubt if she will attend, but we shall welcome her should she do so.'

'Good evening, Mr Swinford-Browne. Do come in.'

William had no time for even such basic familiarities as this. His attitude was that if the Rector hoped he'd have forgotten his grievance by today, he was much mistaken in his man.

'I'll come straight to the point.' Keep it dignified. 'Either you get rid of that woman or I get rid of her for you. She's off her head.'

The Rector looked at him coolly. 'And by 'that woman' you mean whom?'

'Your sister, as you well know. The Honourable Matilda Lilley.' An *honourable,* as Edith had been wailing at him for two days now. He couldn't make out whether she was more upset that that old hag was an honourable or about her accusation. He hoped the former, but either way Miss Matilda had burned her boats – and if he wasn't damned careful, his as well.

'On what grounds do you wish to get rid of her, as you put it?'

'For slanderous accusations for which she has no proof.'

'You had no qualms about Ruth Horner's accusations about Jamie Thorn, with again no proof.'

'Not my concern. That young jackanapes is getting what's due to him. He's a young lad who's been playing with too many lasses, and I'm a respectable married man.'

'Do I take it you intend to sue my sister if she doesn't leave the village forthwith?'

'You do not. I wouldn't waste my money on such a farrago of a case. Women like her ought to be locked up, and locked up she shall be. I'm not a nobody, Rector. One word from me to the Chief Constable and she'll be back in Holloway Prison tomorrow.'

'Then why not make this threat to her? Why come to me?' He supposed it had been a vain hope that Tilly could find some period of calm at Ashden to recuperate physically and perhaps reconsider her views on militancy; it was inevitable that someone would recall her name, and discover her background. That it should be Swinford-Browne was, again, perhaps inevitable. Tilly had warned him she might prove a cuckoo in the nest here as well as at Dover. He had told her it was a risk he was prepared to take, and he was prepared to give battle.

'Because my son is supposed to be marrying your daughter. Do you think I want him marrying into a family of felons? But I come to your house and get abused. Not a good start, is it? No dowry, I don't mind that. What I do mind is if young Isabel might have inherited the family traits. Do I make myself clear?'

'I understand you perfectly, Mr Swinford-Browne. Now let us be clear that you understand *me*. Let us consider for a moment the hypothesis that my sister spoke the truth in what she said.'

'Go on.'

'Truth is, as you know, an absolute defence in law.'

'Not without proof.'

'But we stand here before God, not before a court of law, and God does not need proof, as we know it. He sees directly into our hearts. I cannot claim that ability, but I would suggest that if as a direct result of your intervention – which *could* be proved – my sister were once again removed to Holloway goal, re-arrested under the Cat and Mouse Act, there to have tubes rammed up her nostrils and be held down, screaming in pain and her own vomit as three doctors, supposedly devoted to the saving of life, and two wardresses do their best to kill her by forcible feeding, my family, friends and a large proportion of Ashden from manor to meadow might wonder why you had taken such prompt action. Could it be, they might ask, that there was some truth in my sister's accusations? As Rector, I, of course, must remain impartial, but village opinion is under no such obligation.'

Swinford-Browne's cheeks grew red with anger. 'Are you threatening me?'

'I state both sides of the case, that is all. If there is truth in the accusation, then it must be for your conscience to look after Ruth, and see Jamie Thorn is cleared. You may think it appropriate to find her a position suitable for her situation and a cottage of her own.' Laurence paused. 'Perhaps even the cottage you are so eager to persuade Mrs Leggatt to leave. Ruth after all claims to have pursued her courtship in the adjoining cottage, Mr Thorn's.'

Swinford-Browne eyed his adversary. As with the matter of the oak trees, he knew when he would get no further. The oak trees, however, were not and never had been that important. This was. 'I'll not forget this, Rector. You can say goodbye to the new cemetery for a start, you and your pious Anglican God.' He thought rapidly. 'The wedding goes ahead. You muzzle that sister of yours. I realise the woman was intoxicated with strong liquor and was joking. I can take a joke as well as the next man,' he informed the Rector grimly, preparing to leave. Laurence stopped him.

'Now I'm forgetting I'm a parson, and speaking to you as a husband. Don't lay one finger on my wife, don't shake hands, don't dance with her, and never take advantage of what you imagine to be a future relationship with us by stepping across the boundaries of acceptable behaviour again.'

Swinford-Browne marched out as if he had not heard, and from the study the Rector could hear his voice loudly flattering Harriet's efficiency as he collected his stick and hat. The battle, however, he knew, was not over. Truth was still evading them and Ruth Horner still unwed. Would 'unknown father' or 'Jamie Thorn' appear on the birth certificate in – when was it? – September?

By Tuesday the bee swarms appeared to have settled back to a reasonable hum. Aunt Tilly had not vanished from the house, and Isabel's wedding did not appear to be under threat. In fact the only ripple in the Rectory was the matter of the guest list. It had been beyond Caroline's powers to persuade even Isabel, let alone Felicia and Phoebe, to help her in writing out the cards, which required the best copperplate. George pleaded school, and Caroline wondered why her own plea of working at the Manor had elicited only: 'I expect you'll manage, dear.' She had even asked *why* Mother thought she could manage, and the reply had astounded her. 'Isabel is Isabel, Felicia is in the clouds, Phoebe too much on the ground. You are the one I rely on, Caroline.' Caroline was flattered and amused, but she was still going to dragoon help if she could. She couldn't.

There had been no sign of either Reggie or Lady Hunney at the Manor this morning, which was not unusual, save that she had not seen Reggie since Sunday or talked to him for *three whole days*. As soon as she had finished the letters, she was seized by Mother to support her in the battle of the budgets for the wedding with Mrs Dibble on the pretext she was known to be good at figures. She was also known to be effective as a punchbag between Mother and Mrs Dibble.

'Fifteen lobsters. That's what we need.'

'We are already at over twenty pounds, Mrs Dibble,' Elizabeth objected. More than they paid Agnes for a *year*, she despaired.

'Spare the pence and waste the pound,' Mrs Dibble announced mysteriously.

'How about ten *larger* ones?' Caroline suggested.

'Mayhap.' Grudging assent.

'Two hundred and three people will never eat as much as one person two hundred and three times.' Caroline could vouch for this rule of thumb from years of sandwich-making for parties.

'I don't want to run short of food,' Elizabeth said doubtfully.

'Have I ever let you go short in this house?' Mrs Dibble drew herself up to her full five feet three inches.

'No, no, of course not, Mrs Dibble. You are a marvellous organiser. We can always send any leftover dishes round to the almshouses.'

'No one leaves my junkets.'

Caroline was thankful for Isabel's absence.

Victory in this assured, Mrs Dibble regarded the list again with a professional eye. 'You've too much butter and too little cheese.'

'I always think cheese is something people never want unless it's there.'

'Mayhap. But there it's got to be, even if we're eating rarebits till Christmas.'

'And what about help, Mrs Dibble? The girls won't be able to assist as much as usual, on the day, that is. We can all help beforehand. Can you cope with just Agnes, Myrtle and Harriet? And Fred, of course,' Elizabeth added hastily.

'I could ask Rosie Trott up at the Manor if Lady Hunney would agree. She's a nice girl, is Rosie.'

'What a good idea,' Elizabeth said warmly. 'And perhaps one or two others from their staff to help with the wine.'

'Percy can manage.' Snap. Mrs Dibble had spoken.

'We don't want to ask the Swinford-Brownes for help,

of course,' Caroline observed brightly, seeing where her mother was leading.

Mrs Dibble stiffened. 'I'm not having none of them Towers' girls, or their smelly footmen.'

'Then I'll ask Lady Hunney,' Elizabeth said conclusively. 'I'm so glad that's agreed.' Afterwards in the drawing room, however, she sighed. 'I'll have to get something from the bonds.'

When Caroline was a child she had assumed 'the bonds' were something provided by God rather like a poorbox, a manna of life to be called upon in dire emergencies. That it had to do with mundane matters of keeping your money in interest-bearing funds she had learned much later, too late to divest the word entirely of its magical properties.

'You're very restless, Caroline,' her mother broke off.

'I was expecting Reggie.' It was a white lie. She was *hoping* to see Reggie. Where could he be? It occurred to her he might have gone to Tunbridge Wells or East Grinstead on business – he often did, in which case he might call in on the way home from the railway station. Unless he'd taken his beloved motor car? No, he was far more likely to have taken a train. She would walk up Station Road a little way, not just to see him, she told herself, for she could call at the Manor after dinner, but because she needed some air. It had been quite cool all day, compared with recent temperatures, so it was a pity not to thank the sun for re-emerging.

'I thought I'd take Ahab for a walk.'

'Phoebe's taken him. It's her week.'

'I'll go anyway. I'll catch her up.'

Elizabeth said nothing more, and Caroline quickly

found her sun-bonnet and jacket, escaping quickly before a cry of 'Caroline, do you think . . .?' summoned her back.

She did meet Reggie, though not in Station Road. She walked into Silly Lane, fragrant with elderflower and dog roses, and saw him coming towards her. He never used the path through the Sharpes' farm, of course; he'd probably get pigswill thrown over him. Reggie saw her, and wavered, but he did not break into a run. Something *was* wrong, it must be. Terror stabbed at her. Was he regretting Saturday already and was afraid of breaking the news? Had it been the whim of a summer's day? His grave face, as he came up to her, confirmed her worst suspicions. He put his arm round her in a way he'd never have dared before and which would certainly have earned even Mother's disapproval if she had seen him doing it in public view in broad daylight, engaged or not.

'Let's go somewhere quiet, Caroline, and talk. Come into the park. We can walk over to the folly.'

The folly, by a small ornamental lake, had been the whim of an eighteenth-century baronet and was built like a small Roman temple with the entire divine population of Mount Olympus crowded in as statuary. Rather poor statuary, but Caroline had always loved the place, even so. They looked a rather jolly group of gods. But today she could not bear the thought of it.

'Tell me now,' she asked abruptly.

'No. I'll tell you I love you, though. Do you still love me?'

'Of course,' torn between relief and even greater worry, and using levity to disguise it. 'I never change fiancés more than once a month. And it's only been three days.' She faltered. 'Oh, Reggie, *tell* me.'

'It's Mother.' He pushed open the gate into the Manor park, hurrying her inside, then grabbing her hand.

She knew at once what had happened. '*Why*?' she burst out, meaning 'Why should she influence what we do?', but he took it another way and dumbfounded her.

'She says I should marry someone more suitable.'

'What does she mean?' Caroline cried, shock overcoming her usual common sense. 'Someone with more money, more looks and less ability to answer her back?'

'She's my mother.'

'I'm sorry, Reggie.'

'She doesn't mean that. She likes you, she says, but how could she approve a marriage into a family that has your Aunt Tilly in it?'

Oh, how the woman smiled and smiled and was a villain. She could *carpe diem* quicker than Scipio Africanus. Surely Reggie must be exaggerating, though. 'Just because of her outburst against Swinford-Browne?'

'It did naturally shock Mother,' he agreed. 'But it's because she's discovered – I'm sorry to have to break this to you – that your aunt is a prominent suffragette. Mother hadn't connected it with your aunt before, since Lilley is not an uncommon name, but now she has. There's no doubt about it, I'm afraid.'

'I knew already about Aunt Tilly's beliefs.'

He exclaimed. 'And your father knows? How can you go on sheltering her?'

'How can we *not*?' she retorted angrily, unable to believe that Reggie of all people could be speaking thus. 'She acts in accordance with what she believes. Surely you believe in women getting the vote? It's only the means they use to achieve it that can be disputed by any rational person.'

'You're wrong. Mother, for instance, is a fervent anti-suffragist.'

She began to laugh hysterically. 'Not like Lady Bathurst who advocates suffragettes should be soundly birched, their hair shaved and then be deported to the Colonies as convicts?'

'Yes. Mother belongs to the Anti-Suffrage League and wrote a letter to the *Morning Post* on that issue.'

'And do *you* believe women like Aunt Tilly should be birched?' She was appalled that Reggie spoke so matter-of-factly.

'Of course not.' He was indignant.

'And that they should not have the same rights as men?'

'I don't believe in *all* women having the vote. Do you see Ruth Horner voting wisely?'

'But do you believe in all *men* getting the vote?'

'There is more of a case for it, because all men work. Women do not. I don't believe the vote should be given just to property owners any more, but wage-earners as well. Women are not wage-earners.'

'More and more are.'

'Then there is a case for those who do.'

'Are women not equal to men?'

'In some things yes, in others no.'

'You don't think me equal?'

He looked at her gravely. 'I can't answer that. I look at you and see the girl I love. I look at you and see the girl I've always loved, though I was too idiotic to realise it. I look at you and see the girl I'm going to marry.'

'Oh, Reggie.' She went to him, and he embraced her, his lips on her eyes, her hair, her cheeks and then urgently seeking her lips. It didn't seem to matter where his hands were then, provided she could be with him, clinging to him, a rock in a tumultuous sea. He drew away, took off her jacket, then his own, and took her again into his arms. 'I can get closer now.' It seemed at some point a good idea to sit down on the grass bank above the lake and then at some point after that to lie down. What a wonderful – but strange – sensation to see his face above her, bending over her, then kissing her, almost lying on her, and then face and sun were blotted out. When she felt his hand inside her dress, she shifted slightly, puzzled, then embarrassed. 'Reggie?' She didn't want him to stop, but he did, rolled away and sat up.

'Did you really say going to marry?' she asked almost shyly.

'Of course. You didn't think I'd let Mother stop me, did you?'

Why was he sounding so gruff? Had she annoyed him?

'On the other hand,' he continued, not looking at her. 'I'm the heir to Ashden. You'll have to live there. Even if you don't like each other, you and Mother must learn to work together.'

'Must we?' Dismay hit her. She hadn't given it a thought. Why did *outside* have to intrude *inside*? Marriage should be private – though Isabel and Robert's certainly wasn't going to be that.

'So what I suggest,' he turned over on his stomach, supporting himself on his elbows so that he could see her, 'is that we keep our engagement quiet while I work on her for a time and until she's got over the shock of Tilly. Could you bear to? Have you told your family?'

'Only Mother and Father know.'

'Your father was top-hole,' he said fervently. 'He and my father understand each other. If only women were more like men!'

'I'll make you regret that.' She promptly kneeled at his side, and pelted him with a handful of grass. 'See how you like birching.'

He put his hands up protestingly. 'Hey, I surrender.' He lay down with her again and kissed her more lightly, but after a while said idly: 'There's no chance of your turning into an Aunt Tilly, is there?'

She considered this gravely. 'It all depends.'

'On what?'

'On what you do to annoy me.'

Agnes dressed with care, even more than if she were off to see Jamie. She didn't want to look too prim and be laughed at, nor did she want to look too cheap, because then she'd lose the advantage of being morally in the right. She wanted to look, she had decided, as if she might be an ally, even a friend. As if she'd ever be a friend of the likes of Ruth Horner! On Saturday night when Miss Tilda shouted out so queerly, Agnes had only belatedly realised what she might be meaning. She debated whether she should ask Miss Tilda if she knew something Agnes didn't, but realised that if she did so, the Rector too must know, and would surely have told her. Miss Lilley might only be guessing, but nevertheless it was a guess that sent Agnes's hopes soaring, if only she could establish the truth. She took one last critical look in the foot-high swing mirror on her dressing table, and departed to fight the foe.

'Evening, Ruth. Can I have a word with you?' she whispered. Ruth was setting the table for supper when she arrived, and Nanny, as usual, was snoozing by the fire. Ruth's shape was very obvious now, and in Agnes's imagination grew ever larger, a monstrous barrier to be overcome. Suppose that thing in there was part of Jamie? Suppose he *had* put it there, whispered to Ruth what he did to Agnes, kissed her like he did her, put his hands over those great lumps of bosom – she tried to avert her eyes – like he did Agnes's own small chest, not underneath of course, over her blouse and stays, but it was nice – or had been till her thoughts had become obsessed with imagining her Jamie and Ruth's repulsive mountainous flesh together. She struggled for control as Ruth jeered:

'And I've a word for you. *Yes*. Yes, it was Jamie. That do?'

Nanny's eyes flew open. 'You go and talk to Agnes in the kitchen, Ruth. She can't eat you.'

'Pity she don't want this lump.' Ruth looked down at her stomach.

'I'll thank you to remember you're in a maiden lady's house,' Nanny snapped. 'Get into the scullery, the two of you. I'm listening to me memories, and won't hear you over the babble.'

Face-to-face with Ruth it seemed much harder to establish the friendly atmosphere Agnes had planned in the privacy of

178

her own room. 'I don't want to be your enemy, Ruth,' Agnes began. 'I just need to sort myself out, that's all. We're both in trouble. Mayhap we could help each other.'

'Share his bed?' Ruth sneered, though only half-heartedly now.

'I don't share his bed, but I want to,' Agnes said firmly, feeling on safer ground now Ruth was talking, 'so I thought I'd come to ask – well, if it *was* someone else and you daren't say who, I could maybe help, get justice done—'

'I want a husband, and the husband is going to be Jamie Thorn.' Ruth sounded as if she were reciting her ten-times table.

'There's folks saying it's Mr Swinford-Browne who's done this to you. Forced you, maybe. And now he's forcing you into saying it's Jamie.'

'See here, Agnes,' Ruth replied quite kindly, 'you're just a bit upset and I don't blame you, surely. But no men are angels. You've got to realise that. Jamie ain't, Mus Swinford-Browne ain't, none of 'em. But I love Jamie, I laid with Jamie, and look what's happened.'

'But why, *where*? It was January. It *must* have been Mr Swinford-Browne.' Agnes was beginning to get desperate.

'In the old gentleman's cottage. Ebenezer Thorn.'

'But that's ours, me and Jamie's,' wailed Agnes, unable to believe her last dream had been soiled. 'You're fibbing.'

'You don't believe me? Listen, the old gentleman's sofa is green cloth and it's got red plush cushions with moth-eaten dogs on 'em.'

'You could have seen the sofa at any time, not with Jamie at all.' Agnes began to cry.

'You're a fool, Agnes,' Ruth shouted. 'What more proof do you want? Do you want me to tell you Jamie has a scar just above his johnnie, about—?'

Agnes yelled out, she couldn't help it, or she knew she'd be sick. She yelled again and again. Nanny Oates had to hobble in to soothe her down. What terrified Agnes most, even through her sobs, was that Ruth wasn't even triumphant. She was looking as though she were sorry for her.

'The Rectory!' shouted Mrs Dibble into infinity as she lifted the telephone from its hook as gingerly as a live crab, after the infernal machine went off. Unable to leave her post, so tightly was she gripping the receiver, albeit held six inches from her ear (Percy having read in the newspaper about the dangers to ears from that electricity hidden inside the howler), she bawled, 'It's Squire.'

The Rector came at once. As soon as he had hung up, he shouted for Elizabeth, who appeared immediately. 'I may miss luncheon, my love. Old Cooper's barricaded himself into his cottage. Swinford-Browne is there with his men determined to evict him.' The Rector's hat was instantly produced for his head, his stick and a Bible thrust into his hands. The latter had been known to help in such cases. 'If I know Tom Cooper, he'll have built up his walls like Jericho.'

'And you're the trumpet to bring them tumbling down?'

'I'm the policeman to see Cooper doesn't tumble down himself.'

'It's Phoebe's birthday luncheon.'

'Tell her –' Laurence sought for a way to reconcile the horizons of youth with the agonies of age – 'it concerns the picture palace.' He was already debating whether he should take the trap, call to Tilly to beg a drive in the Austin (no, red rags to bulls) or rely on his own two feet in order to travel quickest. He decided on the trap, and rang the bell sharply enough for Percy Dibble to obey promptly. He might be glad of Percy's stolid presence.

Cooper's cottage lay on the edge of the hop gardens, reached most easily by a long track from Station Road. The nearest way from the Rectory lay up Bankside and along Mill Lane to a steep track down the hillside, but Poppy was too old to risk her obstinate refusal at steep inclines. As she laboured over the track where lack of rain was exposing the stones and flints, the Rector pondered on his approach. There would be no talking Swinford-Browne out of this one, not with the law on his side. He would be even more determined to win his way over the picture palace to impress Ashden in view of Tilly's outburst. Tilly had been contrite – naturally not for speaking out, but for breaking her promise to him; the damage had been done, however, and no one could be sure where it might lead.

'They be good hop-poles!' Dibble cried, outraged, seeing the barricades Cooper had erected round his beloved, if tumble-down, cottage, and across the door and windows. 'Hell and Tommy, they got baby hops on 'em. He must have torn 'em out. Tedious waste, that is.'

'He is an old and bitter man, Percy. We both might feel the same.' The Rector glanced at the black Daimler drawn up further along the track, outside the pale of the cottage.

In front of it, nearer to them, was a wagon, four farm-hands sitting waiting. The wagon appeared to be otherwise empty, save for farm implements, a hop dog, pitchfork . . . then he saw why, as he stepped down from the trap and went to the gate. The barricade here had been broken down, and round the cottage were bales of dry straw. His heart sank. He would not be called on as mediator, for there was to be no mediation; all he could do was protect the guiltless.

'Not about good hops, surely,' Dibble grunted.

From the upper window the Rector could see Tom glaring down at his landlord's Daimler. He could see a bottle in his hand, not for drinking, but, judging by the number of pieces of shattered glass lying around, ready to be aimed at any intruder. He wouldn't put it past Cooper to use even more dangerous ammunition when the bottles ran out.

'Tom,' he yelled.

'I hear you, Rector. I don't be daffy yet.'

'The law's on his side, not yours.'

''Tis a bad law, then.'

'No matter. You will lose all. I'll find you somewhere else if you don't like the almshouse for a home.'

'I got a home. 'Tis 'ere, Rector, like I told Squire, and like I told 'im.' A contemptuously jerked finger indicated Swinford-Browne, sufficiently emboldened by the Rector's presence to climb down from the motor car.

'See, the Rector's on my side, Tom,' he shouted.

'Then he can have a bottle over his head and all, William,' yelled the infuriated Cooper.

The Rector hastily backed away. 'It's *your* side I'm on, Tom. But I don't want to see you hurt.'

'Good for you, Rector. I won't be hurt, staying in me own home, biding me own business.' Another bottle crashed to the ground in the lane just in front of Swinford-Browne, who retaliated swiftly.

'Smoke him out.' He turned to his three men, keeping well in the background.

'You can't do that.' The Rector was outraged.

'Why not? It's my property.'

'Suppose he refuses to leave, and the thatch catches fire?'

'I'll rebuild. I want him out. Chop down the rear door, Stokes,' he ordered the bailiff. 'If the man doesn't come out then, it's his own risk and you're all witness. Hear that, Rector?'

Tom replied for him with a string of oaths followed by a shot fired in the air.

'Light up,' roared Swinford-Browne.

Appalled, the Rector watched as bales of straw were dampened and set alight, acrid smoke immediately curling into the air under the open cottage window, its fumes even reaching him at the gate, making him cough and splutter. Angrily, he made his way into the rear door of the cottage, smoke already snaking lasciviously under doors and into windows. He rushed up the stairs to find Tom.

'Don't be a fool, Rector.' Swinford-Browne's shouting voice outside held a note of alarm, not, Laurence knew, for his own sake, but for Swinford-Browne's reputation, as the Rector was almost universally popular with church and chapel alike.

Crouching by the window, Tom winked at him. 'Give as good as I get, eh? I'll have that bugger in the belly next time.'

'Your language, Mr Cooper.'

'Think I should speak nice and behave dirty like that Fat Jack outside, eh?' he jeered, pulling himself up and making faces out of the window through the smoke.

'You have made your point, Mr Cooper.' Coughing, the Rector tried to humour him. 'Come, now I have joined my lot with yours, so you must at least consider my life and let me lead you out.'

'You're as daft as he is if you think I'll do that. You'll not be catching me.'

The smoke outside, caught by sudden winds, was fanned into flame, leaping perilously near the thatch, and blowing new fumes into Tom's leering face that sent him collapsing back in a heap of coughing, gasping for breath on the floor.

'Dibble, come here!' The Rector thrust his head out, and Percy, spurred at last into action, rushed into the cottage to his master's aid. 'Swinford-Browne, extinguish those fires or you'll kill us both. The man's old and he's sick.'

Smirking, Swinford-Browne said something to his men, who slowly began to fling earth and sand on the burning hay.

'Help me get him to the trap, Percy. We'll take him to Dr Marden.' Percy looked with distaste at the heap on the floor, then at the Rector's face. He remembered his Christian duty.

'He can come to the missis, afterwards. We'll care for him till you get him sorted, Rector,' Percy offered handsomely, taking half Tom Cooper's weight as they half led, half dragged him from the cottage.

The Rector nodded. 'Thank you,' he had not doubted

it. The Dibbles were forever a trial in fair weather but a lifeboat in stormy seas.

'I showed the old bugger, didn't I, Rector?' Tom crowed hoarsely as Poppy plodded into Station Road.

'You did, Mr Cooper, you did.'

Saturday morning found Tom fully recovered, eating his way jauntily through a plateful of kedgeree with a side plate of kidneys returned from the Rectory dining room chafing dishes. He announced he would be walking back to his cottage now if that was all right with the Rector. It took all morning to persuade him that a man of his fragile constitution should be in a nice warm almshouse and not in a damp, ill-maintained cottage. At last, unexpectedly, he agreed. He claimed to have been swayed by the voice of God speaking through the Rector, but in fact it was Elizabeth's apparently casual comment, as she passed through the morning room, that the empty almshouse was the one next to old Mrs Pilbeam, young Aggie's grannie, that saved the day. On summer evenings they could sit outside their respective front doors and have a chat, Tom reflected. Or inside, come to that. There might be the odd pudding in it, or stew.

'You done me a lot of good, Rector,' Tom informed him generously. 'So I'll do something for you now. That new cemetery you want. Tallow Field. Rented to Swinford-Browne, ain't it? I heard tell he won't give it back and you can't force him.'

'Correct. Gossip, it seems, is the speediest means of travel in Ashden.'

'You can tell him it's yours any time you like. He reckons because he pays his rent it's his for aye. Not so. 'Tis glebe land held by candle auction. That's why 'tis called Tallow Field.' Tom paused to pour tea daintily into his saucer and slurp it approvingly.

'I've never heard of it. What is it?'

''Tis your right to hold one every two years. He who makes the last bid before the candle goes out gets to rent it for two years. No more. The old rector afore you came, he were a lazy blighter. Liked his fishing more than attending his faithful flock, and he couldn't be bothered to keep holding auctions. He fished on the Towers estate so he let the owner rent the field without troubling about him. It'll come as a shock to Silly Billy Swinford-Browne, won't it?' he cackled.

'Is there any proof of this?' the Rector asked doubtfully. 'I've seen no records.'

'You wouldn't. I got 'em. I've always been one to let sleeping dogs lie, and besides, me son had his eye on Tallow Field for new hoppers' huts. But now he's been given the order of the sack, why should I care? Him being a lettered man, my dad were churchwarden, see, at the time o' the last auction, and he kept all the papers, and I found 'em arter he were gone. The old Rector weren't interested, so I hung on and forgot 'em till this 'ere cemetery come up.'

'Where are the papers?' A sudden thought struck the Rector.

'There's a china ornament my old mother won at Brighton. A cottage, tedious noble it is. Lift the roof off and there's all the papers. I'll be off now to pick it up.'

The Rector started to laugh. He couldn't help it. He

almost doubled up with the pain in his sides, as tears of mirth rolled down his cheeks.

'Smoke still getting to you, Rector?' Tom asked anxiously.

'No,' the Rector spluttered. 'I was thinking of your former landlord. His last threat was that he was going to carry all your possessions over to the almshouse today. I trust he takes care of the china.'

'He will surely,' Tom said gloomily, unable to see the joke himself. 'Mus Swinford-Browne won't want to pay me no compensation, will 'e?'

The day of the tennis match had turned the cranking handle to the summer. The cool cloudy days of early June had ignited into the resplendent sun and warmth of the later half. A strawberry half June, Elizabeth had announced with satisfaction, as the first punnets appeared in the village from Hector and Eileen Roffey's market garden.

For Caroline June was blazing a trail along which she moved supremely happily, swept along by the special momentum of the Ashden summer this year made glorious by her own personal joy. The month was crowned by Reggie's birthday on the 27th, following the village pageant in the afternoon. Every year the Manor held a midsummer dance with a real band for Reggie's birthday. No uneven paving slabs here, but, unless they were very lucky, no Huggie Bears or ragtime either. Even Lady Hunney, however, could not stamp her aura over the entire evening; it was as if the Manor permitted her to indulge in her role of social hostess, then persuaded her to step back and allow the real Hunney atmosphere to take over.

Aunt Tilly's Austin lurched up the long drive to the Manor. The others were walking, but her aunt had declared that Caroline should arrive in style. Perhaps she had guessed? Oh, May is for the lilacs, but June puts forth the roses. Caroline sniffed appreciatively as the Austin crunched to a stop. No roses were allowed to ramble here where they would, as in the Rectory. Here, before the Manor, they stood to attention like the liveried footmen, a household cavalry drawn up to salute their monarch. It didn't seem to spoil their rich smell. Nothing could spoil tonight's glory. Sir John made a special point of coming forward to greet them in the entrance hall, and not to be outdone, Lady Hunney herself. How odd the dictates of society were. You are not good enough to marry my son, Caroline, and I thoroughly disapprove of everything you do, Miss Lilley, yet I shall greet you as though you do us the greatest honour imaginable by visiting our home. Social life was like a stately dance: when the music stopped one found oneself alone, she reflected.

In the ladies' withdrawing room they found Isabel and Eleanor, the former enthusing about Eleanor's dress – which was strange, firstly that Isabel should notice and second because the dress, Caroline surmised with practised eye, was Lady Hunney's choice: black net over a terrible biscuit-coloured taffeta. Wonderful for her ladyship but hardly for Eleanor. The dress looked as if it had a mind of its own, and Eleanor was not to its fancy. Eleanor winked at her. 'Ghastly, isn't it?' she said mournfully. 'You should have seen the one she *really* wanted me to have, though. Even a zebra would have balked at it.'

'Mrs Swinford-Browne wouldn't.'

'Really, Caroline.' Isabel drew herself up, offended. 'You are a bad influence on Eleanor.'

Caroline tried to feel contrite, as Isabel, followed by a giggling Eleanor, left them alone. 'It's not like Isabel to stand on her dignity.'

'I expect she's envying you,' Tilly put forward.

'She doesn't know about me. And I didn't know you did.'

'The Rectory walls leak more than damp.'

'Phoebe, I suppose,' Caroline said, resigned. 'What she *doesn't* know is that Lady Hunney has put her elegant kid-shod foot down.' Would Aunt Tilly guess the reason?

'Are you sure you want to become another Lady Hunney?'

'I'm going to be the first of the Free-Thinking Lady Hunneys.'

'A suffragette squire's wife?'

'Look at the Countess of Warwick. She's become a follower of the Socialist cause.'

'Only now gentlemen have stopped following *her*.' Notably his late Majesty, King Edward, Tilly might have added, but as usual, refrained. The less you spoke about inessentials, in Tilly's view, the more you would be listened to on matters of importance.

'If Reggie and I truly love each other, as we do, we can carve life in our own ways and find a meeting point. There is an answer, there *always* is.'

Tilly said no more.

* * *

189

Isabel slid her hand into Robert's. 'We must entertain like this.'

Robert looked round at the gracious surroundings of Ashden Manor, mentally compared them with The Towers, and laughed uneasily. 'Mother and you could do it together.' It wasn't the best of efforts on his part and it failed miserably. He longed to talk of Wimbledon, but Isabel never seemed interested.

'That will be nice, of course,' Isabel replied after a moment. 'But on our own would be even nicer. Not so many people, of course.' She was trying to analyse just what it was about Ashden Manor and the crowds here this evening that differentiated them from her own engagement ball. She gave up the struggle, deciding there was no difference and she had merely been tired on the evening of her own ball. She'd make up for it after she was married. It would be wonderful. And it would be *just* like this. How about a Michaelmas ball? She couldn't possibly wait until Christmas.

Phoebe pirouetted in the garden, happy with herself and the evening. She was feeling as though she wanted to cry and laugh both at the same time. It was so still out here it felt as if the evening were holding back, waiting for her to join it. She supposed she was restless because this was almost the last time she'd see Christopher Denis, and although it was satisfactory to think his precipitate action might possibly be due to her charms, it was annoying to think he did find her resistible. Now there'd be a new curate, Father said, someone known to Sir John was coming. *That* was bad news for a start, for he would be sure to be a lot older than her. On a night like this *someone* in the world must be waiting for Miss Phoebe Lilley. If only, if only, she could reach him, tear through the garden, the fields, the woods, and rush into his arms. But what if those bushes, so still and mysterious, hid a Len Thorn, just waiting, waiting, for her? Ever since their encounter in the stables she had been half fearful, half intrigued at the idea of seeing him again. Sometime she would bump into him again and he'd look at her, his eyes watching her, roving over her from top to toe. What for? She could see that look on his face now, the half smile, a knowing smile. But what could he know, he of the powerful rippling body and the strange, scary eyes?

'Knossos hasn't long been discovered, of course. Evans only started digging around the turn of the century, and then there were lots of delays with the Cretan authorities. They were too busy having wars to care about the past. But when they did, there it all was – *is* rather – and I'm going to see it. A labyrinth, just as the myth relates, and pictures drawn on the walls of a whole civilisation no one knows much about. The Minoan, gone in a flash in an earthquake – or the roaring of the bull monster, however you like your myth—' Daniel broke off, aware that lectures on Greek mythology were not what most eighteen-year-old girls would want to hear on a sultry June evening. 'I don't know why I'm telling you all this.' He threw a pebble into the pond and a moorhen, disturbed from sleep, squawked in protest.

'I like to know,' Felicia said somewhat indignantly, upset he treated her as just another girl.

'You're surprisingly easy to talk to.'

'Why surprisingly?'

'I've never been sure what to talk to you about. Or what you're thinking.' Tonight Felicia had acquired a mystery together with beauty.

'I'm not thinking, I'm *absorbing*,' she told him seriously, 'so that when you're away I can imagine where you are.'

'I'll be somewhere else by then.'

'Where, for instance? Tell me where.'

'All right, Desdemona.' He gave in. 'I'd like to go to Turkey. I want to stand where Schliemann stood at Hissarlik, look down and say, 'This is Troy. Helen's Troy. Priam's Troy.'' He looked at Felicia's dark hair, her pale oval face, the eyes fixed on him so intently, and continued, his voice a little husky now. 'I'd like to fasten the golden necklaces around your neck, the diadems on your hair, and say as Schliemann did: 'These are Helen's jewels.'' Then he hurried on, afraid: 'I want to go to Greece, to see Mycenae—'

'Agamemnon?'

'Yes. His tomb, at least. Go to Mount Athos. Perhaps I'll enter a monastery and become a monk.' He shot a sideways look at her.

'I would think God might turn you away and say, 'Go, my son, there is work for you in the world.''

And women, he thought. He summoned in his imagination lines of dark Greek maidens to sway in grace before him, French soubrettes danced to ensnare him, black Africans beckoned, dusky Polynesians laughed, and when all was done then English roses should put forth their perfume. So much time, plenty of time. Out there waiting for him were old civilisations, new emerging countries, and the lure of the East; each had their own way of life, their own culture. He had to *know* his own was best, that Felicia was best; that the promise of her lips as he kissed her was no illusion and would last. After all, he had not yet set out on his long journey. Odysseus was halfway home when he heard the sirens call.

'You're tired of me.' Reggie felt Caroline flinch away from him.

'No. Your arm was hurting me – you're holding me too tight.'

Reggie released her, horrified. 'I'm sorry. I can't get over how differently I see you now. I'm afraid you'll disappear. Did I bruise you?' He kissed her arms in penitence, secure in the knowledge that they were far enough away from the Manor to escape attention.

'There's one advantage in having been friends for so long. No one seems to think I need a chaperone.' There was satisfaction in her voice.

'They're wrong.' He flicked the lace of her bodice absently, his fingers rubbing though the holes on the bare flesh beneath. 'Very wrong.' His lips followed the fingers. 'Do you want a chaperone?'

Thump went her heart. 'No. I want to know –' she continued with difficulty – 'what comes next.' There was a silence and she had a sudden fear she had said something irreparable.

'When we're married?' He sounded puzzled.

'Yes – no. I mean, just to be *alone* with you.' She floundered. Her body seemed to be racing on and leaving words far behind, yet surely he must be feeling what she was feeling?

He was. He embraced her again, his voice hard against her face. 'To hell with my mother. I want to marry you *tomorrow*. Then in fifty years' time we can wobble through these gardens on our sticks, and kiss in this same spot.' He let her go, and looked round at the large rhododendron bank that divided the formal gardens from the rest of the park. 'These *same* gardens. That's the glory of England.'

'I shan't use a stick,' Caroline declared, glad the tension was broken.

'I'll be too feeble to carry you. I'll get the children to do it. Shall we say six?'

'We'll say nothing of the sort.' Children, children born of her and Reggie? Another enormous thought to consider. 'The gardens don't have any hop-bines.'

'Plenty of gooseberry bushes.'

'Mother used to say –' Caroline's tongue ran away with her and she could not draw back – 'under the hop-bines was where babies were found.' His hand was very heavy resting on her shoulders, and he was looking at her intently again. Had she embarrassed him? 'I was joking. I do know about babies,' she managed to say.

'Soon, Caroline, I must marry you *soon*. Look, I've an idea to outwit Mother. Isabel's wedding is only just over a month away. After Isabel and Robert have gone to Paris in the evening, we'll just *announce* our engagement! Mother won't be able to say a word if the whole of Ashden knows.'

194

'She'll blame me.'

'No matter. It will be done and Father won't let her undo that!' He caught her to him again, kissed her in a lengthy embrace, but as a tremor of feeling shot up through her body, he let her go. 'I'm sorry. My hands seem to have a mind of their own.'

'Why sorry? It was—'

'Because I'm going to marry you.' He seemed surprised she should ask.

'But I liked it,' she said uncertainly. 'Shouldn't I have done?'

'Yes, but not yet.'

Flabbergasted, she stared at him until he saw the funny side. He gave a hoot of laughter, and caught her as she thudded into his arms again. 'Kitchener never had this problem with *his* dervishes.'

'Maybe he never had time to kiss like you.'

'He's all the time in the world, and so have we.'

Chapter Six

Harriet felt as though she were suffocating. How could old Dibble work in this stewpot of a kitchen? The range emitted great belches of warmth all day long, because the Rector had to keep his strength up with good hot meals, praise the Lord. The windows and doors might be open, but that only let a fresh blast of heat in from outside. Mrs D. looked like a turkey with her thin neck red with heat sticking out from her high black collar. Greatly daring, Harriet had undone the top button of her print dress, only to have the sainted Miss Pilbeam yell at her. Now old Dibble was, judging by her expression, about to do the same thing. The Rectory, Harriet admitted grudgingly, wasn't a bad situation, but any position in service meant long, back-breaking hours whether the sun was scorching or Jack Frost was freezing you. Perhaps she could go and work in a factory; some girls did. Or be one of them typists? She was good with her hands. She wondered vaguely how she would go about this, and when no answer was forthcoming, dismissed the idea. She could always marry Bert Wilson if things got too bad here. No, on second thoughts, she might end up with a tray on her head like his Auntie Gwen.

Old Dibble had had it in for her ever since the affair of Fred. Harriet still felt aggrieved. There had been a shadow outside the window, she was almost sure, and who could it have been if not Fred? Percy had no interest in women, only his blessed garden. How Fred and his brother and sister ever got born, beat her. Old Dibble must have lain down and covered herself with compost to lure Percy into digging in her with his dibber. No, it must have been Fred peering in, and she was righteously offended that his word had been taken against hers.

'Did you order them raspberries, Harriet?' Old Dibble's querulous voice broke in upon her thoughts and her dinner.

'Course I did,' Harriet lied indignantly. She hadn't exactly forgotten, but who was going to walk out to Grendel's Farm halfway to Withyham in this weather to order raspberries? She'd been expecting to see Uncle Seb, who farmed it, in the village but must have missed him. Plenty of time. She'd see him at the flower show on Saturday.

'White ones, mind.' Old Dibble was looking at her suspiciously.

'If he can,' Harriet hedged.

'Drought.' Mrs Dibble's teeth clicked together after delivering this judgement. 'You mark my words, we'll have trouble with them raspberries. I'll have 'em straightaway, tell 'im, if there's any danger of 'em being finished early. I'll do 'em up with sugar in bottles. They'll keep ready for the ices.'

'I'll get them,' Harriet said shortly, stirring her tea viciously.

'Mind you,' Mrs Dibble sat down gloomily. 'I say if this weather keeps up we'll be lucky if there's enough ice left in the Manor ice-house to keep the butter firm, let alone keeping that there champagne cold. Seems to me I'd best get the freezing machine out and the ices done quick and into the refrigerators. Or back in the ice-house if there's no room. Covered, against the dust.'

Harriet grinned involuntarily. She had a sudden vision of Percy going into the old ice-house at a crouch like you had to, carrying tray after tray of ices. Mrs Lilley had arranged with Lady Hunney to use the ice-house, provided Percy did all the work. The Manor never used it now, only filled it each year from Stickleback Pond as an emergency, and sometimes stored blocks of ice from the ice-man there too. She supposed Mrs Lilley hadn't liked to ask The Towers for the use of their freezing machines to help out, after Miss Tilda shouted out that way. Harriet hadn't heard her, but she'd been told all about it by Myrtle, and the implication had been breathlessly discussed in whispers in Myrtle's bedroom. Harriet didn't know what to think; it had been pleasant to know Agnes Pilbeam's carefully laid plans for marriage were spoiled, but if it had really been Swinford-Browne then he shouldn't get away with it. Or should he? He couldn't be all bad. He was going to give Ashden a cinema once they'd moved that stubborn old fool Ebenezer Thorn out of the way. Harriet had only been to the cinema twice, to see *Sixty Years a Queen* – who hadn't – and later to see a funny film about the Keystone

Cops. What she remembered about that most was the heady excitement of sitting in the dark next to Len Thorn, the warm sensation of his hand moving up and down her thigh – and what had come after that, in the hop-field, taking the short way home from the station. He hadn't given her the time of day since, though, the bastard. Lucky she hadn't had a kid in the basket as a result of that.

'The speed everyone's moving around this house you'd think we'd turned into snails. Time you were in your black and laying luncheon, Harriet. It'll be me and Myrtle doing all the work at this wedding, that I can see.'

Harriet's eyes flickered. 'You'll have Fred, Mrs Dibble. He's all right, is he? Hot weather does funny things. You ought to keep your eye on him.'

'Any more of that and I go to the Rector,' Mrs Dibble warned.

Her inimical eyes made Harriet aware she'd stepped over the agreed line. So what? 'I'm sure we're all fond of Fred. Perhaps it wasn't Fred I saw. But there was someone, Mrs Dibble. There *was*.' The horror of it. She was quite sure now that the shape had been a face staring in through the window, seeing her with no clothes at all, in the bath. No one saw her like that. Not Len Thorn. Not even herself. She'd been brought up properly and always covered herself like she should. And there *had* been someone at the window. And Fred *had* meant to lurch into her in the garden that day. She didn't make mistakes.

'And you keep a watch on them raspberries. If this heat keeps up, we'll all be hunting for blackberries instead.'

* * *

Caroline propped herself up with cushions on the rug in the garden. There was no escaping the heat inside or out (for St Swithin had obliged on July 15), but outside she could at least escape the word 'wedding' for a time. She pulled her sunhat firmly over her head, and rejoiced that she was alone. Phoebe had taken to riding one of the horses from the Manor, George was at school, Felicia was out with Daniel, and Isabel was as usual at Hop House or The Towers, anywhere where she would not get involved in tedious detail. Caroline regretted this, for she had looked forward to these last months when they would all be together as a family at the Rectory. Irritating though Isabel often was, she added a spice of drama to daily life, and Caroline knew she would miss her.

She picked up her books, but somehow neither Mr E. Phillips Oppenheim nor Miss Phyllis Bottome succeeded in gripping her today. She began to feel guilty at abandoning her mother to the now daily Dibble debates about The Wedding. She lay back on the cushions and decided to contemplate life – or herself. First she thought of Reggie, hugging their secret to her, then tried to think what her future would be like as the next chatelaine of Ashden Manor. That thought brought the question of Lady Hunney rushing back into her mind again, so she firmly switched back to Reggie. If she closed her eyes, this was a delightful way of passing the time, and entirely compensated for the indisputable fact that in the Rectory her sole role appeared to be as Solver of Minor Problems, Producer of Alternative Solutions and Chief Scribe and Clerk to the Grand Vizier and the Sultan of the Domain of the Wedding. If it wasn't the wedding under discussion in one or other of its hydra heads, it was what had happened at the flower show, what would happen at the fête tomorrow, the Sunday School treat, or Phoebe's departure to Paris, or the new curate Charles Pickering, a most humourless gentleman, whose attitude implied he was doing Ashden a great honour by joining their community.

What was *not* under discussion, Caroline realised ruefully, was Caroline's twenty-second birthday which fell in ten days' time on the 27th. Birthdays in their sprawling family occurred so frequently that they were not major events, but some effort was usually made to signify that on the whole the rest of the family was pleased that their relation had arrived in this world. This year the Rectory seemed to be dancing furiously round a maypole on which Caroline's string had somehow become misplaced as the music grew faster. Reggie hadn't forgotten, of course. Caroline wriggled a toe luxuriously. They'd agreed to go boating on the river in a Henley regatta of their very own, or else to the seaside, and she was looking forward to it, especially since neither Father nor Mother had yet suggested any need for a chaperone, despite the changed relationship between herself and Reggie. Although she relished this pleasure to come, she nevertheless felt her nose to be slightly out of joint, however hard she tried to straighten it.

Perhaps now she would contemplate life, even the world. Together both presented, she decided, a set of concentric circles, spinning independently with little or no reference to each other. Closest and most precious was her own circle with Reggie, the one they'd spin in for the rest of their lives. Encircling it was that of the Rectory and Ashden, and this, although it included Reggie and her, was complete in itself. Outside it, rarely touching it directly, was a bigger circle, the world Father read about in *The Times* every day, a world which chillingly grew worse each day and, unlikely as it seemed, threatened civil war in Ireland. That would be terrible, and almost as if Kent and Sussex were to declare war on each other. What tragedies and problems it would bring where families were divided between Catholic and Protestant, between Ulster Volunteers and National Volunteers, both arming themselves as the Government tried to push the Home Rule Bill through with the temporary exclusion of six of the northern counties to appease the Protestants. Poor Mr Asquith seemed to be doing his best to please everybody and ending up pleasing nobody. She tried to translate this into Ashden terms, by imagining her father and the minister so bitterly divided over the parish council that they came to blows outside the Norville Arms. It would never happen, of course. Every issue could be discussed and settled, Father believed, where there was common desire for peace, and so it must in Ireland, surely. Perhaps the King could do something – though she was forced to admit he was doing his best to ignore the other big issue: women's suffrage. There'd actually been a bomb found in the church of St John the Evangelist in London on Sunday, the fuse had even been lighted when it was found.

Outside the British Isles, there was yet another circle spinning around, that of the world outside Britain, which touched them even more rarely, only when the Empire needed help or protection. Events like the assassination of the Archduke Ferdinand of Austria at Sarajevo in Bosnia the day after Reggie's twenty-fourth birthday dance were terrible, but that circle did not collide with theirs. Their duty here was to do well by Ashden and their own path in life. But if that were so, Caroline wondered, why had that bird of freedom fluttered within her when she attended a suffragette meeting in Tunbridge Wells with Tilly and Penelope a few days ago? She had wanted to go to London and attend one of the rallies at Kensington Town Hall, but her chief interest – to see the Pankhursts – was frustrated by Mrs Pankhurst still being in Holloway, and planning, if released, to go to France to join her daughter Christabel and to recover her health. The Tunbridge Wells group, she knew from the local newspaper, was very active, very militant, and she was taken aback by the obvious pride in her aunt's voice as she talked almost non-stop on the railway journey to Tunbridge Wells.

'McKenna said in the House last month that the public had four suggestions as to what to do with us: let us die if we refuse to eat, deport us, treat us like lunatics – or give us the vote. That coward informed us he will do none of these, but it is obvious the country is with us – the vote it must be.'

It hadn't been obvious to Caroline. Bravely though the speakers had addressed their audience, their reward had been a shower of rotten eggs from men *and* women. It was only afterwards that Penelope had casually mentioned that there was a non-militant group in the town, with some prominent members, including a novelist; Caroline resolved that she would attend one of their meetings in the Victoria Hall in Southborough. Not now, for all-important at the moment was her engagement. Much as she tried to ignore it until Reggie's planned announcement at the wedding, it was proving impossible. It coloured everything, for in the middle of her own personal circle was a deep, deep happiness that crystallised into Reggie.

'Caroline.'

At the unexpected voice, she sat up, blinking into the sun with surprise. It was Patricia Swinford-Browne, looking even larger than usual in a yellow muslin dress complete with mustard-coloured sunshade.

'I expect you wonder why I've come skulking through the bushes,' Patricia continued cheerfully.

'It does seem somewhat strange.'

'I like you,' Patricia said unexpectedly. 'May I sit down? The rug will do. We'll share it.' Patricia lowered herself cautiously to the rug and sighed. 'I loathe this weather.'

'Your skin doesn't suit it, that's all.' Tactful and correct. Patricia had the kind of complexion that erupted eagerly into spots and rashes, and grew excited at the faintest ray of sun.

'I don't know why. I throw everything from pigswill to arsenic on it. I'm Mother's despair.'

'I suppose you want to talk about the wedding?' Caroline enquired, since Patricia seemed hesitant to continue.

'To escape from it would be nearer the truth. It's a race who will drive me mad soonest, Ma with her constant wailings, Robert with his happy smile, or your sister with her 'anxious-to-please' helpfulness. But in fact I came to give you a warning. Promise me you'll never tell.'

At this childish plea, Caroline stopped feeling defensive about Isabel and began to feel rather sorry for Patricia. 'I won't without your permission.'

'You won't get that. Pa would kill me. It's about your aunt. She's going to burn a church down.'

'*What*?'

'Not yours,' Patricia reassured her. 'Missenden in Kent, it's near Goudhurst. The vicar is a pal of McKenna's and he gave a sermon about the place of women in the home and how we're all inferior beings. On Sunday he's going to preach God's word on what to do with lunatic females.'

'But my *aunt* burn a *church*?'

'They've burned others,' Patricia replied. 'It's property, isn't it? Anyway, the point is that Father's found out somehow. I heard him talking to the Chief Constable. They'll all be arrested, and your aunt will go straight back to Holloway. You did *know* she'd been in stir, didn't you?' Patricia produced her slang with relish.

'Yes,' Caroline said shortly. 'Now tell me why you've come.'

Patricia was taken aback. 'I thought you'd want to prevent her going.'

'Yes, but why *you*? Are you a suffragette too?'

'Hell's bells, no,' Patricia informed her elegantly, 'much as I approve of your aunt. I hate The Towers, you see, and every so often I have to kick it. I'll probably have to stay there. The kind of men who appreciate my charms would be seen off as a son-in-law by Pops with a boot in their rear, the kind of men who think my money would compensate for having me thrown in too *I* would see off with a boot in their rear, and as for true love, well, no Prince Charming's going to come running after me with a glass slipper, is he?'

Caroline was appalled at Patricia's matter-of-fact diagnosis of her future, and said so.

Patricia shrugged. 'They only care about Robert. Once they saw they'd bred an ugly duckling, they left me to waddle about on my own. If you get any information on how to turn into a swan, you might let me know. I've tried mercolised wax on my face – Ma said I'd been let loose from Madame Tussaud's. If I became a suffragette I'd *terrify* Asquith into giving us the vote.'

'Are you sure you aren't tempted to join them?'

'Quite sure, thanks, Caroline. If it came to a choice between soapbox and suds at the kitchen sink, I'd choose the suds.' She paused. 'I hope it doesn't, though. There must be *something* else I could do.'

'Yes,' said Caroline firmly, taken aback by Patricia's mournfulness. 'But you must look for it. It won't come waltzing up The Towers' drive looking for you.'

Patricia giggled. 'It's more likely to be ragtime if Ma and Pa throw me out, as I gathered happened to your aunt. You'd better hurry, by the way. Father's already galloped off in the Daimler wielding his tomahawk.'

Full of anxiety about Aunt Tilly, Caroline hastily thanked her, and raced back to the house. There was no sign of her aunt though the Austin was in the garage, which relieved her greatly. Surely Tilly would have driven, not gone by train, if she were going to Goudhurst?

Nevertheless, she sought out her mother. 'Where's Aunt Tilly?' she asked her mother as casually as she could.

'She went up to London earlier to the theatre, and she's staying overnight with a friend. Why?'

'Nothing.' Caroline's heart sank. Theatre? Friend? Patricia's story could possibly be true. Her aunt had shown no signs of knowing the Tunbridge Wells group well – in deference to the promise Father had extracted from her, Caroline supposed. Or it might be genuine; her aunt belonged to the London groups. Should she tell Father about it? No, came the answer. He couldn't reach the church any more than she could, and the very idea of his sister burning a church would appal him. There was only one thing to be done . . .

'If this is some wild goose chase,' Reggie said threateningly as he cranked the Lanchester's starting handle.

'You'll what?' Caroline could have cried with thankfulness at Reggie's reasonably unreluctant agreement, especially since he could not bring his beloved Perry, as it was only a two-seater. He had been forced to bribe the Ashden chauffeur into turning the other way while he checked the battery was charged and sneaked his parents' motor car out.

'Point out your reputation is hardly going to be improved.'

'I never thought of that.' Caroline was amused. 'I told Mother I was going to see you anyway, so she won't worry.'

'Suppose the Lanchester breaks down and I can't return you till morning? It has been known.'

'Oh, Reggie, what a *good* idea. You'll *have* to marry me then, and even your mother couldn't refuse. *Do* let's break down.'

'We'll have your Aunt Tilly with us. That will put a stop to your dastardly plans, woman. You'll be in the back seat, so *my* virtue is going to be quite safe – unfortunately.'

'That's better. You're smiling.'

'Getting your crazy aunt out of scrapes is more fun than listening to Daniel drone on about the mysteries of the East.'

It was strange to be driving so far alone with Reggie in the hot warm evening, just the two of them side by side, sailing through villages she'd heard of but never seen, passing inns and public houses full of light and noise, and the warm smells of the countryside in between as dark began to fall. She watched his long slim hands on the wheel, thought of them caressing her yesterday, his hands against the light chiffon on her dress, and wondered how anybody could be unhappy in this world with such wonders of love within it. Soon when they were married there'd be no chiffon between them, no underclothing, perhaps not even a nightdress, nothing between those hands and her skin. Perhaps too nothing between her own hands and Reggie's body. Her chest suddenly tight, she tried to imagine it and felt herself blushing.

'I told you you should have worn goggles.' Reggie glanced at her. Belatedly she realised the dust on the road was sweeping into the open motor car and stinging her face.

'We're here now.'

Caroline shivered as the Lanchester drew up some thirty

yards from the church. It was out of sight, but their noisy arrival could hardly have gone unnoticed in this peaceful still night. The church was a little way from the village centre surrounded by yew trees. Somehow she sensed the presence of other people, though there was no one to be seen. At least there was no sign of the police – or William Swinford-Browne. *Would* he come? Was he here, lurking in this twilight, waiting his moment? She took a deep breath, as she jumped from the motor car and ran to the church porch, Reggie close behind her. There were others to be saved besides Aunt Tilly, she had to remember – though that depended on how one looked at it. Perhaps all of the suffragettes would be only too glad to have the police come, to be arrested, or in Tilly's case, be re-arrested under the Cat and Mouse Act. Their object of publicity would be achieved either way. It suddenly occurred to her that it might not be easy to persuade Aunt Tilly to come home.

Reaching the porch door, Reggie shouted: 'Miss Lilley, come out.'

'It's me, Aunt Tilly.' Caroline supported him, checking the bushes lining the approach to the church.

'How on earth did you get here, and why?' Tilly emerged not from the bushes, but from the church itself, flushed and very angry. She seemed a stranger. Surely this wasn't the same woman who read *Alice in Wonderland* to her as a child?

'What's more important,' Reggie interrupted, 'is how *you're* getting back.'

Caroline rushed to the church door. 'All of you, wherever you are. The police are on their way.'

There were three of them. Cloaked figures emerged, unalarmed, undaunted, waiting impatiently for this situation to be resolved. Aunt Tilly was obviously the group's leader.

'We must hurry then,' Tilly said grimly. 'We should have something to show them. This for instance.' She gestured to what one of the group was holding – a tin canister with strings and straps attached to it, and something trailing from the top. 'Over five pounds of gunpowder,' she added triumphantly as Reggie made an unsuccessful grab at the tin.

'*You* can't stay. You'll be arrested. And you can't, you *can't* let that thing off.' Caroline was appalled.

'Why do you think I've come? To give up *now?*' Tilly snapped.

'But this is a *church*.'

'And you told the police?'

'No!' Caroline felt outrage.

Tilly said impatiently, perhaps an apology in her own way, 'For all I know your feelings on churches outweigh those towards an aunt.'

'Or yours to a brother.'

'If so forced. And I am.'

Surely this could not be her beloved Aunt Tilly, saying these terrible things? Caroline tried again, while Reggie argued with the rest of the group.

'You *must* come with us, Aunt Tilly. It's Swinford-Browne who has arranged for you to be re-arrested. He might even come himself. Do you want to be humiliated before him?'

Tilly paused for a moment, taken aback. 'The cause is

more important. What is one more prison sentence? Mrs Pankhurst has been imprisoned countless times, myself only thrice.'

'Because it would mean Swinford-Browne winning.' Caroline was getting desperate. 'It would be defeat for you, not victory. He'd have got what *he* wanted. You can't want that to happen.' For a moment she thought she'd convinced her aunt, but she was wrong. Tilly ran back into the church to join her fellows.

'Have you any thought for Caroline and what she's risking by coming here?' Reggie shouted angrily after her.

'It is of less importance than the cause,' Tilly shouted. 'I'm going to light a fire that *all* will see.'

'You blasted well won't,' Reggie yelled at her, then turning to Caroline: 'Crank up the Lanc.'

She stood bemused for a second, then ran for the motor car, aware of a scuffle behind her. She turned briefly to see Reggie gripping a struggling Aunt Tilly firmly by the arm and slamming the church door behind him in the face of would-be rescuers. He then picked up Aunt Tilly bodily – no mean feat for she was a tall, strong-boned woman – and stumbled after Caroline towards the Lanchester. Like an automaton Caroline seized the starting handle, cranking furiously. She'd never done it before, and could only pray that the gods that ruled motor cars would smile on her. Reggie tumbled Aunt Tilly into the passenger seat – fortunately without the bomb – but once he had taken his hand away from her mouth, the noise and struggles began. Mercifully the engine responded, and somehow Caroline managed to scramble into the back seat as the Lanchester began to roar down the lane. It was some few minutes before they passed a police van and a Daimler on the Goudhurst road speeding in the opposite direction, and Caroline shrank down out of sight. Turning back, she could see a thin spire of smoke above the trees, and a little later a fire engine chugged purposefully past them.

'You can remove your arm, Caroline. I am not foolish enough to leap from a moving motor car,' Tilly remarked drily. Caroline obeyed; she had not been aware that her hand was gripping her aunt's arm so tightly still.

'I take it you approve of your future husband's masterful habits?'

'I will not have Caroline—' Reggie began.

'Caroline does have a voice of her own, does she not?' Tilly interrupted. 'Or are you proposing to control her mind as well as body when you marry her?'

Before Reggie could reply, Caroline said clearly, 'I believe Reggie was right to have brought you away.'

'I am sad that you think it right to frustrate the cause of woman's advancement, Caroline. I had expected more of you.'

'And I of you, Aunt Tilly. You are blind to every moral standard save that in which you choose to believe. How could you burn God's house?'

'It ceases to be the house of God, and turns into mere bricks and mortar when it is misused.'

'In your mind, perhaps,' Reggie said. 'How about the people who have worshipped there for years, who were baptised in its font, were married before its altar, and whose loved ones lie buried there? Is it mere bricks and mortar to them?'

'When men and women are seen as equal, we can build anew.'

'And what about your family in the meanwhile?' Reggie enquired.

'Unfortunately sometimes the individual must be sacrificed for the greater good.'

'What about Father, and your mother?' cried Caroline. 'Do they mean *nothing*?'

'My mother?' Tilly turned angrily round. 'My mother has always cared only for her own wishes. She seeks to impose her views on everyone; she can hardly complain if now her daughter follows her example – especially as she has made it clear I no longer *am* her daughter in any but the legal sense and that, too, she is trying to circumvent. Very well, then she is no longer my mother. Her actions, as yours,' Tilly looked scornfully at Reggie, 'render her unworthy of respect from anyone.'

'I disagree,' Reggie said calmly. 'You expect *your* views to be respected, if not shared. Your mother is entitled to the same treatment.'

'You are wrong. I do not expect my views to be respected. Those who intend to change society cannot bother with such niceties. Caroline, I blame myself for failing to make you understand. I know you felt you had to act as you did tonight, but I am sorry for it.'

Caroline was not.

William Swinford-Browne had the last laugh. Caroline woke late the next day, for it had been midnight when she arrived home, and she and Reggie, to his tight-lipped fury, had to face Father and Mother, who remained unconvinced by stories of punctures. Tilly had unwillingly agreed at Caroline's pleading to slip in through the drawing room window. Now Caroline realised to her dismay she had probably missed breakfast, and calculated the chances of appealing to Mrs Dibble's heart. The hot water in her jug had long since grown cold. It was not a good start to the day and she knew it was going to get worse as soon as she emerged from her room to go downstairs.

She could see Father below her in the entrance hall talking in a low tone to Mother. Felicia was hovering at their side, and she had obviously been crying. She looked up, and, seeing Caroline, hurried up the stairs towards her. 'Something terrible's happened,' she cried. 'Mr Ifield and two more policemen came, and they've *arrested* Aunt Tilly. They say – oh, how *stupid,* that she's a suffragette and that she's already been in prison several times. How can they be right? Oh, poor Aunt Tilly.'

Caroline's heart plummeted. All their efforts had been to no avail. William Swinford-Browne had won and Aunt Tilly had been taken from them to face yet more forcible feeding in prison. What would it do to her health this time? She had barely recovered from the last onslaught. She felt torn apart between her old love for her aunt, her horror at Aunt Tilly's militancy, and the knowledge that somewhere, in between, lay a reconciliation. As yet, it was a reconciliation whose nature she could not grasp or even define.

Her first task was to explain to her sisters and George that Aunt Tilly was neither martyr nor monster, and that would be difficult – save, perhaps, she suspected, with George who since the tennis match had idolised her aunt and might see this latest development as another feather in her hat. And, indeed, Caroline reminded herself, Aunt Tilly herself might see it that way.

'The police are right, Felicia. Aunt Tilly is a suffragette, and has been for some years. It's what she passionately believes in, darling, so don't be too upset. *She* isn't – for she sees it as another step towards the vote. She *wants* it this way.'

'But Aunt *Tilly* of all people.' Felicia looked dismayed.

'Yes. We never really knew her, did we? We took her for granted.'

'We'll see her again, won't we?' Felicia cried in alarm, swinging round to her parents. 'She'll come back here.'

Laurence waited for Elizabeth to answer, and she did. 'Of course. This is her home now.'

As the days passed, the ruffled waters of the Rectory seemed to smooth over Tilly's departure. Perhaps she would be out again in time for the wedding was Mother's invariable response. Isabel, on the other hand, made it quite clear that she hoped nothing of the kind; she was only too relieved that such a potential source of danger to her plans had been removed from the household, though full of lamentations as to how the scandal of a suffragette aunt in prison might affect her plans as a future Hop House hostess. Disgusted for once, rather than amused by her sister's self-centredness, Caroline questioned her father closely. He would only say that Aunt Tilly had returned to Holloway to serve out her eighteen-month sentence, of which thirteen months still remained.

'But, Father, I read in the newspaper that fewer and fewer suffragettes are re-arrested under the Act now because forcible feeding is horrifying the public so much. Why is Aunt Tilly an exception?'

'I fear, Caroline, though as yet without proof, that Mr Swinford-Browne could answer that question for us. We can but pray for her. I shall speak in Church on Sunday.' Would he get proof, he wondered. *Should* he get proof? As so often, the man shouted yes, the servant of God must debate.

Would he pray for her if he knew how narrowly Aunt Tilly had avoided being one of the group who set fire to Missenden Church? Knowing Father, in some ways more than he did himself, Caroline knew the answer was yes.

'Take your stockings off, Aggie. Paddle your feet with me.'

'No, thank you.' She instinctively shrank from such intimacy. 'Anyway, Jamie, it's time we had the picnic.' She hurriedly began unpacking the basket on to the rug, making great show of chasing away an early wasp, and ignoring Jamie as he removed his bare feet from the Medway and rolled down his trouser legs. She was aware that he was watching her, as she unwrapped the sandwiches she'd made that morning under Mrs Dibble's scathing eye. Everybody thought she was a fool for still seeing Jamie. Everybody's eye followed her in the village. Everybody knew he was still refusing to marry Ruth. And everybody thought he was no better than his brother, and using her, Agnes, as an excuse to get out of either paying support to Ruth's child or marrying her. What did *she* think, though? Aggie just didn't know.

It would have been nice in this heat to feel the cool water trickling over her toes, but to do that she'd have to pull up her skirts in front of him to take her stockings off, or go behind a tree and have him think . . . No, it wasn't worth it.

'Would you like a sandwich? It's fish paste.'

He took one in silence and proceeded to munch his way through four of them, together with a tomato and an apple.

'What's the matter, Aggie?' he pleaded. 'You're doubting me again, surely.'

No, no, she wanted to cry, but it wouldn't be true. 'I saw Ruth,' she managed to blurt out at last. She saw him flinch. Why, if he had nothing to hide? Her heart suddenly pained her.

'She's going to sue me, she says, for breach of promise.' His face was full of misery.

'How can she if she's no proof?' Agnes struggled to be practical, but inside she was being torn to bits.

'I don't *know*, and she don't need me or money now anyway. Old Swinford-Browne's going to give her a cottage, so Rector says, and set her up as a laundress. I reckon he's the father, that I do. Folks are saying—'

'He's not the father.'

'How do you know?' He was taken aback.

'I told you, I *saw* her. She says it's you.' Agnes could hear the water trickling, trickling, cool. Not like the trickling sweat down her back making her dress cling to her.

'And you believe her?' His voice rose.

'She says – things.'

'What things?' She saw the fear in his eyes. Why, if he had nothing to hide? She could *smell* fear, like a hedgehog standing rigid waiting for danger to pass by.

'Things she could only know if – personal things.'

There was a silence. He should be asking: what things, and how did Agnes know they were right? But he didn't. Instead he began to shout at her. He'd never done that before.

'If you don't believe me, Aggie, I'd best marry Ruth. You said you'd believe me, you said you loved me, but you wouldn't let me touch you, not like I wanted to, not before we were married. So you don't love me, not like I loved you. Well, I don't love you any more, because you've betrayed me. You don't love me at all or you wouldn't have wanted to wait.'

She began to sob, her tears falling on to the slice of cake he wouldn't eat. He just stomped off and left her alone with the picnic basket. She felt numb, dead really. All she could register was that he hadn't put his stockings back on. They lay there, two brown symbols of her rejection. Him of her. Or was it her of him? She could have said nothing mattered but him. She could have said she'd do what he wanted, here and now in the warm grass. Only that would be lowering herself to be like Ruth. *Besides, what if she saw a scar*? Ah, what then, what then? Trust in the Lord, the Rector said. Sometimes it was easier to trust in a God you couldn't see, than a man you could.

'Well, Miss Harriet Mutter, who d'yer think I ran into this morning in Tunbridge Wells? Your Uncle Seb, him of Grendel's Farm, and you know what he told me?'

218

Retribution faced her, with its arms akimbo, and the turkey neck poked forward for the final peck. 'He told me you ain't never ordered no raspberries.'

'He's forgotten. He always does.'

'T'ain't him that's forgotten,' Mrs Dibble snapped. 'If we don't have any raspberries for our wedding, it'll all be your fault, Harriet, that Miss Isabel's day is ruined.'

'I'll get your silly old raspberries.'

'Don't you talk to me like that, miss. You Mutters are all the same. All lip, no work and lazy as spit water. And no raspberries either, unless we're lucky. No chance of the whites now. They'll be reds and we can be thankful for them.'

'At least I baint dinlow,' Harriet retorted spitefully and unwisely. 'Good job your Fred can't climb trees. He'd be staring in and frightening Miss Felicia or Miss Caroline, afore we knew where we were.'

Mrs Dibble turned red with rage. 'That's a disgusting thing to say. You made it all up and you know it.'

'Made it up? When his face was leering in at me, staring at *me*. Like that?' Harriet shuddered theatrically, telling herself she hadn't felt right about having a bath since. 'A young girl ain't safe in this house, not with him around.'

'What is all this noise about?' Elizabeth Lilley materialised, deducing the noise level was not going to abate.

'It's just the heat, Mrs Lilley,' Mrs Dibble replied promptly. St Swithin had answered her prayers only too well. 'Tempers are a little frayed.' She cast Harriet a filthy look. 'Aren't they, Harriet dear?'

'Yes, Mrs Dibble,' Harriet answered sullenly. 'That's what it is. The heat.'

Even so, she polished the brass more vigorously than usual as she puzzled as to why old Dibble didn't split on her. Then the answer came to her in a burst of triumph. She knew Harriet was right about Fred, that's why.

'I don't see how it could be hotter than this even in Greece, do you?' Daniel lay on his back on the grass in one of the open stretches of the Forest, and thoughtfully chewed a long piece of grass.

At his side, Felicia clasped her knees through the light voile gown, trying to imagine Greece. 'Father thinks there might be trouble out there,' she said.

'In Greece?'

'Near there. In Serbia.'

'Oh, that will all blow over. The Serbs have apologised to His Great and Imperial Majesty in Vienna for that Sarajevo business. Anyway, Austria would simply march into Serbia and it would surrender overnight. You'll see. Why,' he stretched out a lazy hand and placed it in the small of her back, 'are you worrying about me? You needn't. I'll turn up again. It will take more than a few Serbs to stop me seeing the world.'

'Isn't Russia in alliance with Serbia, though? You talked of going to St Petersburg.'

'You do know a lot. I thought they only taught girls about Harold burning the cakes. Or was that Canute?'

'Or possibly King Alfred.' Felicia smiled. 'They teach us to respect our minds, too.'

'Like your redoubtable Aunt Tilly? I don't see you as a suffragette somehow. And I certainly wouldn't like to see you behind bars.'

'What do you see me as?'

He considered. 'A princess in an ivory tower waiting—' He broke off in case she thought he meant for him. That would be pointless, wouldn't it. He'd set his heart on conquering the world, not Felicia. True, he was fascinated by her, and not just by her beauty. There was something about her that was unusual in the women he knew, something indefinable. Perhaps it was that he sensed she already knew her way, sure-footed, through life. Faith should be her name, not Felicia. Still, he knew what he wanted too. They had that in common. He rolled over and drew her down to him, kissing her lightly, gently – for both their sakes. Hers, because he was leaving Ashden, and didn't want to mislead her; his because the body was unpredictable, warmth distanced tomorrows, and the seemingly impossible might prove temptingly possible.

'Shall you marry me, Daniel?'

Had he heard right? He sat up quickly, snatching at another piece of grass to cover his shock and thinking to shield her embarrassment. When she sat up too and laid her hand on his arm, there was no embarrassment on her face, however. Merely enquiry.

'Shall or will?' he managed to joke.

'Shall. Will has too much freedom of choice in it, so I would not ask you that. Shall is merely what is written in the book of fate.'

Daniel laughed, though uneasily, for he was for once

221

completely nonplussed. He'd thought, after Reggie's birthday, that the two weeks' OTC camp training at Aldershot would banish all thoughts of Felicia from his mind. Once back he found it hadn't. Now he desperately calculated how long it was before he could leave again; should he go now, without waiting for Isabel's wedding as he had promised? He knew he would not, however. That meant some kind of doubt was still claiming him. And Felicia was waiting for her answer. 'How can I answer that? We, none of us know what's to come. That book of fate can twist, turn and lead you back or on at its command.' He was getting as serious as her, but there was no help for it. 'But if fate *did* lead me back, and for good, there could be no lovelier bride it could choose for me.'

She dismissed the compliment impatiently, and he felt rebuked, rather to his annoyance. 'I did not mean—'

He interrupted her. 'Fate usually takes one on, not back.' He had tried to warn her – and perhaps also himself. Had he succeeded? Was there any way of reaching Felicia when she retreated as she had now? Not, he realised, in confusion, but in a certainty, so fixed it did not need help. Fleetingly he wished he could follow her, change his own path and stay. But the wish was born of a summer moment, and it vanished with the setting of the sun.

'You've come then, Miss Phoebe.'

Len Thorn perched a foot indolently on the anvil. Phoebe knew he was doing it on purpose to provoke her, but all the same the smell of the sweat pouring off him and the sight of his body rippling in the light of the forge fire took her aback, solidifying in flesh the formless shape that had haunted her nightmares. Dark shapes, as she tossed and turned in the warm nights, had climactically resolved themselves into the devil's head of a grinning Len Thorn. Now that head had a body too, and it was displaying itself before her.

'Only to ask you from the Rector if you could shoe Poppy tomorrow.'

'I might.'

'Can you or can you not?' Phoebe was outwardly calm. She was after all the Rector's daughter, and Len Thorn could not read her dreams.

'Yes.' He seemed disconcerted, she noticed with relief, for that meant she was winning the game. 'I'll be up tomorrow for Miss Poppy. I'll be seeing you then. Ten-thirty.'

'I shan't be there.' She spoke too quickly, and he sensed victory.

'Afraid of me then?'

Phoebe rushed away in confusion, aware she was wrong. She wasn't winning, and she wouldn't be anywhere near the stables tomorrow. She'd go to Tunbridge Wells – or would it be better to face her fears? She'd see how she felt tomorrow.

'Where do I put this ham, Mrs D?' Harriet wiped the sweat from her eye and picked up the ham in one continuous movement.

'In the larder, miss. Where do you think?' Mrs Dibble called from her stillroom, as she liked to call it. Old cupboard was more like it in Harriet's view. 'And I thought

I told you to do them dustbins out with paraffin and soft soap again. Them flies is tedious busy.'

'I'm a housemaid, not a kitchen skivvy.'

'This week you're a kitchen slave like we all are, Miss Hoity-Toity. Mrs Lilley told you that.'

The wedding was only a week away now, and the tempo and the temperature were both increasing.

'I've a job for you, if you don't like kitchens.'

'What?' Harriet was suspicious of jobs.

'Go down to the village and speak nice to Mrs Lettice.'

'Why?'

Mrs Dibble delivered her broadside. 'Because we ain't got no raspberries, that's why, thanks to you. They're all gone. He couldn't keep 'em back in this hot weather. Shrivelled and turned.' There was complacent gloom in Mrs Dibble's voice. 'If you'd ordered them when I said—'

'I did. He forgot.'

'Get down to Mrs Lettice, girl. It's eight o'clock already. She'll be closing. Her brother out at Hartfield does raspberries. Happen he'll have some left. He'd better, for your sake, Harriet.'

Smarting with injustice, Harriet crammed her old straw hat on, determined to get her own back somehow. The chance presented itself as she saw Mary Tunstall passing the Rectory gate, she who did for the Miss Norvilles, poor simple soul. 'Hallo, Mary. My you're brave.'

'Why's that?' Mary was unaccustomed to girls as smart as Harriet speaking to her.

'Walking back this time o' night with him around.'

'Who?' Mary gaped.

'That awk Fred Dibble. Ain't you seen him hiding in the bushes when girls go by? He'll jump out one day, you'll see.'

'Whatever for?' Mary was bewildered.

'Ain't your mother ever told you? He likes to see girls,' she whispered in Mary's ear, 'without anything on. Nothing at all. He looked in at me once. You want to be careful.'

Mary thought about this. 'I don't walk around with nothing on.'

Harriet forgot about patience with poor Mary. 'He'll tear 'em off you, like he does to others,' she shouted. 'Ain't he ever even touched you? Can't you sense him *watching* when you walk up that long lonely path to the Castle?'

Beware the beast, flee the bear, don't face it.

'I just came,' Phoebe announced airily to a remote corner of the stable, 'to tell you Poppy's not very well, so Father says—'

'Father says stay away from men, eh? That it, Miss Phoebe?' Len Thorn spoke very softly. 'Pity. A lovely girl like you is just waiting to be kissed. You must be fifteen now, I'll be bound. Won't be long to wait now.'

'I'm seventeen.' Phoebe was indignant.

'Is that so? You're a woman, I see, now I look further.' His eyes travelled down slowly, then up again. 'Did you ever wonder, Miss Phoebe, what life is like outside this Rectory here?'

'Of course. I'm going to finishing school in September.'

'Will they teach you to finish this?'

Face the formless bear. She had no choice. He stretched

225

out his arms for her, kissed her, not like the curate, but taking her breath away and forcing her mouth open, sucking greedily, surrounding her with hot breath. She seemed to be clamped to his chest, yet she was certain she could feel his hand on her leg. How could it be, for it seemed to be her stockinged leg, and then before she could react, it was clamping her between her legs, and a pain, well, not a pain but something, shot right through her. What was he doing now? Whatever it was, she was quite certain she didn't want him to do it, and moreover he *shouldn't* be doing it. Then suddenly she was free, her skirts falling back.

'There now, Miss Phoebe,' he said hoarsely, 'you're too pretty, that's the trouble.' He stared at her and she knew she should run away or cry out, but she seemed curiously immobile. He ran one hand over her chest, almost absently, and bent forward to kiss her again. She knew she should move, but she didn't. This time he didn't try to force his tongue into her mouth but kissed her quite gently, and the feel of his lips on hers was rather nice. This time that pain, or whatever it was, was exciting as it travelled down her. 'Pretty, pretty, Miss Phoebe.' His tawny eyes seemed to be searing into her; he released her, and this time she did move away.

'Will you tell your father, Miss Phoebe?' The note of cocky defiance wasn't in his voice any more, but she couldn't seem to take advantage of it.

'No. If you don't do it again.'

'Not unless you provoke me, Miss Phoebe.' His nonchalance was coming back now, and he whacked Poppy on her side, as if to reiterate his point.

His face haunted her dreams that night, not so terrifyingly as before. The formless blank shape came curiously, excitingly, but insidiously, creeping towards her, around her, into her, merging in the black shadows that were dancing outside the Rectory windows.

Next day a deeply troubled Mary told her mother about the shape in the bushes who would jump out and tear off her clothes; the mother told her neighbour, who warned her daughter, who giggled about it with her friend, who was so scared that Mary had been stripped mother-naked on her way to the Castle that she told her sister, who told her brother, who told . . . and pretty soon even Joe Ifield knew Fred Dibble was up to his nasty tricks again.

She hadn't seen Jamie. Agnes tossed and turned in her bed; counting sheep, counting pies, nothing worked. He hadn't been at the gate in Silly Lane as he usually was on her half-day off, and pride had kept her from marching up to the ironmongery to seek him out. What if she'd sent him straight into Ruth Horner's arms again, what then? Had she cleaned the slicing machine? One dark thought after another chased through her mind. A drumming inside her began to beat insistently, growing louder and louder. Bang, she'd lost him, bang, he'd marry Ruth, bang, he'd kill himself – it *wasn't* inside her. It was outside, an insistent beating, men's voices, women's too. Outside the Norville Arms, was it? She lay there rigid, unable to be sure this was not another nightmare. Then she was sure; it came nearer. They must be in the High Street, banging, shouting, clapping – not a drunken rabble, though. She sat up in bed, rigid with fear. This was far more sinister: determined, menacing, organised threat with the sound of marching feet. Then it stopped for a moment as though it were gathering strength. It was a little further away now, further up the High Street, by the ironmongery. And then she knew: *Jamie*.

It was as if the whole of her insides were turned into one gigantic silent scream. Rough music. Her ma used to tell her about it, how it hadn't been done for many a long year, how all the villagers turned out of their homes to gather in front of someone's door to show their disapproval by banging anything they could lay their hands on, then attacking the cottage itself with brooms, tin pails, anything. It were worse, so ma said, than anything the village policeman might do. It hadn't died out, though, for tonight they were doing it to her Jamie.

She moaned to herself, her arms clasped round her, rocking to and fro in agony. When that didn't help she drew the sheets over her head, to distance the noise, but nothing could extinguish the sound of Jamie's voice in her ear crying, 'Are you one of them, Aggie, *are you*?'

She heard a door slam. That would be the Rector going out to calm them down. Tensely she waited, counted each step he must be taking, calculating the time it would take him to reach the crowd and shame them into silence. It took fifteen minutes longer than she had thought before the dull roar became a low rumble, and then nothing, as the protesters slipped away into the darkness and at last she fell into a troubled sleep.

* * *

'No, Laurence, I fear you are wrong, sadly wrong. My department looks not to Ireland for the dogs of war, but to Europe.' Sir John paced up and down his study, his brandy and soda as yet untouched, which was a sure sign of his agitation, the Rector realised.

'But even if Russia mobilises in support of Serbia, how are we affected?'

'If Russia fights, Germany joins Austria. It will follow, as the night the day.'

'And if so?'

'France has a treaty with Russia, and moreover may welcome the chance to regain what she regards as her honour, lost in 1870.'

The Rector stared at the Squire. He was tired after his interrupted night. When the troubles of Ashden were so time-consuming, he lacked the energy to grapple with those of the outside world, especially those that could not affect England. Nevertheless he tried. 'And because we are morally bound to France by a mutual understanding, we may be drawn in? Surely not. It is a European war. France would not be so foolish as to expect it, and even if she were, she will realise we cannot support her, because of Ireland. And even if there were no Irish problem, there would be no public support to ally ourselves with France in this present difficulty. No, all this is mere sabre-rattling.'

'The Kaiser has wanted to rattle a sabre at England for many a long year.'

'But not to take on our Empire. He is foolhardy, but not foolish, surely.'

'Foolish? If he believes that England faces the other way,

faces Ireland not France, he might well wish to take his chance to humiliate her, or, worse, count on our neutrality to pursue his own plans of Empire. When he is master of Russia and France, he might reason, he can pick off England at will.'

'Your theory is just that. It can have no realistic basis.'

'At the moment the Cabinet agrees with you. I trust with all my heart you and they are right, Laurence.'

'Caroline.' Isabel hurtled through the door. 'Come and help me.'

It was an order. Reluctantly, Caroline left Cicely Hamilton's *Marriage as a Trade*. She had escaped to her room only five minutes ago, creeping out of a tense discussion between her mother and Mrs Dibble over, of course, the likelihood of rain on *the day*, as the weather had perversely grown cool and close, and the worrying rise of a shilling per sack of flour in Liverpool because of the current uncertainty. When the talk turned to raspberries, she had fled to her book.

Her aunt had spoken of Miss Hamilton with disgust, as a renegade to the militant cause, since she had left the WSPU to join Mrs Despard's Women's Freedom league. Nevertheless she had lent Caroline her book and *that* was shocking enough. Marriage, in Cicely Hamilton's view – and, Caroline supposed, Aunt Tilly's – was no better than prostitution in that women were forced into it for economic reasons. As Ruth Horner had just avoided, Caroline was bound to agree. Not herself, though. Never. With Reggie, it would be an equal marriage. For Isabel . . .

'Smell *this.*' Isabel marched her to her own room where she had set up her home-made perfume apparatus, a glass funnel suspended between two supports over a glass bowl. The Rectory's best blooms stood wilting in a jug (naturally Isabel had forgotten to give them water). 'It doesn't smell at *all*. It's all Percy's fault. He wouldn't get me the pure alcohol I wanted. No one *cares*. I *hate* being poor.' She sat on the bed sulkily while Caroline sniffed cautiously at the results.

She glanced at Isabel. 'It's not the perfume that worries you, is it?'

Isabel bit her lip. 'No. I've decided I'm scared,' she announced dolefully.

'Of what? Robert?' Caroline could not take her seriously, and was inclined to be impatient. Compared with poor Agnes's problems, Isabel's were slight indeed – and entirely of her own making. Did she even know, Caroline wondered, what had been going on in the village this week, and would she care? Guilt overcame Caroline for she was all too well aware that the dark shadows over the village, much as she sympathised with Agnes and Jamie, were failing to touch her as they should, such was her own happiness.

'Of marriage. But I do want to get married, don't I?' Isabel burst into tears, and, alarmed at this proof of sincerity, Caroline went to comfort her.

'I can't answer that, darling, because I'm not in your head, in your heart or in your shoes. Perhaps you're a little worried about sharing a bed with someone?'

'Perhaps,' Isabel muttered, then loftily, 'of course, you wouldn't understand.'

Caroline would. She felt caught up in a web of mystery and excitement about her own wedding bed which filled her with strange feelings. Even the words 'wedding bed' sent a happy shiver of anticipation through her. But what if her guess was right and Isabel didn't really love Robert? Then she could well understand how Isabel might dread it as an ordeal. 'Robert will be kind and gentle, I'm sure.'

'That may be the trouble,' Isabel said under her breath, covering it quickly with, 'He's wonderful of course.'

'Suppose you play a game and imagine these aren't just normal fears but real. How would you feel in two weeks' time if you were still here and not in Paris, if there were no wedding because you'd changed your mind?'

Isabel considered this, then brightened up. 'I do feel a little better. You're a dear, Caroline, you really are. I hope you're as happy as me one day.'

I am now, Caroline thought to herself. Much happier, in fact. She was surprised it was not written all over her face: *'I love Reggie.'*

In those final days before the wedding, Caroline's concentric circles spun furiously and independently. The King's intervention to break the Irish deadlock had failed, and the bitter episode of the gun-running *Asgard* and the Dublin Shootings poised the country on the brink of civil war, Father told them gravely. Meanwhile, Austria disregarded Serbia's apology and seized the excuse to mobilise and invade; Russia snarled and the Kaiser snarled back. Goodwood took place in stifling heat without the King's presence, but society floated on in chiffon, satin and top hats waiting for the date when it could thankfully retire to the seaside. Her birthday passed with scant Rectory attention – unsurprisingly since she chose to spend the day on a picnic with Reggie, her excuse for being alone with him *all day* being that she would feel selfish dragging her family away from the Rectory at such a vital time. Eleanor dutifully failed to put in her 'offered' appearance as chaperone. The Rectory larders groaned, the refrigerators and ice-house filled with raspberry ices (red, not white, though, Mrs Dibble snapped), bridesmaids' dresses were fitted and pressed, the bridal gown allotted a room of its own. Now the wedding fever had gripped Caroline too, quite apart from her own reasons for looking forward to it. Within her there lay a deep nugget of joy, as, bursting with excitement, she waited for Saturday when Friday's grey skies would lift and the long hot summer would reach its climax.

Chapter Seven

'Praise we the Lord!' In the interests of the rest of the household Mrs Dibble refrained from bursting into song and maintained a continuous and energetic hum of gratitude. Not only had the Almighty dutifully provided a warm, dry day (the sun would undoubtedly soon be shining), but He had also arranged for her junkets and jellies to set, a matter about which Mrs Dibble had been uneasy. Cautiously she went to investigate her snow cheese left in the larder to drain all night, with strict instructions that that blessed dog was to be kept out of the kitchen. There had been one terrible occasion when Ahab, strolling into the kitchen from his appointed bed in the scullery in search of nocturnal amusement, found the snow cheese merrily draining away its surplus liquid, ate the lot and was promptly sick, lying wanly and reproachfully by the cause of his downfall when she arrived in the morning.

This time all was well. One by one Mrs Dibble tweaked off the muslin covers from the lemon cheesy mounds to find a satisfactory amount of liquid beneath each sieve.

She drew in a satisfied breath, made herself a strengthening cup of tea, and prepared to finalise the tactics for her battlefield while the troops slumbered on.

'Morning, Mrs Dibble.' She was wrong. Even Harriet was prepared to be down early today, her handsome face for once looking excited rather than sulky. Myrtle tumbled in a few minutes later, just as Harriet had finished her tea and was setting forth to start on the drawing room armed with Globe polish, cloths, tea leaves and brushes.

'And disinfectant in the pigwash tub, if you please, Myrtle. We don't want an army of bluebottles joining in the party. And I thought I told you, Myrtle, to empty the grease-bucket strainer. I can *smell* it from here. And change the fly-papers. And you'll need some more Monkey soap out.'

'Morning, Mrs D.' Agnes came in, trying not to yawn, ten minutes later. Once again she hadn't slept, but she was determined to do her best for the Rectory today.

'I want a word with you, girl,' Mrs Dibble said as Myrtle departed to the scullery, in what passed for her as a motherly tone. She pushed a cup of tea towards Agnes. 'Young Jamie Thorn's coming here today to help Percy out.'

Already Agnes was back in torment and it was only twenty to seven. 'Here?' she repeated stupidly. She'd been trying to see Jamie for days, but he wouldn't open the door, not even to her, not after the rough music. He was never in the shop, never at home apparently, and the door was never left open now like it usually was. His mother always pretended not to know where he was, but she must, she *must*.

'The Rector asked him to come and help Mr Dibble with the wine.' Mrs Dibble offered no further explanation.

Agnes nodded as if the news were of no interest to her, though she was filled with instant hope and despair at the same time. She didn't care now if he'd done it or not, she still wanted Jamie. She realised this was the Rector's way of showing Ashden what he thought of their nasty habits; he was allying himself openly with Jamie Thorn. She wondered vaguely why, and then forgot about the Rector in the dilemma of her own affairs. *He* would be here; she would see him, that was all she cared about. Today somehow or other must settle things between Jamie and herself; every problem had a climax, and today was hers and Jamie's.

She rose to her feet. 'Thank you, Mrs Dibble,' she said, and went to lay dining room breakfast. 'Breakfast for us at seven-thirty today, Agnes,' she heard Mrs Dibble shout after her. 'And Miss Caroline's going to take a tray up to Miss Isabel at eight o'clock, remember.'

'I'll remember,' she shouted back.

Old Dibble had called her Agnes, she suddenly realised. That meant a lot. She was on her side, then. Right. Agnes straightened her shoulders. This would be The Day.

Caroline jerked awake, took a second to realise that this was really The Day, *her* day, jumped out of bed and rushed to the window. The sun wasn't out, but on the other hand there was no sign of rain on the terrace. It was going to be a glorious, glorious day, it had to be. Happily she seized her water jug, splashing water with alacrity into the bowl, and glad she had had a bath last night for this morning no one would dispute Isabel's right to the bathroom. She decided she'd go down to the kitchen to collect Isabel's breakfast, and remembered family prayers at eight-thirty this morning. She'd have to dress properly. Bother. Today of all days she didn't want her usual rush. She opened her door and craned her head out, sniffing in the atmosphere. Already the Rectory was excited. She could hear George crashing about in his room, the comforting hum of her mother's voice downstairs, despite the almost tangible tension. They could make enough electricity from the Rectory air to light Piccadilly – or Ashden. That would be the day; they hadn't got gas in the village yet, let alone a public electricity supply. Not that she minded. She loved the glow of oil-lamps, the sight of Fred slowly working his way round the Rectory lamps each evening; and who would give up the warmth of the fires of the kitchen ranges even for the excitement of gas stoves? To be fair, she thought ruefully, Mrs Dibble would. It must have been terrible for her all this hot summer to have to cook on the range; she never complained, though there were frequent raised voices in the servants' quarters.

Fifteen minutes later Caroline dashed downstairs, complete with wedding camisole, petticoat, knickers and stockings and her old yellow dress. She stopped short on the threshold of the kitchen, beheld its mountains of ordered chaos and tried to bite back laughter.

'Mrs Dibble, it looks like the Carlton's kitchens. Mr Escoffier himself couldn't do better.' Mrs Dibble visibly preened herself. 'Master Dabb didn't need to help you out,'

Caroline added for good measure, and was rewarded by seeing Mrs Dibble blush with pride.

Servants' breakfast had been relegated to the servants' hall in order to make as much room as possible in the kitchens where china, cutlery and the best damask table linen were all laid out to Mrs Dibble's despair. Time after time she'd pointed out to those dratted girls sometimes to fold the napkins in three, sometimes four. That way linen lasted longer, for creases didn't grow into holes. But would they listen? No. And it was she – or rather Agnes – who sat mending it with 'flourishing thread'.

Trays of pattie cases were lined up, hard-boiled eggs lay cooling in preserving pans, the boiled lobsters were assembled for shelling and creaming, pies and canapés lay awaiting garnish and toppings. Bowls of pastry mix stood purposefully on the table for cheese straws and anchovy puffs.

Even as Caroline surveyed the scene, there was a thump on the tradesmen's door, and Joey Sharpe staggered in with two huge buckets full of cream taken off his yoke. 'Reckon the Ritz will have to do without till Sunday. Ashden do have it all, surely,' he joked.

'Be off with your cheek,' Mrs Dibble replied automatically, eyes darting suspiciously over the cream to ensure it was a satisfactory colour.

Agnes hurried in from the servants' hall, complete with tray for Isabel, decked with teapot and a rose.

'Her favourite,' Caroline said appreciatively. 'Thank you, Agnes.'

'When you gets married your trouble begins,' observed

Mrs Dibble without rancour. 'That's what they do say. Best enjoy life while she can, poor lass.'

Kidneys were unlikely to do much to alleviate Isabel's problem, Caroline thought ruefully as she negotiated the staircase carefully and arrived with the tray relatively unscathed save for a minor slop of milk. She wondered if she too would be excused family prayers on her wedding day. This, she hugged to herself with excitement, was her own engagement day, though as yet only she and Reggie knew it.

'Good morning, beautiful bride.' Caroline set the tray down on a side table in Isabel's room and drew it up to the bed.

Isabel, still fast asleep, awoke and struggled up, yawning and stretching her arms luxuriously. 'Lovely. Just think, I can have kidneys for breakfast every day from now on if I like.'

'Almost worth getting married for.'

'It certainly is.' Isabel tucked in with relish, all sign of her earlier nerves vanished. People, Caroline decided, were extraordinary, especially one's own family.

'Shall I come to help you dress?'

Isabel considered rather too long for tact. 'Just you and Mother. I don't want Phoebe jumping about or Felicia mooning around.' Happy families, thought Caroline, in such a good mood she was amused rather than irritated on behalf of her sisters.

'Come along in, Rosie, don't be shy.' Mrs Dibble waved the girl into the kitchen, neatly dressed in the Ashden mauve

239

print, her black for this afternoon carefully tied in a parcel. She looked her up and down. Skinny, small little thing she was, yet a hard worker. 'Servants' breakfast is in the hall. Have you eaten yet?'

Rosie Trott shook her head, her great brown eyes looking round her in wonder. She'd never been in the Rectory kitchen before, and it was nothing like the kitchens of Ashden Manor. This looked so old-fashioned with its copper saucepans and pots hanging on the wall – those that weren't over the two-ovened Hattersley range or on the tabletops. An old cabinet refrigerator, a tongue presser, meat screens – in Ashden Manor it was all seamless steel and smart black gas stoves. It was a different sort of kitchen and she rather liked it; she felt comfortable here, for all she'd heard about Mrs Dibble being a terror.

'That would be lovely, Mrs Dibble.'

'You know Harriet, Myrtle and Agnes, of course,' Mrs Dibble hurled at her as she bustled the girl along to the servants' hall.

Rosie nodded. 'I were at school with Myrtle.'

'In with you then.' Mrs Dibble decided not to overdo the friendliness. 'There's a lot to do here, and I've heard you're not afraid of hard work . . .'

'What is the news, Laurence?'

Elizabeth, unusually, went anxiously into the study where, again unusually, her husband was reading *The Times* before taking family prayers. Matins had been especially early today, a fact Ashden rewarded by leaving the Rector to recite to himself – to his great amusement. 'The children must not be upset, but I want to know,' she continued.

'It is not good, Elizabeth. The Lutine bell was rung at Lloyds yesterday to announce that Russia had carried out its threat and mobilised. There is little hope now that Germany will not retaliate and declare war on Russia. Belgium has recalled its army, and fears German invasion naturally enough if –' He broke off. 'And in France, there is bad news also. Monsieur Jaures, the influential French Socialist, who has done so much to try to avert war, has been assassinated.'

'Then there is little hope for poor Europe,' Elizabeth sighed. 'It will once again be dragged into war. Thank goodness we are an island.'

'There is worse news. The Stock Exchange in London was closed yesterday afternoon in response to the international financial crisis.'

'But what has it to do with England?'

'Let us hope nothing.'

There was a pause. 'Then *we* might be drawn in? And France? Oh, *Laurence*!'

'It cannot be coincidence that Winston Churchill has sent the British Fleet into the Channel on manoeuvres. We are rattling our own sabres, and Sir John has telephoned already to say he cannot be with us today. He is needed in Whitehall during the present crisis. He is close to Haldane, you know, the former War Minister, who did so much to restructure the army.'

'Oh, but that's terrible.' Unable to grapple with the wider horror, Elizabeth seized on the particular. 'Today of all days. I take it Lady Hunney is coming?'

'Yes. I doubt if a mere international war would keep her from adding her lustre to our celebrations.'

'That is not like you, Laurence.' He must really be worried, she realised.

'Exports of food from France and Germany will be stopped.' Laurence was not listening. He was still reading on. 'The bank rate has risen to eight per cent and the country has only a month's supply of meat.'

'I shall speak to the farm immediately,' Elizabeth declared. 'There may be a rush. We are fortunate in Ashden to be so near at hand to our supplies.'

'The price of bread goes up one halfpenny a loaf next week. Gold is being called in –' Laurence lay down his newspaper. 'The situation is very serious.'

'Any European war must be serious for our imports. Thank goodness we have the Empire to supply us. How *can* they take our gold coins away? That is *our* money.'

'They will issue us with paper money instead.'

'I don't like the sound of that,' Elizabeth declared, then bravely came to the heart of her fear. 'Laurence, Isabel and Robert are going to *France* tonight.' There was a question mark in her voice.

'France is a long way from Russia, my dear.' But there was little to reassure her in the Rector's voice. *The Times* had written of England's duty, and that the Empire stood ready. Furthermore, what he had not told his wife was that although the Foreign Office had so far issued no formal instruction to travellers to stay at home and was reassuring those already abroad that there was no danger, merely possible inconvenience in countries that had mobilised, Sir John had privately suggested he advise the couple to stay at home. He must speak urgently to Swinford-Browne and Robert.

Percy Dibble happily hummed down in the cellars as he carefully rearranged his treasured bottles, his moment of supreme happiness before him. A Frenchie had once come to see the Rector, and complimented Percy *in person* on his rhubarb wine. He was a *sommelier*, he said, and whatever that was precisely it was obviously a splendid thing to be, so Percy duly elected himself *sommelier* of the Rectory from that time forth. He never bothered to mention this to Daisy. He still called Margaret by this pet name even though seventeen-year-old sparkling, pert little Daisy was now forty-five and they'd three kids, two of them with kids of their own. But there was Fred of course. Percy carefully blew the dust off a bottle of Chateau Margaux that the Rector had been saving for something special. 'Rest you there, my lovely,' he crooned. 'Today's not special enough.' Today, as well as his fruit wines, there'd be foreign wines, not to mention the cases of champagne lined up in martial order, the bottle necks sticking out like so many hens in a wire coop waiting for supper. Miss Matilda's gift, so Mus Lilley said, and now Miss Matilda wouldn't even be here. Not right a lady like her being in prison. Hardly bore thinking of what the world was coming to. Percy's view was that everybody should know their place and stick to it, otherwise the world got in a valiant pickle.

'Mr Dibble!'

That would be Daisy. Percy sighed as he went to the foot of the cellar stairs. Sometimes Daisy was a mite too formal, but then people was all different. He looked up, but the angle of the steep steps and the overhang meant all he could see was Daisy's black boots and part of her skirt and apron. How could disapproval make itself so evident with so little?

'The Good Lord may have to tolerate hard liquor today, but He don't require us to drown in it, Mr Dibble. Time to get the crystal polished.'

He opened his mouth to say that was Harriet's job, then remembered that as *sommelier* he was responsible, and that he had Jamie Thorn coming to help too. Sometimes the Rector stuck his neck out just like them champagne bottles, and one day, just like them something would go off pop.

Isabel reluctantly emerged from her bath. She told herself this was because it was the last time she would be enjoying this luxury here in the Rectory, but in fact it was to delay the moment when she would don the new lace brassiere and nainsook knickers she had so proudly bought last week. No one else in Ashden had ever worn a brassiere, she was sure of that, as she wriggled to fasten it behind her. Once done, she admired her own shape in the mirror, the way it divided her breasts, then sobered as she remembered that tonight, even if it was in a cabin on an overnight steamer, someone else would be admiring it too. She would keep her nightgown on. Surely he wouldn't expect her to take it off? She had tried to ask her friends, for she wouldn't dare ask Mother, and had comfortingly been told that no gentleman would ask such a thing of her. But she wasn't so sure. The thought of that terrible man at her engagement ball, Frank Eliot, slipped into her mind for no reason at all, and she shuddered deliciously. Quickly she pulled on the girdle, which she had decided could be her 'something old'. No new corsetry for her today, she thought practically; she wanted to be comfortable. She sat down on the stool and lovingly stroked the white artificial silk stockings on to her legs. Her very first pair. It belatedly occurred to her that perhaps she should have bought some for the bridesmaids too. Oh well, their legs wouldn't be seen. Sensuously, she stretched out one leg after the other, arching her feet to admire them. Then she clipped the suspenders into place. Perhaps she should wear a pretty garter too? She quickly dismissed thoughts of the confined space in which she would be undressing tonight; perhaps they wouldn't undress . . . not till they reached Paris and she had a dressing room of her own.

Mother would be here any moment to do her hair, and then it would all begin. There was nothing she could do to stop it, marriage would tick relentlessly nearer. Anyway, she didn't want to stop it – did she? There was Paris to look forward to.

Phoebe searched impatiently for the white stockings Agnes had laid out for her. She couldn't find them. Anyway, who needed to wear new stockings? She rummaged to find a respectable pair of old ones, then hopped around in a sort of Indian war dance she had concocted to assist in the lacing-up of corsetry and donning of hosiery, and suchlike fiddly things. Growing up had meant sacrifices, she had discovered. It was all very well putting one's hair *up*, but having to bone your stomach and hips *in* after the comparative freedom of her earlier light corset and liberty bodice was no joke at all.

Nevertheless she drew in her camisole as highly as she could under the bosom. It made a satisfyingly large bulge of the latter, almost as good as Mother's.

Hair next. Where was Mother? Phoebe debated her chances of escaping a wigging if she pulled the bell for Agnes to seek out Mother, and decided they were slim, so she pulled on the nearest old skirt and blouse and dashed out herself. After all, it was no use telling her she had to wear a silly transformation at the back to support the ridiculous lump of muslin and flowers deemed suitable for bridesmaids if Mother were not going to help jam the thing on. Or she could ask Caroline. She was almost as obliging as Mother. *Someone* must help. She couldn't see the back of her head except by lying semi spread-eagled over the stool, looking into her dressing-table mirror and, if she were lucky, catching a glimpse of the back of her head in the wall mirror opposite.

There was no sign of Mother; she must be with Isabel or old Ma Dibble-Dabble. And no Caroline either. Very well, she'd do it herself and *then* she could put her pink gown on, ready for the wedding. With great glee Phoebe contemplated the narrow skirt with its over-tunic – how cross Isabel had been that they all had narrow skirts and she looked as if she were 'wearing a crinoline', she had moaned, her gown was so full. Phoebe was looking forward to the wedding, though she wasn't sure why. She supposed it was because some-thing was happening at last. Moreover, it was a something in which, though there was no Christopher to tease and the new curate was no Anthony Wilding, at least there could be no Len

Thorns to distract her with thoughts of powerful bodies rippling with muscles over their firelit anvil.

Felicia was dressing almost absent-mindedly; unlike Phoebe, however quickly and with whatever lack of attention she dressed, she still looked graceful – not that she greatly cared, but she knew it pleased Daniel. She deftly braided up the long dark hair and slipped the cool satin over her head. She liked this shade of green and the matching silk gloves, carefully dyed from white. Soon she would be ready, and that would help make *it* come all the quicker. *It* was not only Isabel's wedding, but seeing Daniel. He'd be leaving in two days' time, and this might be the last time she saw him, yet it was impossible. What if she never saw him again? Suppose he married a dusky princess of the Nile, or a classic Greek beauty? No, God could not be so unkind. It was He who had marked them for each other. Daniel still had to find that out, that was all. She was lucky, for she had known what she wanted all along: Daniel.

Agnes hesitated, then took the plunge and made an excuse to go by Rosie's station where she was busy shelling eggs and creaming the yolks. 'You're friendly with Ruth Horner, aren't you? I wondered—'

'Not really,' Rosie quickly interrupted. 'I know her, that's all, and, oh Miss Pilbeam, I'm ever so sorry.'

Agnes stiffened, then tried to relax. Genuine pity she must accept, and she and Jamie had few enough friends left, that was for sure. 'Kind of you, Rosie. Mind, not too much curry powder in the eggs.'

'No, Miss Pilbeam. I'm sorry – about Jamie, I mean.'

'What for?' Agnes said sharply. 'It makes no difference, we'll be wed anyway.'

'Even after what I said I'll have to say?' Rosie stared at her.

'What's that?' Agnes was bewildered.

'Ruth asked me, you see, and I had to say yes, 'cos I did.'

'Did *what*?' Unconsciously Agnes clutched her wooden spoon like a weapon.

Rosie looked alarmed. 'I thought you must know by now, that Jamie would have told you. That's what caused all the rough music, see.'

'*What*?'

'I had to say I saw them going into the old gentleman's cottage, Ebenezer's, I saw her and Jamie. 'Cos I did, going back after my evening off.'

'You *saw* them?' Agnes whispered, feeling as if she'd been hit in the stomach. No one could doubt Rosie. If Rosie said so, it was the truth.

'My mum said speak the truth and you'll never go wrong, Rose.' Rosie looked anxious all the same. 'Now look what I've done.' Rosie tried to grapple with this ethical problem.

'It isn't your fault,' Agnes managed to say. She'd never really believed it, not even after what Ruth had said. She'd told herself all the boys swam naked in the river, Ruth could have seen Jamie like that any time in the last ten years. But now that remaining strand of hope was broken too, and the rough music drummed incessantly at her heart.

Twelve o'clock. One hour to go. Late for a wedding, particularly since they were to receive Holy Communion.

Laurence had disapproved when Elizabeth told him of the time being set back so that a full luncheon was not required. Our Lord should not take second place to household economics, he had pointed out, but Elizabeth, practical as always, pointed out that Our Lord had performed miracles at weddings to help supply the provisions, and this would be another one in its way.

Laurence entered his cool church, which smelt of the fragrance of flowers and the wisdom of ages. Ostensibly he had come to check his cope and white stole were lying ready for him, and that all was ready for the Celebration. He knew it would be. Bertram had proved a most efficient sacristan, except for the day after his birthday. Teetotal the rest of the year, he claimed the Lord owed him the privilege of a bottle of port wine on the day of his birth. Unfortunately this year his birthday had fallen on a Saturday, but the churchwarden took over his Sunday duties, without a word being spoken.

Laurence tried to analyse the root of his worry. Marriage was a celebration he'd carried out countless times. He'd married the children of couples he'd married as a young man himself, he'd baptised their children, and now he was to marry his own firstborn. Soon the other five would follow. Four, he automatically corrected himself. He sometimes saw Millicent as a living entity in the family, a presence that would not fade. She would have been nearly twenty-four now, possibly even married. They might even have been grandparents. Impossible to think of his firefly bewitching Elizabeth as a grandmother. With Isabel married, they might not have to wait long now.

But that brought him back to the heart of his concern. He had doubts about the wisdom of Isabel's marriage, but all his talking to her had shaken her resolve not a whit. She was twenty-five and what if her motives were more selfish than desirable? Had marriage not always been a matter of position and property, an economic arrangement? He and Elizabeth had married for love but who was to say which marriages were happiest? Isabel would make a splendid hostess, and mother – here, Laurence's imagination broke down. He could not see Isabel as a mother, but it was fashionable for the wealthy to leave the task of rearing their children to others and England produced worthy sons none the worse for it. Just because his own views were different, he could not condemn others. All the same, his prayers to God were more personal than usual.

At twelve-fifteen the bell-ringers arrived, collected their beers, ready waiting thanks to Bertram, and, as their boots clumped up the wooden stairs to the bell chamber, he reflected that they were as much a part of it all as he and Elizabeth, for marriage was a social event as well as a religious one. He remembered this afternoon he must persuade Robert not to travel to the Continent in such troubled times, and that inevitably meant discussion with Swinford-Browne, who would be as concerned as a father as he was. Relations between them were strained, to put it mildly. Without proof he could not accuse Swinford-Browne outright of involvement in Tilly's re-arrest. He had, however, made his suspicions plain to the man – who had piously denied any knowledge of the matter. Now they must meet as parents with a common anxiety. He put it out of his head again; the coming service would affect the rest of the young couple's lives, the loss of a holiday in France would not.

'Ta-ra-ra-boom-de-ay,' carolled Elizabeth, leading the way with *the dress*; Caroline was half crouched at her side holding the skirt and train gently over her arms, managing the odd kick on the 'boom' when she could.

Isabel sat in splendour at her dressing table, her fair tresses looped stylishly *à la Vallière*, after Elizabeth's ministrations; there had been no need of a transformation after all, thanks to her mother's careful brushing and judicial use of pins. Like a high priestess, Isabel slowly raised her arms towards her wedding dress.

'Isabel,' Elizabeth jerked the dress away as she drew closer and observed the shocking truth, 'have you been *enamelling*?'

'Only a little lip rouge, Mother, and a little on the cheeks,' Isabel declared, studiedly off-handedly.

'You look like a painted doll.'

'This is my *wedding* day, Mother.'

'All the more reason for you to look as God intended, my child.'

Caroline decided to intervene, seeing deadlock fast approaching. 'I should take it off the cheeks anyway, Isabel. It doesn't suit you, but the lips look rather nice.'

She earned a glare from her mother. 'It will mark the gown.'

'I'll be careful.' Isabel scrubbed at her cheeks with the nearest handkerchief – a carefully laundered one from Grannie Overton's linen reserve with embroidered roses and violets.

'One two three *go*.' Caroline shouted as the gown floated

251

down over Isabel's head and shoulders, settling, then falling over her hips. Caroline was despatched to the rear to do up the army of tiny covered buttons; Elizabeth tweaked in front. The Overton pearls were duly placed round her neck, gloves were donned, train and veil arranged and at last Elizabeth pronounced herself satisfied. She pulled the cloth off Caroline's mirror, carried in specially for the occasion. 'There!'

Isabel surveyed herself, from flowery topknot to the satin shoes peeping out under the detested full skirt. At last she turned round to face them. 'I look beautiful,' she told them in awe-struck wonder.

Elizabeth said nothing, but her silence said all. Caroline provided the words: 'Lovely – have you got the old, new, borrowed and blue?'

'I've put my blue garter on, but –' Isabel's face grew round in horror – 'not the something borrowed.'

'You've Granny Overton's pearls.'

'No, they're going to be mine anyway – I'll have to borrow the jet buckle after all, Caroline. I'll pop it in my Dorothy bag.' She beamed, all resolved to her satisfaction.

Caught out, Caroline could not refuse. 'I'll go and fetch it.'

'And change while you're there?' Elizabeth said.

'Why?'

Elizabeth laughed. 'Look at yourself.'

Caroline did. She was still wearing her old linen gown. Isabel caught her eye, and burst into laughter. Caroline hugged her. 'Be happy, Isabel. Be happy.' She surprised even herself by how much she meant it.

'Listen,' Isabel said suddenly. 'The bells have started.'

* * *

252

The peal rang out over their heads as Caroline, Patricia, Phoebe and Felicia gathered at the door of the church waiting for their sister.

'We're her rainbow tea-set,' as Phoebe put it, looking at their different coloured dresses.

Inside the church the Rector and his wife prayed for their daughter's happiness. In the Rectory gardens, Jamie Thorn carefully placed the last glass in position, concentrating as hard as he could on this simple task for it saved thinking of other matters. Percy nervously rearranged bottles of champagne in buckets, bowls, and two hipbaths of ice. Rosie rushed around the trestle tables from the village institute checking plates and napkins. This was easy compared with earlier tasks. She'd shelled so many hard-boiled eggs, banging them on the side of a basin, she felt like a young thrush who enjoyed his snail breakfast on the flagstones underneath her window every morning.

The kitchen stood empty, its doors firmly closed against Ahab. The Dibbles and the rest of the staff were in church, seated sedately side by side in a pew at the back, thoughtfully arranged by the Rector, ready to depart to their posts at the close of the service. Their thoughts were divided between the coming wedding and the thousand and one details they might have left undone. Far in front of them, Robert sat awaiting his bride. He at least had no doubt that this was the happiest day of his life. In the pew behind, Edith Swinford-Browne stole furtive glances across to the bride's side to try to spot the Earl of Buckford and his family, and was disappointed to see no one who could possibly be the dowager. Not *all* the bride's family was present. Fortunately there had been no reprieve for that terrible woman, an honourable or not, Miss Matilda Lilley. William had boasted to her that despite the Rector's earnest representations to his brother to intervene as a member of the House of Lords, nothing, he winked conspiratorially, was to be done. The woman remained in Holloway. Edith hoped this was because of the Earl's disapproval – surely William would not be so unkind as to block her release. She herself disapproved of suffragettes (she ignored any other possible reason for William's anger) but there was no doubt they were brave women, and forcible feeding sounded most upsetting. She cheered up as a gentleman who was undoubtedly the Earl inclined his head politely to her. A stir of restlessness through the church. Not long now. Only Jamie Thorn, his task reluctantly concluded, but who had refused to come to the church, noticed that the overcast sky was worsening.

'The King of Love my Shepherd is . . .' The St Columba tune swelled up to the beams above them. It's all so unreal, Caroline thought, dazed. In a few minutes I'll wake up and it will be a normal Sunday. Isabel looks beautiful; sitting on that stool at home she looked like an Arthur Rackham illustration – usually that's Felicia's role, but today Isabel did too. It must be marriage, mystery. *Shall I look like that?* No, don't think of Reggie. Think of Isabel and Robert. It's their day.

'Dearly beloved friends . . .'

They were, they were. Everyone was here, save Aunt Tilly. Caroline had felt Reggie's eyes on her as she walked up the aisle behind Isabel. People always cried at weddings; she didn't want to even though it was all so beautiful and perfect. Tomorrow they would be just Isabel and pleasant dull Robert, today they were symbols of something greater. Robert looked very handsome in his grey morning suit and oyster waistcoat. Not as handsome as Reggie, though. Her thoughts flowed on, until she dragged them back to her father's voice and the service.

'... With this ring I thee wed; with my body I thee worship ...' Soon it would be her, and Reggie, and at that thought she had to concentrate on Isabel and Robert even harder.

It was all a ritual the service, Communion, even down to the rose petals and rice at the door, and the photographs to be taken at the Rectory. But then life too was a ritual, from which it was sometimes impossible to escape, a friendly prison. Her father's short nuptial address moved her to tears, which this time she could not hold back; it was simple, the embodiment of the love of a father for his child, the love of a priest for his communicants. It seemed to her it marked something momentous, as though by his words he tolled a bell that spelled a watershed in their lives. Isabel Lilley was no more. Isabel Swinford-Browne had been born. She had moved away from them, just as surely as soon Caroline would be Caroline Hunney.

And she watched the slow stately pageant move on, like the Rectory year itself, until they were back at the Rectory. 'Hurry,' someone called, 'it looks like rain.'

Caroline saw her mother glance up at the sky, and afterwards the image remained in her mind, stamped by random selection on her memory. Then she moved to organize guests for the photograph, or in fact several. Phoebe fidgeted while they were taken, but at last, with the wriggle of a posterior edging out from under the camera cloth, they were released for the banquet. Faces in such large group photographs conveyed little, Caroline often felt. 'Why not take a photograph just of the hats?' Caroline whispered to Reggie as she caught up with him. 'They're often far more memorable than the faces underneath. Look at Edith's – it must have danced round the stage with Lily Elsie in *The Merry Widow*.'

'Perhaps she wishes she were.' Reggie snorted so loudly she had to shush him. 'If it rains, it'll be like Kew Gardens on her head as the roses grow.'

'It's going to rain, you mark my words,' they overheard Mrs Dibble warning Percy dolefully, as he opened his umpteenth bottle. 'We're going to need *the plan*.'

Surely even Mrs Dibble could not believe the weather would stoop to confer such an indignity as rain today . . . Caroline giggled.

'That champagne is making you tipsy already,' Reggie told her in an unloverlike manner.

Caroline considered this. 'You may be right. It is, perhaps, stronger than I had thought.'

'I had to stop Nanny Oates taking a second glass,' Reggie told her virtuously. 'She thought it was lemonade with fizz in it. I say, those lobster things look quite decent.'

'Thank you kindly, sir.'

'Don't mention it, my pretty maiden.' He lowered his voice. 'This evening then, as soon as they've gone?'

Something caught at her, intensified by the switch from banter to love. 'Yes.'

'No grey skies for us. The sun will shine all the day long, just you see.'

*   *   *

Margaret Dibble glowed with pride as she watched her mountains of food vanishing, and the threatened rain did not come. She felt Queen of the Rectory, but fast on that thought came that of the accompanying responsibility. Those patties were disappearing all too fast. Were there any more trays left inside? She promptly dispatched Rosie, and watched Miss Isabel flitting around her guests. She always had been a pretty little thing; it was a pleasure to do things for her. Always so appreciative. And now she was married, and into riches. A valiant, handsome young man, too, so polite. Miss Isabel would live happily ever after. She saw Fred ambling around grinning as if nothing had happened at all. She owed that to the Rector again too. She'd heard that after the rough music for Jamie Thorn stopped, the Rector demanded anyone who'd been assaulted by Fred *themselves* to step forward. He hadn't been angry, just asked. Puzzled, they'd looked at each other. 'Your children then,' the Rector had pressed. 'Send them to my house tomorrow evening. We must put a stop to this.' He did, for no one came, so Joe had had to release Fred again, free from official stain as a public nuisance. Margaret vowed she'd make the Rector's favourite pond pudding as often as he wanted from now on no matter what the season.

No one was taking any notice of Fred today; Jamie Thorn was here, too, and no one seemed to care about that either, perhaps because there were a lot of foreigners around. She watched Agnes go over to speak to Jamie, saw her rebuffed. He just walked away from her. Men were like that, Mrs Dibble thought fiercely, disgusted.

Like children. As self-centred as her mother's stale lardy cakes, and today of all days, Miss Isabel's day.

Isabel floated from one person to another, in a progressional dance of her own, moving back to Robert every so often with a beatific smile. The smile was caused by her overwhelming relief; it had all been so easy. A few words and she was married, across that mighty threshold and safe for ever. She could have wept for happiness, though that would spoil her looks, so she smiled instead.

'My own Mrs Swinford-Browne,' Robert observed tenderly, squeezing her waist, and daringly kissing her cheek. 'This is the first day of *our* life.' Isabel was no longer a princess; she was his queen.

'That housekeeper of yours is better than the quartermaster at OTC camp.' Daniel grinned, as he led Felicia out of range of the all-seeing eye. Not that she needed much taking. He had tried to stay away from the Rectory, but found he was as drawn to her as flies to a fly-paper and now he was stuck fast. Until Monday at least. Then, just when everyone else was enjoying the bank holiday, he'd be leaving. The crowds would be streaming back across the Channel, while he would be setting off. It wasn't quite the route he'd intended. It was a nuisance, this European business, but he'd agreed with his father that the sensible thing to do was to take a railway train from Paris to Marseilles and pick up a boat for Greece, rather than to travel slowly overland. It was still a compromise, for his father had wanted him to cancel his plans altogether, but Daniel refused point-blank. His whole life was itching to start, and he was determined not to put it off. What if the Austria–Hungarian Empire had mobilised, what if Russia was growling? In the end they'd let the Austrians and Serbia fight it out. At least it made something more interesting to read in *The Times*, he told his father nonchalantly. Better than the correspondence on dogs in railway carriages which had preoccupied it in July. He intended to eat, drink and be merry today. Even now he could not take it in that old Isabel was married. He and Reggie had teased her all their lives, and suddenly she had had the last laugh and wed into riches – of a sort. She was easy to tease, for she never laughed at herself, unlike Caroline. Still, he was fond of Isabel and wished her well. She looked a stunner today – and so did Felicia. Careful, Daniel old fellow, he told himself, steady on the champagne or you'll land up in Ashden Church yourself. Looking at Felicia now, that didn't seem such a bad idea.

Time for the ices. The quartermaster made her decision. Young Master George would be glad. He always liked his ices. Always a lear in his belly, as her granny would have said, a hole in it. Well, why not? Boys needed feeding up.

Young Master George was congratulating himself that he could hold his drink like a gentleman should, and, after all, that's what he now was: grown up. He'd given Isabel away (all too willingly, he smirked) successfully; Father had said he was proud of him. His new morning suit made him look like one of the fellows, *and* he'd been chosen over and above Uncle Charles, Earl of Buckford, to do the honours for Isabel. That had been one in the eye for Grandmother (probably why she hadn't come), even though Isabel had kicked up a stink when she heard. He didn't know why: his voice was well and truly broken now so, as far as he was concerned, he was adult and it was all plain sailing to the grave. Even that speculation about girls with the fellows at Skinners could be put to the test now – within the limits of being a gentleman, of course. He appraised the assembled company through his new adult eye. Unfortunately the eye fell on no luscious temptations of the East; all the stunning-looking ladies were too old for him, all those of his own age looked too young and too silly. There was always Eleanor, he thought. She was pretty decent, and she wasn't that old. Not that he thought of her as a luscious temptation of the East, but he at least could stick dancing with her this evening. He imagined himself placing his white-gloved hands on Eleanor's back. Good – oh, the ices were coming out.

Mrs Dibble looked at the remaining two raspberry ices, already beginning to melt. She wrestled within herself and won. It was to be a day of reconciliation. 'Have one of the ices, Harriet,' she said graciously, pushing it towards her. 'All turned out well, didn't it?'

'Yes, Mrs Dibble,' Harriet beamed. She wasn't sure what the 'it' referred to, but accepted the offering for what it was. The Rector had given them all a glass of champagne, and that headiness combined with Bert Wilson's hot breath, as he delivered the evening bread order and took advantage of her proximity over an armful of Viennas, had bolstered her self-esteem. 'I'll take one to Fred, shall I?'

Mrs Dibble took this in her stride. 'If you'd be so good.' She watched, frowning, as Harriet set off to Fred and handed it to him, cool as a cucumber. She could see Fred examining it in that way he had, beaming, and then pumping Harriet's free hand up and down, before he plastered raspberry ice cream all round his mouth. She felt like weeping. It looked like Ashden was coming to its senses at last; that rough music was over, with only Aggie and Jamie left to sort out. That too must be possible. After all, today even the threatened rain had obligingly kept away; it was a day for happiness, and she saw no reason why young Aggie shouldn't have what her young ladies were enjoying. *Mrs* Isabel, Miss Caroline and Miss Felicia, eyes shining bright as good deeds in a naughty world, and Miss Phoebe – where *was* that dratted girl?

Phoebe had, on her mother's instructions, gone to the stables to release Ahab from his incarceration and take him for a short walk. She was pleased about that; she had grown tired of the endless chatter, the champagne, of which she had had two glasses more than her mother had specified, had left her feeling sick and unable to confess this to anyone, so escape seemed an excellent idea. She took Ahab into Silly Lane and down towards the forest; that way she wouldn't have to go past the forge. Not that he would be there late Saturday afternoon. Everyone knew you'd have to go to the Thorn cottage if your horse was lamed after five on a Saturday . . . He wasn't there – he was *here*. Coming towards her. She stopped, as the sickness grew worse in one great lurch of her stomach; she was caught, a bright bird of paradise in her pink bridesmaid's gown, trapped in alien land. She marched on steadily, until he barred her way.

'Going somewhere, Miss Phoebe?'

She could not answer, could not speak. The whole lane seemed to be filled by the impenetrable barrier of this one man.

'I'll set Ahab on you,' she cried at last.

'It's not Ahab I be wanting, surely.'

She'd heard somewhere that if you stood at the back of a ship and watched the waves long enough you'd jump in, drawn, magnetised. If she stood here, she'd be sucked in, further and further towards Len Thorn; swallowed up. With one enormous effort she let go of Ahab's collar, commanding 'Go boy,' and dashed past *him* in Ahab's pursuit. Silly Lane had a bend in it as it turned towards the track that led to Forest Gate. It was just as well, for she was out of *his* sight by the time she was violently sick in the ditch.

'Time for your punch, Percy dear.'

Daisy calling him dear? Percy grinned. The punch had been ready, and the glasses, even while the teapots were still rushing to and fro. He was glad she was enjoying herself. She'd worked hard. She always did, of course. So did Mrs Lilley, only in a different way. Percy greatly admired Elizabeth Lilley. She was a strange one, for a rector's wife, but this were a happy household and that was her doing – however she chose to make it so.

'I do so admire your gown, Mrs Lilley.'

Elizabeth was surprised and truly grateful for the genuine

warmth in Edith's voice, and felt ashamed of her own hypocrisy as she duly admired Edith's own quite extraordinary gown; its stark and startling combination of black and white would put a zebra in the shade and the hat with its black and white roses hardly helped. Elizabeth had spent a lot of time with a paper pattern ordered from *The Lady*, carefully amended by Mrs Hazel, and concocted her gown from several remnants from Weekes', and a lot of lace, binding and flowers. This blue suited her, as did the close-fitting matching silk hat, but it was hardly like being dressed by Lucile. It occurred to her how odd it was, or perhaps it was a mother's thankless lot, that it was Edith who had admired her toilette. Not one of her daughters, wrapped up in their own concerns, had thought to mention it.

Mrs Dibble flew into the kitchen to begin the task of ensuring all was clear for the next battle in her masterly campaign: supper. Out of the larders should come the pies and pickles, roast hams and fowls, ready to be taken into the dining room. Preoccupied as she was, she almost didn't hear the infernal machine ring. Annoyed at the distraction, she marched into the hall and gingerly lifted the receiver from its hook . . .

'Laurence, what is the matter?' Elizabeth asked sharply, seeing the expression on her husband's face as he hung the receiver up on its hook again. 'It's nearly six o'clock. Isabel and Robert will be leaving at any moment. You did talk to Robert, didn't you?'

'I did. His father informed him there was no need for

anxiety. Robert chose to believe him and not me.' It had not been a smooth discussion and he had not wished to upset Elizabeth with its worrying results. To his amazement, whereas Robert had clearly been anxious about the journey, Isabel had point-blank refused to be talked out of her honeymoon with Swinford-Browne (to spite him? Laurence couldn't help wondering) pointing out that hundreds of holidaymakers had left for the Continent yesterday, without intervention by the Foreign Office, and today there was still no formal warning to cancel travel plans. Every argument Laurence put forward had been ignored, not answered, by Swinford-Browne, and with Isabel backing him and Robert neutral, there was nothing he could do.

'Oh, Laurence.' All Elizabeth's carefully suppressed fears rose again.

'Now Sir John has telephoned again. There is grave news at the Foreign Office. Germany issued mobilisation orders yesterday. Today it has declared war on Russia. He warns there may be worse to come. He wished me to advise Isabel and Robert that it would be most unwise now to travel to the Continent. We must speak to Swinford-Browne, Isabel and Robert again immediately.'

By the time they were all gathered in his study, somewhat annoyed at the interruption to their plans, William Swinford-Browne had drunk a great deal of champagne. He had been surprised that the Rector could produce such a good one on the amount his living was worth. He was confirmed in his view that The Towers' estate was paying over far too much in tithes.

The Rector explained the serious position and the advice

he had received, with Elizabeth anxiously at his side.

'Not go?' Isabel cried in dismay. 'But we *must*.'

'What do you think now, Father?' Robert asked anxiously.

'Scaremongering.' Swinford-Browne was purple in the face. He'd already made his views plain earlier today. Now the girl had joined *his* family, he was in authority and he fully intended to make that clear from the beginning. Despite his triumph over Matilda Lilley, he was still smarting from the Rector's victory over Tallow Field and the new churchyard. Candle auctions indeed. This country was archaic; it needed to look to the future, not medieval nonsense. The Rector was living in the past, and was no judge of the international scene.

'It is better to err on the side of caution,' Laurence said.

'If every bally man thought like you, Rector, we'd have no Empire.'

'William, your language,' Edith said faintly, fastening on the one area to which she could contribute.

'Keep out of this.'

'I feel Edith and I as mothers have some say in this matter, Mr Swinford-Browne,' Elizabeth declared quietly, to Edith's undying gratitude but considerable alarm.

'With respect, Mrs Lilley, it's a matter of *fact*.' William Swinford-Browne slapped his hand down on the desk to indicate this was man's work. 'What if Germany does declare war? She can't fight in two directions. She'll be fighting Serbia and Russia; she needs allies at her posterior not bayonets. You'll excuse my language, I'm a plain-speaking man.'

'You are indeed,' the Rector agreed, the muscle in his

cheek pumping furiously. 'I too. Have you forgotten Sedan?'

'That's ancient history, man. The Franco–Prussian war was way back in 1870.'

'France will *never* forget. If Russia demands they come into the war, honour would not let them refuse.'

'Honour? Poppycock. Revenge maybe.'

'As you like. But if France mobilises—'

'Isabel and Robert are English and civilians,' Swinford-Browne interrupted scornfully. 'They can just come home again.'

'Oh *yes*.' Isabel clutched gratefully at the straw being offered. 'Your father's so right, Robert.' She was glad she was a Swinford-Browne now.

'I suppose so,' Robert agreed doubtfully.

'You *suppose* so, do you Robert?' Father eyed son. 'Let me tell you, it's panic like this that leads to trouble. If the Kaiser and that old fool ruling Austria–Hungary want to take on the Tsar, let them. In England we've got enough to do with the bally Irish problem.'

'I still appeal to you not to go, Isabel.' The Rector ignored Swinford-Browne.

Isabel stared at her father. 'It's my honeymoon,' she replied piteously, and when she saw no signs of this influencing the situation, added a petulant, 'I'm married now, Father.'

Swinford-Browne chuckled, well pleased now victory was assuredly his. 'Good champagne, this.'

The Rector could not resist. 'Indeed it is. All paid for by my sister, Miss Matilda Lilley, who unfortunately could not be with us today.'

* * *

Caroline could hardly believe the time had come at last, so bursting with excitement was she. Isabel and Robert had just been driven off in the Swinford-Browne Daimler to the railway station at Tonbridge, and the gathering was about to disperse to change for the informal evening dance. There would be an interval of an hour, and Reggie had teased her by refusing to tell her when he was going to make the announcement. She had promptly said that in that case she would deny it all, but for some reason he had not believed her. On frabjous day . . . Oh dear, *how* she remembered Aunt Tilly reading 'Jabberwocky' to her and now she couldn't be here. Then all thoughts of her aunt passed as she saw Reggie climbing on to the terrace parapet waving a glass and stopping everyone from drifting away.

'Don't put your glasses down,' he yelled with precious little formality. 'You'll be needing them again. Miss Caroline Lilley has done me the honour of agreeing to become my wife.'

It was out, pop, like a champagne cork. And now for the fizz, she thought, somewhat dazed, as people seemed to be rushing to her from all sides, her sisters, her father (looking just a little disapproving) and her mother reaching her first. Eleanor, Daniel – hundreds of kisses that must wear her face away like the pilgrim steps in Canterbury Cathedral, and her hands pumped up and down like Nanny Oates' well. And then came Lady Hunney, the cool cheek laid against her own, dripped poisoned honey. 'My dear Caroline, what a –' pause – 'delightful surprise. How sad my husband will be to have missed such an announcement. We shall all meet to discuss it.'

267

Shall, Caroline noted, as Reggie's arms encircled her waist in flagrant challenge to his mother. 'Thank you for wishing us well, Mother,' he said quietly.

It was *over*! She was engaged, and now she could relax and enjoy the evening with Reggie on her own cloud of happiness.

'How clever to announce it now, my darling,' Elizabeth whispered, trying only to let Caroline's happiness dismiss her anxiety over Isabel.

'What a perfect end to Isabel's wedding,' Felicia said.

'You'll be lady of the manor one day,' Phoebe pointed out, agog – not a statement calculated to thrill Lady Hunney, who was well within earshot, Caroline saw with amusement.

'I say, Reggie, if you're going to be in the family, you can teach me to drive the Perry.' George suddenly got excited.

'I can keep you in order too, young man.' Reggie aimed an amiable cuff at him. George dodged.

Mrs Dibble did now permit a tear to fall. Such a wonderful day. The rain had held off, Miss Isabel was on her honeymoon, Miss Caroline engaged to the young lord of the manor, and the ices had held out. Only Agnes was left. The latter was becoming a point of honour.

'I told Jamie he can go,' Percy said casually, strolling up to help her fold up the trestle tables. 'I can manage now.'

'You *what*?' His wife dropped the table end. 'Get him back this minute.'

'But—'

'Get him back, Percy, *please*. And tell him I want to see him in the servants' hall.'

If Daisy said please, it must be important, he supposed, even if it didn't make sense, so he obeyed more promptly than usual.

Mrs Dibble set out briskly in search of Agnes, and found her doing a load of dishes in the scullery. 'I want you to go to the servants' hall, Agnes, and mind you look busy.'

'What for?'

'Don't ask why, girl. Just do it, please.'

If Mrs Dibble said please, it must be important, so in the interests of the Rectory on this unusual day of days, Agnes went, highly puzzled.

Two minutes later, Jamie marched in, greatly relieved that he could stay after all, and didn't have to leave the sheltering walls of the Rectory for the unkind jungle of house and village. When he saw Agnes desultorily dusting the picture of the 'Unseen Guest at Every Table' which dominated the room, he stopped short. 'Where's Mrs Dibble?' he demanded truculently.

'She's not here, Jamie. I am.' Agnes in one gigantic leap seized the opportunity God or Mrs Dibble had thrown at her pain. 'And before you go and be cruel to me again, I'm going to say something.' She quickly manoeuvred herself between him and the door.

The boy's face grew mutinous, and he got away as far as possible from her. 'I don't want to hear nothing from you.'

'Yes, you do. I'm going to tell you this even if you never speak to me again. Rosie Trott tells me she's going to speak for Ruth, and give evidence that she saw you two going into Ebenezer's cottage.' Seeing he showed signs of protesting, she swept on: 'No, don't say *nothing*. I believe her, but shut up, Jamie, till I've finished. I've decided I don't care. I love you, Jamie Thorn, and I think you love me, and that's all that matters.'

He said nothing, just looked at her dumbfounded.

'And what's more,' she added quietly, 'I'll prove it just like you always wanted.'

Jamie began to rock to and fro on his feet, his face crumpling as he tried to hold back tears. He managed, but only just, and by that time he found he was in Agnes's arms and she was holding him like he'd always imagined, soft-like, not stiff.

'I'll tell you what happened, Agnes, honest then. Rosie did see us, me and Ruth. I was angry with you, you wouldn't do nothing and Len was going on at me for being – never loving a woman like he had, and it got really hard, Aggie, what with wanting you, and Ruth was eager, she always did like me, so one day I thought why not.'

'So it *is* your baby,' Agnes forced herself to say. She'd told herself she could face anything and she would.

'*No!*' The word burst out from him. 'I couldn't tell you, I couldn't. In the cottage I was all ready, I was going to, I wanted to, but at the last minute, well, I couldn't.' He flushed red.

'You realised you loved me?'

He swallowed, snatching at the easy way out. 'Something like that.' How could he explain to Agnes it wouldn't stay up at the last moment? What if he failed like that with Agnes? What if she jeered at him like Ruth had for being no man? 'Yes,' he agreed. 'I was all ready, and then I thought of you.'

She shuddered. 'I believe you, Jamie.'

'You said that before, Agnes.' There was no reproach in his voice, just hope this time.

'I sensed you were holding something back, I suppose. Now I know you're not.'

He drew a deep breath. He could be brave too. 'Look, Agnes, this time, this place ain't right. Someone might come in.'

'Yes.'

'Come for a walk bank holiday?'

'I'd like that, Jamie.'

The moths were already fluttering round the oil lamps as George began his sterling work with the gramophone. Greatly daring, he started with 'Dixie', until Caroline laughingly came across and said: 'Later, George, later. We've still got the old folks here.' Not Lady Hunney, thank goodness. Daniel had escorted her home, and then returned himself.

'Here's your rotten old waltz then.' George gave in cheerfully. He spotted Eleanor on her own. *Now* was his chance. He rushed across, bowed. 'May I have the pleasure?'

She curtseyed solemnly. 'Sir, you may.'

Caroline's euphoria swept her through the evening in an endless succession of 'Alexander's Ragtime Band' and 'Hitchy Koo', interspersed with 'The Merry Widow' waltz and 'If You Were the Only Girl in the World'.

'You are, you are.' whispered Reggie, he and Caroline so absorbed in each other they didn't even hear the telephone ring, late that evening, when the light had passed and only the oil lamps and their fluttering attendants illuminated the shadowy dancers of summer. There weren't many left by then, just family and close friends, as the Rector came out on the terrace and for no discernible reason, without a word from him, the dancers stopped, silhouetted statues.

'Sir John has telephoned me again in case there were still time to call back Isabel and Robert. There is not, and France mobilised late this afternoon.'

A heart-rending cry from Elizabeth: 'Isabel!'

'There is worse.' The Rector's voice was steady. 'Sir John met Lord Haldane who had just left the Admiralty. Winston Churchill has mobilised the fleet of Great Britain to protect the western shores of France. There is little doubt but that the Cabinet will ratify his decision tomorrow morning.'

'What does mobilise mean, Daniel?' Felicia whispered.

His face was grave. 'It means war.'

Chapter Eight

'All people that on earth do dwell.'

Here, in St Nicholas, with the organ booming out and
the voices of the congregation responding, Caroline found
it impossible to imagine that England could soon be at war.
There hadn't been a *real* war for a hundred years; wars took
place in far-off lands like South Africa, India, Abyssinia;
they were engravings in the *Illustrated London News*, or
memoirs written by officers or the occasional 'voice from
the ranks'. Wars meant a column of soldiers who from time
to time marched through the village bound for Aldershot
or the Channel ports, not something so close at hand as
France, and not to fight Austria or Germany, whose people
were so friendly and welcoming. True, the village and even
Father had joked about the 'German Menace' for years,
but only in connection with Dr Marden's dachshund.

While her father had been taking early service, Caroline

had volunteered to go in search of the newspaper which had not yet been delivered. It had not proved a difficult task to find the reason. Inside and outside Timms, the newsagent's, a large crowd of villagers was too busy discussing the news to allow time for delivery, and Tom Timms, trying his best to be apologetic though he had been the centre of the excited circle, explained that special editions of the newspapers were to be published throughout the day as more news became available. Whether they'd reach Ashden or not, he couldn't say, but his youngest was up at the railway station now, and his eldest was cycling into the Wells. Caroline remembered the day the news had come that the old king was passing through Ashden, and so the whole village had marched en bloc up to the railway station to cheer him as the train slowed down to acknowledge the doffed hats and shouts. Then, as now, intangible excitement leaped from person to person like signals along telegraph wires. It was evidence that Ashden was part of a larger world; something they preferred to ignore much of the time. This time it was different, however, for there was underlying anxiety evident in the group. Tom Timms, now, hadn't he been a soldier? Perhaps he was on the reserve list, and might be recalled. And wasn't one of the Mutters a Territorial? He too might even be involved if there were war.

The news in *The Observer* had not been reassuring. Nor had family prayers, with Mother bursting into tears over Isabel's safety halfway through the Twenty-third Psalm. Caroline had been more alarmed at that than at Isabel's plight. 'The editor strongly believes,' Father said, 'we should join the war to support France and Russia. Gavin is much respected. His views will carry weight.' It was a measure of the seriousness of the situation that Father spoke of the news at all, especially on a Sunday.

'Why should we?' Elizabeth asked vehemently. 'Would France do the same for us?'

'If France and Germany go to war, my dear, remember Belgium and Luxembourg lie between them, and Germany's first step would undoubtedly be to sweep through the smaller countries to attack France. We are pledged to defend Belgium's neutrality.'

'Politics,' his wife snorted. 'What of *Isabel*? What does Mr Gavin have to say on that?' Fear made her angry.

'The French government have taken over control of the railways, but they are planning to run a few trains to bring home British civilians today. The Germans are a long way from Paris, Elizabeth.'

Caroline saw Mother took this as a reproof, for she went silent the way she did when she disagreed with what you said, but had decided to wait for a better moment to say so. In any case, it had been at that moment that Mrs Dibble had come in, ostensibly to clear the china, though the pinkness of her cheeks suggested a different story.

'You look concerned, Mrs Dibble.' Laurence laid down *The Observer*.

'I thought you should know, Rector, the baker's just delivered. There's talk of the bread going up yet higher. The railway trains are packed with all those foreigners scuttling back home like rats, and, oh sir, I know my Lizzie's Rudolf was a bandsman when she met him on that trip to Brighton, and a bad day that was, but I'm sure she said he'd been a soldier in the German army. Will he have to go?'

'Is he naturalised, Mrs Dibble?'

'He married my Lizzie.'

'I fear that is not the same thing. But let us hope the war will be over so quickly he will not be needed.' The Rector hesitated, but saw no point in disguising the truth. 'He may have to leave for a little while, of course.'

'Showing themselves in their true colours now,' Mrs Dibble observed sharply. 'I always said there was something funny about him, being a German. Nothing they like better than a good war.' She looked at a dish of congealed eggs as though it held some kind of answer, and bore it menacingly out.

'Where are you going, Laurence?' Elizabeth asked, as he rose without finishing his toast.

'To think again about my sermon, in the light of what Mrs Dibble has said. The Archbishop of Canterbury has ordered special prayers for peace to be said today. If all of England feels as Mrs Dibble does, I fear the chances are not high. I must think how best to speak to Ashden.'

'"Peace I leave with you, my peace I give unto you: not as the world giveth, give I unto you. Let not your heart be troubled, neither let it be afraid". This is more than a text of scripture; this is *my* address to you, in St John's words.' The Rector paused, looking down at his congregation, larger than usual. He had been perturbed by the words he caught at random outside the church, some eager and excited, some anxious, as was he, for relatives abroad, but many dismissive, as though Ashden were not involved in what was happening around it. Over the centuries kings had come and gone, religions changed and politics raged. Ashden life, and that of hundreds of villages like it, had been essentially unchanged. Change had been a slow, cumbrous beast, as imperceptible as the erosion of water on stone. One day a farm might be run by Master Tom, the next day he'd become 'the old gentleman' and young Alfred, his son, had become the new master. Squire was Squire whether Sir John or Sir Reginald. He had heard Arthur Sharpe growling to Cyril Mutter earlier this morning: 'Makes no difference whether it's war or peace. Harvest is harvest, and muck is muck. Still go on, they do.' Laurence hoped he was right, with all his heart.

Less than a month ago some well-intentioned man had written to *The Times* suggesting every church used the tune 'Austria' to show sympathy with the Emperor for the loss of his son, the Archduke. He wondered from how many churches 'Praise the Lord, ye Heavens Adore Him' had rung out that day. St Nicholas was one. It had seemed a small enough gesture. Yet now, thanks to Austria, the loss of the peace of Europe was probable. The Emperor and his ally the Kaiser had struck the tinderbox to begin the conflagration. Ashden itself was an example of how easily it could happen. Take Jamie Thorn: one small incident that resulted in rough music and a reopening of the Mutter–Thorn feud. He had damped down the fires but not quenched them. They smouldered on.

'Peace has a semaphore of its own. If we in Ashden heed St John's words then Ashden will survive. "Not as the world giveth, give I unto you". If England heeds these words, she will survive, and if Europe heeds them, it too will survive. If there is a war, and there is a just cause for us to fight it, then we do so for the sake of every innocent man, woman and child, whether they be in Europe or here, Germany or Ashden. But to do so, Ashden must find its own peace. No more rough music, or the drumbeat we shall follow will bring destruction.'

Looking round at the faces of the congregation, Caroline wondered if it understood what he was trying to say, or whether the wider implications were lost in the immediate message of 'no more rough music'.

'I quite agree with the Rector.' A shrill voice croaked out behind, a shockwave ran round the congregation, and two hundred necks craned round curiously to see who had dared interrupt the service.

'It's the Misses Norville,' Phoebe hissed with excitement at Caroline's side. 'Look! It *must* be them. Who else could it be?'

Caroline needed no bidding to turn round. In the Norville pew, empty for so long, stood the two Miss Norvilles dressed uniformly in black, save for white lace dotted strategically at necks and wrists; they wore the black bonnets and full skirts of the mid-Victorian period, and stood side by side like two forbidding rooks, their gloved hands gripping the front edge of the pew. Then one of them sank back almost out of sight as she sat down, and left the 'stage' to her sister.

'My sister and I have an announcement to make.'

'That must be Miss Emily, the elder of the two.' Caroline was so fascinated by the sight of them, she hardly took in what they were saying. She hadn't seen them in church since she was about eight.

Miss Emily promptly sat down. Miss Charlotte stood up. 'We understand there is some question of war with Germany. My sister and I have therefore decided to fortify Castle Tillow.'

The Rector, as taken aback as his congregation, thought quickly. They were old, they were recluses, they should not be figures of fun. 'The battleground is in Europe, ladies,' he answered gently. 'And today we pray that there will be no battleground.'

The sisters promptly changed places again, as Miss Emily rose: '*We* may have peace in our hearts, Rector, but do the Germans?'

The Rector saw a ripple of comprehension run round his congregation. There must be an end to this, quickly. 'The same God is Father to all peoples, and like any father can bring peace to His children, if they but stop to listen.'

'But our dear *mother* told us,' Miss Charlotte retorted shrilly, rising like a jack-in-a-box, 'that Old Boney would get us one day. This Kaiser is quite clearly another Bonaparte. There *will* be an invasion.'

The mischief was done, as suddenly the congregation realised the full drift of what the Norvilles were saying. The Rector could almost see the word 'invasion' running along the pews.

'Wire netting,' Miss Emily cried excitedly, 'and Johnson is digging a moat. Everyone is welcome to shelter in the Castle. We have ammunition and chickens and we will issue passwords –'

The ripple of fear suddenly turned to laughter, as the idea of the Misses Norville defending Ashden with bows and arrows against the Germans took the congregation's fancy. The Rector was about to seize his opportunity, when Lady Hunney, quicker still, determined to secure her position as the lady of the manor.

'Unfortunately the Misses Norville dwell in the past,' she announced from her pew, not condescending to stand. 'The Hunneys do not. My husband is working in Whitehall trying his best to avert this crisis; *that* is positive, to concentrate on defence is an invitation to be attacked.'

'Let us remember that this is the House of God in which He alone rules. It is time we gave Him leave to speak,' the Rector thundered, incensed that Maud was turning this into a political debating ground. If in this church people could not be calm, what hope for Europe? 'Let us pray. And let us all remember that in Germany and in Austria too, people are on their knees praying to the same God, the only God, for *peace*.'

God sends meat, and the Devil sends cooks, the Rector thought as he made his way back to the Rectory later. Perhaps those words written in the seventeenth century could be the basis of a sermon one day. This morning had presented an extraordinary crisis, not just to his authority, but God's. The Devil's cooks had come in the guise of two eccentric old ladies, but their words could spread the deadly poison of fear through the community. Had God sent the laughter to dispel the poison? Did not laughter grease the wheels of daily life? He heard through the open door as he approached the sound of Caroline's laugh followed by a bellow from George, and rejoiced at the Rectory's normality. Could the Rectory supply the strength he needed without the sound of the girls' voices,

George's cheerful shouts, his wife's ever-present soothing command within these walls?

That evening after evensong there was a concert on Bankside given by the village band; the warm evening was still with an air of expectancy and, as the last sounds of the brass died away, the band spontaneously broke into the National Anthem. With one accord the audience rose from the grass and makeshift chairs. As it finished, Cyril Mutter looked round at him from the row in front. 'No rough music, eh, Rector?' he said gruffly. 'Eh, Alfred Thorn?'

'The Towers has had no news.' Laurence hung up the telephone receiver early on Monday morning. It had been a vain hope that Isabel and Robert might have returned already. Even in the best of times, they would scarcely have had time to arrive in Paris, and take a return train and steamer. With every form of transport heavily overcrowded in both directions, normal schedules would have been abandoned, he reasoned, and there would surely be more trains arranged for foreign civilians. The telegraph office at Ashden railway station had been open day and night, as was the post office, and it was some comfort to hear that no civilian telegraphs were coming in from overseas. Isabel and Robert might arrive at any moment.

'No harm can come to them, Elizabeth,' he reiterated for the umpteenth time. Common sense told him so, but sometimes sense could be outridden by emotions.

'Has the newspaper anything to say, Laurence?' was her only reply. Elizabeth stared through the window, as if she hoped to see her daughter running down the path. She had no strength of will to do anything else. All her energy was being spent on worrying about Isabel.

'Germany has declared war on France. But Elizabeth, there is still Belgium to cross, and as yet Germany has not done so.' He did not tell her German troops were already in Luxembourg, and were rumoured to be massing on the Belgian border.

'There will be war, I know it. The bicycle shop has already run out of oil, and the Lettices' stock is severely depleted. Mrs Dibble had great trouble in obtaining haricot beans. The Sharpes tell her they have sold all their cheese in *advance*, and Mrs Marden tells me even Harrods is running out of provisions. Women are taking *dustbins* in to fill with stores. And most of our sugar comes from Germany and Austria. I shall speak to—'

The Rector interrupted, seized by sudden fear. He could not do what he might have to do for Ashden if Elizabeth, his strength and love, were not at his side in spirit as well as physically. The wheels of the Rectory had to continue turning smoothly, but there was more to that than the simply material. He too was beside himself with anxiety over Isabel, but there were other calls on him – and therefore on his wife.

'Elizabeth, come back to me.'

She turned at last. 'I don't know what you mean, Laurence.' But she did, and had not the strength to face it. For the first time in twenty-seven years, the interests of Ashden, the Rectory and motherhood were not as one. There was no clear path for her, and God had chosen to flicker His lamps so that they danced confusingly over all.

'If the store runs out of beans,' Laurence continued doggedly, 'we shall gather dandelions, if of sugar, we shall use honey and glucose, and if the bicycle shop of oil we shall make candles – together, Elizabeth. But what shall I do, what will Ashden do, if *we* run out of hope and purpose? You have chosen your own wise path, here, my love, avoided essentially purposeless commitments in a greater need, but if war comes, Elizabeth, the whole of Ashden will be our family and it needs you as well as me.'

'I cannot, Laurence, I might not have the strength,' she pleaded.

'Together we do, my love, you and I and God.'

She took a deep breath and tried. 'I hear dandelion leaves are extremely nutritious.' She thought she would not mention to Laurence that Mrs Dibble had successfully obtained the last sack of potatoes from Farmer Lake.

Always Isabel. No one thought of *her*, Phoebe sulked. Even now Isabel was married, she was still managing to dominate the conversation. It was all: 'how will Isabel get home from Paris' and never 'how will Phoebe get *to* it.' She was still determined to go to finishing school. No rotten Kaiser was going to stop her. It simply wasn't fair. Anyway, she consoled herself, the hullabaloo would probably be over in a week or two, and there would be plenty of time to travel to Paris in September. Meanwhile how was she going to exist through boring August?

Somehow, Caroline reflected gloomily, she and Reggie seemed to have got squeezed between the concentric circles she so blithely dreamed up only a few weeks ago. So far from being concentric, they now appeared to be on a head-on collision course.

The whole village, confident that fair weather would continue for ever, and planning to embark on its usual bank holiday occupations of cricket (either discussion of the Oval match or playing in Ashden's), lazing outside the Norville Arms, at the Tunbridge Wells fair, or on a day trip to the seaside, was prepared to indulge also in ever-mutating discussion groups on the war news. Views ranged, so far as Caroline had heard, from expectation of imminent invasion by hordes of German troops in horned helmets, up to those prepared to set off today to fight the foe with hop-dogs or hammers, and down to those who suggested Great Britain should mind its own Pygmalion business and get on with the harvest. Tension grew as news filtered through of naval reservists having already left the village. The two Tilbury brothers had departed yesterday, and what were their wives to do now? Nothing about pay, nothing about allowances, just report for duty.

But Caroline listened with only half an ear; the other half, the more prominent of the two, told her that today she would see Reggie. There had been no sign of him yesterday, but she had not expected it, for he had warned her that his mother had commanded all three to attend what should have been Daniel's last Sunday luncheon in the Manor. When he arrived earlier than she expected, Caroline ran downstairs eagerly. They had been planning a trip to the seaside, but to her disappointment he had different ideas. 'I thought we might get news of Isabel quicker,' he said to her ingenuously, 'if we went up to London, and called on Father.'

She acquiesced, but she had longed for a day away from Ashden, and with Reggie, not surrounded by the crowds of London, especially at such a time. Moreover, he suggested travelling by train not motor car, and she was dressed for the seaside, *not* London, in a light blue voile gown which had seen several seasons but remained a firm favourite. Elegant it was not, comfortable it was.

'I don't believe this is your idea,' she said glumly on the way to the station.

He grinned shamefacedly. 'Pa hasn't been able to telephone, and we don't feel we should interrupt him by telephone, so Mother has despatched me to call in and find out when she can expect to see him again. What a question at such a time!'

'With *me*?'

'Accompanied by Daniel was her suggestion. But Daniel's so furious he can't go to Greece, I told him to push off and find Felicia.'

'Lucky Felicia, if he's in that mood.'

'She has a good effect on him. He becomes a more reasonable human being when she's around. Haven't you noticed? In fact, he *behaves* like a human being, and not like a young Apollo.'

'Does he want to marry her?' Caroline asked bluntly.

He hesitated. 'Daniel is set on travelling. I think he has some idea of rushing round the world and coming back to claim her like Jacob and Rachel in the Bible.'

'Jacob waited fourteen years.'

'Only because he got palmed off with the ugly sister. No danger of that now I've – ouch!' He dodged as she whacked him with her handbag.

'Is your mother still speaking to you?' she deemed it safe enough to venture.

'Yes.' He seemed surprised. 'Why?'

'Our engagement,' she reminded him, taken aback.

'Mother is the best Lord Nelson I ever met. She doesn't like it happening so she assumes it isn't. Her blind eye is so confident she's not even annoyed about it.'

Caroline felt dismissed, a woman of no consequence, and somewhat cross with Reggie, although she could think of no logical reason why this should be so.

The train from Tunbridge Wells was late and already full. Only with difficulty did she manage to squeeze into the compartment, and Reggie was left standing all the way to Victoria. At East Grinstead, even more people crowded in, and at the thought of another hour and twenty minutes at least ahead, her heart sank. She tried to pretend it was fun, but the heat soon sapped energy, and she was glad when they arrived and could take some refreshment. That too was a struggle, for Victoria was packed with naval servicemen, and still lots of foreigners, judging by the babble of French and German. They weren't even at odds with each other, preoccupied with their individual problems and their own leave-takings, special trains running, heartbreaking scenes of women clasped in foreign husbands' and sweethearts' arms. Caroline wondered if any of them was Mrs Dibble's Lizzie's Rudolf. The crowd was swelled by holidaymakers whose trains had been cancelled, taken over by the Government for troops. They were easy to spot for they, like her, were in seaside attire, boaters, blazers, light summer dresses. It was as if Brighton Pier had been dumped in Victoria Station by a large wave. Most of them, it seemed to her, were making for St James's Park, just as she and Reggie were. She was used to seeing the Park full of nannies out with their charges in perambulators, now it was swamped by holidaymakers, sweethearts and sightseers, pulled there by the general humming of the air.

'Exciting, isn't it?' Reggie hugged her, as they at last found a bench to sit on.

'Yes.' She meant it. It was hard not to be infected by the energy that seemed to be flowing through the crowds around them. 'Do you think we'll be drawn in, Reggie?'

'I don't think it will come to that. The Kaiser is a madman, so they say.' Reggie put on a funny face, placed his forefinger under his nose, jumped up and strutted along the path, goose-stepping, to the amusement of strollers-by.

'Don't joke.' She caught his arm in sudden alarm and he sat down again. 'It *is* serious.'

'We don't make it better by long faces.'

A burly young man walked by with his arm round his lady-love, and she found herself longing to feel Reggie's round her again, but he seemed preoccupied. She felt she was at the back, not the forefront of his thoughts, and it alarmed her.

'A soldier and his lass,' he observed.

'He looks more like a plumber to me.'

'I meant me.'

'You?'

287

A terrible chasm opened before her. Reggie and Daniel both had OTC experience. Suppose in due course they had to join in this war? Worse, suppose they *wanted* to? With alarm, she remembered Reggie's thwarted desire for an army career. Surely the Regular Army would be enough to protect Britain? And, if not, the Reserves and the Territorials? After Lord Haldane's reforms, its organisation and manpower must be quite adequate to protect France and Belgium against Germany, formidable though Germany's army was said to be. In Ashden Caroline's feet had felt securely on the ground. Here, she felt thrown out of her depth, at one moment sucking at an ice cream (forbidden in Ashden) as though this were Margate on a perfect bank holiday, and at another in the midst of a major crisis. What was worse, it affected *her*. Reggie might go. Was that why he was so preoccupied, so exhilarated? She recalled all the times he had spoken so wistfully of how he had wanted an army career. Suppose that was why he was here, to beg his father to let him go to war? Daniel would be here now; he could run the estate, Reggie might argue. She fought to subdue panic so that Reggie should notice nothing, and concentrated on the crowds around. Everywhere they lined the streets, watching the motor cars passing in to Downing Street, or towards the Houses of Parliament, and Whitehall. All those people locked in conference on a scorching hot day like this. Did the Kaiser not take time for a summer holiday, she thought irrelevantly, to distract herself.

Halfway through the afternoon, the crowds began by a sort of osmosis to head towards the Mall, and hearing a whisper: 'His Majesty', they followed, caught up in the surging mass. They arrived at the Mall just as the open car went by carrying King George and Queen Mary with the Prince of Wales. Caroline found herself waving and cheering with the rest, a lump in her throat; it was impossible not to be moved by this symbol of their own great country and Empire. His father's work for peace in Europe may come to nothing, King George seemed to be implying, but I am still here, and here I shall remain.

Reggie grabbed the latest edition of a newspaper as soon as the motor car had passed. 'Shall we stay on this evening, Caroline?' he asked casually. 'I'd like to try to see Father, and I don't feel I can barge into the War Office at the moment. He's staying in Queen Anne's Gate with Lord Haldane and Grey, too, the Foreign Secretary. It's possible he may have news from Paris. Look, I can whizz into my club and telephone him to see if we can meet him, and I can telephone your parents.'

Caroline hadn't even given a thought to what her parents might be thinking. Now she did: a late train home, and just possibly no train home if the situation deteriorated. A few days ago it would have mattered so much, her being alone with Reggie. Now it seemed immaterial. She was not 'with Reggie'; he had slipped from her; he was hearing not the birdsong in St James's Park but some siren voice calling him to the Colours, thousands upon thousands at his side, all marching in pursuit of some vague concept named honour.

'It's worrying, all this talk of war,' Agnes said primly, trying to think of something to say, when there was so much needed saying.

'Won't affect us, will it?' said Jamie solidly, lying back

on the grass with his hands behind his head. 'Never does in the country. Wars and politics are for townsfolk, not us. But it's us keeps the country going while they get on with their games.'

She laughed at him. 'What if another William the Conqueror strolls in?'

'The Tommies can deal with him, while we get on getting corn in, and shoeing horses. They still have to be shod and, before you say it, Aggie, I know there aren't so many now. I don't want to work in a shop all my life. They'll all be motor-forges soon. I reckon that's what I'd like to be, a motor-forger.'

'You're daft, Jamie Thorn.' She leaned over and, greatly daring, tickled his nose with a piece of grass. 'You've never ever even been in a motor car, I'll be bound.'

'I have so. Lots of times. Anyway, you don't have to have kissed a girl to know you'd like to. Or that you'd enjoy it.' He grinned wickedly. 'Only I weren't going to say kissed.'

'Jamie Thorn, I'm surprised at you.'

'No, you're not, Aggie.' A pause. 'It's very quiet here. No one about.'

'Apart from boats up and down the river, and them fishermen over there.' Something in her chest seemed to be hammering at her.

'We could move further back, get out of the heat, among the trees.'

A longer pause. 'It *is* a little warm here,' she admitted. She jumped to her feet and began to gather up their belongings, following his rigid back into the woodland. It

290

felt strange beginning to undress before Jamie, until she saw he was as shy as she was. That made her feel a little better. 'Do we have to take off everything, Jamie?' she managed to blurt out.

The thought of it made him so hard he had to turn away. 'Be quick, Aggie,' he almost choked. 'Just . . . just.' He couldn't say it as he fumbled with his trousers and when he looked round there was a neat pile of calico and Aggie sitting down hugging her skirt round her knees. Somehow that made him even harder, and he sat down by her side. 'Sure, Aggie?'

'Yes, Jamie.'

'Suppose it happens again like it did – that time?' He tried to explain and she listened.

'We've the rest of our lives to make it all right.' So they had, so they had.

Awkwardly he pushed at her skirt, and then her arms were round him and it was all fumbling and pushing until he found the place. He didn't stop to wonder if it would be all right; he knew it would be and it was. At first he was afraid of hurting her, but he couldn't do anything about it, so he pushed on. She let out a yelp, but all she said was, 'Go on, my lover, go on.'

There wasn't any need to worry this time, and he was past thinking anyway, just full of a roaring and a loving that swelled up higher and higher, taking him over completely until he burst into her, and saw she was there, his beautiful, beautiful Agnes, and then she wasn't because he was crying. Not for long though.

'I'll have the biggest and best motor-forge in Sussex,' he vowed jubilantly, lying back on the grass afterwards.

'That's because you'll be my missis. You could serve teas and ices.'

'Oh, *yes.*'

'The nippers can help you,' he offered boldly.

'Get on with you, Jamie Thorn.'

Sir John returned briefly to see his son at Queen Anne's Gate in the middle of the evening. He greeted Caroline courteously enough, but she knew she was an irrelevance. His words were for Reggie, not because he was his son but because this was war and men's business. Dazed by the unreality of the circumstances, she felt this justified, but as the group talk continued she began to feel excluded. Did not women suffer as much in war as men, though in different ways? And why should those ways always be different? Sir John was grey-faced from lack of sleep and the gravity of the situation, and was clearly anxious to return to the War Office.

'Germany has demanded free passage through Belgium. It will not be granted, of course, and we shall issue an ultimatum this evening giving them twenty-four hours to guarantee Belgium's neutrality.'

'Will they do so?' Reggie demanded.

'Luxembourg is already invaded. That is your answer. Our own mobilisation orders are agreed, and will be issued tomorrow morning.'

'But what about Ireland? Suppose they seize their opportunity for civil war?'

'John Redmond has pledged Ireland's support in this crisis. They will fight with us.'

'And France?' Caroline did not dare ask directly about Isabel in the light of such awe-inspiring news.

'Paris is calmly resigned to war. There are already skirmishes in the east.' Then Sir John did recollect what had been happening in Ashden. 'You must forgive me, my dear, for my preoccupation. I understand you and Reginald announced your engagement on Saturday. I must congratulate you, though I could have wished—'

'*What*, Father?' Reggie interrupted angrily.

'A better time, my son.' He paused. 'You will no doubt be discussing the situation with Daniel when you return home?'

Innocent words, but the look father and son exchanged terrified Caroline. She did not speak lest the sickness in her stomach overwhelm her, after they left Queen Anne's Gate. She realised that instinctively they were walking not towards Victoria Station, but towards the Mall, where crowds were surging up towards Buckingham Palace, obviously for an expected appearance by King George and Queen Mary. When at last the doors opened and they came on to the balcony, the whole crowd around them seemed to explode in one vast cheer. The sound of 'Rule Britannia' and 'God Save the King' enveloped them, Union Jacks and tricolours were waving on all sides, picking up the blood red of the geraniuims bedecking the palace, and caught up in the euphoria they found themselves singing too.

'Why should we want to sing?' she asked Reggie, as they fought their way through the crowds back to the railway station. 'Is it for war?'

'No. I think it is for England.' he replied soberly, but

as she turned to look at him she sensed that, beneath his serious expression, excitement was still pulsating.

The train did not reach Ashden until well after midnight, and as they picked their way in the darkness down Station Road, Reggie's arm around her waist, all was quiet after the uproar of London. Only one remaining cottager still kept a vigil. On Bankside old Jacob Timms, father of the newsagent, was sitting in his chair outside his cottage, the oil lamp glowing within, picking out his dark silhouette. He had been there for many, many hours, and until midnight there had been a hushed circle of people listening as he read out the news from London, as each special edition arrived.

On his way home from the War Office late that night, Sir John Hunney called in to the Foreign Office to see the Foreign Secretary. He found him with a friend. The ultimatum to Berlin had been given, now came the waiting. 'I'll turn down the lamps,' he offered. 'Then you can see the people more clearly. It is a strengthening sight.'

The Foreign Secretary moved to the window, and looked out into the darkness. 'The lamps are going out all over Europe. We shall not see them lit again in our lifetime.'

Caroline could not sleep that night, though little enough remained of it. Perhaps it was the fast-moving events of the day, whose end was not yet known, perhaps the knowledge that the happiness that had been so nearly within her grasp had slipped an inch or two away. In the morning she rose to face the inevitable recriminations for her late homecoming, but to her surprise there were none. Her father was engrossed in *The Times,* and Felicia was reading over his shoulder. Why? Caroline wondered instantly. Felicia was never normally interested in world events, but she had spent the day with Daniel. Nonsense. Caroline tried to take hold of herself. She was overtired and her imagination was galloping as usual well in advance of facts.

'Is there news of Isabel?' she asked anxiously.

'None. Your mother has gone to calm Mrs Swinford-Browne.'

Mother calm her? Father looked at her in that way of his which said: I know what you're thinking. Keep it merely as a thought. So Caroline did. She seized the paper after her father left for Matins, finding a perverse comfort in the way *The Times* maintained its formal order: a front page of personal advertisements, page after page of statistics and law reports, and in the very middle the war news. It seemed to help keep it in perspective – temporarily.

Felicia continued to read over her shoulder, interspersed with prowls around the room. Finally she observed, 'The Honourable Artillery Company is seeking what it describes as 'eligible recruits' because it is not up to strength. Will many regiments do that, do you think?'

Caroline laid the newspaper down, detecting the overdone casualness in her sister's voice. 'I don't know, Felicia.' She meant, and Felicia knew she did, I don't know if Daniel will want to go to war. I don't know if Reggie will. 'How's Mother?' she asked, determined to keep off those imponderable, terrifying unknowns.

'Better.'

'Even if Isabel has an uncomfortable journey, she will

get back,' Caroline pointed out. 'She's not in Brussels, she's in Paris.'

'Perhaps,' Felicia said quietly, 'but if she were being sensible she'd be back by now. The last of the special trains has come in, and they weren't on it.'

'When was Isabel ever sensible? But that doesn't mean she's in danger, merely that she's decided not to sacrifice her honeymoon to the Germans. And darling Edith will have instructed her that it isn't nice for a young gel to send postcards on a honeymoon.' If Caroline had hoped to make Felicia laugh, she was disappointed.

'A column of soldiers came through yesterday. They had full packs and they were watering the horses at the pond. They were singing "It's a Long Way to Tipperary" just as though there were no emergency. They sounded so cheerful.'

Caroline followed these inconsequential comments exactly, and braced herself. 'British soldiers always do,' she commented lightly.

'That's what Kipling says in his verse. I wonder if it's really true? I tried to think of the men yesterday under fire—'

'Don't, Felicia, please. Didn't Mother say we should visit the wives of the Tilbury brothers to see if they are in need with their husbands going away so unexpectedly.'

'Yes, she did. We'll go after breakfast. I'm sorry, Caroline.'

George was out for the day with a friend from Skinners, and Phoebe had decided to visit Philip Ryde's sister, Beatrice, with whom he lived. When Felicia and Caroline too had departed, Elizabeth, returned from The Towers exhausted from her endeavours, seized the chance to return to her sole preoccupation.

'Edith is distraught, Laurence. Could we not telephone Sir John to cable the British Ambassador in Paris? Isabel *is* our daughter?'

'How many other daughters, how many sons,' he replied, torn apart. 'I cannot do it, Elizabeth. All cable lines to Paris are needed in the general good. The ambassador would have notified the Government if there were danger to or casualties among civilians. Today is not the day to press our investigations. France's railways are needed for troop movements now they have mobilised. As soon as the immediate need is over, their government will return to civilian problems.'

Elizabeth battled with a situation she had never envisaged, and the need to maintain the calm Laurence demanded of her. So easy to demand, so hard to live up to. 'Without let or hindrance, her passport says,' she burst out. 'These Germans will stop at nothing. They will sweep through Belgium, and on to Paris. Will one British passport stop them?'

'Have mercy, Elizabeth,' he shouted, losing his own control. 'I do not *know*.'

'No. We neither of us do.' There was bitterness in her voice. 'I suppose I should speak to Mrs Dibble about luncheon.' The curate and church officers were coming unexpectedly. So easy once. Now, with the sudden and horrific threat of food shortages hanging over them, it was a terrifying prospect. 'Consider the lilies of the field,' Laurence would say. Well, they were the Lilleys of the Rectory and *she* was the one who had to plan luncheon. That had nothing to do with patriotism, only common sense. Elizabeth felt as if she were bursting out of her clothes with pent-up emotion. Was there nowhere in this huge old rectory where she could cry alone? No, everywhere she would be under the eye of God, she told herself. A sympathetic eye, no doubt, but an inexorable one. She must stand firm.

Margaret Dibble had sensibly not consulted the Rector or Mrs Lilley on all matters integral to the well-being of the Rectory. She was making her own arrangements. Now was the time for good customers to reap their rewards. She'd start with Sebastian Grendel and the Lettices.

Caroline could not bear the waiting: waiting for Reggie to call, waiting for news of Isabel, waiting for war news on the telegraph or newspaper. Twice on the Tuesday morning she and Felicia walked up Station Road to wait with countless others for the train from London and East Grinstead. Tom Timms hardly had time to get the latest editions back to his newsagent's shop before they were all sold to people grabbing them en route. There seemed to be general satisfaction that the die was cast in the form of the ultimatum to Germany, and talk turned to Jack Hobbs playing at the Oval today, where Surrey was playing Nottinghamshire, and whether he'd make his 800th run. When the midday editions reached them early in the afternoon it caused little further excitement, for everyone had expected the news they read – that German troops had crossed the Belgian border.

'Old Kaiser Bill will get his whiskers singed, eh?' she heard Len Thorn shouting. Caroline hoped Kaiser Bill was taking due note. Len was a powerful man.

By three o'clock she was fretting because there was still no sign of Reggie. To her horror, she suddenly realised it was Tuesday and she had completely forgotten her job at the Manor. True, the bank holiday had been extended for two days, but she suspected Lady Hunney would not recognise this as any reason for her absence from her post of duty in the library. Moreover Reggie would be expecting to see her there. She part ran, part walked, and arrived breathless to find Lady Hunney advancing towards her, as Parker let her in, with all the menace of a troop of Prussian cavalry. *Why* oh why had she foolishly used the front door. Appearances were deceptive, however, for Lady Hunney was lacking her usual fire.

'Reginald is not here, Caroline. Neither of my sons is. They are in London.'

Caroline was taken aback. 'But we came home last night.' It was a foolish rejoinder, but Lady Hunney answered.

'They have left again. I think, Caroline, they *wish* to be in London for some reason.' Her voice lacked its usual barb, which Caroline found almost more terrifying than the usual honeyed serpent of her tongue.

'Shall I carry on working in the library, Lady Hunney?' It was all she could manage. Caroline realised now they shared a common fear, but it was one that could never be voiced between them.

'If you wish. The time may pass the quicker. I envy you.'

Envy? More worried than ever, Caroline made her way to the library, but for once even this failed to take her mind off the outside world.

'Caroline, if there is a war –' Felicia began, as Ahab bounded off in haphazard pursuit of whatever rabbits were foolish enough to remain at their sunset supper.

'I've decided not to think about it. It may not happen,' Caroline butted in firmly.

'It will, now Germany is invading Belgium. How could we not fight such an aggressor? Suppose this were France, and we were Belgian or French, watching rabbits jump around just before we went to bed? Suppose we were terrified that this meadow would be crushed by tramping German boots tomorrow? It must be terrible – all the menfolk leaving home, leaving wives to look after children alone. And who will do their work while they are away? Farmer *Lake* is a Reservist. He'd have to go. Suppose German troops came marching up Silly Lane and took over Owlers farm, demanding all their food?'

Caroline thought about the Miss Norvilles, and the astonishing events of Sunday. It seemed funny in retrospect, but it hadn't at the time, and just suppose it wasn't such a joke? Suppose the Germans *did* come? No, she would not think that way. Britain was still an island even if we did enter the war, the Channel was the greatest barricade we had, and the British Navy manned it. The Kaiser would be banging his head on a brick wall if he tried to send invasion ships across.

A special family prayers that evening after 'Rector's

Hour' was taken by Father, who led prayers for the peace of the world. Mrs Dibble was crying, Caroline noticed, puzzled until Felicia reminded her that Joe Dibble was a Territorial. She reproached herself that she had been worrying so much about Reggie she was forgetting the others of the household. Surely Territorials weren't being called up? If they were . . . Her fears deepened, and later she manufactured a reason for herself to meet the incoming trains from London, hoping against hope to see Reggie. All she saw were the usual groups, sometimes silent, sometimes animatedly arguing over whether or not Ashden should be involved in the war. As though it could declare itself neutral, she thought dispiritedly. No, for once Ashden had to face the fact – as she did – that they were part of England, that England was part of Great Britain, that Great Britain was part of an Empire – and that the Empire was about to clash with the rest of the world. She watched packets and newspapers being flung out by the guards. The excitement of yesterday had evaporated now, and people read the news quietly. That England would be at war by midnight was taken for granted.

And it was. Major-General Sir John Hunney in the War Office was informed that at eleven o'clock the cable line to Berlin had been cut, and that the navy had been ordered to commence hostilities against Germany. He put on his cap and prepared to leave. Sleep would come easy tonight, but what of tomorrow and all the morrows that followed it?

Elizabeth tossed and turned by Laurence's side, trying not to disturb his sleep, but frantic at her inability to solve the problems crowding in upon her: Isabel stranded in Paris, perhaps crying for her mother who could not help; the bank rate up to ten per cent, the price of bread and wheat up – which meant *everything* would go up. How would the poor manage? How would *they* manage? Who would tend the farms? What would happen to Phoebe now? She reminded herself she had four other children besides Isabel; George was still a child, and all of them, not to mention Laurence, needed her strength, not her weakness. I'll try harder, she told God desperately. I'll try harder, she told Laurence with more conviction. He mumbled something in his sleep, and she thought how much she loved him.

The telegraph and post offices had never handled so many telegrams at once; they all had more or less the same message – and the same shock impact. Joe Dibble, the Dibble's eldest son, was a gardener in Forest Row. He was also a Territorial, and he looked blankly at the telegram.

'What's the matter, Joe?' His wife had heard his cry.

'Stone the bally crows. I've been called up.'

'Called up where?'

'The army.'

Muriel Dibble, in the family way with their second child, stared at him uncomprehendingly. 'You'll be back tonight, won't you?'

'I – I dunno. Have to see what they say, won't I?'

'Is it this war?' she asked with sudden understanding. 'You ain't even got a rifle. What good are you?'

'Just a formality, like.' He stared at the buff paper as though the bald words could provide the answer. What he'd never told Muriel was that in a fit of bravado, he'd signed the General Service Obligation. Didn't that mean they could send him overseas? Still, most like it would never happen.

Another telegram went to Farmer Lake at Owlers Farm. He'd almost forgotten he was on the reserve list. Dazed, he looked at the fields of corn as yet ungathered. Who was to get the bloody harvest home this year? Perhaps they'd wait a bit, if he explained. He'd been running the farm so long now since his brother was killed when a wagon crushed him, he'd completely scrubbed the whole army from his mind.

Another went to Jim Lettice, the Ashden postman. The telegram said nothing about allowances or pay and that was hard with three babes under six. Still, if the country needed him he'd go and be proud of it. He went upstairs to the cupboard where he kept his mementoes of service days. He'd been twenty when the South African war ended. Now he was thirty-two, but all the better fighter for it, he reckoned. The Kaiser would have second thoughts now he knew the British lion was roaring.

'By Jove, this has woken the old country up.' Reggie was jubilant as he and Daniel left the War Office and sauntered into the Park on Wednesday. This was a new Britain. War had been declared and it was a country reborn with a new purpose, to defend gallant little Belgium. He knew his father was aggrieved about this as a reason for war, seeing it as Prime Minister Asquith's ploy for inducing a reluctant country to fight a very necessary war, but so far as he was concerned, *that* was indeed why he was going. That, and the chance of some action, he admitted honestly to himself. But it was a war of right against might, and how could England turn a blind eye? He watched a soldier kissing his sweetheart as if he wouldn't see her for a hundred years, and guiltily remembered he hadn't told Caroline he was coming up to London again. He'd meant to. He would have to talk to her about marriage before he left. Then he was overtaken by the immediacy of the moment again, as he caught Daniel's eye.

'Soldiers of the King, eh? Here, you, have this shilling!' He tossed a shilling at a surprised and grateful beggar. 'I'll be getting another one any moment now. Bestowed on me by His Majesty the King. It's rotten we can't serve together. I can't think why Pater's against brothers serving in the same regiment. Bad for discipline? Balderdash.'

'We may neither of us be serving anywhere,' Daniel warned him, but his excited face betrayed his own lack of doubt. 'We've still got to go before the board in Oxford, tomorrow.'

'Only for a rubber stamp.' Reggie dismissed this. 'They won't turn us down. The Pater must be right about these temporary university commissions for fellows with OTC experience; we're lucky that with the Pater we've just jumped the gun a day or two before Kitchener's official announcement. All we have to do is look like the keen, manly university types we are. Easier for you than me. You still are. I'm a careworn man of the world.'

'In that case I'll go to the Royal Sussex, and you can take the King's Own commission.' For once their father had done them proud, sympathising with their immediate desire to volunteer and devoting time in the War Office to finding out immediately two crack regiments that were not up to full active service strength.

'Dash it, no,' Reggie complained. 'Anyway, we don't *know* either will take us.'

'Pa checked with the CO. They can take us, if the board passes us. Me for the Royal Sussex then.'

'I'll toss you for it,' Reggie said generously. 'I won't insist on my rights as elder brother.'

'You've chucked your shilling away now. I've got one.' Solemnly Daniel flicked the coin up into the sunny blue sky.

'Tails,' called Reggie, craning over Daniel's hand, as he slowly withdrew the other one.

'Tails it is.' Daniel pulled a face, and clapped Reggie on the back. 'Well, the King's Own is a decent regiment too.'

For a moment, Reggie was tempted to say you take the Royal Sussex. Daniel had after all had the disappointment of his travels being cancelled, but then he changed his mind. Daniel could go to Greece as soon as this bother was over, whereas Reggie would never get another chance of a bash in the Royal Sussex.

'I don't mind, old fellow,' Daniel assured him, grinning, then chanted: 'The Royal Sussex is going away, Leaving the girls in the family way.'

'Not me,' his brother assured him virtuously, as Caroline leaped into his mind again. She'd understand, though. They could wed as soon as he came back. These university commissions were for single fellows only, of course, but the Pater reckoned it would all be over by Christmas, and he'd have made her proud of him by then.

* * *

305

'Just think, Caroline, a chance of a real crack at a real enemy with the Royal Sussex.' Reggie lay back on the grass in satisfaction. For a moment, she thought she did not know him, so little was he with her, so much carried away by this new adventure. 'Three cheers for Kitchener and university commissions.'

'I'm not cheering.' She could not force herself to be glad for his sake.

He sobered instantly. 'No. You do see I'd have to go, whether I want to or not, though?'

Did she? She battled with herself, and could not trust herself to speak.

'As I see it,' he went on gravely, when he received no reply, 'it's a question of honour. What would you think of me if I shirked it?'

I'd have you here, everything inside her cried. 'You're the Squire here in practice, and it's even more important with your father so involved at the War Office. That's your job, and your honour. Not fighting.'

'Oh, but fighting is. It's all part of it. Daniel and I and countless other fellows like us were born, whether we like it or not, into the families that lead the country. You could say we're lucky or unlucky. Either way if we don't set an example and *lead,* who will? Pa says they're going to ask for volunteers for a whole new army of men, so how can I hang back? The leaders of the nation have to lead. That's how I see it,' he finished awkwardly.

'When are you going?' She knew her reply was stilted, but how could she pretend an enthusiasm she did not feel?

He hesitated. 'Tomorrow. I'm joining the 2nd Battalion

of the Royal Sussex at Aldershot. It's my guess they'll be leaving for France any moment.'

'*Tomorrow*?' she repeated, unable to take it in.

'Look. These commissions are only for single fellows, but as soon as I'm back, and it's not going to last long, we'll be married by one of those special licence things. We'll have a Christmas wedding.'

'Don't you *care* what this is doing to us?' She knew it was unfair, she knew she was behaving childishly, but out it came.

'Yes. As it happens, I do.' There was stiffness in his voice. 'For the last six weeks I have been thinking of little else but the day I could marry you. Or, more truthfully, if you must know, the night after I'd married you. I'd pictured us together, not in the Manor, but in the Rectory, where I could just have *you, alone,* and *mine.* And now, through no fault of mine, I have to go off to fight for the country I was born in, *without* that night.'

'Do you,' her voice seemed to be swallowed up by the pagan forest around them, 'have to? I mean, *without*?'

He didn't pretend not to understand, nor was he shocked as he might have been once. 'God knows I want to, Caroline, and I think He wouldn't mind *too* much, but I can't. It's all to do with bally honour again, I suppose. If this is an honourable war, and I believe it to be, I have to behave honourably in all things. And that, young lady,' he turned over and grinned at her, suddenly light-hearted again, 'means waiting till Christmas.'

'Will you be sent abroad?' Felicia asked. She might almost have been asking when he'd next be going up to Oxford, from her polite voice. Daniel now knew her better than that.

'Probably. The battalion's stationed at Dover at present. Very handy. It's just another sort of adventure, Felicia, and I've got to have it. Once this mess is sorted, I can set out on my travels afar. It means I'll be seeing Northern France and Belgium before Greece, that's all.'

'All?'

A brief silence ensued while he tried to deflect the swift arrow of Felicia's reply, which sliced as usual through the irrelevant direct to the heart. Heart? *Was* it involved after all? 'I'm not going alone,' he tried to laugh. 'The whole of the Regular Army and the Reserve are coming with me. I don't think even my swollen head could take on the *Feldmacht* unaided.'

'The what?'

'The lads in grey. The German Army. Kaiser Bill's minions.'

'They're good soldiers, so I've heard.'

'Not so good as the British Tommy.' He knew Reggie had a few reservations on this aspect, believing that stalwart hearts could never conquer stalwart weapons, but he did not share them. He was a historian, not a classicist like Reggie. Every so often there was an eruption in Europe, like Napoleon. It was like the recent eruption of Mount Etna; after a while it settled down again, and so would this flare up once it was made clear to the Kaiser that there was sufficient strong opposition. He was, therefore, surprised to find himself saying: 'Why don't you give me a photograph of yourself, just in case I'm away for more than a couple of weeks and miss my birthday? I can kiss your picture instead.' Embarrassed, he laughed awkwardly.

Ashden station had never been busier; true, there had been as many people when the old King had passed through, but they had been patiently waiting, not jostling about, fussing over luggage for want of words to express their feelings during the interminable wait for the steam train. It was hard to believe all this activity stemmed from Ashden. It was as if the village were taking a brief holiday from itself, and tomorrow or the next day it would step back to resume its normal pace. Caroline tried to tell herself that this was only like another of the Hunney trips, another episode of derring-do; in the old days she had walked back to the Rectory to wait for a postcard, or maybe two or three, depending on how many thoughts Reggie spared on her. Those days were past; now she did not doubt that he would spare thought for her, but how could she bear the waiting? There was only one way, she decided. She must do something positive to help win the war. The next time she saw Reggie he would be in uniform; would he get leave, or would she have to wait till Christmas when the war was over to see him? The clock of life had gone berserk, first rushing round frantically, kaleidoscoping years of emotions into a few days, and now holding out the dismal prospect of slowing down to suit the slowest tortoise.

On the station window was pasted the new poster: 'Your King and Country Need You'. The recruiting offices in Tunbridge Wells and East Grinstead were said to be overwhelmed by the response to the call for a hundred thousand men for a new army, and many of the men on the platform here without baggage, she supposed, might be on their way to offer their services.

And now the tempo speeded up again. The signal was down, and almost immediately it seemed, with a belch of triumph at its prowess, the train puffed in alongside the platform. For one glorious moment Reggie's lips were on hers, and then he was gone, he and Daniel, swallowed up by the demands of the outer world. Some other Caroline smiled, some other Caroline waved, and then the train bore the Hunneys away, leaving herself and Felicia on the platform.

'I'll be back down the chimney at Christmas, Caroline, just like Santa Claus.'

Reggie's last words rang in her ears, just as a voice grunted beside her. It was Freddie Bertram's, the sacristan's son, an ox of a young man. 'Kitchener wants a new army.' He wasn't talking to her, but to one of the Mutters.

'You're talking dinlow, Freddie. Who's going to cut the corn? Kitchener coming to do it, is he?' There was a roar of laughter from the Mutter clan, but Bertram proved obstinate.

'You say what you like. I be off to fight the Belgians.'

The laughter grew. ''Tis the Germans we be fighting, the Kaiser.'

Freddie grew red and more obstinate still. 'Beating the Kaiser is important.'

'Who's to bring in the harvest if Kitchener has his way?' The banter gave way to something more serious in the atmosphere, not only because Freddie had had a score to settle with Norman Mutter for a long time. 'Women could do it, I reckon. Don't need a man, do it?'

'Women could do most of the jobs men can do,' Felicia observed quietly to her sister, as they decided it was time to leave. The argument bode fair to become heated.

'They could,' Caroline agreed, 'but if men would let us.'

'If they won't then we must do it anyway.'

Caroline was surprised at the decision in her sister's voice. It struck her that perhaps not for the first time she had underestimated Felicia. Perhaps she too had plans for enduring Daniel's absence. But this was not the time to press her. Caroline felt so full of uncertainty and emotion herself that for the moment she had none to spare.

Last night she had been to visit Nanny, and returning when dusk had fallen had been an eerie experience. Where she was accustomed to see the dim comforting glow of Ashden's two street lamps had been only the darkness of night. She had returned to the cottage to borrow a torch from Nanny, who told her Alfred had gone to the wars.

'But he's old.'

'He's what they call a Reservist.'

Caroline hadn't even known his name. He was just the lamplighter, and he travelled all the villages round here each morning and evening, always talking hopefully of the day soon when 'the gas would come'. Now the war had come instead. She was so used to the familiar sight of him carefully trimming and lighting the lamps that it seemed, as with the travelling clock winder, that he was part of the fabric of the village. For many a late-night drinker at the Norville Arms the lamps had been a polar star to guide them safely home, and now the lamps were out.

Now she felt her eyes fill with tears for Alfred, for Reggie, for them all; for the pain of separation and the darkness of waiting.

Mable Thorn thumped the rabbit stew on the table and sat herself down, taking up the ladle like a truncheon. She pursed her lips, feeling her jaw slip into its familiar shape of belligerence. She had no choice as the only woman in a household of thick-headed men.

'I hear your Bertram is volunteering, then. A credit to his family.' A long pause. 'You thinking of going, Len?' A longer pause, and more ominous: 'Jamie?'

Len sniggered, relieved the spotlight had shifted so quickly. 'Might as well. Better than wedding Ruth, isn't it, Jamie, but less fun than bedding her, eh?'

'I ain't got no call to the army,' Jamie said stolidly, determined not to be riled by Len. He had the strength to stand it now there was Aggie. 'I got responsibilities.'

'Yeah. We know. A bastard.'

'No.' Jamie gave a simple denial, nonplussing his brother.

'I heard Rosie Trott give evidence for Ruth.' His mother sounded non-committal, but Len sniggered all the same.

Jamie had forgotten all about Rosie, in the flush of love for Aggie, and was taken unawares. 'I ain't done *nothing*, as I keep telling you. Don't any of you believe me, me own *family*?'

Silence was his answer, and the slap of rabbit stew on the china plate.

'I got the shop to look after.' Jamie said aghast, frightened now at the way they were looking at him.

'Ma can do without your kind of help,' Len informed him.

Jamie looked at his mother, who stared at the stew on her plate as though it were a crystal ball. 'You want to be rid of me?' He couldn't believe it.

'Nothing wrong in fighting for your country,' his mother muttered.

Jamie pushed his chair back and stood up. He saw it now. Whatever he did, whatever he said, only Aggie would *ever* believe him. No one else. For the rest of his life, to Ashden he would be the father of Ruth's bastard, and if he married Agnes she'd suffer too. And the worst of it was, they were right in a way. He *had* intended to bed Ruth; it was only his John let him down. So far as he could see, he'd lost his good name in the village, and any hope of respect from his family. There was only one way to get it back, and that *before* he married Aggie.

'You can lay about here all you like, Len. I *am* going off to fight.' He kept his voice quiet so they'd know he meant it.

Len gaped at him. He never thought Jamie would be such a fool. 'Yes, well, like I said, you've got a lot to run away from.'

'I ain't *running* away, I'm marching. Because I got something to come back to. And I'll make you respect me if it's the last thing I do.'

'Come with me, Felicia. I'm going to Tunbridge Wells.' Caroline's face was full of excitement.

'Shopping?' Felicia was amazed.

'No. I'm going to do something for the war effort. Like Reggie. Apart from being a temporary lamplighter, that is.'

Felicia did not laugh, but she looked sufficiently interested for Caroline to press her further.

'I'm going to train for a VAD – a Voluntary Aid Detachment. Elementary nursing.'

'But that's what I'd decided to do.' Felicia grew excited. 'I thought I'd make a good nurse.'

'I won't,' Caroline said ruefully. 'But I shall do the training all the same, because it could be a passport to something much more useful. I have to get a first aid certificate first, and they're doing special three-week courses in the Wells.'

Would Felicia make a good nurse? Perhaps yes, she would. How odd that one thought so little about the people one was closest to. In the Rectory they were held by bonds so tight, united by shared experience and need, that Caroline had never deeply questioned how each of them might function if left to go their own separate ways.

Because of the war, the Rectory was becoming a hub from which each of them might move to be a separate spoke. The thought alternately daunted and exhilarated her, but above all it papered over that numbness within her that Reggie's sudden departure and the possible danger to Isabel had caused. For the moment that was enough.

'I'll come,' Felicia declared.

Mrs Dibble looked grimly round her empire. War had come and it was under threat. It was as if the Kaiser had galloped out on a personal offensive against Margaret

Dibble, putting prices up, removing food from the shops, cutting off imports – well, he wasn't going to get the better of her. He'd snatched Joe, and he'd taken Lizzie's Rudolf – not that he was much loss – but her own enclave was standing firm. If the Kaiser was fighting with flour, the Rectory would turn to potatoes; if he was after their bacon, the Rectory would cure its own; if he stopped oranges getting to them, they'd eat more apples. Anyway, now dear old Lord Kitchener was back at the War Office, the Kaiser would be trembling in his boots. She'd not been herself after she got the news about Joe, but hearing of Kitchener and going into the general stores and finding out Joe was regarded as a hero doing his duty and fighting for England had cheered her up. Now she too was armed for the battle.

Carefully she propped in the kitchen window nearest the tradesmen's entrance one of the cards Mrs Lettice was handing out for people: 'This house has sent a son to fight for right.'

As the days passed, the face of Ashden was changing. Many young and not so young men slipped away, mothers and wives appeared behind shop counters, the Rector performed hasty baptisms, and two hasty marriages by special licence. It was like a chessboard, Caroline decided. Every time you opened your eyes, someone had jumped into someone else's place, and the numbers on the board were slightly fewer.

More women and schoolchildren were working in the fields, and somehow the wheels of the village still spun. The haywagons trundled up Silly Lane to the rickyard, marrows, beans and tomatoes appeared in the shops as usual. And overseas, *somewhere*, some unknown somewhere, was Reggie. Caroline clung to that as she travelled daily to the first aid course, at which predictably Felicia's nimble fingers and steady hands were faring better than Caroline's enthusiastic but definitely less agile ones. Nevertheless, the alternative was far more daunting. Edith Swinford-Browne had flung herself into committee work, exhorting Caroline to knit, so far as she could gather, babies' socks for sailors' wives. Edith had constantly pleaded with Mother to start an Ashden knitting circle and, when she refused, started one herself. It took her mind off Robert, she explained bravely. The couple had been gone nine days and there was still no word. Even Mother was silent about it now, while Caroline clung to the belief that Isabel's sense of self-survival would not let her down now, when she most needed it.

'I could not love thee dear so much, Loved I not honour more,' Aggie read out from the back of the locket. 'That's beautiful, Jamie.'

'I wrote it for you.'

'*Wrote* it?'

'Down, I mean. I found it in a book.' Jamie hastily defended himself against misunderstanding.

'Why?' But in her heart she already knew, and dreaded hearing confirmation.

'Because old Kitchener will only need 999,999 men now that he's got one signed up in me.'

There was pride in his voice, a pride she had not heard

these last six months. She forced herself to voice enthusiasm. 'A King's man, are you now, then? I've got a soldier for a sweetheart.'

'I'll be back just as soon as I've a medal to show you all.'

She stared at him unbelievingly. He hadn't said a word about whether she minded or whether she'd be all right, or when he expected to get this medal. He was going away, going away and leaving her. Inside she wailed, but all she said was: 'We'll all be proud of you, Jamie.'

He was a little disappointed. Didn't sweethearts cry, and weep on your shoulder? 'They said the Royal Sussex might be needing men for a new battalion.' He was determined to impress her. 'That would be a valiant thing, surely.'

'Valiant,' she repeated hollowly. The Royal Sussex is going away . . .

Laurence laid down *The Times*. It was already mid-afternoon and this was his first opportunity to look at it. 'McKenna has come to his senses. He's releasing all the suffragettes remaining in prison. Tilly will be free.'

Elizabeth considered this mixed blessing, with so much else to worry about. 'Will she return here?'

'Will there be a welcome here if she so chooses?'

'Of course.' Elizabeth's voice was less than enthusiastic. She was tired, so tired, of trying to adapt to the new situation. She had tried to push Isabel to the back of her mind, while she grappled daily with the demands of the household – at least the Government had stabilised food prices for a few days, though their deadline was today, the 10th, and what would happen now? – and the demands of the help she was giving Laurence in Rector's Hour.

It was more like two hours at present, with calming distraught women whose reservist husbands had suddenly disappeared without any assurances from the Government about separation allowances, girls whose sweethearts had vanished without a word, farmers whose hands had followed Kitchener's dictates with the harvest left undone. Much of the work was the result of the necessary cessation of Squire's Days, for there was no squire with Reggie and Daniel away to the war and Sir John in London most of the time. Laurence was doing his best on the practical side of temporary parish relief for the poor hit most by rising prices of food, galvanising reluctant officials like Horace Trimble into working with an unaccustomed speed, making constant telephone calls to London to do what he could, difficult enough in itself with telephone operators so busy.

Elizabeth had become lady clerk to her husband, the comforter of the sad, the field marshal of the household, and organiser of an emergency relief fund for extreme cases of poverty. It was unreal to her; she did it mechanically, but with no heart in it, the unreality prolonged by the return of the hot weather. She had not been pleased when Edith Swinford-Browne almost demanded her presence at her newly formed Knitting and Sewing Circle. Elizabeth's task, she had informed the Rector's wife, was to obtain patterns from the Red Cross for men's pyjamas, bedjackets, skirts and nightingales. A mere one shilling and threepence each. Elizabeth had refused. Not only could she not afford one shilling and threepence, which would have fed the Rectory for two days before the emergency, but she was wise enough to see that nightingales and bedjackets were of less use in

318

war than bandages and, with winter approaching, heavy British army warms and weatherproofs.

'Laurence,' she continued now, 'I had a visit from Maud this morning.'

'A *visit*?' His eyebrows rose, and the corners of his mouth twitched, then he suppressed it, realising that such a unique event must stem from great distress. 'She is naturally concerned for Daniel and Reggie?' he probed gently.

'Perhaps, but she would not unburden herself to me about that. No, it was the Manor. Sir John has offered it to the Government for a hospital for the wounded, and they have accepted.'

'Many country houses have done so. It is not unexpected.'

'But to Ashden it is. And to Lady Hunney.'

'It is only temporary. They have the old Dower House to live in. Surely she is not so unpatriotic as to resent that?'

'She does, but realises it is inevitable. She is brave within her own limits, Laurence. She has a Roman stoicism.'

'I had not associated her, I must admit, with a faculty for looking on the bright side.'

Elizabeth managed to laugh. 'But she does. Her very last words to me were – ' she mimicked the precise crystal sharp tones – '"I do take comfort in the fact that Ashden will be a hospital for *officers*".'

Chapter Nine

George was in his element. At last there was something decent to do in Ashden, even if it hadn't yet spawned its cinema. What's more, he was helping the war effort. Spies were being caught and shoved in stir all over the place, so there was no reason why Ashden shouldn't secretly be hoarding some. Hundreds had been shot out of hand at barracks all over Britain, the coastline was crawling with traitors semaphoring to U-boats, signal boxes were being taken over by enemy agents intent on wrecking trains, and German governesses were showing themselves in their true colours. Moreover Russian troops were on the move, on the railways, with the snow still on their boots. It was an alarming thought – even if the Russians were supposed to be on our side – and it was small wonder the scouts had been ordered to guard the railways, especially the bridges.

George couldn't, he admitted, quite see how any of the villagers could have turned into spies overnight, and there was no one with a suspicious accent or he'd have heard it long since. Even Lizzie Dibble's husband at Hartfield had gone back to fight for the Kaiser, and good riddance to him. It was true Rudolf had always seemed a pleasant sort of chap when he came to visit old Ma Dibble and Percy, but that only went to show how cunning these Germans were.

He liked this job; it was an adventure, like in John Buchan's books or E. Phillips Oppenheim's. *Real*. The scouts had been given the task of guarding the highways, as well as railways and bridges, and his patrol route was along Station Road, keeping a careful eye on hedges and ditches, where they had been warned German soldiers might be hiding; then he marched to left and right of the railway line, through Three Oak Farm and the hop farm respectively; then he did a stint on the bridge, especially when railway trains steamed through, in case any Germans disguised as passengers had any ideas about blowing it up – and then down the other side, again to left and right, through open farmland. George was a little concerned about the river a mile or so away. It wasn't in the patrol area he'd been allotted, but it seemed to him there was scope for enemy activity there. Still, here in Station Road he had a very definite part to play and to his excitement he realised *he could play it now*!

'Stand away, please!' he bellowed. 'Keep well away from the ditches, *if* you please.'

Two tiny tots, busy investigating the stickleback content

of the River Crain as it emerged from underneath the shallow bridge of the road and across the line of the ditch, obediently scuttled for safety.

Tilly regarded the Common balefully through the windows of the imposing house on Mount Pleasant. Tunbridge Wells was neither one thing nor the other; not the battleground of London, nor the quiet thinking ground of Ashden. At least once upon a time girls, boys, and whole families had enjoyed themselves walking on the Common here; now, it seemed to be an ants' parade ground of uniforms, discussion groups and workers of every class. Everyone, it seemed, had something to do – save her. She was gathering her strength after being released from Holloway, but she and her fellow suffragettes were still worried that this was yet another of the Government's traps and that, whatever was said when they were released, they might still be re-arrested. She must avoid it, she had reluctantly decided. Her spirit might be strong enough to undergo the ordeal again, but she was forced to admit her body was not. Earlier this year the doctor had forbidden her to go on hunger strike again, and she had ignored him. If she went on at this rate, he said, her constitution would be so weakened she would be a prey to any disease she came across: tuberculosis, pneumonia, fevers. She could not risk it yet again, there was still too much for her to do.

'Have you read Mrs Pankhurst's letter?' Penelope came bursting into the room.

'What does it say? Pa pleaded with me to launch this knitting circle or I'd have been here earlier. You should have heard me nattering on about scarves for the war effort when all *I* was longing to do was to find out what *Mrs P.* was going to do.'

'We're to suspend militant activities until hostilities are over.' Mrs Pankhurst's letter had been circulated to all groups on the 13th, and the Tunbridge Wells group to which Tilly had speedily allied herself had delivered one to her as promised.

'You sound rather blasé about the prospect. It makes sense, doesn't it? We want to make people *think* about women and the vote, and at the moment all they can think about is the Kaiser and the cost of bread.'

'The question is, Penelope, how long will hostilities last? Weeks? Months? Years even? Memories are short, especially in politics. We will lose all the ground we have won towards gaining the vote. Even the publication of *The Suffragette* is to be suspended.'

'We must support the war effort,' Penelope pointed out reasonably, 'or it shows us in a bad light. Look at the Women's Freedom League. They've already established the Women's Suffrage National Aid Corps to help the poor. If Mrs P. doesn't come up with something like that, I'm off to offer the Corps my invaluable services, or if not them, *someone*. Trained to do nothing, ma'am; willing to run the whole bally shooting match, ma'am. There's us ruling classes for you.'

Tilly managed to grin. 'How right you are.'

Penelope paused, not knowing quite how delicately she should tread. 'Do you have plans for when you're fully better?'

'I did. I read that the War Office through the motoring

organisations was appealing for motor cars with or without drivers. I offered my services. I was told that the motor car would be welcome, but that as a woman I could be returned to the bosom of my family – unwanted. I drove off *in* my motor car and came straight here.'

'Idiots. I'm glad anyway, because I want you to stay here as long as you like. Pa thinks you're a corker. A misguided one, but a corker all the same.'

'Even though I'm leading his daughter astray?' Penelope's offer of shelter, after she had come to see her in Holloway, had been accepted gratefully and immediately. It had solved Tilly's biggest problem. She was not well enough to live on her own, nor able to return to Dover, nor, for the moment, was it advisable for her to go to Ashden. Laurence had nobly suggested it, but he had enough to do in the current crisis without hauling the cuckoo back into the Rectory nest. She had been amused to see slight relief on his face when she refused; this was what she had always loved in her brother – that he was a human being as well as a man of God. Or perhaps the two were the same? Anyway, time enough for Ashden. Give Swinford-Browne enough rope and she would be back.

Lord Banning was an amiable, vacant-looking man, who greeted her pleasantly and courteously every time he met her in the house with a faint air of surprise as though it took him a moment to recall who she was; it made her feel like an injured bird, welcome, but transitory.

'I don't need leading. I *run*.'

Tilly relaxed. 'Forgive me. I am forever treading on eggshells at Ashden, because of my brother.'

'He disapproves of your activities?'

'Of course. Therefore I'm somewhat inhibited in what I say to his daughters.'

'You mean Caroline.' It was a statement, not a question.

'Yes. You heard she was engaged to Reggie?'

'No! By golly, she'll do him a power of good.'

'And what about he to her?' Tilly asked drily, relieved to see there were no signs of regret for Penelope's own lost opportunity. She'd be a wonderful supporter for the cause. *That* was her metier.

'They'll live happily ever after.'

'Penelope!'

'Very well then. They *could* live happily ever after.'

'I'm going to press you. I love my Caroline. Why your doubt? Because of the war?'

'Yes. The question is: which war?'

Belgium, everything was *Belgium*. For the last couple of weeks *Paris* had been the talk, that, and the sainted Isabel. Phoebe worried about Isabel too, but not all day and every day. She knew she must be safe, or they would have heard, whereas all those poor people in Belgium were having terrible things done to them; babies were being killed and nailed to doors, women's breasts were being cut off, and from what she could gather, *worse* things were happening to women. Phoebe did not like to speculate on that for it pushed her back into her own darkness. What was *she*, Phoebe Lilley, going to do? Not what Caroline and Felicia were doing, she was sure about that, but everyone around her was rushing around talking about the war effort.

Phoebe wasn't going to knit or sew, *and* she was too young to be a VAD, thank goodness. She wasn't sure what it entailed but it sounded messy and she hated blood. Philip Ryde had said she could help him when school started again in September, but that wasn't exactly a war effort, and besides, Philip was old and dull, *and* he had a limp. He was safe, of course, unlike – no, she wouldn't think of *him*. She quickly decided to walk over to The Towers on the pretext of asking Patricia if there were any news of Isabel. She wouldn't walk up Station Road in case she saw *him* lounging outside the forge in the High Street; she'd go the long way round past the hop farm. She wondered whether hop-pickers would still come from London this year, or whether like everything else that too would change.

She set off across the Withyham road into Mill Lane. She liked this winding lane, which led up the hill to the mill; then she could turn off on to the footpath skirting Gowks Wood. The hill made her feel as if she had passed out of Ashden and into some brave new world of her own, a kingdom ruled by Phoebe Lilley. The corn was only stubble now, with sheaves dotting it like wigwams, and prickly as she lifted her skirts to jump the ditch into the wood. Gowks Wood, unlike Nye Wood, near the Forest, was a friendly place, filled with bluebells in spring and yet with enough room between the trees for grassy clearings. Once, as a child in her favourite glade, she'd found a fairy ring, which appeared for the mornings and vanished before nightfall. It had become a ritual to stand in the middle of it, and make a wish.

Today, her heart jumped painfully, someone else was standing there: Len Thorn. She stood still, like a cat spotting an adversary in the dark of the night, trying to ignore the thudding within her.

'I saw you coming, Miss Phoebe. I've been to the hop farm. I thought I'd wait for you here.' He grinned.

'Why?' she enquired, surprised that she managed to sound so calm.

'This and that.' He ambled out of the ring that once had enchanted her.

'Don't come near me.' His slow tread was more sinister than if he had rushed at her.

'You're not afeared of me, are you?' He put a hand on the sleeve of her voile gown and slowly ran it up and down the length of her arm. She felt powerless to move, feeling the heat of his touch through the thin material. He stared at the rounded flesh as though it mesmerised him. 'Just a kiss, Miss Phoebe.' He turned those tawny eyes on her, and she felt her face inclining to his as though she had no control over it; his lips were on hers, lightly at first, then his arms were holding her closer and words something like, 'You're a witch, Miss Phoebe, and no mistake,' tumbled out. He held her against him hard, then released her. 'There now, that weren't so bad, were it?'

'No,' Phoebe agreed, doubtfully.

'You sit by me, my lovely, and tell me what's amiss that you look at me as though I were the devil himself. You sit by me and talk to your heart's content.'

To her surprise, it seemed quite natural to pour out her feelings about her sisters and the Rectory and about how she was always being left out. He said nothing, but, chewing on a piece of grass, he listened.

'I'll never ever have anything to do, now that I can't go to Paris in September. The war might go on for months and nobody cares at all. I'm not important to *anybody*.'

'Everyone's important to someone, so my old grannie said.'

'Not me.'

'You're important to me, Miss Phoebe. Every time I see you, with your rosebud lips and eyes like a young doe, and hair like the wind through the forest trees, I want to kiss you.'

After all, it was rather nice, with her arms round his neck, and his lips pecking gently at her. She closed her eyes, enjoying the sensation of his lips darting from neck to eyes, to ear, to chin, and even inside the unbuttoned neck of her gown. The sun was pressing in upon the blanket of her closed eyelids, pleasantly warm in the still, quiet glade. But then she became aware that it wasn't quiet. The warm breath was turning into harsh gulps, and the gentle kisses becoming harder. She was aware of the grip of his hand digging the boning of her girdle into her; she opened her eyes in protest, but, as the hand shifted and the pain receded, the other hand moved down her body to grasp her between her legs, kneading the thin voile dress and cotton of her petticoats. An ache shot up through her body, just as terror gripped her. What was happening to her, to him? His face was inches from hers, gleaming with sweat and a kind of triumph in his staring eyes. Just so must demon monsters have looked in fairy tales when they seized their prey. And she was his; she couldn't move. She was held so tight, held in the reality of her nightmares.

She was Phoebe Lilley, she tried to tell herself, struggling in vain, and nightmares didn't happen. They *didn't*. She hit out instinctively wherever she could, using struggling arms, feet, knees and almost by accident teeth, which dug themselves firmly in his chin. Taken by surprise, he howled in pain and relaxed his hold. She was free to run from this horror, this darkness of the unknown.

Stumbling and panting she fled along the footpath, not stopping to glance behind her until at last she could plunge off it and lose herself among the rows of bines, heavily laden with ripening hops, providing a sheltered arbour of acrid dry scent. She drew deep breaths as she stopped, shuddering, terrified she was being followed. She was surrounded only by the deep silence of the fields. Or so she had thought.

'Are you all right? Miss Lilley, isn't it?'

Her heart sank. Pushing through the bines, alerted by her heavy sobs, was that terrible hop man Eliot, cap on his head, red kerchief at his neck, and with that threatening moustache. Instinctively she backed away, and he stopped still in his tracks.

'Don't worry. I'm not going to hurt you. Tell me if there's anything I can do.' He looked so concerned that she burst out crying in earnest.

Frank Eliot wavered, undecided, cursing his luck for strolling up at this moment. Cautiously he came closer, for he had no alternative. 'Shall I escort you back home to your father?' he asked quietly, alarmed to see her dishevelled state.

'No!' How could she face Father or Mother like this?

'Have – did—' Frank broke off, perplexed. He had never been in such a situation. A man, for sure, and in one leap he guessed who it was, but what to say next that would not embarrass her coming from another man? Had the fellow raped her?

'I've some beer here, Miss Lilley.' He swung his luncheon bag down from his shoulder. 'Sit down and have some.'

'No, thank you.'

She spoke so sharply, he realised what she was fearing. 'You stand then. But have some. It will steady you, and then I'll take you home.'

She grabbed at the old lemonade bottle, in which some horrible looking liquid had replaced the lemonade she longed for. Fleetingly it crossed her mind he could be a white slaver, but she didn't care. The beer tasted bitter and rough, but it did steady her, enough to say eventually: 'I'm all right now. Thank you. I don't need to go home.' She was rigid with shame.

'Look, Miss Lilley, I'm a man. It's not right I should be asking you outright, but I must. If there's some tramp or *anyone* been doing things he shouldn't to you, PC Ifield should know of it.'

Phoebe looked at him with fear in her eyes. He was a man and, what's more, Isabel had said he was a dangerous man. She shouldn't trust him, but then there was no one else. 'It wasn't a tramp.'

'Whoever it was, did he—' Frank was nonplussed again. The girl needed a woman. Then he had an idea. 'I'll take you to Miss Patricia, she's a friend of yours, I know, but before we go I must tidy you up a bit.' He pretended not to notice as she shrank back against the bines. 'Here,' he produced a comb from the bag, 'let me use this.'

Warily, Phoebe let him approach, and he tried to bind the heavy strands of dark hair up into some semblance of order, as he had once loved doing for his now dead wife. Then, as she seemed incapable of doing it herself, he twirled her round, buttoned up the neck of her dress, and tidied the sleeves and collar.

'I reckon just now, Miss Phoebe,' he said quietly while he was doing it, 'you think men are all beasts, but we're not. We're most of us just like you women, scared sometimes, bad sometimes, but meaning well. And you must think what men want of women is a violent, dirty thing. But it's not. It's the most wonderful gift God gave us when it's used right. It's like electricity: used wrong, it kills you, but used proper it glows with the brightest and sweetest light you ever did see.'

Bang, right on the head. The last nail. Percy eyed his handiwork with some satisfaction. Daisy had explained it was to help the war effort, and here it was, as neat a container as you ever would see. This was the sixth, and hidden behind the log piles. There was another in the coalhouse, two buried deep in the bushes down by the compost, one in the stable hayloft and another behind Fred's workroom. The decoy one in the Rectory cellar was the one the Germans were meant to find. At first he'd misunderstood, and thought that, despite Mrs Lilley's instructions, these containers for food was the food hoarding he'd read about which was unpatriotic. The Government had said so, and more importantly so had the Rector. Now Daisy had pointed out to him that they had been ordered by the King to deny the Germans access to everything; transport, money, petrol – and of course food – if they invaded. After all, if the Germans came marching in demanding billets, they couldn't fight 'em off with Master George's water pistol, could they? They'd have to be cunning, welcome them in, and deny them food. So all the Rectory supplies would have to be hidden. All the same, Daisy had said, the Rector need not know about it just in case he got confused too.

Ten to one it was a lot of fuss about nothing, Percy thought. The British Expeditionary Force was protecting us now, and every day the newspapers were full of the glorious success our boys were having against the Germans. War had been declared over two weeks ago and no Germans had arrived in Sussex yet. Not troops, anyway. Plenty of spies, though, until the Government started rounding up and interning all the ones they'd planted years ago, pretending to be bakers, and butchers, or – Percy stopped short. He'd been going to say bandsmen, and then he remembered Rudolf. He had liked Rudolf, German or not; he pondered this problem for some time and concluded that his Lizzie must have knocked the evil out of him, so that he was almost English really. Still, suppose the Kaiser got hold of Rudolf and made him talk; persuaded him to tell him all about Hartfield and Ashden. They'd know where to come then. Perhaps the Misses Norville had been right to fortify Castle Tillow.

*　*　*

'I'm sorry, Mother, but we *have* to go to do our VAD training. You know we signed on for six months minimum. It's nearly the end of August, and our three weeks' first aid course is finished on Friday. Provided we get our certificates we have to go on to the next stage.'

'But on Saturday, so *soon*. And both of you. Felicia is so young, and you *are* volunteers. You are not being paid.'

'I am eighteen, and we *are* going together. And we have a duty, payment or not,' Felicia answered.

Elizabeth was not reassured, but as Laurence came in from afternoon visiting, sought an ally. 'Laurence. Caroline and Felicia say they have to leave us on *Saturday* for training in a hospital. That's only four days.'

'Where are you going?' Laurence asked sharply.

'To Shooters Hill in North Kent. The Royal Herbert Hospital is one of those that will receive wounded soldiers, if there are any, and they need VADs immediately, fully trained or not.'

'To nurse *men*.' Elizabeth looked shocked.

'I doubt if they'll want either of us to perform operations yet a while,' her daughter reassured her cheerfully. 'Felicia's the one with the cool touch on the fevered brow, anyway. It's as much as I can do to roll a bandage. The victims run away when they see me approaching.' The victims had been volunteers, scouts, schoolgirls, young women all eager to be bound into mummies with bandages by would-be nurses with more enthusiasm than aptitude.

Laurence relaxed. 'Where will you live?'

'We'll be billeted somewhere nearby.'

'But we don't know anyone there,' Elizabeth pointed out alarmed.

'We know each other,' Caroline said firmly, thinking how unlike her mother this anxiety was. She must be worse affected by worry about Isabel than she had realised.

'Three of them absent,' Elizabeth said to her husband, as though they had already left. 'It is frightening.' She did not say: how will I cope? For she knew somehow she would.

'There is more worrying news,' Laurence said soberly.

'About the army?' Caroline cried. She meant the British army, she meant Reggie. She had heard not a word since he had departed, though Sir John had reassured her this was natural with the army travelling.

'The British have just had their first major confrontation with the enemy near a village called Mons. Apparently the engagement went well. Even so, the army may have to pull back a little way into France.'

Elizabeth broke the silence. 'Withdraw? The British army *withdraw*?' We shall be invaded, was Elizabeth's immediate fear, but she did not voice it. 'Laurence, let us pray. All of us. Caroline, please ask the servants to join us, and Felicia, find Phoebe and George.'

'No.' Her father spoke so firmly that Caroline stopped halfway through the door.

'We are one family.' Elizabeth was astounded.

'All the more reason for us to think of them, my love. If we summoned them to prayer now, at four o'clock, they would immediately think invasion was imminent, or a catastrophe had taken place in Europe. It would be tantamount to erecting barbed wire around the Rectory itself, and that we cannot do. But we four can share our fears with our Lord, that He may give us strength.'

After some hesitation, Caroline decided to bid goodbye to Lady Hunney that very evening, and to go alone.

The Manor itself was in the process of being turned into a small, fully equipped hospital with twenty-four beds, staffed by a matron, surgical and nursing staff, and part of a VAD detachment. Some of the Ashden heirlooms were stored in the cellars, others studded the Dower House. At first sight Maud Hunney looked smaller and less formidable in the Dower House, but it proved an illusion only, at least so far as Caroline was concerned. The iron-clad figure who rose to meet her arrayed in dinner gown and diamonds was as unbending as ever. If Caroline had had any hope that she and Lady Hunney would be drawn together by their common worry she found she was greatly mistaken.

'Could I ask if you have news of Reggie or Daniel?'

'I have not. Soldiers, Caroline, have other thoughts to occupy them than the women they leave behind. You must bear that in mind.'

She might have been talking of some slight acquaintance for all the emotion in her voice. Caroline smarted, yet it was her sons who were so far away. Did their silence not worry Lady Hunney as it did her, did she dislike her so much that she would betray nothing of her own feelings before her, or was she so hidebound in convention that her iron self-control would not yield even at such a time?

'I bear in mind, Lady Hunney, that letters are hard to send with an army on the move.'

'Possibly.' Lady Hunney paused. 'Or indeed an army in battle.'

An arrow of fear leaped through her, stinging Caroline with fear and pain. 'You think Reggie and Daniel are involved in this confrontation in Belgium?'

'I cannot tell you that, for I do not know. My husband may, but he is not at liberty to discuss it with me. All I know is that Reggie left England on the 12th with the Royal Sussex, and Daniel a week or so later with the 1st King's Own.'

'Thank you,' Caroline said quietly. The ice in Lady Hunney's voice had not melted at all. Even *The Times* was more forthcoming, but she forced herself to grant that somewhere deep within her, Lady Hunney might possibly be human. In a sudden rush of compassion, she kneeled down beside her and took the cold hands in hers. 'We are both suffering,' she said earnestly. 'We both love him, can we not help each other through this terrible time?'

Wrong again, she realised immediately she had spoken. Her appeal was flung back in her face as Lady Hunney stood up, coolly disengaging herself.

'Certainly. How good of you to call, Miss Lilley.'

The next morning, as Caroline was packing, an unaccustomed noise filled the Rectory. The Rector was *shouting* – shouting for his wife, his daughters, his servants, anyone and everything. It was Ahab who reached him first, and even he got a hug for which he slobbered gratefully over Laurence's boots.

'They are *safe*!' he yelled, as startled heads shot out over the balustrade upstairs and people rushed towards him from all directions on the ground floor.

Elizabeth was already racing down the stairs. 'Isabel?'

'Mrs Swinford-Browne the younger and husband returning today. Sir John has just telephoned; he had been in contact with the British Embassy on our behalf, though he could not tell us that at first. The steamer arrives at Folkestone this afternoon.'

'Oh.' Elizabeth hurled herself into her husband's arms, and his happiness gave him the strength to whirl her off the ground and round in the air, to Harriet and Myrtle's gaping astonishment and Agnes's openly displayed satisfaction.

'At last the governments of Europe have become sufficiently concerned to arrange for British civilians to have special railway trains. The Swiss Government sent 800 people by train to Paris yesterday, and Thomas Cook have organised their onward progress to England. The train left Paris at midnight, and the Embassy arranged for it to take some stranded holidaymakers in Paris. Our Isabel is one of them. The bad news from Belgium has concentrated everyone's minds wonderfully in Paris, thank goodness!'

'There is panic?'

'Apparently not; only great determination.'

'To do what?'

Laurence gave her a warning glance, conscious of listening ears. He did not reply to her question. *The Times* today had revealed that, success or none, there had been two thousand casualties at Mons, and that the British and French armies had indeed stopped advancing and were pulling back a little. If they were pulling back, then the

Germans would be advancing, from Belgium and from the east. Where after all would the Kaiser's armies be moving other than to converge on Paris?

By the afternoon it was raining and Caroline and Felicia had left for Tunbridge Wells, where they had arranged to stay for two days while they finished the course and took the certificate. Elizabeth acknowledged the good sense of this, with train schedules so uncertain nowadays, but nevertheless, even the knowledge that Isabel was returning failed to make the Rectory seem other than a large and almost empty shell. This was war, Elizabeth reminded herself. Countless families were suffering so. Sons had gone to the wars for hundreds of years; now daughters, for the first time, were following too. Laurence said the war might last till Christmas. Very well then, on Christmas she would set her hopes.

Meanwhile there was Isabel to welcome home – although, Elizabeth remembered almost with surprise, the Rectory no longer *was* her home. She despatched Phoebe, who was most unwilling, to the railway station to find George, still hunting spies with his official badge, and meet all the late afternoon trains. The Swinford-Brownes had promised to telephone as soon as there was any news, but Elizabeth did not trust them.

Rightly so, for it was fully an hour after Phoebe had arrived breathlessly back at the Rectory with the news that the pair had returned that the telephone call came through from The Towers. Not a happy pair, Phoebe reported with some glee. Isabel, she related, was furious because they had

had to stand in the railway train from Paris and, worse, she hadn't been allowed to bring any luggage.

'But she's unharmed.' Elizabeth came anxiously to the point.

'Oh yes. She's just the same.'

Laurence took the unprecedented step of cancelling Rector's Hour as they waited. At the sound of a motor car they rushed to the front entrance. One look at Isabel's face told them that she was indeed cross. Moreover the gown she wore was one that she had left in her trousseau, not one of the Paris ensembles she had expected to acquire.

'It was terrible,' she told them pitifully, ensconced in pride of place in the drawing room. 'Our *honeymoon*! Nothing but war, war, war talk. The couturier to whom I'd been recommended had left for the wars, the *pâtissier* had left for the wars, the porter at the hotel had left for the wars, even the cobbler left for the wars. Cafes shut early, restaurants, theatres – oh, there was *nothing* to do.'

Laurence listened grimly. 'And yet you stayed on.'

Isabel caught his tone. 'It was our honeymoon,' she said defiantly. 'It could have been a false alarm, anyway, and we knew it was *impossible* to get sense from the embassies. Imagine, one had to *queue* for *ten hours* for papers to leave the place.'

'Did you see any Huns?' George interrupted, bored with papers.

Isabel was swept away by her own grievance. '*Then* they said we were lucky to get on the train! Lucky!'

'So you were,' Elizabeth said thankfully.

Isabel turned a baleful eye on her mother. 'The jet was

among the luggage. Caroline's not going to like that. Where is she, by the way?'

'She and Felicia are training to join a VAD unit. They are in Tunbridge Wells till Friday and then leaving for the Royal Herbert Hospital at Shooters Hill.'

'Whatever for?'

Laurence lost patience. 'Because there is a war being fought, my dear, which you were fortunate to escape. Because wounded men are expected to arrive at the ports any day now.'

'You mean all those rumours in Paris just as we left were *true*? It was said the British had been wiped out on the field of Waterloo.'

Elizabeth went white. 'But Reggie and Daniel may have been there.' She turned to her husband. 'Laurence, can it be we are not being told the truth here?'

'There are many, many regiments in the British army, Elizabeth. The Hunney boys are probably in reserve safe behind the lines. Besides, this is mere *rumour*.'

'But if it *is* true, where will the Germans go next?'

'Paris!' cried Phoebe and George in unison, for once unreproved by Laurence.

Isabel digested this information. 'Perhaps it's as well we left when we did, then.'

Phoebe prowled round the garden, at the moment a most welcome cage. No one noticed her, for there was so much else going on. The Rectory grounds were safe; outside she might meet *him*, and the thought made her feel sick with fear. She was not sure whether it was fear of Len Thorn, or fear of an

340

unknown and untraversed gap between the safety of 'now' and the hitherto confidently regarded future of marriage, and there was no one she could confide in. Caroline was not here, and pride had prevented her asking Patricia for enlightenment. She was in a limbo from which she could see no exit. She had tried to help in the kitchens until she grew bored, and now to her amazement found herself watching Fred carve animals. Funny, everyone said he was odd about girls, but he never bothered her and she rather enjoyed being with him, as though the world outside had beaten both of them. He missed Felicia and, though Phoebe's hands were no substitute for her sister's, he seemed to like her company. At least someone did, she thought ruefully.

'I volunteer,' he told her proudly in his hesitant speech.

'You?' Phoebe stared at him. She was so taken aback she forgot about being tactful.

'Be soldier,' he informed her, stroking the wooden squirrel that had appeared between his cupped hands. 'Like Joe.'

'Yes, but –' Phoebe, torn from her own problems, and concerned for once with someone other than herself, thought quickly. 'They won't take men who have important war work here.'

'What's that?'

'For some men the jobs they do here are more important than their going off and getting killed abroad.'

'Killed? Joe get killed? Like rabbits?'

Bother. Now she'd done it. Not Joe, she assured him hastily. 'Only . . . only . . . officers,' she produced in desperation.

'Oh. This war work?' He held up the squirrel.

'Yes. So they won't let you go.'

'You important war work?'

'No, I'm a woman,' she replied automatically; it occurred to her that socks and saucepans were all men wanted from women. She couldn't boil an egg and she wasn't going to knit socks for anyone, particularly Edith Swinford-Browne. A vision of Edith in khaki socks hit her, and she grinned. Fred obligingly grinned back. There should be something women could do, she pondered, though there'd never be anything in Ashden; she'd have to go away – well, *that* would be good – but at seventeen no one would take her anywhere interesting. Dark, large outside worlds loomed over her with frightening shadows. She'd never, never have the courage now to go anywhere or do anything, yet if she didn't she'd be marooned here, imprisoned alone with Ma and Pa. Even Aunt Tilly turned out to be doing something, if it was only burning things down; Caroline and Felicia were going away; Isabel was married, which excused her from living, the way she appeared to see it. Her parents were wrapped up in home and parish. Panic began to set in. She'd have to stay here with Fred forever, two misfits left alone. She *couldn't* stay, yet she didn't have the courage to go.

Phoebe excused herself from Fred, who didn't notice her leaving anyway. She walked over to the tennis court, which looked as lonely as she was nowadays, and found herself crying at her own predicament. She must *force* herself out of this limbo. She'd walk up to the station and find George, that's what she'd do. It would take bravery – it had the other day, even though she had gone with George then, and seen all those thirsty faces staring out of the train windows. They were hop-pickers on their way to Groombridge. Train journeys took a long time now. Then *her* idea came to her – so simple, so *important* if soldiers were travelling, and refugees, and even hop-pickers. The answer was: *lemonade*!

Mrs Swinford-Browne appeared briskly early on the morning of the 27th, far too early for an At Home, even if the Rectory held such events. She wished to imply that this was urgent war business – as it was.

'I do hope you will forgive my calling when you have so much else to do. I am the local organiser, you see.'

'Of what?' Elizabeth asked, dragged unwillingly from the kitchen, where she had become involved in a question of whether the doubling of the quantities of marrow jam was worth the rising price of the extra sugar.

'The Belgian refugees, naturally.' Edith produced this with pride.

'You need money? Clothing? Blankets? I have given all I have spare to the Red Cross.'

'My dear Mrs Lilley, perhaps you haven't read the newspapers. Lady Lugard, Lord Hugh Cecil and the Honourable Mrs Alfred Lyttelton have formed a committee to find accommodation for Belgian and war refugees, and have requested local reception committees. Naturally I have volunteered. I believe Belgians are quite civilised.'

'You are to have lodgers at The Towers?'

Edith hesitated. This was one point she had not yet discussed with William, awaiting the right moment, and so she avoided a direct answer. 'I have several offers of help from most respectable houses in Hartfield and Withyham. Lady Hunney has had to refuse, of course. She has done enough for the effort, poor soul. But the Rectory now, I am sure you have room.'

'I shall discuss it with my husband.' Elizabeth's voice was non-committal.

When Edith had gone, she sank back to reflect on the situation. Caroline, Felicia and Isabel had left home. Suppose the first two were sent to France, where she had now read the Red Cross were sending VAD detachments? In Ashden village, now the corn was in, more men were volunteering. Agnes had told her that Jamie Thorn had gone to training camp, and the ripple that that had caused had sent others rushing after him. The feeling seemed to be, from what she could gather, that if a no-good blackguard like Jamie could fight for King and Country, it needed a few good men to follow him to even the score for Lord Kitchener. Elizabeth's own work in the village was increasing, as was Laurence's. Meanwhile people still fell ill and had babies, elderly folk still died of old age. To open the doors of the Rectory as a refuge for foreigners for the sake of the country was a twist she found too much to grapple with, but it had to be done. Mrs Dibble, she supposed unenthusiastically, must be consulted.

'Belgians?' Mrs Dibble was doubtful. 'Who's to do their boots? Fred can't. He's doing the lamps *and* clocks now the clockwinder's gone to the wars.'

'They will wait on themselves, and cook for themselves in the kitchen.'

Mrs Dibble stiffened. *'That* they will not, Mrs Lilley. My kitchen's my own.'

'Of course. That was a foolish suggestion of mine.'

'How much are they paying?'

'Do you know, I haven't the slightest idea.' Trust Edith not to mention this small point. 'I'd better find out, I suppose.'

'I'll do the cooking. But not for no heathen, mind. Nor no Romans.'

'I'm sure they will be good Christians, Mrs Dibble.'

'Praise the Lord.' Mrs Dibble sounded unconvinced.

Phoebe shifted from foot to foot nervously at the railway station, waiting for her first train from Tunbridge Wells. The Stationmaster, Mr Eric Chaplin, had been agreeable for a trial period, and on her trestle table stood home-made lemonade essence, glasses and jugs of water, and a sign written out by herself: 'One halfpenny a glass. Free to servicemen and refugees.' The washing-up she would do in the stationmaster's kitchen sink with buckets of water from the well.

'Them hop-pickers are a rough bunch,' Mr Chaplin warned her. 'I'll be keeping an eye on you, don't you worry, young lady.'

Hop-pickers didn't scare Phoebe in the slightest. Nevertheless, when she saw the signal down and a puff of smoke in the distance, she wished she could turn and run, but the thought of an 'I told you so' grin on the stationmaster's face made her determined to stick it out. The railway train steamed in to the platform, shrouding her in white smoke, and carriage doors began to open. Of course there was no sign of George, just when she needed his help. People spilled out all along the platform, surrounded by battered cases, paper parcels, even sacks of belongings. Their sharp voices disconcerted her, so different to the slow Sussex drawl. Whole families of all ages milled around, from toddlers to ancient grannies.

'Lemonade!' She cleared her throat and tried louder. The sound still came out as a squeak. Then one man, in green scarf and shabby cap, saw the notice. 'Cor, stone the crows. A halfpenny. It ought to be free.'

'I'll have one, if you please.'

She jerked her head up at the voice. It was Mr Eliot. Of course, he was the manager, here to meet the hop-pickers. She was instantly confused and nervous, but managed to put on her best business voice. 'That will be one halfpenny please. For the war effort.' She raised her voice, this time to a shout.

'Good girl,' he said approvingly, taking the glass. Whether he spoke of the lemonade or something else she did not know, and had no time to speculate as the cry went round 'for the war effort': half-pennies and pennies were thrown at her from all directions. Late that afternoon she made her way home, well content, clutching a net 3s 7d in a paper bag, like a talisman. She needed it. She hadn't yet told Father what she had been doing. Perhaps tomorrow she'd come to a business arrangement with the stationmaster's wife to do the washing up, though.

'I suppose we have to, Elizabeth.' Laurence pulled a face. It would feel like invasion, having strangers sharing their home; even if the war were over in a week or two, it would take time to repatriate all the refugees. They could be here for well over a month, perhaps even two. He struggled to reconcile the man with the vicar of God. He had no choice, of course. 'Perhaps God will be merciful and send me one who enjoys chess, now Caroline's left us.' She was the only one of his family who had any interest in playing at all.

'Caroline!' Elizabeth exclaimed.

'Please, Elizabeth, do not worry—'

'No, Laurence. It has occurred to me: who is to write the parish magazine if Caroline is not here?'

'I must, I suppose.' Laurence was even more dismayed. It was a time-consuming job but an important one.

George poked his head out from the sofa where he was rereading William Le Queux to get some tips on spy-catching. 'I will.'

'Please be serious, George.' His mother was impatient.

'Why not?' George was instantly aggrieved. It had been an idle offer, but now he felt sure it was the only thing in life he'd ever wanted to do, apart from catching a spy. It's simple. Do let me, Pa. You can read it through afterwards to check my spelling and all that.

'Why not?' Laurence was amused. 'Why not indeed?'

'We're nearly there. It's the next station.' Felicia peered out of the train window at Lewisham.

'Somehow Blackheath and the Royal Herbert don't seem so far from home after Penelope's news,' Caroline replied.

Yesterday evening, to celebrate their gaining of first aid certificates, they had dined in Tunbridge Wells with

Penelope and Aunt Tilly. The news that Aunt Tilly was there at all was shock enough, since Caroline had thought she was in London, but Penelope's news was even more startling. She had casually announced that her brother was now caught up in the fighting and that she was off to Serbia in a few days' time with a hospital unit led by Lady Paget.

'I'm no use at anything, I told them,' Penelope had explained. 'But they must have thought I'd do for something or other, even if it's only scaring away the Austrians. Bold Englishwoman goes into battle armed with Keating's Powder and a tin of Zambuk. We're leaving for Skopje early next month.'

Caroline had seen the look of envy on her aunt's face, and it was all she could do to persuade her to regain her own health before rushing off to foreign parts to help others do the same. Caroline sympathised. Shooters Hill now seemed dull beside Penelope's exploits, and it had taken Felicia's common sense afterwards to readjust her thinking that training widened their usefulness.

The train began to slow down, and Caroline felt her heart pounding.

It was about to begin.

Chapter Ten

Isabel walked into Hop House with unexpected trepidation. The early enthusiasm she had felt for a house of her own had mysteriously vanished and, instead of the kingdom she had looked forward to, it had become a land that might hold uncharted obstacles and pitfalls. They presented themselves as soon as she and Edith went inside. The last few days at The Towers, recuperating from her ordeal, had blinkered her against this moment; she had merely reflected that they had been gone nearly a month, and Hop House would therefore be completely ready by the time she and Robert decided to move in. Instead, she was greeted by the smell of emptiness, a house lonely and unoccupied. The furniture, she could see through the door Edith enthusiastically threw open, was there, but pushed higgledy-piggledy around and still covered with dust sheets. The curtains were heaped in piles on the floor while the windows yawned their nudity. A telephone set perched unattached on the mantelshelf, and the walls, newly wallpapered (to Edith's taste), smelled of distemper and cast out a chill that found its target in Isabel's spirits.

'But where are the servants?' Her dismay made Isabel abandon her customary diplomacy with her mother-in-law.

'Mrs Bugle starts on Monday, Isabel – dear.' Edith decided to leave a pause before the endearment.

'And the others?'

Edith bristled. 'There *are* no others.' There was reproof in her tone. 'The men have volunteered.' Not all of them, in fact. William had commandeered the Hop House butler as a Towers footman, to remedy their own sudden shortages.

'Volunteered for what?'

Edith's lips stiffened patriotically. 'The army, Isabel. They'll be back soon, I'm sure, now our boys are pushing that Kaiser back where he belongs.'

'How could they volunteer without your permission?'

'They had it.' Edith stretched the truth somewhat in view of Isabel's querulousness. 'We must do our little bit for England.'

Isabel was appalled. 'How am I to manage?'

'I am sure Mrs Bugle will find a reliable girl from the village.'

'I mean, how are we to manage till Monday? Just look at this.' Isabel swept a despairing arm round the room.

Edith decided the time had come to take umbrage. In her youth as a butcher's daughter she had spent many a long, tiring morning helping the cook-general with household duties and somewhat resented the fact that others had escaped so lightly from life's inequalities. The blue taffeta rustled as she kissed her daughter-in-law goodbye. 'Such pleasure, playing housewife for the first time. I do so envy you.'

Six hours later Isabel felt as though every dust particle in the house had burrowed through the pores of her skin. The dust covers were off, but the furniture remained where it was. One curtain hung gaping out from the only two hooks she could find. Two single beds bulged with inexpert bed-making; her gowns hung neatly in the wardrobe. Robert's wardrobe remained empty, not as a pointed gesture, but simply because the unpacking and hanging of gentleman's clothes baffled her. Never had she been so glad to hear his step.

'Darling.' She rushed out to the entrance hall to burst into the tears she had been holding back specially. 'I've had the most terrible day; the house is disgusting and there aren't any servants.' She clung piteously to him.

'I daresay we'll pull through.'

Surprise at this lack of support made her loosen her hold and stop crying. 'Don't you *care*?'

'Not very much.' Robert walked into the drawing room, and flung himself in the nearest armchair.

'Is something wrong with you?' It dawned even on Isabel that this was unusual behaviour.

'I'm sorry, kitten.' Robert made an effort at normality. 'I expect we'll get servants soon, once they're back from this war. I'll have to call *them* sir, then, no doubt.'

Isabel wondered why his normally placid face was looking so downcast. It made her uneasy; it was almost as though they were back in Paris, except that then his anxiety had had an edge of excitement, as he insisted on buying every single edition of every single newspaper and talked endlessly of distant places like Brussels, Namur or Liege. She had been so sure Robert would regain his interest in everyday life once they got back home, yet, just when she needed him to organise the house, he'd relapsed into moodiness, especially when he read that one or two bombs had fallen in Paris and the government had left for Bordeaux. He'd cheered up when the next issue of *The Times* informed him that the new Governor of Paris had decided to defend the city. General Gallieni had stopped all this nonsense of editions of newspapers being published every hour or two, and newspaper sellers were no longer allowed to cry out in the streets. Pity it couldn't happen here, too, then Robert might cheer up and help her. Perhaps she'd be very nice to him tonight. The sexual side of marriage was a mystery to Isabel. She couldn't see a lot to it, it wasn't frightening or repulsive as some friends had claimed, merely rather boring. She in fact found it hard not to giggle when Robert made such a fuss about not having babies when there was a war on. Such a to-do putting on that horrid, uncomfortable looking thing; he'd thought she wasn't looking, but she was.

'Pa won't let me go.' Robert interrupted her thoughts.

'Where?'

'To volunteer, of course.'

'*You* volunteer?' Shock made her gape unbecomingly. 'But you can't leave me now.' She meant with the house to arrange, but he took it otherwise.

'It's because I love you, dearest, that I have to go to fight. Every decent man should, to protect his womenfolk.'

'You could do that much better here.' What on earth

was the sense of going to Belgium to prevent Germans attacking Hop House?

'It looks as though I'll have to. Father won't let me go. He says he needs me at the moment at the brewery, now so many have gone to war.'

'There are enough men going without you. The menservants have all left.' Isabel was terrified. She tried hard to think of the war effort and patriotism but all that really registered was that she'd be here alone.

'Do you think it is right they should go to war and not me? A fine example that sets. The Hunneys have both gone, so has Peter Jennings. Even Philip Ryde volunteered, only they wouldn't have him.'

'We've only just escaped with our lives,' Isabel pointed out. 'I think you owe it to your parents to stay here.'

Robert did not reply. In theory his father could not stop him, in practice he most certainly could. He could remove his 'job', such as it was, and his house, leaving Isabel homeless, and worse, he had made it clear he would stop his allowance.

'What time is dinner, Isabel?'

Isabel's stomach lurched uncomfortably. 'Here?' she asked stupidly.

'Where else?'

'We have no cook. We'll have to go to your parents, as I did for luncheon.'

'I'll bally well starve first,' he told her violently.

'Then we'll go to the Rectory. Mother won't mind.'

'But I *do*. We'll eat here. Our house. Let me have some bally thing to call my own.'

Trained to recognise male danger signs in Father, Isabel went for the first time into the Hop House kitchens. She bitterly resented it, but was also experienced in knowing when self-survival demanded silence. What she found was not encouraging. Tinned peas, Liebig's extract, blancmange powder, a sack of potatoes, another of onions, and some eggs. No milk, no bread. She was about to inform Robert that he would have to ride down to the general stores, when she thought better of it. With no telephone she could not even ask Mother for advice. A dim recollection of seeing Mrs Dibble make a vegetable omelette came to mind. She would need milk, or was it water, or both? She could walk to the farm, but she wouldn't. Then she had a good idea. She would borrow milk from her nearest neighbour – no matter if that were Frank Eliot.

Monkey Brand soap, Monkey Brand soap, more Monkey Brand soap, and soda. It made a rhythm as you scrubbed the basins, and took Caroline's mind off how tired she was. Surely it must be eight o'clock by now? She had begun her working day, like the other VADs, at seven this morning. She began by scouring, she ended by scouring. The middle of the day provided welcome relief, as she laid trays for the patients with knives, forks and spoons all in regimental order to pass Sister's eagle eye. She performed the same duties all night long too, in her sleep; sometimes in her dreams she was laying cutlery on upturned basins, and sometimes carrying in trays with empty basins stacked up on top. How could Felicia enjoy such apparently contented slumber? She must be equally tired, even though she had been appointed to the grand position of a ward orderly. Grand but not enviable, for she had to be at everyone's beck and call to fetch slop buckets and remove slops, or buckets of soiled bandages now even more casualties were arriving, all to be dealt with simultaneously it seemed. How little she had known of her sister's mettle when the Rectory walls were their boundaries. Here was Felicia, seeing blood, pus and even gangrene and amputated limbs, and all Caroline could manage was to scrub a few pots and lay trays. Or was that all? She had found out much about herself too; that her strength was greater than she had thought and would carry her through, despite her fears. Perhaps there was more of her father in her than she had realised, or perhaps God was making sure that Ashden Rectory did not disgrace Him!

She waited as Felicia slipped the dark serge overcoat over her print gown and light blue overall to walk home to their billets near the crest of Shooters Hill. The peaked caps they had to wear suited Felicia but made Caroline look like a cross cockatoo.

'Another trainload came in today – did you see them arrive?' Felicia asked her. 'They aren't such serious cases as the last one, thank goodness. I could not bear—' She broke off, as if admission of failure let her down.

'How *do* you bear it?'

Felicia looked surprised. 'Every time I see those dressings being changed, or a wounded soldier brought in, I imagine it's Daniel, and that I might be able to help him by doing what I do. Don't you think of Reggie?'

'It's rather different with scrubbing bowls,' Caroline said ruefully. 'But every time I get tired, I think of him fighting for England over there; it acts as a Master Dabb on me. I start scrubbing twice as hard. Even so, I'd like to be doing something more significant to help.'

'You're just like Aunt Tilly. You want to do what men do best, instead of what women do best.'

Did she? Caroline couldn't believe it was so. All she knew, even more clearly since she had left Ashden, was that somewhere out there was something and someone calling her name, softly now and far away, but ever there. The someone was Reggie, but what was the something? And why didn't it call louder instead of leaving her feeling as though she were threshing around in a field of corn looking for the one blade for her?

Felicia was saying, 'I feel as if I'm taking part in a theatrical charade when I go to their ward. They are so self-conscious and act more like schoolboys than officers. The Tommies are far more natural and just let the nurses and doctors get on with it. They joke with me while their dressings are being changed, and I've stopped feeling so useless merely standing by with the bucket.'

Caroline wondered at how quickly and how far they – who had been brought up never to look too closely at their own bodies – had come in so short a time. What would Mother say if she knew Felicia was in such close contact with men's bodies; whatever it was it would be irrelevant. This was a different world, and when the war was over it would either vanish as they returned to Ashden, or prove the threshold of a new kind of life. Meanwhile, she decided, she would not allow herself to think of Ashden, for fear of finding just how much she missed it. She would instead reread the one brief letter she had had from Reggie – reread it for the twentieth time. Or was it the thirtieth? How sweet even the baldest statements could be, how loaded with inner meaning each mention of platefuls of snails or brawn, how charged each word of love. She knew from the newspapers there had been another big battle, this time on the Marne, not far from Paris. The 'withdrawal' had been a 'retreat', everyone was saying, but now the British army really *was* triumphant again, and pushing back the Germans across the river. Let it be so, oh let it be so, she prayed, and dear Lord, keep Reggie safe.

George was becoming bored with his job. The first flush of honour at representing DORA, the Defence of the Realm Act, had worn off, there was a limit to the excitement to be gained by patrolling the footpaths and railway track of Ashden with a large stick, home-made lasso and whistle. Yet there seemed nothing else he could do for the war effort; Phoebe had suggested he help her serve drinks and buns, but that was woman's work. He'd helped erect the barricades round Castle Tillow, and the rest of Ashden didn't seem to require protecting from invasion. Together with a fellow scout on a neighbouring watch, he'd been sleeping in a tent for two days in order to maintain a twenty-four-hour guard, but the delights of the hard ground and rough fare provided by some hop-pickers were beginning to pall.

George jumped over the stile from Station Road, and began to stroll along the footpath towards Hodes meadows. He hadn't proceeded far when it happened. He saw him standing out like a sore thumb in the English countryside. No hop-picker this. A thrill of excitement caught him, and

George ran behind a tree to observe his quarry more closely. There was no doubt: the black Homburg hat pulled far down towards the beady eyes, the dark suit, heavy moustache and beard, and, to clinch it, he was actually writing in a notebook. He was obviously gathering vital information from passing trains, and had cleverly positioned himself just near the signal but out of sight of Mr Toms in the signal box. If trains halted by the signal, he could assess the numbers of troops, perhaps even their regiments. Or worse, George tensed up, he was planning to *take* the signal box in a few moments, just as he'd read about; he'd overpower Mr Toms and then *wreck the train*!

George decided on his plan of action. He must surprise the enemy, creep up behind and give him some sort of fright. The man would instinctively reply in his native language – which would be *German*. With one hand George grasped his scout stick firmly like a shooting rifle, and looped the lasso ready for action over the other wrist. Then he emerged cautiously from his cover. The German was still engrossed in recording information. George was hardly able to believe his luck. Slowly, slowly, catchee monkey spy, he told himself. This was what he'd been waiting for; this was the stuff of Rorke's Drift.

Three yards, two yards, one yard, and *wham!* The stick was poked in the back, and then he swapped hands with the lasso now ready for action.

There was an incomprehensible cry of pain and shock as the man struggled to his feet, only to find his arms firmly pinioned. Good work, George, he congratulated himself, for the shout was indisputably guttural. He grabbed his whistle and gave the three loud blasts he had discussed with Mr Chaplin, hoping he was still within earshot. He was, for George could already hear shouts and the sound of running feet; that would be the porter while the Stationmaster would ring ahead to PC Ifield. Meanwhile old Hunny here – he grinned at the pun – was making the dickens of a noise.

The porter, Arthur Mutter, came rushing up. 'PC Ifield's on his way, sir.' Not much older than George, he was thrilled to see evidence of his first spy.

'Good,' commented George curtly. 'Give me a hand, will you?'

With Mr Chaplin's and Arthur's help, the man was prodded up into the station cart; George sat proudly at his side, his stick visibly at the ready in case the prisoner showed superhuman strength and burst his bonds, and the old horse plodded off down Station Road with Arthur at the reins. The Ashden telegraph proved quicker than the horse, however. By the time PC Ifield had grabbed his helmet and reached the junction of Bankside and Station Road, half the village, spearheaded by the Norville Arms regulars, had spilled out from its normal occupations to hiss at the German spy. It was George's supreme moment. Already he could see his name in the Skinners' news-sheet and the *East Sussex Courier*.

Even the Rectory had heard the news, for Mother was at the gate to witness his homecoming. She was looking upset; perhaps she'd thought he'd been hurt? That must be why she was rushing over to old Ifield and talking so earnestly. Together they accompanied the cart past the Rectory, past Tillow House and into the grounds of the police house.

They waited till then to break it to him. It turned out the spy was a Belgian after all, and the reason George couldn't understand him was that the fellow spoke some peculiar language called Flemish. A very natural mistake, PC Ifield declared. Mother was not so understanding, as she forced him to apologise to the man and sent him back to the Rectory while she smoothed things over. It turned out the fellow was actually staying in their house with his family and had only just arrived. George now recalled some vague talk of Belgian refugees, but how was he to know they were actually *coming*, and after all he'd been at his post of duty for the past two days and nights. Somebody should have *told* him.

Smarting with chagrin, George went straight up to his room on the pretext of starting the parish magazine. He might as well have a go at that; there was nothing else to do in this place.

Shortly afterwards, Elizabeth, full of sympathy for the poor man's ordeal acquainted her husband with the story of George's iniquity. Laurence tried not to laugh and failed, and reluctantly Elizabeth gave in and laughed with him.

'It's all very well for you,' she informed her husband, 'but I had to apologise and try to explain with scarcely a word of a common language between us. After all that trouble Mrs Dibble and I went to in organising their rooms to make them feel at home, the poor people had only been here an hour before our son assaulted the father. After all they've been through he must have been terrified.' Try as she would, another giggle escaped her.

'Where are they now?'

She made a face. 'He retired to their rooms with his

wife *and* the two children. I don't know what to do.'

'Leave them there. When they emerge, warn me, and I'll appear in cassock and surplice to impress them.'

'Suppose they're Roman Catholics?'

The Rector peered out of the morning room window. 'It seems to me that may be irrelevant,' he commented. 'Look.'

Elizabeth rushed to join him. Down the Rectory drive marched a family of four, the 'spy' in front carrying one battered bag, his family behind. All their backs had the truculent, stolid look of those who have no intention of returning. 'But where can they be going?' she asked in concern. 'Should I run after them? They are our responsibility.'

Laurence watched for a moment or two as they disappeared through the open gate. 'No. They look as though they know exactly where they're going. And I would say it's to one of the few places they know. The railway station, or,' he paused for effect, 'The Towers, where they were taken when they first arrived.'

'The *Towers*?' Elizabeth's lips twitched.

He put his arm round her. 'The Belgians are the losers. Indeed I almost feel it my duty to implore them to stay. Perhaps, on reflection, we should go after them.'

She looked at him, startled at the seeming gravity in his voice. She braced herself. 'Very well. If you are sure that is right, Laurence.'

'We could perhaps wait a little while.' He laughed, his conscience pricking him slightly. Was it for the Lord's work or his own sake that he so desired the Rectory to have an open door for those in need but to be able to close it when necessary? He saw Elizabeth's relieved expression, and knew she was battling as was he.

'I think we could,' she agreed thankfully. She waited guiltily for the sound of the telephone bell; it came several times, but not from The Towers.

Frank Eliot, opening his front door at Hop Cottage on the maid's evening off, was completely taken aback to find the Rector's wife on the doorstep. He wondered whether Phoebe had told her of their encounter, and was relieved when he found, after inviting her into his parlour, that all that was at stake was her son's services as a hop-picker. Opportunely, troops were being detailed to take over the scouts' duties. 'And possibly my daughter Phoebe, when I have spoken to her, may accompany him,' Elizabeth added.

'Does not her work at the railway station rule that out?' he asked in surprise.

From the look on Mrs Lilley's face, he realised he had blundered.

'What work, may I ask?'

There was no help for it now. A full explanation would serve better than half-truths. He told her, therefore, emphasising how necessary Phoebe's work was and what a valuable contribution she was making to the war effort.

'Thank you, Mr Eliot. I understand.'

By no sign did she reveal how hurt she was. He was a stranger. To her husband, however, she did not conceal her horror. 'She cannot possibly be allowed to continue, of course.'

'Why not?' he asked. 'It seems to me to show enterprise.'

'But serving troops and hop-pickers. It's not fitting for her to be dealing with them alone.'

'Two of our daughters are tending soldiers in some capacity or other. Would you say that was fitting?'

'That is war. This is not.'

'For Phoebe it *is* war. If she meets trouble, she will either deal with it, or give up. Either way, let her try.'

Even Mrs Dibble, Elizabeth discovered to her increasing chagrin, had known about the lemonade, but had not seen fit to mention it. For the mistress of the Rectory, Elizabeth seemed to be singularly ill-informed. It was a situation she must deal with, war or no war.

'I could do with Grandfather's cottage, surely.'

Mabel regarded her elder son with something rapidly approaching dislike. She hadn't realised how much she'd miss Jamie till he'd gone. He'd been a shame to her in Ashden, but Len was no substitute for Jamie's companionship, and even less for his work. Not that she'd been wrong in telling him to go. He'd done ill and must pay for it, but that didn't mean Len was going to profit by it. Ebenezer Thorn, while drinking to the Kaiser's downfall in the Norville Arms a week ago, had collapsed and died. There was general sympathy, for Ebenezer had been popular in the village, even – during periods when the feud was dormant – among the Mutters. It was, Mabel reflected sourly, just like Len to be asking what he could get out of it without doing a stroke towards the work of the funeral and clearing out the poor old man's clutter.

'Your father's going to sell it, and we've been offered a tidy price. A hundred and fifty pounds, that's double what it's worth. Where are we going to get that kind of money again?'

'I do a decent day's work.'

'A decent day's laze, I call it. It's only your father pulls you through. And what if you go to war too?'

'I'm needed here. I can't go to war.'

'Then stay here. You've a roof over your head, haven't you?'

'And what if I wed?'

'Bring her here and all.'

Len had a mental vision of Phoebe Lilley tucked up in the attic, helping his mother out, humping buckets of well water in and out, and frustration made him belligerent. 'Who are you selling to?'

'As if you can't guess.'

'Old fatty Billy boy?'

'Quite right, son. If you don't get earning, you lazy splodger, the picture palace ain't going to see you, surely.'

'Caroline, come quickly.' Felicia rushed breathlessly into the hospital kitchen.

'I can't. I've still got nineteen trays to go. Can't it wait until I do the ward rounds?'

'No. There's a Tommy here from the 2nd Battalion of the Royal Sussex, and he's in *Reggie's* platoon. He *knows* him.'

Caroline forgot all about trays sixty-two to eighty, and endeavoured to walk sedately with Felicia in order to avoid notice by the Sister on the ward. Private Joe Pinfold, recuperating after a bullet in the leg, was propped against his pillows, obviously regaling the occupants of the adjoining beds with his views on the nurses, for he promptly stopped as Felicia approached.

'This is my sister, Joe. She's Lieutenant Hunney's fiancée.'

Fiancée? Caroline was whisked back into the world of Ashden, which she only visited in her dreams at night now. Here, in the hospital, the word struck her as strange, for here she was Caroline Lilley, a VAD trainee, and that was all.

'Is Lieutenant Hunney all right?' she burst out after expressing her sympathy for his wounds.

'Come to see me in the dressing station himself. It would take more than a few Germans to knock him out, don't you worry, miss. And me,' he added for good measure.

'What do you mean? Did they try?' What a stupid question she thought, even as she said it. Only a matter of days ago a *Times* special edition had proclaimed the engagement at Le Cateau: 'Fiercest fight in History. Heavy losses by British troops'.

'Oh yes, miss. At the Marne. Advance guard we were, off to meet old von Kluck himself one fine morning. Pissing – raining hard it was, they never ought to force you to fight when it's raining. Ain't got the heart for it. Well, there we were, all wearing our waterproofs, and no one could tell who was fighting who. So we copped a packet, not only from the Germans, but our own artillery, coming up behind.' He had put it more graphically to his mates.

'That's when you were wounded? And what about Reg – Lieutenant Hunney?'

'You stay with me, Pinfold, he says. I was on the stretcher, see. I'm going that way myself.'

'Why?' Caroline asked sharply. 'Was he wounded?'

'Only a scratch, miss. Bullet grazed him. He was in

there less time than it takes to flip a tiddly-wink. Don't you worry now. Gentlemen like Lieutenant Hunney pull through. They're in the lead, see, and the one at the front always gets through.'

Caroline considered these words of wisdom dubiously. She wanted to ask fatuously: did he mention me? That was nonsense; how could he have done? *Was* it only a scratch? She would have to go on waiting, clinging only to the knowledge that a week ago he had been safe. War, she now knew, was not a daring charge by a cavalry of immaculate red-jacketed soldiers, but a group of wet men in waterproofs being machine gunned by their own side.

'Elizabeth, can you spare a moment?' Laurence poked his head round the corner of the boudoir door.

'Of course.' Elizabeth abandoned the pile of parcels of knitted comforts awaiting despatch to the War Office. The boudoir was now a packing room with a considerable turnover, which Fred ambled down to the post office or carriers to despatch at least twice a day.

Was Ruth Horner's baby born already, she wondered. Had the police come for Jacob Halfpenny, whom the whole village knew to be a deserter and with whom all sympathised since he looked after his widowed mother who was nearly blind and confined to her chair, crippled with rheumatics? Had Grannie Johns gone at last, she who was so old no one knew *how* old, save that she remembered the 'great battle'? Waterloo? Had Laurence discovered yet another of Mrs Dibble's hoards? Elizabeth was still feeling like a fish floundering out of her depth in her own home. 'There is very bad news from the Manor, Elizabeth. Sir John has come down briefly to stay with his wife for Daniel is on the missing list.'

'Daniel?' she repeated stupidly. The lists of those missing were names published in *The Times* under the heading Roll of Honour, not people they knew. 'Does that mean –' she grappled with the horrifying idea – 'that he is dead?'

'Possibly, or wounded, or is a prisoner of war. It is too soon to be sure.'

'But that is *terrible*. Poor, poor Lady Hunney.' Elizabeth watched Laurence pacing round the room. 'He is so young. It was his twenty-first birthday only two weeks ago. He wants to do so much, and now missing in a war that is not of our making. Who else?'

The same thought was in both their minds: Reggie.

'Where is he missing?' she asked confusingly.

'There was some delay in notifying the War Office, because of the retreat and the swiftness of the German sweep towards Paris. Daniel is in the 1st Battalion of the King's Own Royal Regiment; the battalion was late in being ordered to France, and therefore was not involved in the fighting at Mons; however, it did join in the retreat, and took part in the engagement at Le Cateau we read about. The King's Own met disaster there when somehow they remained visible to the enemy, who machine gunned and shelled them as such an obvious target. A great many were killed, and then the battalion fought valiantly on throughout the day before being ordered to withdraw.'

Elizabeth shuddered, and Laurence tried to keep his voice even as he recited the known facts. 'The men were buried in a mass grave. It is possible that Daniel may have been one of them, though Sir John thinks it unlikely, since he would have heard if so.'

'Poor boy,' Elizabeth said, her tears already falling. 'How is Maud?'

'She has taken it badly – or well, as you may think. She simply refuses to believe he is dead, and insists that there has been some mistake.'

'I can understand her. I would feel that myself.' Elizabeth paused. 'Laurence, what of Felicia? She is so fond of Daniel.'

'Neither of us can leave the parish at such a time, Elizabeth. I will write to Caroline to break the news gently to her.'

'He is well,' Caroline crowed triumphantly, as they walked back to their lodgings that evening, twirling round to demonstrate the point.

'That's wonderful news,' Felicia said.

'What does fighting a battle conjure up to you, Felicia? To me, it's derring-do, Kitchener and Omdurman.'

'All it means to me is a pile of soiled bandages. I don't believe I care for King and Country.'

Caroline stopped short in amazement. 'I would have thought that of all of us you would be the most duty-bound.'

'Would you, if that were Reggie in that bed?'

'No.'

'*Every* man there is a Daniel for me.'

They walked in silence in the starry night on the more wooded side of the roadway of Shooters Hill, where thick bushes recalled the area's famous highwaymen days; days when gallows stood ready at the foot of the hill, and staging coaches stopped with relief at the Bull Inn. The mounting steps were still there, but used now only for the occasional horseman. Sevendroog Castle, a weird and romantic tower on the hill top, gave it an atmosphere so different to that of the hospital lying at its foot, but all sense of excitement vanished as they reached their lodgings. There was only one letter awaiting them – for Caroline. She opened it and Felicia, eagerly waiting for news from home, saw her face change.

She would go to the hop-fields to find George. Mother was worried about him; she must be, Isabel told herself. George was only fifteen and the hop-pickers were a very rough crowd. Shopkeepers had barriers and shutters erected against thieving hands, and the Norville Arms always consigned hop-pickers to the barn behind the inn. Besides, she deserved a temporary escape. Robert was totally preoccupied by how much he hated his new work at the brewery, necessary now that so many of the men were volunteering, and when he wasn't complaining about that he was still bewailing the fact that he could not volunteer himself. She found it hardly flattering. Every day she feared he might sneak off to the Drill Hall recruiting centre in Tunbridge Wells to offer his services, and he had told her that every time he saw his father he tried again to make him change his mind. Fortunately William Swinford-Browne was standing firm.

The day was warm for September, and Isabel decided it justified her wearing the new light voile gown that she had purchased to compensate for the loss of all her baggage in France. The light, open-sided T-bar shoes she had chosen flattered her feet but made each step agony along the uneven stony paths to the farm, and the worn-down field paths where each spike of dried-out grass seemed to select her white silk stockings for its target. Few of the hop-pickers recognised her, rather to her chagrin. Most of them were East Enders or other foreigners intent on their own raucous songs, shouts and guffaws, as they sat with bines across their knees, nimbly stripping off the hops – or, in the case of the men, it seemed, standing by and leaving the task to the women. She suddenly realised with a throb of excitement that George would be hard to find amid this rabble and that would mean – after all, why not? She *was* Robert's wife.

'Where will I find Mr Eliot?' she demanded of the first Ashdenian she could see – she had a vague idea it might have been a Mutter. He certainly wasn't very polite. A jerk of the thumb and the barest gesture of removing his filthy cap were all she received. He was, however, accurate. Following the direction of the thumb, she saw Frank Eliot at the gate to the next field. He was looking at his pocket watch, and certainly had not seen her, so that panther lounge was natural, not for her benefit. She longed for him to look up and walk to *her*. It wasn't her place to approach him. Except of course in case of emergency like the borrowing of the milk. He had been most polite then, most helpful, though all the while she had had an annoying feeling that he was somehow mocking her.

He did look up. Naturally she didn't notice, and naturally he was walking towards her to greet her. She would speak first, though she would take a long time deciding to do so – until he was almost up to her. But he did not wait for her to speak.

'Good afternoon, Mrs Swinford-Browne. I'm honoured.' He swept off his boater – how unsuitable for a farm manager. She would speak to Robert.

She gave a theatrical start. 'You did give me a fright.' She managed to imply he would be forgiven.

'My apologies.' He ran his eye over her, reflecting how strange it was that she was Miss Phoebe's sister: Miss Phoebe who looked so provocative and yet was so innocent, and this one, who pretended to be so aloof and dignified and yet – he was sure – was deliberately placing herself in his path. True, her husband was a weak sort of fellow, but he was his employer's son. Frank was torn between wishing to avoid trouble and the feeling that Mrs Isabel should be taught a lesson, for everyone's sake. If she didn't choose to learn it, then his conscience would be clear, he decided. Quite what he'd do then, if anything, he didn't know. Meanwhile: 'I came to pay my respects, ma'am. I expect you are looking for young George. I will escort you.'

'Thank you. I'm interested in my father-in-law's concerns.'

She enjoyed her feeling of power as the hoppers in the alleyways, some of which were already cleared of their hops, made way for them. Every so often Mr Eliot would scoop a child up under his arm and place it firmly to the side, or even on occasion into the huge hessian bins used for the picked hops, whence the child was quickly pulled out.

'They don't like that. It presses the hops down too much, and they have to hover them up again before the measurer comes round.'

'Indeed.' It was double-Dutch to Isabel, who picked her

way, smiling at the seated women when she remembered, but always conscious of the man at her side.

'Smell, Mrs Swinford-Browne,' he said suddenly, picking a hop from a bine still on its wire.

'I can, thank you.' The air was heavy with their acrid, heavy smell. It made her feel trapped within it, repelling yet robbing her of the ability to walk away.

'Smell it.' It was an order, and he thrust it beneath her nose.

'Very nice,' she managed to say stiltedly.

'It lulls your senses.' His voice grew soft. 'Like a woman.'

She gave a cry of outrage, but he apparently didn't hear for he was surrounded by a group of hoppers. She stood to one side, showing her impatience at being ignored. Not for long.

To her horror, one of the hoppers, a huge, rough giant of a man, made a sudden swoop towards her, and she found herself swept up and suspended over one of the large bins of hops, to the great delight of the hoppers who gathered round shrieking with laughter.

'Footshoe money,' he shouted, foul breath hitting her in the face, 'or I drop you in, missis.'

'Put me *down*!' Tears of anger welled up. 'Mr Eliot, *order* him to put me down.' But to her fury he made no move, despite the apparently shocked expression on his face.

'More than my job's worth, Mrs Swinford-Browne. Can't go against the old custom. Mr Swinford-Browne knows that. You're a stranger here, and you didn't stop to have your shoes rubbed with hops before you walked the fields. That means you have to contribute to the hop party fund.'

She longed to refuse, but from her humiliating position

was quite unable to do so. 'Very well, I will. Put me down first.'

To the crowd's cheering she was promptly replaced on the ground, and the ridiculous boater was waved in front of her. She fumbled in her handbag and dropped one of the new paper notes in it to a round of clapping.

The crowd drifted away, and she stared icily at Frank Eliot. 'You will pay for this, Mr Eliot.'

He bent down and picked up the crushed hop spray. 'You look after these hops from the day they're planted, building up the hills round them, protecting them from the wilt and mould, like little babies, and then they grow, twining themselves round their poles and wires, ensnaring your heart with their young beauty and their fresh green leaves. A poor man has no say in it. He just hears their call, like Odysseus did those sirens.'

'You're mocking me!' Isabel cried angrily, unable to believe it.

'Me? I wouldn't dare, Mrs Swinford-Browne. I'm just a farmer.'

He looked so startled, she almost believed him, but she was saved from answering by George's indignant shout. 'What on earth are *you* doing here?'

She hurried gratefully towards him.

Frank Eliot watched her go, regretting that the Almighty had so arranged it that those to whom one's body was attracted did not necessarily exercise the same appeal over the mind, and grateful that her position probably put the matter out of his control anyway.

* * *

373

'My cinema. My *palace*.' William Swinford-Browne complacently viewed his kingdom to be. No one had got the better of him in Ashden, not even his own son. All this balderdash about wanting to volunteer, even after he'd seen the casualty lists. No, he was still intent on breaking his mother's heart.

Nor had Isabel made any headway with him. Love's young dream did not seem to be working out to madam's satisfaction. He wished he had the training of her. It was either money or the marriage bed causing the trouble. It couldn't be the first so it looked as if Robert was not giving her what she needed. That was his diagnosis, and the young fool proposed to deal with the problem by running away to war. William couldn't allow that, especially since Edith would promptly take over Hop House for refugees so that she could kick them out of The Towers, and that would mean moving Isabel in with them. William did not fancy this arrangement. She would be too close in every way. Sex was one thing, but personal security was another. He had had a narrow squeak with Ruth Horner, and did not propose to be caught out again. He'd take his amusement in London in future, well away from home ground.

Turning to more pleasant thoughts, he began to wander round the two cottages. Hovels is what he'd call them. One was empty, the other full of lumber. He'd told the Thorns to get rid of it by the end of the week. Then he'd tear the cottages down and in their place would arise a palace of white plaster and black beams, with a clock tower built in the centre. Ashden needed a village clock. That would show the Lilleys. He'd arrange for it to strike half a minute after the church clock, or perhaps *before* would be more subtle. Here shortly Charlie Chaplin would be delighting the whole of Ashden, and they'd be grateful to *him*, William Swinford-Browne. To think that Matilda Lilley had thought she could get the better of him. He didn't usually have much time for doctors, but the fellow who had pointed out that one in two women went mad in middle age had his full support.

In Tunbridge Wells Matilda Lilley was reading *The Times* in the morning room. At her side were the ancient suitcases that accompanied her peripatetic life. She looked up as the door opened, expecting to see the butler, but it was Lord Banning.

'Er – there appears to be a cab at the door for you.'

'That is correct. I must apologise. I had thought you were away, Lord Banning. You must now consider me most impolite in leaving without thanking you for your hospitality.'

'No. I was wondering why you were going, that's all.'

Tilly was surprised. 'Now Penelope has left, naturally I presumed that you—'

'You are concerned for your reputation?'

'Of course not.' She had been going to continue, 'for yours', but then realised she could hardly say this without putting herself in the role of 'helpless womanly woman'. From his quizzical expression she also realised that he both appreciated this dilemma and had engineered it. It amused her. 'Lord Banning, I have imposed on your hospitality long enough,' she told him.

'That is not for you to say, Miss Lilley. Now that Penelope has left, I should be grateful for your continued presence. I have grown accustomed to your voice and appearance. I like them, rather.'

The words seemed familiar, and after a moment she recalled Shaw's *Pygmalion*. She spoke briskly. 'So, Lord Banning, have the police, and I shall not diminish the number of their opportunities.'

'I understood Mrs Pankhurst had suspended suffragist activity. And pray, Miss Lilley, do not grasp that suitcase handle so firmly. The footman would take it as a slight to his professional status.' He took the case from her hand and set it down.

'That is so. But Christabel Pankhurst has made their attitude quite clear. I heard her speak in the London Opera House. If the Kaiser were to win this war, all hope of the vote for women would be lost. Besides, we have sought for a long time to be regarded as men's equals in our daily lives. It follows we must be part of this war; if not marching with the troops then doing everything we can to support them, and to encourage them to go.'

'Help recruitment, you mean?'

'Certainly. Too many men will do nothing – it is their nature – unless shamed into going by their womenfolk.'

'And what of those who do not believe in violence, Miss Lilley? And pray do sit down. I feel I am at a public meeting, and I cannot sit unless you will.'

Against her will she laughed, and obeyed, recognising a foe who, although he did not use her weapons, was worthy of her mettle. 'You want me to say there is a difference between fighting to defend the cause of right and fighting on the offensive, so that you can point out there were no such moral issues when I burned churches. I won't oblige you, Lord Banning. I merely say I must help beat the enemy by encouraging recruitment at the moment and, when I am completely well, by using any and all means at my disposal.'

'You're not looking your best,' he agreed. 'I daresay Holloway is to blame.'

'Do not tease me, Lord Banning, if you please. I assure you that aspiring to be a womanly woman is not part of my convalescence. Planning how other women are to be made a little less wretched is.'

'I assure you, Miss Lilley, that working for the WSPU, the Women's Emergency Corps, the Women's Convoy Corps, the FANYs, the Women's National Service League, or any of the other thousand or so organisations now fighting for the war effort, has no bearing on whether or not you are a womanly woman.'

'And what has? The trailing of admirers calling at my door – or rather your door – with bouquets of flowers?'

'No.' He smiled at her.

'What then?' she asked, impatient with such trivialities.

'Yourself alone. The same imp of self that has sent my daughter galloping off on her white metaphorical charger to Serbia with Lady Paget's mission.'

Tilly trod carefully on this delicate ground. 'It must be a great worry to you, Lord Banning, but she is a resourceful as well as a brave girl.'

He said nothing for a moment, pressing the tips of his fingers together in a clichéd gesture, she noticed. Whatever would come would be a diplomatic cover over deep water. 'Her decision was made on humanitarian grounds, to help the Serbs, not the cause of women's role in society. Male surgeons accompany the unit. Leila – Lady Paget – was the most unlikely person, so it seemed, to have organised such an enterprise. But that was a verdict I made based on my acquaintance with her before the war. Now everything and everyone must be reappraised in the light of changed circumstances. We are all called to our personal colours, Miss Lilley. Therefore how can I presume to comment on yours? And in such a spirit I suggest you remain under my roof.'

Tilly eyed him doubtfully – and took up the challenge. 'You are kind indeed, Lord Banning. I shall remain – regardless of our joint reputations – until my activities displease you.'

'Then I may send the cab away?'

'You may.'

'I have in fact already done so. A glass of sherry, Miss Lilley?'

Chapter Eleven

'He is still missing.' Felicia sat on the edge of her bed on the Monday evening. 'Sir John can't tell me *anything* other than hard to get information with the army across the Marne and on the move. I suppose it's encouraging –' her voice trembled for the first time – 'that he's not on the casualty lists for the first four weeks, but then I remember that the new lists are only for those lost during the Marne battles. Daniel was lost much earlier and if there *were* terrible news it wouldn't now be in the lists. So Sir John says,' she added forlornly.

'He might be a prisoner.' It was hard for Caroline to sound positive about this, faced as she was with Felicia's stoical attitude, and feeling all the worse because of her own relatively good news about Reggie.

'No. He's lost – at least to me.'

Caroline longed to ask how Felicia could be so sure, but

she knew it would be no use. Felicia probably did not know herself, so how could she explain? If it were Reggie, she too might have that certain knowledge. Caroline pushed that fear away; it prowled in circles round her continuously, kept away by the bright campfire of her own determination. If she let her guard down, the nightmare would close in. The idea that had been formulating in her own mind, however, suddenly gained strength. What if Felicia were to come too? That might prove the way for her to endure this time of terrible suspense. 'Felicia,' she urged, convinced she was right. 'You remember I told you the Red Cross are asking for volunteers to travel with Mrs St Clair Stobart to set up hospitals for the wounded in Antwerp. I want to apply, so why don't you come too?'

'Me?' It was hard to tell Felicia's reaction from her tone.

'I know what we are doing in the Royal Herbert is valuable work and that we have to be trained, but someone will be needed to scrub basins and empty bedpans there too. Why not us, if the Red Cross would sanction it? Just as Reggie and Daniel felt they ought to go abroad to fight the enemy, so should we. If women are equal to men, we too should go to the front line, even if we're not carrying muskets. Lots of this year's debutantes have already gone abroad. The Munro Corps is leaving at any moment for Belgium, taking an ambulance unit. Lady Dorothie Fielding is going with it – remember her? – and one girl, Mairi Chisholm, is your age, eighteen.'

Felicia said nothing but Caroline could see she was listening, and grew even more enthusiastic.

'I'm going to apply, Felicia. That way I feel I'm standing

at Reggie's side. Mrs St Clair Stobart is leaving on the 20th, and I'm determined to be with her. Do come. We could even suggest it to Eleanor.' They had been amazed to hear that Eleanor had actually defied the Gorgon and offered her services as a VAD in Tunbridge Wells, and was just about to get her initial certificate in first aid.

Felicia spoke at last. 'Yes, 'I'll come if they'll have me. It will be one way of shouting "No" to the Kaiser, just as Daniel did.' She jumped off the bed. 'We'll do it tomorrow.'

'Elizabeth.' Laurence didn't stop to ask if she were busy this time. He almost ran into the boudoir to find her; as usual she was surrounded by heaps and heaps of knitted garments donated by enthusiastic volunteers, ranging from scarves that could have enfolded entire platoons from their length, gloves, 'comforters', and baby clothes for sailors' wives. Why the latter should be particularly necessary now was a matter of bewilderment to Elizabeth, but she had obediently followed Edith Swinford-Browne's excited instructions. 'I have the strangest news from Sir John.'

'News of Daniel?' Elizabeth dropped the pile of comforters.

'No. Maud has disappeared.'

'*What?*' Elizabeth sat down faintly in the basket chair, conjuring up an image of a pantomime Maud vanishing in a puff of smoke.

'Eleanor returned from her first aid course after three days away to find her mother gone, and the staff ignorant as to her whereabouts. Sir John is alarmed for her sanity.'

'You mean suicide?' Elizabeth was blunt. 'No, Laurence, Maud is not of such stuff as that.'

'She may be very disturbed.'

'Which would spur her on, not defeat her. Remember the year the peach trees were so diseased the gardener insisted on burning them down, and she personally sprayed them with soap and water, willing them to survive, and they did?'

'This is not quite the same as peach trees.'

'It is her reaction to crisis – relative, of course.' Elizabeth remembered her own emotions and the terrors that had raced through her mind when Isabel was in Paris, and multiplied them several times. She realised what must have happened to Lady Hunney. 'If I were she, Laurence, I would go in search of my son.'

'Even Maud could not storm her way through to the battle front: it is still on the move. She would find herself in German-occupied territory.'

'Only the advanced dressing stations move with the army, surely.' Elizabeth was convinced she was right. 'If he is still alive, he could have been moved. Has Sir John made enquiries at the Foreign Office to see if she has applied for permission to travel to France, and a passport?'

'I do not know. All that is known is that the Lanchester was found at the Tunbridge railway station, but the chauffeur did not take it there.'

'Then Maud drove herself, and has taken a railway train.'

'Times are out of sorts indeed.' There was no humour in Laurence's comment; he meant it, and Elizabeth understood him perfectly. Two months ago the idea of Lady Hunney driving herself to take a train would have been ridiculous. Now it seemed quite rational.

'I will go to see Eleanor immediately.' Elizabeth ignored the afternoon pile for the post office and went to find her hat.

Mrs Dibble waylaid her on her way out and from the look on her face there was no gainsaying the summons.

'We'll have to make do, Mrs Lilley.' The folded arms and ominous tones meant time had to be found to deal with this problem. 'Mrs Thorn's put banister brushes up to one shilling and sixpence. And we're running low on tea. Costs going up and my budget going down. It's not right, surely.'

'It's the war, Mrs Dibble. Our *income*'s going down. So many farmers really won't be able to pay their Michaelmas tithes this time because of hardship. We must be prepared.'

'If they don't pay you money, stands to reason they should pay you in kind. We'll have the corn.'

'I'm afraid they don't see it that way any more.' Indeed the farmers did not. There was already enough resentment over paying tithes, without the extra burdens that war had unexpectedly thrust upon them. Rents, yes, that was considered fair, but tithes were a different matter.

Mrs Dibble paused, awaiting her moment. 'And there's poor Mrs Hubble.'

'What of her?'

'She's had one.'

'One what?'

'I heard in the post office only an hour ago. The telegram.'

'What—' Elizabeth broke off. 'Not her son?'

'Killed in action. God rest him.'

'I shall go to her.' Eleanor must wait; shared anxiety must give way to present grief. Until war had come, one decided one's own priorities; war now took command and decided them for you. Tim Hubble had helped Percy out in the Rectory gardens on occasion before he signed on in the Regular Army, they all knew him, and now he was dead.

This afternoon the carrier would be delivering the green window holland she had had to order for blinds for the whole of the Rectory to conform with the Emergency Light orders. She was unsure whether this was to save fuel or in expectation of the enemy in the air. Surely the former, for the idea of the latter was inconceivable. How the Germans would see their dim oil lamps from the sky was a mystery to Elizabeth, and surely no aeroplane or Zeppelin would dare cross to England anyway. But laws were laws. Unfortunately cost was cost. Try as she would, she could not avoid the uncomfortable feeling that Percy was up to no good on the matter of fuel. The coalman had paid a suspicious number of trips to the coal cellar yesterday, after there had been rumours of the price of coal rising steeply. They must burn wood, she decided. It was a pity they were not sufficiently near the Forest to claim the right of estover, in gathering peat for fuel and wood for burning.

Sometimes she glanced with some amusement at the 'What women may do' column daily in *The Times*. There seemed to be so many vital tasks for women that she wondered how the country had managed to fare without these helpful hints before. Very few of them had any relevance to her. Or perhaps 'Keep calm and hopeful' was aimed at Elizabeth Lilley. Or sewing nightingales as inspired by Florence for the wounded in the Crimea. Or making comforting puddings. No, there were no rules. *The Times* had no guidelines for the vast majority of women, merely eager ideas, and those spouted out in profusion all around her and all over the country. It was becoming patriotic not to indulge in luxuries, and as a result the luxury food market was collapsing bringing hardship to many thousands who worked within it; it was becoming patriotic not to clothe oneself extravagantly, and already Mrs Hazel was complaining of the slackening trade as women decided not to order dresses for the new season. Once there was a river of life in the Rectory which flowed swiftly but safely with herself at the helm. Now there were two, no, three rivers of daily life in which the currents were dangerously unpredictable: their private family life, which had suddenly split asunder; the life of Ashden; and what was going on in the catastrophe that had embroiled Europe. It was a situation that needed a greater navigator than herself.

It was five o'clock on Friday 18th September when Caroline and Felicia arrived home unannounced after a tedious train journey with two changes. The railway trains were crowded, and their arrival bore little relation to timetables. Felicia bore it calmly. Caroline did not, and was hot, cross, and not the least excited about their coming departure from England. By the time they arrived at the Rectory, her spirits and enthusiasm had somewhat recovered.

'Antwerp? Tomorrow?' Elizabeth cried. No sooner was she over the shock and delight of seeing her daughters back than this terrible news was broken. 'But that's in *Belgium*.'

'Of course, Mother. That's where the war is.' Caroline laughed. 'It's no use going to a nice safe hospital in Boulogne – it's at the front that we are needed.'

'But you are both so young and inexperienced.'

'And both so strong and willing,' Caroline countered firmly. 'There's no danger. It's a port, so we can be taken off by ship at a moment's notice.' It sounded good but she didn't have the faintest idea whether it was true or not.

'But darlings, men will be wounded.' Elizabeth felt helpless. How could she point out once more that the men would have to be washed and administered to in intimate detail, and not in a clean scrubbed hospital, perhaps, but straight from a battlefield into a tent? Her imagination ran riot. She had been so careful to shield her daughters' modesty, and George's too. 'Who is in charge? The Red Cross?'

'The Belgian Red Cross.'

'Then Sir John might be able—'

'No, Mother, we're just two very ordinary as yet untrained orderlies going over to help. We don't need help ourselves. Mrs St Clair Stobart is a superb woman. She refused to be presented at court – just like me, you see. She's worked in the Transvaal, running a shop, she launched the Women's Convoy Corps several years ago, where she drilled and trained women just like us. She went to the Balkan Wars two years ago, and set up a hospital. She knows exactly what she's doing, and now she's started the Women's National Service League. Eleanor wants to apply too, she's passed her exam.'

'Lady Hunney has vanished. Eleanor may not be able to come.'

'Vanished?' Caroline giggled, taken by surprise.

'The family is very worried,' Elizabeth said reprovingly.

'I hope she returns – Eleanor will be so upset not to come.' Caroline was horrified.

So was Elizabeth. '*Hope*? Really, Caroline, have you young people any idea of the agony mothers go through, or do you think it irrelevant? Poor Lady Hunney has gone on a no doubt fruitless mission to find her missing son. She will not find him –' a small exclamation from Felicia – 'and what kind of a homecoming to find the daughter she relies on for support gone to Antwerp, possibly to be in danger herself?'

Caroline was ashamed. 'I'm sorry, Mother. I didn't put that well. But I'm afraid I think Eleanor's right to go, despite all you say. Women, and that's what we are, not just daughters, have a right to follow our duty just like men. Surely you can't think that a woman's duty is to be subservient to what her family wants?'

'Like me?' Elizabeth was still angry.

'No!' Caroline was truly contrite now, and put her arm round her mother. 'Of course I didn't mean you. Oh, how can I explain? You stay here, we depend on you, because you have chosen that. We want choice, too. What choice has Eleanor if she must subordinate her will to her mother's?'

'The choice of choosing love, perhaps.'

'That love will be stifled if given no air.'

'Do I,' Elizabeth asked stiffly, 'give you air?'

'You allow it,' Caroline said seriously. 'It is almost the same.'

'Tomorrow,' Elizabeth observed, mollified, 'the blinds will be installed over the Rectory windows. Mrs Dibble and I are to finish sewing them tonight. Perhaps they will stifle us here in the Rectory.'

'Not while the door is open for all in need to enter and for all who must to go out.' Caroline hugged her mother.

'Where's Phoebe?' Caroline looked round the dinner table, disappointed that on this, their one night at home, there was no sign of her sister. She had been here earlier, so why go out now?

'War work,' George pronounced grandly, eyeing the roast chicken hurriedly cooked in honour of the unexpected guests. The stewpots of the hoppers had smelled tantalisingly good in the fields, and made him run back to the Rectory at the double for dinner.

'She's joined the Foreign Legion and gone to the Sahara?' Felicia enquired, straight-faced.

'No. She's gone to Ashden station, dishing out lemonade. There's a late troop train coming through. It was her idea,' George informed her, generous when credit was due. 'I give her a hand now and then.'

Phoebe? How things were changing, Caroline realised. Such a short time, and already the Rectory seemed different. Or rather, not the Rectory, but its inhabitants. Thank goodness, for the Rectory itself should be immutable. Ashden had shown tangible signs of change, however. Not only was Mrs Lake sitting on the tractor in place of her husband but right in the middle of the village, two cottages she'd known all her life had vanished, and the foundations of the cinema were laid. 'The Tower of Babel,' her father had grunted when she asked him about it. 'William Swinford-Browne's contribution to the war effort, or so he claims, though the village seems to think it's going to be a valiant thing.'

'Chicken,' cried Caroline delightedly, as her father flourished the carving knife and fork. It was obviously time to change the subject.

'They're falling in price now nobody entertains any more,' Elizabeth said. 'It may be grouse when you come home next.' Hovering in the air was an unanswerable 'when will that be?'

Laurence was inexpertly carving off a leg when the door flew open and Phoebe rushed in, still with her hat on, and stumbling over the mat as if to match her incoherent speech. 'They're back.'

'Who?' Laurence enquired, thrown off his stroke.

'Lady Hunney and *Daniel*.'

'Oh.' Felicia rushed to her in delight, so overwhelmed with relief she did not notice Phoebe's slight withdrawal. 'Where was he? Where did she—?'

'I don't know,' Phoebe cried impatiently. 'She wouldn't talk to me. They simply put the stretcher into the ambulance, and off they went. I just came to tell you.' Her voice tailed off as she saw their faces and realised what she'd said.

'Stretcher?' Laurence voiced their fears.

'Yes, he's wounded.' Phoebe looked round uncertainly.

'How badly?' Felicia demanded.

'I don't know,' Phoebe wailed. 'I thought you'd be pleased they were back.'

'We are,' Felicia said quietly. 'No matter how bad the news, he is alive.'

A sudden arrow of agony struck Caroline unawares with that one word, and plunged her back into doubt. How could she know if Reggie were alive or not? His last letter had been cheerful enough, but there was a long time and many bullets between the writing of a letter and its arrival. Suppose she were away when he came home on leave? He would understand, wouldn't he, that she was doing it for him? It was not going to be easy either for herself or Felicia to leave Ashden and go so far afield. Penelope, who had left so confidently for Serbia, was used to living independently, whereas, though Caroline had always longed for the opportunity to ramble through the larger world, now that the opportunity had come she found it daunting, and was glad that Felicia would be with her.

On the following morning, the day they were to leave Ashden, Felicia was nowhere to be found – in the Rectory, at least. It was obvious to Caroline where she had gone, and her anxiety grew. What would Felicia find at the Manor, and how would it affect her – and their plans? At ten, while she was packing, with Mother's help and Harriet at hand to be despatched to the village for last-minute requirements, Eleanor arrived. Caroline's heart sank. It was not hard to guess the reason.

'I can't come, Caroline,' she burst out as soon as they were alone in the garden. She had been planning to apply to the Red Cross and hoped to follow them out shortly. 'You understand, don't you? Is Felicia still going? She's very keen on Daniel, isn't she?'

'Of course, Eleanor. I don't know whether she's coming or not. I haven't seen her this morning, and she said nothing yesterday evening.'

'You wouldn't go if it were Reggie, would you?'

'No.' Caroline did not even have to consider the question. Then her place would be here. The closest she had come to the deep grief of bereavement was when Grandma Overton had died, and then she had been supported by sharing it with her family. If it were Reggie she lost, others would sympathise, but they could not truly understand.

'Mother simply said no when she discovered about Antwerp,' Eleanor continued. 'I had to tell her.'

'You let her persuade you?'

'No.' Eleanor was definite about this. 'I would have gone. It is for Daniel I want to stay. Not that he asked me to, for he is hardly capable of it. It was seeing him, and realising that war is here, as well as in Antwerp. How could I go, Caroline?'

'You had no choice.'

'I'll do my best to be assigned to the Manor in due course. Mother will hate it, but I don't care. I'm sure the Red Cross will be sympathetic. I'm not much good at nursing, but I can fetch and carry like anyone else, and normally I'm good at being placid.' Her voice broke.

'How is he?' Caroline asked gently.

'Oh, Caroline, he's paralysed below the waist, and a wound in the lower leg is simply oozing pus. It may have to come off.'

It was like a bowl of cold water thrown into her face. Never had Caroline imagined anything so terrible. A broken leg, a broken arm would mend. But this? And to

Daniel, the good-looking daredevil who had planned to travel so far and do so much.

'He wasn't wounded in the big disaster that overtook the King's Own near Le Cateau, so naturally he wasn't on that casualty list. He was hit later in the day as they were involved in sporadic fighting, and then immediately the retreat began. He was taken to a dressing station, and in the confusion names got muddled and he ended up in one of the three Paris military hospitals – oh, what does it matter? He's terribly, terribly wounded.'

Yellow telegrams to break the hearts of those at home, and stretchers. At the Marne, the Lancers had galloped into battle; on the Aisne the army had been met by the new Krupp howitzers, she'd read. What use were gallant cavalry charges when met by shrapnel, and shells, and bullets that tore and mangled flesh without the enemy even showing its face? Anger filled Caroline at the futility of it all, and made her all the more determined to strike her own blow. The sudden doubts she had had at the realisation she might lose both Eleanor and Felicia's companionship vanished. If it had been right for her to go with them, it was right to go alone, no matter what collywobbles fluttered within her.

'Mother had quite a time of it in France.' Eleanor tried to be light-hearted, 'I gather she found she had no right to be on the military trains, could not bluff her way through, and had no money that the French would accept; so she sold her pocket watch and ring, and with the proceeds hired a horse, cart and driver and was driven to the front.'

'To the *front*? Didn't anyone stop her?'

'They most certainly would have done so if they'd caught

her before it was too late. It's lucky she didn't get shot. It seems she came up behind the reserve lines and demanded to see the colonel of the 1st King's Own, who had apoplexy on the spot. He confirmed Daniel was missing, and good old Mother, who never takes no for an answer, then went on a tour of *all* the hospitals from field tents to fully equipped outfits, and eventually found Daniel down in Paris. Mother simply ignored all protests and stayed. Daniel must have been delirious, because he apparently thought he was back at Ashden with her here.' Eleanor failed to keep up her brave effort and broke down.

'Your mother is a very brave woman,' Caroline comforted her.

'I know.' Eleanor managed to grin. 'I'd so love to be able to hate her. But I don't.'

'I shall not be able to go to Antwerp, of course.' Felicia looked anxiously at her sister. 'I don't know what the Red Cross will say, but I doubt if they'd want unwilling candidates. I'll speak to them immediately. The Matron at Ashden says she can do with even untrained help at the moment, so they may not mind too much.'

'No, I'm sure they'll help.' Caroline tried to be reassuring, but Felicia eyed her doubtfully. 'Are you sure it's wise for you to stay here, Felicia?' she continued gently. 'Perhaps it would hurt him even to see you?'

It was a mean argument, but Caroline meant it. If Daniel was so badly wounded, the sight of Felicia, whom he had come at least close to loving, might remind him all the more of his changed life.

'There is that chance,' Felicia conceded, following her reasoning instantly. 'But I shall stay nevertheless. I know I can *help* him, and that is more important than his liking or not liking me to be there.'

Caroline hesitated, reluctant to pry but longing to know. Daniel was friend to them all, part of their circle. 'Did you see him?'

'Yes.'

'Did he – was he – did he know you?'

'He did. And you are right, he turned his head away.'

'How could you bear it?' Caroline cried, in agony for her sister.

'I could not, until I realised I was belying my own purpose if I gave up so easily. I told him I would come again, and again, until I was as much part of his daily view as the sunflowers on the curtains at the windows. And then just as the sunflowers turn to face the sun, so would he.'

Her voice was so matter-of-fact it took a moment for Caroline to realise how much it must have cost Felicia to endure this, and then to recount it. 'And what did he say to that?'

'He said –' she delivered the words with pride – '"do as you damned well please".'

Should she go in? Caroline hesitated while passing the Manor House, and decided against it – not while Daniel was so ill. The Manor, now fully equipped as a hospital, had an atmosphere of purposefulness and expectancy. This place was of the present; the days of feudal manors were past until after the war, when all they were fighting for would have been achieved and Sussex could resume its sleepy ordered peacefulness.

The Dower House's generous eighteenth-century proportions had been reduced to a cramped dolls' house in which the staff and inhabitants were manoeuvring round each other with disapprobation and discomfort.

'I've come to say goodbye again, Lady Hunney,' Caroline declared as cheerfully as she could manage, when she was admitted into the presence.

'*Goodbye,* Caroline?' The elegant eyebrows arched as though they had never seen the battlefields of France.

'I'm going to Antwerp, as a VAD. Eleanor must have told you.'

'Why?'

'To work there.'

'You have employment here. We have brought many of the books that require cataloguing to the Dower House, and no doubt the Manor would still afford you access to the main library. Do you intend to walk out on your obligations without a word? It seems strange behaviour.'

Caroline felt as if she had bounced down Alice's rabbit hole into Wonderland. Surely Lady Hunney could not be serious? 'I'm sure you would agree that everyone must do what they can for the war. I must, and you have. It was a very brave thing to find Daniel and bring him home.'

Lady Hunney stared at her. 'Not brave, it was my duty as a mother. I suggest you do yours as a fiancée. I believe you consider yourself engaged to my elder son?'

Hadn't boxing without gloves been outlawed years ago? Caroline mentally staggered under the ferocity of the assault. 'I love Reggie and I shall marry him. What my duty is to him is for me to decide.'

'I fear you do not understand what marrying into a family such as ours entails. When a woman marries she accepts the requirements of her husband's family. As Reginald's fiancée they are incumbent on you.'

'And what are those?' She was seething with anger now the initial shock of attack was subsiding, but pleased that she was managing to control it.

'To do your duty as Reggie's wife and the future lady of the manor. *She* cannot shed her responsibilities as lightly as you seem about to, Caroline. She is there, *of* the village and *for* the village – just as your father is to a lesser extent. He could not gallivant off to be an army chaplain with talk of doing what he could for the war. Such lack of discipline is disgraceful. The rule of self will lead this country to destruction.'

She was the Red Queen, she was monstrous, she must be beaten. 'Reggie would wish me to do what I know to be right.'

'Then you do not understand my son. He is a Hunney, and that guides him through life as firmly as the Ten Commandments.'

It would be an Old Testament comparison. There was nothing of compassion in Lady Hunney. 'I cannot accept your precepts. Nor am I bound to.'

'Reginald will be most disappointed in you. It was bad enough your gadding off to that hospital; to know you are in Antwerp, possibly in danger, can only cause him distress.'

'And you will tell him, won't you?'

396

'It is my duty to do so.'

'Then you must follow that, Lady Hunney, as I shall mine – in Antwerp.'

'You are mistaken. Hearing of your outrageous plan from my daughter, I have been in touch with Mrs St Clair Stobart, and informed her and the Red Cross that you will not be going.'

'How *dare* you?' Caroline was white with anger. 'How *dare* you interfere in my life?'

'It is not *your* life, Caroline. You have a position to maintain, and you will maintain it.'

'What shall I do, Father?' Caroline paced up and down her father's study. 'I don't want Reggie upset by my problems, but I must do what I feel is right.'

'And what does God tell you is your duty?'

She answered readily. 'To help bring this war to an end by doing what I'm training to do, menial though it is.'

'Did He mention Antwerp?'

She managed a smile. 'Not quite so loudly.'

'Very well then.'

She threw her arms round him. 'How do you always manage to cut through to the heart of a problem and find a solution, Father?'

'I don't, my love. God does it for me; my task is to find and then convey it.'

'And how do you know that you've found His answer?'

He considered for a moment. 'How do you decide what and what not to include in the parish magazine?'

'I stumble and hesitate over everything, put them in this

order and that, and when I finally decide on the right order I wonder how I could have been so stupid as not to see it in the first place.'

'That's how I do it too.'

She laughed, her mind at ease now, for she knew on what lines to think. 'Talking of the parish magazine, how was George's effort?'

'I took a few liberties in correcting his style and spelling, and toning down his more melodramatic cries of war, but he has interesting ideas. Oh, and I left in one of his caricatures to please him. It was finely observed – Kitchener's finger pointing from one side, Cyril Wilson with his miller's hat from the other, the Kaiser's fist threatening overhead, a bewildered creature bearing a remarkable resemblance to a Mutter scratching his head in the centre, claiming, "I be valiant dinlow surely". Pictures are more telling than words at times. He has some talent.'

Agnes sat down harder than she meant to on the edge of her bed; she didn't even notice the iron side hard against her legs, nor did it register that it was twenty minutes to seven and she was ten minutes late downstairs. All she registered was that her monthly flowers still hadn't shown. She should have had her monthlies three weeks ago and no amount of pretending in the world could persuade her it was all the upset over Jamie's going away. She had been put up the spout, was, as her mother would say, expecting, and there wasn't going to be a father. She was, it struck her with sickening force, in exactly the same position as Ruth Horner, now waddling round the village bold as brass and only days to go. But Ruth was lording it in a cottage of her own with money enough to keep her, by generous gift of her former employer. She, Agnes, was parlour maid in a *rectory*, whose occupants, however kind, could hardly be expected to house her in her present condition, unblessed by the Church. Nor would her parents tolerate such shame under their roof. She would be the laughing stock of the village. Jamie was in camp, preparing to move to Dover, then go overseas, with never a mention of leave, only cheery words about his mates. He wouldn't be very cheery when he heard about this. She supposed she ought not to tell him. He'd be upset, and there was nothing he could do about it. Her contribution to the war effort, she thought wryly, would be not to worry a fine upstanding soldier. Perhaps he wouldn't care; perhaps he was already stepping out with another Dover lass. She'd heard women were supposed to be encouraging their menfolk to join up, so she must be the only one that wasn't. Men and women were parading the streets in Folkestone, and now other places, encouraged by some admiral or other, to hand out white feathers to young men not in uniform. They should come to Ashden and give them to the likes of Len Thorn.

With resolution she stood up. If she hadn't had her flowers by next week when the next one was due, she'd have to do something. What, she wasn't sure yet, but that was her deadline. She slipped her print gown over her head, covering up the location of the problem. She'd put it out of her mind for a week or so.

'Morning, Mrs Dibble,' she said brightly as she entered the kitchen, moving towards the teapot always ready at this time of the morning.

'You're looking pale, Agnes.' Mrs Dibble looked at her sharply, interrupting her rendering of 'The seedtime and the harvest, Our life, our health, our food'.

Agnes poured her tea, then caught sight of the kedgeree and breakfast dishes being prepared for the family breakfast; vast globules of food that made Agnes's throat close up even to look at. Eggs, enormous in size, broken into dishes ready for cooking, seemed to wink evilly at her; armies of kidneys lined up in menacing columns. She took a hasty drink of tea, but in vain. 'Excuse me,' she said primly, rushing outside to the privy they used during working hours.

Mrs Dibble watched her exit without comment, noted the time she was away, and the even more wan face that came back in, and decided it was time to speak.

'Milk or water. Kaolin. One of them will settle it. Your stomach, I mean. Not the reason for it.'

Agnes slumped in her seat. 'Thank you, Mrs Dibble.'

'Don't thank me. Thank the lad that got you into trouble.'

Agnes raised anguished eyes. She could not speak. Her whole body seemed one mass of choking worry, stifling every word.

Mrs Dibble's eyes softened. 'What you and me need, Agnes, is a nice chat. You get on with your work, can't have the Rectory suffering, and this afternoon when you're feeling better, we'll have tea.'

Agnes nodded and, making a brave attempt at normality, picked up the Keating's powder.

* * *

400

Felicia reported for duty at Ashden Manor nervously. It had all seemed too easy, a step towards an end. Now she began to realise that the step in itself would not be easy. Long hours, night duty, perhaps actually helping to nurse the men in time, not just fetching and carrying under orders. A fully fledged operating theatre complete with X-ray apparatus had sprung up in the grounds, built within the disused carriage house at the end of the stable block. All this within a few weeks, she marvelled. Such a little time to turn the manor house she knew so well into a strange and awe-inspiring citadel, where she knew no one – save Daniel. The thought strengthened her. She was the lowest of all ranks and, although there were only half a dozen patients here at the moment, there was already a regimented, disciplined atmosphere. Soon all twenty-four beds would be filled, for more casualties were arriving all the time at the Channel ports. She rang the bell hesitantly; last time she had been a 'visitor', now she was a worker. The formidable face of the middle-aged woman in dark blue who opened the door did little to reassure her.

'Good morning. I'm Felicia Lilley, a VAD.'

'No, Miss Lilley. A Voluntary Air Detachment is composed of approximately fifty persons, a commandant, medical officer, quartermaster, lady superintendent, pharmacist, and forty or so other ranks. You are a probationer nurse *in* the VAD. Kindly remember that. I am the superintendent. Follow me.'

'I'm sorry, ma'am.' Felicia stepped inside, following the broad swaying back up the well-known stairs, bleak without the Hunney family ancestors adorning them, into the 'office', the library where Caroline used to work. Many books still remained, looking down at these intruders into their quiet domain.

'We are not yet fully operational – and I emphasise *operational*, Miss Lilley. We are run on military lines and I expect military discipline.'

'Yes, ma'am.'

'I understand you know Lady Hunney. And our patient, Mr Hunney.' The tone of voice suggested this would be no benefit to Felicia.

'Yes, we are neighbours. I live in the Rectory.'

'Then I emphasise even more strongly that we are a military hospital and the owners of the house have no authority or influence here. Is that clear?'

'Perfectly.'

The superintendent looked at the composed face in front of her, and foresaw trouble ahead, but in the days that followed she found she was mistaken. The girl proved competent, willing, and surprisingly strong. She was assigned to kitchen duties, as far from the patients as possible, and carried out her work uncomplainingly, proving adept at collecting contributions from the village in the form of bedding, kitchen equipment and even some matting for the newly tiled floor in the large ward. As an experiment, she got her reward – if reward it was. She was put on night duty when one of the regular nurses was ill.

Felicia sat by Daniel's bed as he slept, just as she sat by those of the other patients for a while, willing them all to fight, and be strong. One night he opened his eyes, saw her and fell into sleep again. The next night he did the same. The night after that he turned his head away from

402

her, towards the window, through which moonlight was creeping through a gap in the curtains. Then he spoke – or rather whispered: 'Agamemnon's moon.'

She did not know what he meant, if indeed it meant anything. 'Yours too,' she whispered back.

'Not now.'

'It shines on everyone.' Foolish words, and indeed he was already asleep again. She crept back to her official post, with its one dim oil lamp. The exchange had meant nothing, and everything; the healing had begun.

Phoebe walked down Station Road, well content. She had donated eleven whole pounds to the post office box for the Red Cross fund now. True, now the hoppers had gone, turnover was dropping, but if Ashden Manor was mobilised as a hospital, it would pick up again. It occurred to her she should liaise with the authorities there, otherwise she could find herself supplanted by one of the VAD vans, though perhaps Ashden was too small a station for that. She was very pleased with herself, and proud of finding there were possibilities in Ashden as well as Paris. When the war was over, as surely it must be soon, she'd be glad she had had this experience instead of going straight to finishing school. She was going to provide more than lemonade as winter approached. She had arranged to borrow a tea urn, and to provide soup, to be kept hot on Mrs Chaplin's range. She could charge a penny, perhaps. What about pies? She walked along, busily calculating costs and profits. She had never been able to see the sense of mental arithmetic at school but now it had a new relevance.

She was so preoccupied that he was there before she realised it. Just her, and *him* strolling towards her, Len Thorn. A wave of panic engulfed her, making her dizzy, until she controlled it by telling herself he would not dare accost her here. She would simply march past him. *Now.* The steps were long ones, and her legs leaden, as if she were running in a dream.

'Good morning, Len.' She continued on her way. Coldness was better than ignoring him.

'Morning, Miss Lilley.'

His obvious wariness gave her confidence. She had faced the monster, and she had beaten it. The monster, she told herself, had only been Len Thorn, and nothing more. Perhaps that was how the troops felt about the Kaiser – he was the bogeyman, and if you sang rude songs about him, it reduced him to size. Kaiser Bill and Len Thorn were the same, really. It was a question of degree and power. Len Thorn had no power over her. Not now. And perhaps what Mr Eliot said was true: there was sweetness as well as darkness between men and women. Christopher Denis and Len Thorn were the past; the future was hers. She marched home to the Rectory with a confident swing, singing to the hedgerows, *It's a long way to Kaiser Billy, It's a long way to go.*

She, too, was a soldier on the move.

The Dover visit had rebounded on her head. Never had Caroline envisaged making it under these circumstances and, worse, alone, since the rest of the family had seized the excuse of war to escape it. When she was offered the chance of a transfer to a Voluntary Aid Detachment in Dover, it had seemed the perfect solution to her problems. Not abroad, but near to the pulse of the war, for it was one of the chief ports for refugees and for the wounded troops. But it had disadvantages and the proximity of Buckford House was one.

On the death of her husband, the Dowager Countess had reluctantly been forced to make way for her eldest son, daughter-in-law and three children; she had moved, not into the Dower House, but into one wing of the main building, and since then her presence had given the facade of Buckford a lopsided appearance in her granddaughter's imagination. It looked to her like a giant, with an all-seeing enormous eye on one side. 'You're being quite ridiculous,' Caroline rebuked herself, as she took the branch path to the porch of the side entrance. The latter still seemed to Caroline to be doing its best to convey that the real hub of the house was here – as indeed it probably was. In Grandmother's entrance hall hung the forbidding portrait of her late husband by Sargent. In life, so her father had told Caroline, the earl had been a man of Pickwickian build and presence, but in death he seemed to have taken on his wife's aura. Caroline made a face of fellow sympathy with him, but the Earl stared gravely back.

'Her ladyship will see you now, Miss Lilley.' 'Pecksniff', as Caroline had dubbed her grandmother's butler, graciously ushered her in. He pretended she was a stranger, as usual, though she had been coming every year since she was born.

Perhaps Miss Havisham in *Great Expectations* looked something like Grandmother, sitting spider-like in the midst of her web. Spiders must presumably look attractive to their prey, and so did Grandmother. Most old ladies of eighty-two were shrunken in size if not in character. Not Grandmother. Most old ladies of eighty-two had lined faces mellowed into wise compassion. Not Grandmother. Most old ladies of eighty-two had long since retired into black silk and lace gowns. Not Grandmother. She was as tall and imposing as the days when she had alternately terrorised and intrigued Victorian society; her features, if standing out more sharply, only impressed more deeply; and her gown, today royal blue, proclaimed she was still an active force in the world. How, Caroline wondered, not for the first time, had Aunt Tilly stood it all these years?

'Am I to understand, Caroline,' the deep voice had harshened with age, the steel beneath the velvet glove more nakedly displayed, 'that you are living *alone* in Dover?'

'Working, Grandmother, and in a hostel with other VADs.' It was a small hotel on the front, nestling by the White Cliffs, which had been commandeered for the emergency now Dover had been declared a military area.

'*Working?*' The word was invested with deep horror and disgust. 'Unchaperoned?'

'Yes, Grandmother, and no, Grandmother. I am chaperoned by thirty VAD colleagues.'

Grandmother never wasted time on lost causes, but always moved promptly to the next. She could give a fine lesson to Sir John French in how to conduct a war. No retreats for her.

'Is Buckford House not good enough for you?' she enquired.

'It is outside the Dover restricted area, and I would have too far to travel on night duty.'

'*Night* duty? You roam the streets?'

'There is expected to be a great influx of Belgian as well as British casualties, and our VAD will then be mobilised, so it is quite possible I shall do night duty. It depends what I am assigned to do. I doubt I will be roaming the streets, though many girls are volunteering now as women policemen, or for Special Patrols.'

'You forget what is due to your station in life.'

'I remember my duty to others.' Caroline smarted at being told yet again of her 'station in life'. War did not take note of 'stations' – as the Rolls of Honour published almost daily testified.

The Dowager gazed at her, always a move calculated to intimidate. 'You are by nature a wayward girl, Caroline. It is not a quality to be welcomed in a woman.'

Grandmother was clever. There was no mention of Mother, which would antagonise Caroline, but only the slightest implication that such inherited traits could not be from her Grandmother's side of the family.

'I'm sure you would like to know, Grandmother, that Aunt Tilly is recovering well from her latest imprisonment, according to her last letter.' Caroline held her breath, half regretting her own descent to strong-arm tactics.

There was a pause. 'I shall expect you every Sunday, Caroline.'

'I'm afraid that will depend on my hours, though naturally I should be delighted to come when I can.' There was some truth in this, for, despite the tension between herself and her grandmother, she enjoyed the opportunity to see her cousins, one of whom, Angela, still lived at Buckford House.

'Inform your superior that the Dowager Countess of Buckford has requested your attendance.'

'I cannot do that.'

The still-elegant hand tightened on the arm of the chair. 'It is distressing that my grandchildren are prepared to grant me merely one visit a year.'

'You would not expect Charles to attend every Sunday.' Her cousin was in the army, stationed at Dover Barracks.

'He is a gentleman, Caroline.'

'And I am a woman, and at work as he is.'

'Bandaging and serving tea like a common waitress is not work. It is self-delusion and self-gratification. What kind of example is that?'

'An excellent one, I hope.'

'It is not the way things are done in England.'

'*Have* been done, Grandmother. Times are changing.'

Caroline left, having consumed the ritual dry seed and Madeira cake. She found to her surprise she was shaking. When she was asked for her pass so that she might enter the Dover restricted area, it felt as though she were emerging from prison into freedom.

That night in her room Caroline was able to look out over the calm night sea. She was alone, for her roommate Ellen, a loquacious young lady from London, as Caroline had dubbed her, was still on duty. Across there was France; you could see it on a fine day. Some people said they could hear the guns of battle here in Kent, and game birds as far as

Sussex were unduly disturbed this year. Somewhere in the middle of the whirlpool was Reggie. She had heard nothing from him for two weeks, and feared that he had been involved in the battle on the River Aisne. The newspapers had extolled it as a great victory. Paris had been saved, and von Kluck and his German army were in retreat. That had been ten days ago, and it was the beginning of October now. Had it been a victory? So much must be omitted from these reports and what was left might therefore turn truth into falsehood. One truth was Daniel lying paralysed in the home he'd left so confidently less than two months ago. And what was she doing to help other Daniels? Her valuable role here had so far consisted of going from door to door begging for saucepans, china, blankets, anything to equip the makeshift hospitals awaiting their first patients. So far the neat iron bedsteads with their pink, blue and yellow bedspreads were mostly unoccupied; but soon it would be a different story.

It seemed men were fighting all over the world now, not just in France. Russia was fighting Austria and Germany in the east. Turkey had come into the war, and so had Japan. Men from the Dominions were being drawn in, Canadians into France. South Africans were fighting Germany for her colonies in Africa, Indians protecting the Persian Gulf, and Australians and New Zealanders defending Egypt. And not only on land. At sea too there was bitter fighting, where Britain had always assumed her position impregnable.

Where her own heart lay, on the Western front, the Germans had not been beaten. They were running not for their border, but for the Channel ports, to which

Antwerp was the key, and the British and French were racing to outflank them and get there first. Sir John French had issued orders for the army to start digging trenches so that they could hold the line from the Swiss border to the Channel to prevent the Germans breaking through. It sounded so simple, but it meant in reality casualties, tragedy and grief. Moreover securing the Channel ports was the key to preventing the invasion of England. Here at Dover the prospect seemed more real than in Ashden. Caroline decided she would redouble her efforts to teach herself to drive. As a nurse she would be mediocre; as a tea dispenser, useful; but as a driver invaluable. She would never be as dashing a driver as Aunt Tilly, but nevertheless after a fashion she could drive already, and this gave her great satisfaction. It was a small contribution to support those men in the trenches – and one in particular.

Chapter Twelve

By mid-October. Caroline was at last becoming used to this 'new' Dover. When she was a child, she had found the town a wonderful place, partly because to walk up the cliffs and to Dover Castle, or down to the harbour where the Calais packets and other shipping docked, was an escape from the rigours of ordeal by Grandmother Buckford, and partly because every step spoke of a long and venerable history. The grey solidity of Dover Castle reminded her of the sketch in her Schoolbook of the ancient Pharos whose light had guided Roman ships to Britain to supply the occupying forces; and the harbour of the stiff-necked picture of Queen Elizabeth, to whom it owed its eminence as a port, reluctantly, though her purse, had been prised open.

Caroline's early memories of Dover were of vast hordes of navvies incessantly working on enormous blocks of stone for the new naval harbour. Impressive though it was, she had seen few ships of war anchored there. Packets and steamers came and went, and merchant seamen were still in the vast majority. Now Dover had mobilised itself, it must surely come into its own. Signs of war were evident everywhere. Restrictions were placed on civilians, a trench system had been dug around the town in case of invasion, cliff paths were closed to the public, and guns were sited on the pier ends. Destroyers and submarines were known to be positioned across the Straits, and further off cruisers with reassuring names like *Cressy* and *Aboukir*. The Astra-Torres and the Parseval airships floated like giant sausages across the sky.

Last night, Tuesday 13th October, VADs all over the south of England had been mobilised to meet the crisis of the vast numbers of wounded Belgian troops and civilian refugees expected today after the fall of Antwerp on the 10th. She might have been among them, Caroline realised with shock, if she had gone to Antwerp as originally planned. How long ago that decision seemed, yet it was only three weeks; those three weeks had transported her to a life so different it might as well have been Antwerp. That she was coping reasonably well was thanks to Ellen, who offered amazed and amused help when Caroline, to her shame, discovered just how much she had been dependent on the Rectory staff.

Caroline had slept deeply that night, but she stirred to hear the heavy thump on the door. It didn't succeed in raising Miss Loquacious from London, and Caroline had had to shake her,

'Wake up, Ellen! We're *mobilised*.'

'I'll mobilise tomorrow,' Ellen muttered, for once far from loquacious as she heaved herself over and went back to sleep, much to Caroline's exasperation. Excitement had brought her instantly wide awake. She dressed rapidly as instructed, with short dashes over to Ellen's bedside to prod her into reluctant movement. Accompanied by a still yawning Ellen, she had hurried downstairs expecting to find a hive of action. In fact, the superintendent was sitting calmly at her desk, detailing duties for the morrow, and then sending them back to bed. Too excited to do so for the moment, Caroline had gone out briefly into the dark night to listen to the lap of the waves pounding on the shore, watching the stars above the dark sea, conscious of a sort of hum, whether actual or imagined, of activity and tension in the town. Here a laugh, a whistle, the murmur of voices, the pinpricks of torches as late wanderers worked their way along past the blacked-out windows.

When she returned to bed she had been too wide awake to fall asleep easily and this morning her movements were lethargic. Not yet an adept enough driver for an ambulance, she was detailed for: general assistance to the wounded; helping stretchers off the ships and on to trains or into ambulances; helping serve tea and soup at the station; and assisting the walking wounded into motor transport for the tented hospital camp. The harbour area now seemed as foreign as France itself, with strange uniforms on all sides, foreign tongues being spoken, harbour workers wearing badges to proclaim their identity lest they were handed white feathers for not being in the forces, Red Cross workers, policemen, and a tea van, yet overall a general purposefulness had instilled its own order. The first ship of the new mass influx had docked twenty minutes ago, and the gangplank had been erected. From the decks refugees, civilian and uniformed, hung over the sides for their first glimpse of what must look to them a strange land. A stir among the groups of workers standing outside the Red Cross supply depot aroused Caroline's attention; the first stretcher was being borne off, and she hurried to her duty position to guide it to the convoy of waiting ambulances.

Later that evening, free for the first time in twelve hours and having missed the hostel dinner, she went out with Ellen in the drizzle, into Dover town to find a restaurant, and was too tired to disagree when Ellen eagerly entered a small smoky fish and chip shop where the other occupants were all harbour workers. Their uniforms, Caroline realised, gave them protection, and awarded them a respect that otherwise could not surely have been counted on.

She had thought she had become inured to the sight of wounded soldiers, but she had not. Not when they came stretcher after stretcher on to home soil or, in the case of Belgian troops, safe soil. Not when in their wake came a steady trail of anxious faces whose eloquent eyes told of the tragedies they had witnessed. And not when the walking wounded, hobbling on crutches, cracked jokes about their ordeal.

When the plate of greasy fish and chips arrived, the look of it revolted her, but the taste of the fish and the solid potato content of the chips calmed her and made her feel better.

'I've never been in a cafe like this. The most Ashden

414

runs to is tea and ices in a corner of the newsagent's.'

Ellen looked amazed. 'What do you do with yourself in a place like that? You said you never worked.'

'Not as you did.' Caroline suddenly wondered what she *did* do all day in the Rectory. She could hardly claim the Manor library occupied a lot of her time.

'I suppose there's a pub in your village. That where you go?'

Caroline laughed. 'No. Remember my father is the Rector.'

'No slipping out for a quick port and lemon, eh? The pubs around Shadwell would go broke if we was all like you. Mind you, I don't go near some of 'em. You got to look after yourself in Shadwell, no one's going to do it for you.'

Caroline looked at her thin elfin face, full of energy, and had no doubts that Ellen could 'look after' herself.

'Mind you,' Ellen swept on, 'I'd like to live in the country.'

'You'd be bored in two seconds.'

'Do you keep cows?'

'Not us.' Caroline envisaged an indignant cow wandering around the Rectory gardens, and Percy's face if asked to milk it. 'Only a dog and a few chickens for fresh eggs.' Even the hens were newcomers, another Dibble 'beat the rising prices' solution.

'I never seen a cow before I come on the train to Dover. Big, ain't they? I always wanted to go hop-picking, but Dad and Mum never would, lazy devils. Sounds fun.'

Caroline thought of the elaborate precautions taken

against thieving hop-pickers in Ashden, and the amount of abuse and blame for every tiny incident hurled at them, and felt ashamed. To Ellen Ashden was as much of a dream as escaping from it had been to Caroline. And now they had met here in Dover on common ground.

'How did you come to train as a VAD?' she asked.

Ellen shrugged. 'My mum died and I didn't fancy looking after Dad, so I hopped it. I said to myself, Ellen, if you're ever going to get out of this place, here's your chance. If I'd gone on working in that sweatshop of a factory, I'd never have got out.'

'But we're not paid, and you had wages there.' Caroline was all too conscious that she was not being paid. Though her parents had not mentioned it, she knew it must be a struggle for them to support her while she was away from home.

'I handed over all me wages to Dad, so it's made precious little difference. My gran gave me a bit, so I thought I'd see the world.'

'Did you want to go abroad?' Caroline thought enviously of the opportunities that had seemed so promising for her and had been snatched away by Lady Hunney. Her ladyship had fulfilled her threat to recount Caroline's iniquities to Reggie. Dover or Antwerp made no difference to Lady Hunney – though she thought perhaps it did to Reggie. In his last letter he had not reproached her, thank goodness, but merely said: 'I could not bear to think of you over here too. If you knew how much it means to the chaps – and, I confess, me – to think and talk about you all in England's green fields while we're stuck in the flat desolation of Flanders, you would realise how glad I am you have stopped at Dover.'

'Not likely,' Ellen was saying. 'They eat snails out there, don't they, and don't know what soap's for. This is as far as I ever want to go.'

Caroline looked round the smoky cafe, and at the remains of the fish and chips in front of her and the streets of Dover outside, thronged with people. This was not as far as she ever wanted to go, but it was a first step.

Half a mile away and several hours earlier, Jamie Thorn had been sitting at a table opposite Agnes in a similar cafe in the High Street, only instead of fish and chips they were having tea and scones. Agnes was concentrating very hard on her cup of tea. She'd asked for a nice plate of ham, nothing too fatty for her, although she was usually all right in the afternoons. She'd stayed overnight at the Maison Dieu, which the Corporation had opened specially for visitors to the troops. They couldn't do enough for Kitchener's First Hundred Thousand when they got here in mid-September, Jamie said. She felt odd being a guest and not working, especially since most of the other guests were well-to-do. But she had decided it was worth the money, and Jamie had been all for her coming to Dover when she swallowed her pride and suggested it. It might be easier to tell him, less real, away from Ashden.

Or so she'd thought until she got here and found Jamie so strange. He didn't seem to care about Ashden and what was happening there; he was just full of what good sport the army was, and the pals he'd made at Shornecliffe, and the officers and the drill and endless, endless talk of war and how he'd be part of it soon. They couldn't go up on the cliffs or into the country and anyway it was raining; they had to keep to the roads because the army had closed off all the footpaths. She'd duly admired the old Castle, but not with much enthusiasm. Dover was a rough place compared with Tunbridge Wells, and as for these Kentish folk – what there were of them among the foreigners – give her Sussex every time. Even the countryside she'd seen on the railway train hadn't been exciting, not like going to London. But Jamie seemed to like Dover. He'd been to the cinema and the pubs, even a music hall where a girl in red spangles led them all in 'Goodbye Dolly Gray' and 'Soldiers of the Queen'. It was a life in which she, Agnes, had no part, and this made her feel awkward. She'd had no opportunity for saying, Jamie, Ruth Horner's had a baby boy and the whole of the village is saying it's got Mr Swinford-Browne's ears. No opportunity to say, Jamie, you're *really* going to be a father. He'd forgotten her, that was clear. He was too busy talking about his puttees and khaki uniform, and new rifles called Lee–Enfields. It had no relevance to Agnes and her problem. Well, if Jamie didn't love her any more, she could not tell him about the baby. Her pride wouldn't let her. Anguished, she tentatively tried again.

'Your mum misses you in the shop, Jamie.'

Jamie looked at her oddly. 'Does she? I sent her a postcard of the castle.'

'Did you?'

'Yes.' Jamie took a gulp of tea. 'I expect I'll be going abroad soon. Off to shoot the Kaiser, eh? He'll be shivering in his jackboots will Kaiser Willy when he meets us First

Hundred Thousand. There's a chap from Scotland here, he plays bagpipes.'

When she did not comment, he went on aggressively. 'Sound like a frog caught by a cat. You should hear 'em, screech, screech, screech. Call that music? I could do better with me penny whistle.'

She felt tears sting her eyes. Why were they talking about penny whistles when time was so precious? She wanted to talk about things that mattered, him and her, but he didn't seem the same Jamie. He was coarser, brasher, not her loving, shy, honest Jamie. He never said anything about getting married or leave or anything. She forced herself to mention it.

'I expect you'll be getting leave before then, Jamie? Coming back to Ashden, eh?' she tried to sound casual.

Jamie lay down his knife and fork and grabbed some bread and butter, stuffing it in his mouth. 'I reckon I ought to see a bit of the world while I can, don't you? You could come too if you like. London. I'd like to see London.'

'That would be nice,' Agnes said listlessly. If she *liked*? Didn't he care? He didn't want to come home, he didn't care whether he saw her again or not. He'd left Ashden behind, he'd left *her* behind, and that was that.

'The Royal Sussex is going away, Leaving the girls in the family way.' Again and again it pulsed through her mind, an endless refrain. Jamie had said he was posted to the 7th Battalion, Royal Sussex, and how fitting that was. 'Going away, going away . . .'

'Have another cup of tea, Jamie?' She pulled his cup towards her with trembling fingers.

* * *

'What's up, mate? Wouldn't let you up her skirt, eh? Quite right, too.'

'Piss off!' Jamie's control snapped. A few weeks ago he'd hardly have known such words, let alone used them. Now they came readily enough to convey his frustration, his bewilderment and anger. All the same, Joe and his other mates were the best things about this place. Agnes had been surprised to see him in his Sunday suit, not uniform. Hardly surprising, they hadn't got any yet. The army had run out. A few of the lads had scrounged old scarlet uniforms, but he wore some old blue makeshift stuff from which the dye ran if it rained. And weapons? The new Lee–Enfield he'd boasted about? That was a laugh. He'd a bit of lead piping to train with, and the officers swung wooden rattles to pretend they were enemy machine guns. Some army. At least they had forks and plates here; up at the Castle Barracks, they didn't even have those, he'd heard.

'You're a mess of bleeding nerves, mate.' Joe Harris was more concerned than offended. Not that he cared much, but he liked things to be cheery around him.

'I got things on my mind.' Jamie calmed down; it might have been an apology.

There was only one thing on his mind, in fact, and that was Agnes. Why did she have to be so offhand and starchy when all he wanted to do was kiss, cuddle and love her? He'd looked forward for two weeks to her visit, tried his best to make her proud of him by telling her how well he was doing, and she'd behaved like a spinster aunt paying a duty visit. Didn't she understand how he felt far from home, that a soldier needed affection? No, all she wanted was to tell him how his ma was, and ask when he was coming back to Ashden. Didn't she realise he couldn't go back there till he'd proved himself? He couldn't face his mother till he'd something to show her, a medal maybe, he thought vaguely. He'd put it on the table in his bedroom along with the wooden horse he'd carved when he was ten and the toy tin soldiers handed down through generations of Thorn children, so battered the paint had worn off most of them. He'd repaint them as soon as he'd won his medal, using the new khaki. Or maybe cast new ones. After all, he lived by a forge. Yes, he'd enjoy doing that, when he went home for good. Maybe everything would be all right then, the village, his parents – and Agnes.

Felicia began as though she were reading a book to a child, leaving the story at a tantalising point, never too obviously, never dramatically. Her subjects were not, after all the stuff of novels, for how could Daniel be interested in fiction when fighting so much cruel fact? She talked of the small stuff of everyday life. 'Percy has made hidey-holes for large tins of stores, and Mrs Dibble goes out by dead of night to take out what she wants. They crept out one night for some sugar, because that's getting so expensive to buy, and Harriet heard them. She must have thought it was Fred again, up to no good, or some prowler. So she armed herself with George's cricket bat – and – I think you're getting tired, Daniel. I'll tell you what happened tomorrow.' She paused hopefully, but there was no reply. Daniel wasn't listening. Nor was he the next day, nor even the day after, as she began the stirring tale of George and the German spy.

'. . . Quite clearly he was sitting waiting for the railway trains to stop at the signal and would then write down details of the troops on each train. George even feared he might be planning to take over the signal box and crash the train. So he positioned himself behind a tree and very, very carefully got his home-made lasso in position. Then he. I'll tell you what happens tomorrow.' Felicia hardly bothered to see if there were any response, or whether as usual Daniel was staring at some unidentifiable object on the opposite wall.

But this time to her surprise and joy there was: 'Did Harriet hit him?'

So he had been listening the other day. Jubilant, and careful not to betray her excitement, she replied casually, 'No, she hit the sugar loaf by mistake and sent it flying into pieces all over the garden. But you wait till I tell you about the spy tomorrow.'

He made no answer, but she did not mind. She was on her way and so was he.

Gradually it came to be accepted, even if frowned upon by the Matron, that Felicia, when her duty finished, would be found at Number Three bed, Daniel Hunney of the 1st King's Own, paralysed and minus one foot. Since she was regular in her attendance it became accepted that she would deliver and supervise suppers for all four beds in Ward Number Two.

This evening, as she pushed the trolley of dirty dishes back to the kitchen, slightly later than usual, she met Lady Hunney outside the ward, coming to pay her evening visit to Daniel. Felicia bowed slightly and continued on her way, but was surprised to be recalled by the imperious voice. Her relationship with Lady Hunney had always been easier than Caroline's because Lady Hunney, like many others, found Felicia's self-containment perplexing. The obvious attraction she held for Daniel she had put down to the whim of a summer enchantment that would disappear as soon as he touched foreign soil. Now that foreign soil had proved so tragic, she had assumed that Felicia's girlish infatuation would vanish, and had indeed encouraged her posting to Ashden. That it had not intrigued rather than dismayed her – for the time being.

Obediently Felicia stopped and turned, waiting for Lady Hunney to approach her.

'I am told you spend much time with my son.' Lady Hunney stared with distaste at the dirty dishes and Felicia's slightly soiled serviceable cotton gloves.

'It is my own time, not the hospital's.'

'No doubt. Why are you so much with Daniel?'

'That is my concern, Lady Hunney.'

'And mine, Felicia. You realise I shall forbid these visits if they are upsetting him.'

'The Matron can forbid me to see him, but so far she has not done so.' The gentleness in Felicia's voice softened the clear implication that Lady Hunney had no authority here now, but it reached her nevertheless.

'Miss Lilley, my son is and will always be a cripple. If I discover you are filling his head with false hope, I shall stop these visits.' She spoke mildly but equally firmly, but Felicia flushed.

'God decides whom He will cure and in what manner.'

'You seem very certain of God's prerogatives, Miss Lilley, but less knowledgeable of a mother's understanding of her son's needs.'

'As his mother, then, you must know that he is tenacious, that he will not readily abandon his plans for life.'

'I wish to ensure he has a life first, Miss Lilley.' Her voice rose, outraged at such assertiveness.

'That you have already done, Lady Hunney.' Felicia's voice was warm. 'He owes you his life.'

Lady Hunney bowed her head in what might have been a slight acknowledgement. Objectiveness and generosity were not qualities she was accustomed to finding in her opponents.

Edith's court shoes pitter-pattered with annoyance as she was directed by a subservient Mrs Bugle into Isabel's morning room, decorated to Edith's mind more like a boudoir with its frills and tassels than a practical place of work. But growing up with such an example as the Rectory, perhaps Isabel was not entirely to blame – save for disregarding her new mama's advice. Isabel was disconsolately leafing through the Winter Fashions number of *Vogue*. *The Times* and the *Illustrated London News* lay unopened on the table. Edith sniffed. If *Vogue* thought winter fashions here would consist of elegant full-skirted black gowns and jackets with tigerskin trimmings and muffs, they were much mistaken. In America, perhaps, but here there was a war on, though Isabel did not seem to appreciate that fact.

'Isabel!'

Isabel looked up at the accusatory note in her mother-in-law's voice. It was becoming distressingly frequent, and Isabel could not understand why. She had been most obliging to the Belgian refugees when they were rehoused at The Towers. She had even had them to tea once, painful ordeal though it had proved. She had imagined her own terrible experiences in Paris would make a common bond in view of their losses, but they had not shown any interest. Edith had suggested she might do more knitting, sewing and so forth. Isabel felt that as a newly married woman, accustoming herself to running her own house (a task by no means as easy as she had blithely imagined), she was doing quite enough already.

'Yes, Mother?' Isabel writhed at the need for such a designation.

'Where is Patricia?'

Isabel was astounded, though relieved that for once she was not at fault. 'I have no idea.'

'She informed me she was staying with you last night.'

'No, she wasn't.'

'Then where is she?' Edith raised her voice. 'You're encouraging her to defy me. I know you are.'

Isabel had several ideas on where Patricia might be, and none of them involved any encouragement of Patricia from her.

'I blame the war,' Edith continued. 'You girls think you can do anything you please.'

'She's probably staying with a friend in the Wells.' Isabel tried to show concern.

'Nonsense. Suppose she's gone to Serbia?'

'Why on earth should she?'

'There is a war on there,' Edith snapped.

'It's far more likely she's in London or the Wells.'

'You don't seem concerned. It seems to me, Isabel, you take your responsibilities far too lightly. Patricia is a young unmarried girl, and as much your sister now as Phoebe.'

'She is an adult,' Isabel pointed out. 'She's twenty-one.'

'Barely. My little lamb.' Edith burst into tears and Isabel tried ineffectually to console her.

The little lamb arrived home at The Towers at six o'clock that evening, and announced herself a proud new member of the Women's Police Volunteers. She arrived at Hop House precisely one hour later, two suitcases following her borne by The Towers' chauffeur. One was for her forthcoming departure to East Grinstead, the other for an overnight stay at Hop House.

'I've been tossed out into the snow,' she informed Isabel gleefully, 'and they even kept the baby.'

'Baby?' cried Isabel faintly. 'You've had a baby?'

Patricia regarded her scathingly. 'Brace up, Issy. I was joking. I've become a woman policeman, and Ma and Pa don't approve. I've been thrown out. I'm a refugee, just like her blessed Belgians she pretends to dote on so much. It's your and Robert's part in the war effort to take me in for the night. Then before I go to swing my truncheon, I'm off to the Wells. Thought I'd drop in to see your aunt.'

'But perhaps we ought not to take you in if your parents disapprove,' Isabel said instantly. 'And what on earth do

426

you want to see Aunt Tilly for? You're not going to become one of those awful women, are you?'

Patricia giggled, but did not reply since Robert came in and demanded to know what was going on.

'I'm a lady policeman, Bobby, that's what. I'm going on the march in patrols round the military camps and in the towns to prevent undesirable conduct, as they say.'

'Soldiers won't take any notice of you,' Isabel said, in surprise.

'The girls will. That's whose most of the bad behaviour is. Won't leave the men alone. I sympathise. I'm looking forward to going.' She burst out raucously: 'On Monday I go out with a soldier, on Tuesday I step out with a tar.'

'Patricia!' Isabel felt she ought to express the genuine shock she felt.

'That's jolly brave, sis,' Robert said quickly. Brother and sister exchanged glances, and Isabel felt excluded from something she could not understand, save that it reminded her of how Robert had been in Paris. 'I'd like to do something like that.' he continued.

'Pa will never let you. You'll have to run away like I did. Why don't you?'

Robert relapsed into silence, aware of waves of hostility emanating from his wife. For Patricia's sake, he'd avoid more acrimony tonight.

The timing had been orchestrated carefully for the grand finale. Now that no street lighting was permitted, nature must be harnessed to man's will. Easy enough to choose a full moonlit night, but a special visit to Chapel was necessary for William Swinford-Browne to ensure, like Mrs Dibble, that the Lord looked kindly on his enterprise and did not spoil the evening by creating unhelpful clouds. Mid-November was later than he had ordered for the grand opening of the Swinford-Browne Picture Palace, but at least at five o'clock there should still be enough light aided by the rising moon to ensure that he was seen as he stepped from the Daimler on to the red carpet. Everything was going as smoothly as beer from a barrel, he congratulated himself. As the Daimler drew up with himself, his wife, son and daughter-in-law, he could see a highly satisfactory gathering awaiting him, including that fellow from the *East Sussex Courier*, and Master George Blasted Lilley as representative of the parish magazine. He never made the mistake of underestimating the power of the parish magazine – or the influence of the Rectory over the village.

He stepped down from the running board and paused, ostensibly to help Edith down, in fact to admire his own achievement from its black and white Gothic frontage to the clock he'd had made in Switzerland positioned in the imposing central gable. Fortunately the clock had been delivered before war made imports a matter of chance, and he was proud of the revolving figure that emerged each hour, of a man striking a bung into a beer cask. It spoke of himself, a self-made man, and not ashamed of what he did. Beer had paid for the cinema, which recorded his achievements for Ashden to admire for ever. Even those bally Belgians had had their compensations. He'd been able to boast in his club of his patriotism in having them under his roof, and then they'd promptly left for alternative

428

lodgings in London (having had the bally nerve to tell him they needed peace and quiet).

Edith had debated long over her gown for this evening, wanting to strike a balance between patriotic restraint and the need to live up to her role as new benefactress of the village, now Lady Hunney had been pushed aside into the Dower House. She had compromised on a sober dark blue gown and an ermine-edged white velvet stole to show up in the gloom. Isabel had shown no such restraint; her Empire-line brocade evening dress was embellished with a wide silk sash, lace, and appliqued beads. She looked charming, though out of place on a November night on Bankside, admired by the habitués of the Norville Arms.

William was gratified to find that the large, expectant crowd, which sprawled not only along Bankside but halfway down the grass bank towards the pond as well, consisted of far more than the estate workers he had ordered to attend. A large part of Ashden was assembled, and would not be disappointed. He would speak.

He paused at the entrance to the Picture Palace, as though it had just occurred to him that an address might be in order. He took Edith's arm firmly in his to emphasise he was a family man, and ensured that on his other side stood Robert, the son, he wished to imply, who stood so steadfastly by him.

'In these dark days,' he began, 'Ashden needs entertainment, and if my money can bring it to you, that is as much helping the war effort as my wife's comforts for the troops. Those of you trying to overcome grief will be comforted, those of you seeking relaxation or education can find it here.' He paused, with a careful grin. 'I'm not going to make a long speech, so I'll just say we've got a splendid opening programme for you: the secret is out. We've a six-reeler, the famous *East Lynne* to make you cry, a Charlie Chaplin to send you away laughing, and everyone's favourite, Pimple, to start you off. Those of you who are lucky enough to have reserved seats can see it tonight, and for the rest of you it will be on for the remainder of this week. No reserved seats then, it's every man for himself.'

'It always is in your family.'

In the sudden hush after her clarion cry, Matilda Lilley, forewarned of the occasion by Patricia's visit, pushed her way through the crowd from Nanny Oates' cottage to confront her enemy. Isabel gave an appalled moan at the unwelcome and familiar voice. 'Other men go to the trenches, not your son. Why? Because *you* won't let him, Mr William Swinford-Browne,' Tilly yelled, intent on not one word escaping her large audience. Then she plunged forward. 'What are you doing for King and Country?' she continued. 'Tearing your heart out like these good folk here by sending your son to fight? Not you. You're bribing the village with *this* –' she gestured at the Picture Palace – 'hoping they won't notice you think you're better than them. Patriot? Swinford-Browne, you're a *coward*.'

Mesmerised, Swinford-Browne failed to act quickly enough. He was too late to stop Matilda Lilley, in full view of the Ashden villagers, brandishing a large white feather mockingly before him and poking it in his pocket.

Then he acted. With a roar he tore the feather out, grabbed Tilly's arm, twisting it, and flung her viciously off. She collapsed, sprawling heavily on the ground, just as George, red in the face, leaped out from the crowd to her defence.

'That's my aunt,' he shouted. 'And she's a *lady*. You *are* a coward, Mr Swinford-Browne. I'll tell my father.' Near to unmanly tears, he bent down to help his aunt up, and the crowd began to move in, murmuring among themselves.

'A lady, laddie?' William snarled, shaking with rage. 'She's a crazy lunatic who belongs in Bedlam. This time I'll see she gets there.'

'No, Father.' White-faced and trembling, Robert tried to hold him back. 'She's right. I should be there.'

'Hold your blasted tongue, sir,' William shouted at his son, while Edith sobbed helplessly at his side.

Tilly scrambled up, shook off George's arm, picked up the discarded feather and defiantly waved it aloft. 'I know it's not your doing, Robert. It's his, Mr One-rule-for-me-and-another-for-you.'

As Swinford-Browne rushed at her, Ashden woke up to the fact that they had been proudly sending their menfolk to the front as the country needed, and a rich, able-bodied young man was still here. Before they could vent their anger, Joe Ifield pushed forward to pull Swinford-Browne back, shielding both him and Robert while Edith and Isabel screamed, keeping well away.

'Let go of me, you fool,' snarled William. 'It's her you're to arrest.'

'What for?' Joe asked stolidly. 'You hit her, I didn't see her hit you, sir.' His voice was raised so that everyone could hear and, purple with indignation, William heard a roar of approval from the crowd.

'Reckon Joe's right.' Harold Mutter, the carrier, was the first to walk away from the Picture Palace, and back into the Norville Arms.

William Swinford-Browne marched into the cinema, followed nervously by his family, and with even more trepidation by some of his estate workers, as they saw others of their fellow workers walking towards the Norville Arms; all but half a dozen of the men were near the end of their working lives, so they changed their minds and followed suit.

The Swinford-Browne Picture Palace was formally open.

'But you can't!' Isabel was aghast. 'Just because of what one crazy woman says?'

'No, because of my own belief which no doubt you think equally crazy,' her husband replied coldly. 'I ought to be out there doing my bit just like everyone else. Just like Anthony Wilding, just like any old Joe Smith. War *doesn't* choose. It takes, Isabel. You didn't marry anybody out of the ordinary. I just feel as everyone else, that I ought to stand up to evil. I've been talked out of it long enough and it took one crazy woman, if that's what you consider your aunt, to show me so.'

'But what about me?'

'The best way for men to protect their families is to go out and fight for them over there.' He looked at the face he'd loved so well, at the tears welling up in her eyes, and softened in pity more than love today. 'Don't be sad, little puss. I'll be back just as soon as the war's over. And that can't be long. I probably won't even get through initial training. I'll fight my war out somewhere like Lincolnshire with my luck.'

'Luck?'

He reddened. 'It would be a pity not to get a crack at the Kaiser now I'm going.'

'I think all men are *mad*,' Isabel said vehemently.

'Do you?' He sighed. 'Perhaps you're right, but I'm still going.'

'But they don't *want* volunteers any more. They've got too many. They made the conditions harder in September, by raising the height requirement.'

'I'm still going. I'm tall enough, and young enough.'

'The newspapers have stopped claiming the war is nearly over. Suppose it goes on till next year?' she continued desperately.

'You'll be all right. Your parents are here. There's always the Rectory.'

A terrible suspicion smote her. 'What do you mean, there's always the Rectory?'

Robert braced himself. She might as well know now, she'd have to some time. 'Father's not too pleased that I've volunteered. Far from it, for I'm afraid he's stopped our allowance, but don't worry, I've enough saved—'

'He can't do that!'

'He can. It isn't fair, because I've worked for most of it. For the last few months, anyway,' he added honestly. 'But how am I to live?'

'On my officer's pay like everyone else.' It occurred to him that she was showing singularly little concern for his safety, only his departure.

'And how much is that?'

433

'If I get a commission, I think about six shillings a day when I'm trained. It may be more.' Robert tried to be nonchalant.

'I can't possibly live on that.' Isabel was appalled.

Nor could he, but he proposed to try.

'But what am I going to do? This house eats money,' she wailed.

'You could live with your parents. Or with mine.'

She burst into tears. 'You don't love me any more.'

'On the contrary. But it's apparent you think money more important than my safety, Isabel.'

'How can you say such a terrible thing?'

'How can you not offer me one word of encouragement? Has it occurred to you how I must feel going away and leaving a bride behind?'

'Then don't go,' she shouted.

He lost patience. 'You, my mother, my father. What bally use is it for the Government to run recruiting campaigns, when you all have so little opinion of me you don't think I'm in my right mind?'

She ran to him, frightened she had gone too far. 'Darling, I'll do anything. You know silly me is just making a fuss because she doesn't want to lose you. Forgive me?'

He stroked the golden hair he loved so much. 'Of course,' he whispered as tenderly as he could. But in his heart a tiny sore spot refused to be consoled.

'No, ma'am.' Agnes sat miserably on the edge of the basket chair in Mrs Lilley's workroom.

'It's Jamie, isn't it?' Elizabeth asked gently.

'I'm not saying, madam.' Agnes tried to stay as calm as she hoped she sounded.

'We don't want you to leave, Agnes.'

'It wouldn't be right, madam, with me having a baby out of wedlock. This is a rectory. What would folks say?'

'It is immaterial, Agnes. It is what we *want*. With the war now there are so many jobs you can do here to help me, without having to tire yourself with housework.'

For a moment Agnes wavered. 'No, madam, I'm grateful, but I've quite decided.'

'We can't let you go without knowing you are going to be all right, Agnes. We feel responsible for you, especially the Rector, both as your employer and as your priest.'

She flushed. 'He won't think too well of me.'

'God judges, Agnes. My husband and I do not. Now, where are you going? Home to your mother, or to Mrs Thorn?'

She shook her head. Impossible, both of them.

'To Nanny Oates?'

Agnes looked surprised and almost smiled. 'No, madam. She's done enough for poor Ruth. I wouldn't wish me on her too, poor old lady.'

'I'm glad. I wouldn't like it either, for it would look even more as though we had thrown you out. Agnes, we want you to stay here and so does Mrs Dibble. She'll help you all she can.'

'It's good of you all but, besides the shame of it, I can't answer the door when I – get bigger,' Agnes said jerkily. 'I'd always feel guilty, like I did something bad, and though the Bible says it is, it didn't feel it at the time. I don't want the village laughing at me, not like they did before.'

'They didn't laugh at Ruth.'

'Maybe not. But it's not the same.'

'Where in Ashden will you go to?' Elizabeth worried, as a terrible thought struck her. 'I hope you've no idea of going to London or Tunbridge Wells, and trying to support yourself?'

'How would I do that, madam, when the baby comes?' Agnes looked bewildered, and Elizabeth did not elaborate. Many girls in her position would go on the streets to earn enough money to live.

'Just a foolish thought, Agnes. I wish you would tell me where you intend to go, though.'

Agnes managed a smile at last. She told her.

It had taken all the courage she could muster to walk up here but, after the bitterness of the last weeks since she returned from Dover, courage had been easier to find, for the simple reason that Agnes didn't care very much about anything. Up here she felt quite different, though, literally above it all and free from the oppression of her own thoughts. With her basket of food she was Red Riding Hood on her way out of the forest. Already she was high enough to see Ashdown Forest in one direction and the hop farm and railway in the other. Down below her were the Rectory and church, and the huge elms that dotted Ashdown Manor Park. Yet so few folks ever came up Tillow Hill. Here stood the beacon to be lit in case of a Napoleonic invasion, rebuilt now by the Misses Norville ready to signal the German invasion of Ashden, and way over on her right was the Devil's Bed, a place of superstitious evil for the villagers. It was said if you came up here after dark alone, he'd rise from his bed and tear out your soul. Well, he could do no harm to her, and if she *were* walking into the devil's domain, she'd give him a run for his money.

Ahead of her was the ruined Norville Castle, its towers and tumbled battlements looking like giant teeth, and far from friendly. Barbed wire now encircled the whole Gothic ruin, and try as she would she could find no way through it. She walked round the building on the far side in case the front entrance by the 'moat' wasn't the real way in at all, and was surprised to find the building in quite good repair, solid enough to withstand the buffeting it must get from the Sussex winds, despite sheltering trees.

Somewhere there must be a way in. She had marched round twice, stumbling over tussocks of grass and with the distinct feeling she was being watched. On her third perambulation she saw the face of old Johnson, the Norvilles' 'man', balefully looking out of a small window above what must surely be the door on the far side of the 'moat'. So there must be a way through the wire here. She scooped up handfuls of grass to protect her gloves, and prodded and pushed. Five minutes later she found a system of hooks in the barbed wire that undid with relative ease, allowing her entry like a gate. Congratulating herself on passing the first hurdle she went in, and jumped when a grinding bang in front of her brought down the drawbridge over the pond that called itself the moat. She wanted to laugh, despite her wretchedness, and she trod daintily across it only to find a locked door on the other side.

'State your business.' Johnson's hoarse voice assailed her from above.

'With the Misses Norville.'

'Entry refused.'

Agnes grew annoyed. 'Tell them Agnes Pilbeam from the Rectory is here, with something for them.' She pointed to her basket.

'Leave it there.'

'No.' She made as if to retrace her steps, half-expecting the drawbridge to be drawn up under her, but it stayed put. She waited curiously, listening to sounds of altercation from within. Eventually the door was opened by Johnson, ancient helmet on his head and bayonet in his hand.

'You can come in,' she was told as though the greatest favour in the world was being offered.

She walked in cautiously. It was cold and damp in this barren stone hallway but the massive wooden door on the right creaked open into a room warm enough, with blazing fire and paraffin lamps.

'What do you want?'

She jumped. She had thought the room empty, for the high back of the Chesterfield had concealed the lace-capped heads of the two sisters sitting side by side.

'I've brought something for you.' Taking her courage in both hands, she marched round to the Chesterfield and stood awkwardly before them, clasping her basket. They looked like a couple of Queen Victoria dolls, sitting there in black with their lace caps and hands neatly folded. Not so pleasant-looking as dolls, though; sharper, with almost birdlike eyes, and clawlike hands.

She put her basket down and drew out a large chocolate cake, a jar of jam and some pickles. Seeing she had their attention, she took a deep breath. 'I could cook for you every day, if you'd let me.'

'We don't need a cook. Mary cooks.'

'I'm better. And she stays home every other Sunday.'

'We can't afford more staff, can we, Charlotte?'

'No, Emily, and nor can I. The very idea.'

'I'll work free. Just my board,' Agnes said quickly. 'I'd live here, you see.'

'How? Impossible.' Their cry was in unison.

'Why?' Agnes tried to keep in control of the situation, and sound reasonably persuasive.

'Who's to do the work?'

'I am. Mary can't do all your cleaning. Look, that table needs French polish. I'm a trained parlour maid. I could do that. And bring you tea and . . . and that pretty blouse needs mending.' She spotted a tear in the lace.

'I'm not going to Buckingham Palace.' Miss Charlotte's sudden cackle unnerved her.

'It still needs it.'

The sisters looked at each other. 'She's a fugitive from justice. Emily.' There was fear in Miss Charlotte's voice, and Agnes was quick to reassure her.

'No. I'm parlour maid at the Rectory. They'll give me a character.'

'Don't they pay you?'

'Yes.'

'There's something very odd about you, young woman. Go away,' Miss Emily ordered. Her sister nodded in rather

439

reluctant agreement, her eyes on the chocolate cake.

'Oh, please.' Agnes began to panic, she had been so sure she would succeed. 'You're so quiet here, and the Rectory is so busy.'

'You'll have followers, a young thing like you.'

Agnes could keep her grief back no longer. 'No, I won't. I'm expecting.' So she had no hope now. She had planned to get a job, make herself indispensable, and *then* tell them. It hadn't worked out like that. 'You won't want me now.'

They weren't listening, but talking to each other. She was nearly at the door when she heard what they were talking about.

'Does she mean a *baby*, Emily?' Miss Charlotte's attention was immediately deflected from cake.

'A baby boy, Charlotte.'

'It might be a girl, Emily.'

'It might be both, Charlotte.'

'We could teach it to talk.'

'*Her*, Charlotte.'

'No, you said it would be a boy. Where are you going, young woman?'

Agnes didn't know, so she stood still.

'You can't go anywhere. We've always wanted a little baby, haven't we, Emily?'

'We have, Charlotte, we have.'

What are you doing, Reggie, while I lie here in this small bedroom, listening to the lapping of the sea and Ellen's snores? Are you thinking of that night last June when you said you wanted to imagine yourself with me in the Rectory bedroom? How different this room is, with its bright red roses on sand-yellow wallpaper. Where are you . . . asleep in a trench? In billets in reserve? Or on a snatched day's leave sleeping in a hotel? It was the not knowing that was so hard, and still the waves lapped on as if they didn't care.

Were you in that big battle at Ypres that the newspapers said went so well? Yet if it did, why did it take so long? It had started in mid-October, and wasn't over till nearly the end of November. It had been a vital battle to win, of course, since if Ypres fell, then the Germans would reach the Channel. Over two thousand officers had been killed . . . no, she would not think of that. His name had not appeared in casualty lists, and there might be a letter tomorrow. Always tomorrow. Like jam. Do you go into battle as one of our patients described, shouting with laughter: 'Early doors ninepence'? He said that was the 1st King's Own at the Aisne – Daniel's battalion. He's not laughing any more, Reggie. Are you?

Are you thinking of me, Reggie, or drinking in an *estaminet*? Are you *anywhere*, Reggie? People were quieter now, no one claimed this war would be over at Christmas any more. Instead, there was talk of how they'd manage at Christmas; she wondered whether she'd get leave or not, for it was only two weeks away. Before her stretched unimaginable horrors. Up until now she had thought of it in terms of stoically enduring Reggie's absence, filling the time with her own work, and when the war was over, everything would be as it was. Now she wondered whether that would be so. Ashden Manor, her future home, was a hospital. It could not so quickly be reconstituted into the old Ashden. A cinema stood where Ebenezer Thorn had lived. Ashden men had gone off to war and she already knew from Mother that some would never return. Ypres, the first major battle, for all its success had killed many men as well as officers. Today had been December 10th. Advent carols in St Nicholas . . . What memories that brought back. The liturgical colours changed for the great day that proclaimed the festival was on its way. Christmas gifts, Christmas carols, Christmas puddings, Christmas in St Nicholas. She must get back, she must.

She awoke early next morning, and was already dressed when, alarmingly, the guns of the harbour defences began to fire. Ellen, needless to say, hardly stirred, but Caroline rushed downstairs to join the huge excited crowd gathering on the Parade. Submarine was the word passed from mouth to mouth, and as the rumour came from the direction of the harbour it was passed on as truth. An hour later, when the crowd had dispersed to spread the story further, the guns fired again. This time it was the eastern entrance and *three* submarines. Their periscopes had been spotted, but despite all the hullabaloo and endless stories going around, no one either then or later that day could tell of damage either to harbour or to submarines; it was generally supposed that the Germans had taken fright and scurried home. She went back to the hostel that night with divided feelings. Dover's defences were good, yet Germans had got as near as the harbour. Perhaps the Misses Norville were not so scatty with their fears of invasion. Soberly, she turned her mind to happier matters. There had been a letter from Reggie she had been saving to read, so that the pleasure was the more intense.

Outside today the seagulls had dipped and called on the beach, oblivious of the dramatic events that had taken place earlier in the harbour. Reggie had written (when? She looked at the date, 14th November) that there was a sparrow chirping somewhere near his trench. He spent much time watching and listening to it. 'And do you know why, my darling? When we walked in Ashdown Forest last spring you told me to listen to the Dartford warbler. I wanted to talk about me and my problems and so I pretended to take no notice. You were rightly annoyed with me, but do you know why I didn't? Because I stupidly thought there was all the time in the world for such things as birds. Now, my love, I listen to my sparrow because I know there is not . . .'

Chapter Thirteen

No wonder Jane Austen kept up such a voluminous and detailed correspondence with her sister whenever she was away from home. Caroline remembered her father telling her, a bored, uncomprehending fourteen-year-old child, of Sir Walter Scott's admiring comment that Miss Austen had that 'exquisite touch which renders ordinary commonplace things and characters interesting'. In those days she could see no virtue in the recounting of tedious stillroom activities, or the detailed doings of neighbours, but now she found herself eagerly seizing on any epistle from the Rectory, welcoming each incident as of epoch-making significance, for they studded the landscape of memory with nails of fact. From Mrs Dibble's plum heavies to Farmer Lake's lost arm at Ypres, everything involved her and was precious.

Today Caroline was rich indeed, for there was another letter from Mother, and yesterday she had had another one from Reggie – though the latter caused as much anxiety as comfort. Reassuring words, she told herself, might cover a nightmare of experience. He wrote with careful detail, and a touch of derring-do, of his fellows, of the cosy dugout in the trench, of the life and character of the villages. It was part of France and Belgium he had never seen before, accustomed as he was to a France beginning at Paris and stretching south into the glorious sun. This bleaker north produced a starker view of a land where the villagers were poor and their homes primitive; they bore no resemblance to Ashden, or any life to which she could relate. It was what he didn't say, however, that caused her concern. He did not mention Daniel, for example, though he must surely know of his brother's fate. Had his parents underplayed what had happened to him or was the horror so great that he kept it bottled up inside himself? She had no way of knowing and she could not raise the subject. Since letters arrived at irregular intervals, sometimes two or even three together, they often commented on letters she had sent him perhaps two or three weeks previously, and it was hard to get a sense of continuity. The line was quiet, she'd read in the newspapers. There was less news in the press of what was happening in Flanders, and more of fighting in the rest of the world. Did that mean, she had wondered at first, that there would be leave for the men in the trenches? It had taken some thought to show her the ridiculousness of this notion, and when no word came from Reggie of home leave, she had sent her gifts off to him; Rupert Brooke's poems, a copy of an extraordinary book of short stories called *Dubliners* by a young man called James Joyce, and a silver pencil.

Resigning herself to his absence, however, concentrated her mind on the nagging feeling she had been doing her best to overcome. She was not, and never would be, a good nurse; therefore they had put her on general duties. Yet what, she had now realised, she was good at was making and understanding decisions, communicating them and cheering people on through their ordeals; all those qualities which as a humble VAD she was not exploiting to the full. This did not perturb her unduly in itself; she had wanted to help and help she would. But when so much needed doing with men still flocking to the colours, there must be something she, and thousands of women like her, could do apart from their traditional roles of housekeeping, teaching and nursing. The Government, however, was giving absolutely no help to encourage women to branch out. Those brave individualists like Lady Paget and Mrs St Clair Stobart won their way in defiance of the Government and not with its help. Oddly, since war broke out she had been feeling much more akin to the suffragette cause in its wider implications for women. She would write to Aunt Tilly, from whom she'd heard little in the last three months, to ask her advice. She'd heard *of* her of course; letters from family and friends (save from Isabel) had been full of the story of Swinford-Browne's comeuppance. But Tilly herself had never mentioned it.

Caroline was worried also on more practical matters. She was unpaid, and for the Rectory, with rising prices and reduced income, especially after Lloyd George's first War Budget in November which doubled the ninepence tax rate for incomes over £500 to one shilling and sixpence, this was an increasingly significant factor. Even with her mother's money, their income was only a little above £500 but, since her father's was harder to gather in these days of common hardship, she felt she was a burden they could well do without. She could always be a nippy or a clippie, she told herself more cheerfully, nippies being the Lyons' teashop waitresses, and clippies bus conductors. She'd read they were grudgingly considering women now in London to replace men who had volunteered. In any case she was resolved that, Lady Hunney or no Lady Hunney, when her first six-month contract as a VAD was concluded in February, she would think very carefully about her future, and if it lay in Belgium, then she would welcome it. Reggie would surely understand if she explained how she felt about it, but so far she had not thought it fair to worry him with her dilemmas.

She longed to be there to experience for herself what it was like. Patients had described it to her, but all the time she had the feeling they were remembering a different place to the one their words were conjuring up for her. It was almost as if they were obliging her with words, when locked inside themselves was a place that they could share only with those who had been through the same experience.

Christmas would be here in eight days, and still she had not heard whether she would be granted leave. She had tried to persuade herself it was her duty to remain, for obviously some of them had to, but then this morning's letter from her mother had reminded her so vividly of Rectory Christmas that she almost wept with longing for the peaceful life she had loved so much.

'We peeked at the Christmas puddings yesterday, including the one from last year which horrified your father because it had so much brandy and stout in it.' Caroline remembered; he had only been mollified when told that it was an old family recipe of Mr Thomas Hardy, a novelist her father much admired. 'We peeked and the alcohol had preserved it as well as an Egyptian mummy, so we'll use that as well as Grandma Overton's recipe, the one with the mashed potatoes you laughed about as a child. Mrs Dibble has, she says, bought sufficient currants.' A line was heavily scored beneath the 'bought'. 'We missed you greatly at the Great Stirring Ceremony. Even Isabel came down for it. She is looking rather peaky; I expect she is missing Robert, unless . . .?' Caroline laughed, understanding the unwritten question: could it be Isabel was not enjoying life at The Towers? 'But she says nothing. I shall wear my old blue, shortened by Mrs Hazel. She is sadly down on new gowns this year, though I gather Edith has decided to patronise her – I suspect under orders from William in order to regain favour in the village. Poor Edith. Phoebe is losing her plumpness at last, and growing quite fashionably slim. Between you and me, I think she is growing a little bored with her job at the railway station, now the cold weather has arrived with a vengeance. I recognise in her the signs of old. How I wish you were here. It's holly-gathering time again and you are always so clever at finding it. George is all for thieving some from the Forest by night, in the hope he won't get caught by the Board of Conservators. They have spies everywhere, I tell him, just like the Germans, and that has put an end to his devilry. We did miss you on his birthday today. He was very pleased with the book you sent, though I doubt if such a busy young man will get round to writing to tell you so.' (In fact he had, or rather, he had sent a drawing which arrived, like Mother's letter, this morning.) 'Sixteen now, and all my chicks hopping from the nest.' Caroline noticed the ink was heavy there, as though the fountain pen had paused – perhaps because her mother had been fearing that, if the war continued much longer, George might indeed be hopping.

'And now, my love, I must tell you something. Agnes, as you know, left us suddenly; Harriet is now parlour maid and doing very well.' Caroline had been astounded at the news and could only put it down to rivalry between Agnes and Mrs Dibble, decreasing the tension between Harriet and the housekeeper, since there had seldom been rapport between any of them. 'Agnes is to have a baby – I am breaking her confidence by telling you this – and, although I begged her to stay, she insisted on going. I was horrified to learn where, but she is still with the Norvilles, I hear, though she is unwed, poor girl. It is clear who the father is. Jamie is in training camp at Shornecliffe, and she told me there is no question of marriage. I tell you this, my darling, in case our Dear Lord takes you by the hand to intervene.'

Caroline lay down the letter. How like mother to make her wishes so plain, so confident she could rely on Caroline as usual. Now she was in the same position as her father had been; questioning whether to persuade an obviously reluctant Jamie Thorn (if she could find him) to wed the mother of his unborn child. How mistaken they had all been in Jamie; she had thought he truly loved Agnes, and surely in this case there could be no doubt of his fatherhood. Back to the old question: was an unhappy marriage better than no marriage at all? Aunt Tilly had said yes, but she considered the wider issues, not the individual bitterness of two people locked for life in loveless intimacy. Quite apart from that, Mother simply did not appreciate how much there was to do *here*. Caroline was surrounded by human problems every day: ruined lives, anguished relatives, writing letters for those who lacked the skill – or the arms – to do so. Each of them had as much claim or more on her time and emotions as Agnes. Or did they? Agnes, who had given her so much help and loyalty, must deserve as much as any of the patients. But how was she to find Jamie?

It took a lot of determined application to the problem; even bullying was necessary to find out which regiment Jamie was in and how she could speak to him. It took time to persuade the camp authorities that she was not an importunate sweetheart of Jamie's but had a personal mission from his home. She wasn't sure that a private room in the Commandant's HQ was the best of places to bring up such a delicate matter, but she could hardly drag Jamie out into a local pub. His face was shot with sudden fear as he recognised her.

'Miss Caroline, what's wrong? Agnes? My mother?'

'They're both well,' she reassured him quickly. 'I'm sorry I alarmed you.' She plunged in. 'You love Agnes, don't you, Jamie?'

His face grew mutinous and her heart sank. So something *was* wrong. When he replied it was guardedly. 'Reckon I do, miss.'

'Then why don't you want to marry her?'

Jamie replied sullenly, 'I do, miss. That is, I did, but she

450

don't love me no more. She's stopped writing. She must have another sweetheart. Not my fault.'

'I'm quite sure she hasn't,' Caroline said vigorously. 'What on earth did you say to her last time you met?'

'Nothing.'

'*Nothing*? When the poor girl's going to have your baby?' Jamie looked as if he were going to faint. He couldn't be putting that on, Caroline reasoned.

'Expecting? *Agnes*?'

'She must have told you when she came here to see you, surely?'

'No, miss.' Jamie tried desperately to assimilate this. 'Perhaps because there's another fellow?' He could hardly get the words out.

Caroline was outraged. 'I always thought you were an honourable lad, Jamie Thorn. How can you even think that of Agnes? You know she'd never do such a thing.'

'She hardly spoke to me when she came,' he said defensively. 'She wouldn't let me kiss her. Nothing. How was I to know she hadn't found someone else now I've gone.'

'Then you don't deserve Agnes if you could think that of her. She's having your baby. Didn't you have an opportunity to talk?'

With some unwillingness Jamie remembered his boasting about a medal. Several times. He'd been full of stupid talk about getting a medal, and all the time she was giving him much more than that: his baby.

'Where did you track him down?' Daniel asked with interest.

'Ahab's a very simple dog. He's like us all; when he realised he was lost in the Forest, he simply sat down and howled. We could hear it even at Friar's Gate, and we rushed in to find him before the Board of Conservators rounded him up as a stray. We arrived at the same time as the Forester. We got off with a stern warning to look after our dog better. I tried to pass it on to Ahab, but I'm not sure he took it in. He was too busy trying to race me back to the Rectory for supper.'

Daniel laughed. 'He's a grand dog. Bring him to see me if you can sneak him past Mother.'

'Better still you come to see him.' Felicia held her breath for his reply, aware she was stepping on to dangerous ground.

'No.'

'It's a very small way from this bedside chair to the invalid chair.'

'*No*!'

'I say yes.'

He glared at her. 'You're not me.'

'I am. I fight with you. I shall fight *in* you.'

He looked at her in tired pity. 'You can't.'

'Not if you don't let me. But you could so easily.'

'Perhaps. But I won't.'

'Why not, Daniel? You know I love you.'

'That's why, Felicia. For once I'm not thinking of me. Don't you think I like seeing your lovely face and hearing your gentle voice by me? But I won't do it. You're eighteen—'

'Don't say, with all my life before me, *please*.'

452

'That's exactly what I am thinking. Mine is a ruined life, Felicia, and no amount of pity and help or even love can change that. I can read, I can think, I can dream, but *I can't walk*; that means I can't travel and nothing, nothing can change that either. And don't tell me God can.'

'I won't. *You* can, though.'

His face was flushed with anger as, throwing off the rug, he pointed to his wasted leg, and then the one that was only half a leg. 'I can change this? Or *this*?'

'*Very* well,' she said steadily, 'we disagree.'

She looked so calm, he thought angrily. How to reach her, make her understand?

'But if you will not let me help you,' she continued, 'my life too is destroyed, for I love you and nothing can change that either.'

'And do you think it would help that love. Felicia,' he seized her hand fiercely, 'to stay with me forever, knowing I can never marry, never lead a normal life?'

'You *can* marry when you are quite recovered.'

'Felicia, don't you understand yet? I never shall. Haven't they told you?'

'Told me what?'

Anger made him blunt. 'I'm paralysed and I'm impotent.' He waited for the look of repulsion or pity he expected, but it didn't come. What did was worse.

'I don't understand.'

He turned his head away, cursing. 'I can't marry you, Felicia. For heaven's sake, you're a sort of nurse. You should understand what that means. I'll never be able to be a husband to you. Never love you as you deserve to be

453

loved. Never give you children. *Now* do you understand?'

A jolt went through her, and as instantly left her again, determined as she was not to show reaction. She took his hands. 'It doesn't *matter,* Daniel. I love you, the adventure of your soul.'

'It matters to me, Felicia.'

When she saw he was choking back emotion, she stood up, to be calm for both of them. Through the window she could see the grey December day of the rest of her life. How was she to say it, how make the sacrifice he was asking of her when everything in her cried out to remain here?

She managed it at last. 'Very well, Daniel. I'll go away. That's what you want, isn't it, so that I don't remind you any more of the past?' If she had hoped he might stop her, that hope was extinguished as he remained silent. 'But if you're casting me out because I'm the old life, then I'll only go on one condition.' He waited. 'I want to see you begin your new life.' He looked up, startled. 'Let me see you in that invalid chair, Daniel.'

But he turned away from her again.

Leave, wonderful leave. Caroline performed a hop, skip and a jump. She had been one of the lucky ones. Forty-eight hours from four o'clock Thursday afternoon, Christmas Eve. *Today!* She would be home in time for supper if she were lucky, and certainly for Midnight Mass, the first Celebration of Christmas Day. She was the happiest girl on earth, and hugged Ellen in commiseration. Ellen was remaining on duty.

'Don't you worry about me, Carrie,' she assured her

valiantly. 'It's a lot more fun here than slaving at Shadwell for me Dad. Two dozen Tommies and a few Froggie Belgians are more than a match for a glass of port in the local back home. That young one from the Naval Reserve, Pip, he fancies giving me a Christmas present or two. I know just what he thinks it's going to be now he's hopping around. He's had his eye on me.'

'Don't let it linger too long.'

Ellen grinned. 'Why not? A short life for a soldier, make it a merry one, say I. More ways of killing the cat for the war effort than knitting two left socks.'

Caroline had thought about this statement for some time last night when sleep came hard through excitement. Were all men the same? Ellen had given her graphic descriptions of just how the soldiers led their merry lives while waiting to go abroad, or even convalescing after wounds, and how standards in her home area had suddenly changed with the advent of war; girls who had kept sweethearts at arm's length rapidly decreased the distance when threatened with their departure. 'It's their bit towards the war effort,' Ellen had explained. At first Caroline thought she was joking, then realised she was not, and then pondered on its morality. For men were men, and if the Tommies felt that way, what of Reggie? All she had given him was a photograph, and it was all he had asked, though she had diffidently offered more. Had there been unspoken hopes in the last passionate kisses he had given her; had she missed them, let him down? And what would her reaction have been? Had he been holding back knowing that to ask might tear her apart even further? If he were to ask now . . . ?

The restlessness in her body at the thought battled with all she had been led to believe in. Did war change *everything*? Certainly this one might, for now it reached out its dirty fingers and touched England itself. Eight days ago the country had been shaken when German warships bombarded the east coast. A girl cleaning a doorstep in Scarborough had been *killed,* and altogether 127 people had died in the attack with over 500 civilians injured, not to mention soldiers and sailors. The newspapers had been full of the appalling events. In Hartlepool a family of eight people had been killed – only the cat had escaped. Yet it was the girl on the doorstep whom Caroline conjured up most vividly; she had her back to approaching death, bending over her daily work. Suppose it had been Harriet or Myrtle at the Rectory, or Rosie Trott at Ashden Manor, peacefully engaged in her daily routine, only to die without warning? This was invasion just as terrible as if the German army had arrived on the beaches of southern England, perhaps it was worse because it was so insidious. In Dover there had been not panic, but an increased tension, an awareness that they too were part of the military front. Here at the harbour, on her last spell of duty, she was waiting to escort a group of patients from the boat into the waiting ambulances for Dover Priory station, for the Canterbury line.

Full of her own thoughts about her return home, she became aware with startling suddenness that there was some sort of commotion going on, people shouting, yelling, excitement – or fear? – communicating itself like a rippling wave through the waiting groups. At last she distinguished the words: 'Take cover, take cover.'

Someone grabbed her by the wrist, pulling her inside the ambulance.

'What happened?' she shouted at her companion.

'Air raid warning. The motor cars have just driven along the Parade with the placards.'

'Another false alarm, like that submarine, I expect.' Caroline rushed to the window just as the clouds lifted and she glimpsed an aeroplane. Simultaneously, it seemed, there was a dull boom. No false alarm, no disappearing submarines this time. There was a moment's pause, then shouting all around. What to do? Take cover? Go to help at the scene of whatever had happened? She yelled at two men sheltering under a nearby van. 'Is there damage? Where is it?'

'Somewhere near the Castle.'

Was their hostel all right, was Caroline's instant fear. Ellen might still be there, for she had been on night duty, and it was only eleven o'clock. She longed to rush over to find out, but their orders were to take cover till an all-clear. Moreover she had a job to do, even if she were uncomfortably aware that a harbour and a railway station would make good targets. Surely the harbour would scare off any more planes? They had felt so confident here, protected by all the new guns and fortifications, yet somehow an aeroplane had managed to drop what must surely have been a bomb right on Dover itself.

When it was evident that no more bombs would fall, they resumed work, and on her arrival back from the Priory station she was relieved to find Ellen waiting for her.

'What's *happened*?' Caroline demanded. 'I've heard everything, from the Castle being in ruins to the entire

Parade being demolished. Thank goodness you're safe.'

'It blew me out of bed.'

'But was anyone killed?'

'Cor blimey, no, it only got one poor devil – he was blown out of a cherry tree, and bruised, poor soul. Serve him right for being up a tree in December.' There spoke the towns woman, Caroline thought to herself, amused, as Ellen continued, 'Guess what the Kaiser managed to blow up, though. I went to have a look at it.'

'The Castle?'

'A field of blooming cabbages. That's grand news for hostel meals. I'll be able to go in without holding me nose.'

'It's very brave of you to come down here.'

'No, it ain't. Our lads went up in the air from Swingate, and a seaplane went from Folkestone to see off Herr Kaiser's gents. Exciting, ain't it?'

'Did they shoot it down?'

'Some hopes. They only had pistols and they probably hold water. That should teach the Kaiser a lesson.'

Mrs Dibble was forced to acknowledge that she missed Agnes's calm competence, odd one though she could be at times. Harriet and she were rubbing along well enough, and the girl had come on wonderfully with promotion, but, apart from the extra work for them all, and they couldn't afford no extra help now, Harriet didn't have Agnes's all-round ability, able to turn a smoky fire to blazing warmth as readily as she could bake an apricot soufflé. Agnes was no mean cook; Harriet was hard put to it to mash a potato. Mrs Dibble pummelled at the basinful of potatoes to reduce them to smooth light consistency and stirred in Harriet's unevenly chopped onion. She vigorously shook salt and pepper into it, inspected it, added more butter, and left it while she attended to the onion and sage stuffing for Mr Goose Number Two. For herself, she liked the mashed potato stuffing, but Mrs Lilley had decreed one of each, so that was that. It would be up with the lark tomorrow morning. Puddings on to boil, stoking up the range fire, which would be kept in all night to ensure no last-minute mishaps, and the oven ready for the geese. *And* the larders would be firmly bolted against that blessed dog. With that job done, it would begin to feel like Christmas. It hadn't seemed natural without all the girls crowding around these last few days, and Mr George, bless him, wasn't much use. But now the geese were stuffed she felt more Christmassy, heartened by the fact that it was up to be a family Christmas after all. Fred would like that, for not only did it upset him when people went away from the Rectory, but it was going to be a family Christmas for the Dibbles too. Lizzie was coming over in the van with the Hartfield carrier, who was going on to his usual Christmas duty of delivering chickens and turkeys cooked in the baker's ovens for those who could not do their own, and picking up Joe's wife and little one on the way.

So Christmas would be Christmas after all in the Rectory, and the devil take the Kaiser, she thought daringly. The Rectory walls were too thick for the Kaiser to barge in and spoil everything – and he could keep out of the cellars, too, where the extra coal was stored, just in case. She burst out into 'Rock of Ages Cleft for Me', then remembered the hour and the season, and hummed 'O Little Town of Bethlehem'. Bethlehem she visualised as another Ashden, where starry skies were ushering wise men and shepherds to St Nicholas.

Upstairs at ease in her old room in the Rectory, Tilly debated on whether or not to attend the Midnight Celebration. She knew very well she had no choice, in fact. Of course she must go, if only to please Laurence. Safe in the familiar surroundings, she did not regret accepting his invitation for Christmas. Simon – Lord Banning – had asked her to stay, but as she knew very well he had invited his sister, with whom she had crossed swords in her suffragette days, Tilly had asserted her independence. Soon she would have left for good, and he must begin growing unaccustomed to her voice and appearance again, she thought with amusement. Their bargain had been 'until she was well again', and now she was. It was time to fly the coop once more. On her last visit to the War Office she had yet again been told to go home and stop bothering them. So much for women's part in the war. *The Times* filled a column a day with helpful ideas; the War Office was too busy to consider the vast source of employment lying virtually idle in the country. She had, like so many others, been forced to go where she could; she had chosen the FANYs, the First Aid Nursing Yeomanry, and after Christmas would be leaving to join them as one of their drivers in Belgium. She considered asking Caroline to come with her; yes, it was not a bad idea. She was being wasted where she was, and only fools now thought this would be a short war. She'd ask her, as soon as the opportunity arose.

Meanwhile she'd give thanks to the Lord for Ashden, changed but unchanged by the war. She had been amused to be cheered when she arrived in the Austin this afternoon, and to find herself somewhat of a heroine. Ashden had obviously swung round to patriotism, though this hadn't, she noticed, stopped the success of the cinema. Pragmatic as ever, Ashden saw no harm in patronising the gift while deriding its donor as Lord Tom Noddy, in their succinct phrase. She crammed on her faithful brown toque, then changed her mind and switched it for the new hat that Lord Banning had gravely presented to her this morning as she left.

'It's fully armoured,' he explained. 'Bulletproof for the Western Front. Your heart has its own armour.'

Surely enough, she could feel a thin layer of tin or some other metal between the blue felt and its bright blue silk lining. Curiously, it was not uncomfortable, and thus fully protected against outside harm she descended the Rectory stairs to join Elizabeth for the Midnight Celebration.

'Are you ready, Felicia?' Phoebe's head shot round the door.

Felicia had been ready for the past ten minutes, and had been sitting in the chair by the window that faced towards the Manor, thinking of her future. 'Yes.' She stood up and put on her hat, while Phoebe fidgeted impatiently. The time had been productive, crystallising Felicia's thoughts into resolution; out of the deep ache of rejection and helplessness, she could now see a path. It was not a path that even a month ago she could have envisaged taking; it was a path that would cause anxiety to her parents and danger and hardship for her. But, unlike the other paths, it led out of the Slough of Despond in whose unfathomable depths she must otherwise surely choke and drown.

'Isn't it wonderful?' Phoebe cried as Felicia joined her.

'Yes,' her sister answered, though they spoke of different things.

'Everyone coming home again,' Phoebe amplified.

And that too. Perhaps most of all, because it was a farewell to the life that had sheltered her. No matter where she was next year, this Christmas they were all together.

George came leaping down the stairs after them, easing a finger round his tall, stiff collar. 'Do we still get mince pies when we get home?' he asked anxiously.

'We *always* do,' Phoebe told him scornfully.

'But there's a war on. You never know, Mrs Dibble might not have been able to get the fruit and stuff.'

'I think you will find,' Felicia assured him gravely, 'that she has managed to do so.'

'Wizard!' George, an angelic look on his face, rushed forward to take his aunt's arm in his.

Isabel had never imagined she would be looking forward so much to returning to the Rectory. She hated The Towers, and realised how big a mistake she had made in moving back here from Hop House rather than going home. Her first rebellion was to insist on Christmas luncheon at the Rectory since Robert was not coming home on leave. There were drawbacks to living under the same roof as her husband's parents. The story of the cinema was dying down, but it was undoubtedly awkward living here while it was doing so. She had been openly laughed at in the post office. She had an uncomfortable relationship with both her mother- and father-in-law, and Patricia was away from home, leaving her to face them alone. What's more, her allowance was negligible and all bills had to be sanctioned and paid by Edith. And lastly, at the back of her mind, was Frank Eliot. He hadn't had the impudence to come near her since their encounter in the hop-fields, but hearing his name spoken of so approvingly in the Swinford-Browne household made her feel uncomfortable. Her second rebellion was to declare she was going to attend Midnight Mass at St Nicholas for religious reasons, and would therefore remain at the Rectory overnight. Edith had not previously noticed signs of devoutness in her daughter-in-law, but had no qualms about losing Isabel temporarily. She was a bad influence on Patricia, who had been greatly changed after Isabel's entry into the family and showed no signs of wishing to return home. As for Robert, Edith could only conclude that Isabel's shortcomings as a wife had driven him to volunteer. For what other reason would he do so? It had taken all William's charm at least to find him a commission in the Public Schools' Battalion which he had then refused. William had not mentioned his name since, and had therefore not been at all pleased to find Isabel was not to be present at Chapel. He needed her there, to emphasise he now had a son at the front, so he had informed Edith.

Halfway down Station Road in the chauffeur-driven Daimler, Isabel passed a girl walking towards the village with the aid of a torch, carrying two bags. With railway trains arriving at odd times, this was not unusual nowadays, and even the scouts had given up challenging them, ever since one got a clip round the ear for his pains.

There was something familiar about this one, though.

'Stop!' Isabel banged on the glass.

Startled, the chauffeur instantly obliged and Isabel was precipitated forward. Without stopping to upbraid him, however, she leaped out of the motor car in her pleasure.

'Caroline! Oh darling, darling Caroline.' She threw her arms round her. 'No one bothered to tell me you were coming home. Oh, I'm *so* glad to see you. Jump in.'

Caroline returned the embrace. Hearing her sister's voice, seeing her again, made her want to cry. Christmas had begun. She wanted to savour every moment of it to the full. 'Let's walk,' she urged. Caroline had looked forward to this solitary slow approach back into Ashden under the Christmas stars, and a Daimler was not the same.

'Oh, well, if you insist. It might be fun. We'll send the bags on alone.'

'Dear Isabel, always so practical.' Caroline laughed between tears of joy.

'What are you crying for?' Isabel asked, surprised.

'Oh, just the unexpected happinesses of life.'

St Nicholas was even fuller than usual this year, the strangers visiting Ashden Manor or relatives in the village more than compensating for the absent faces, some of which would never return. The congregation waited quietly in the dim candlelight, improvised blinds hiding the mediaeval stained glass; so far it had been a more austere Christmas than usual, with fewer celebrations. The Lord of Misrule was doing his best to ruin their lives over in Belgium and Serbia, and all the other countless countries now drawn into this

464

war; he was too busy to preside over Christmas festivities here, in the old traditional manner. Besides, Bill Hubble, who usually did the honours dressed up in his jester's costume, didn't have the heart for it this year, what with Tim gone. Even the carol-singing procession had been abandoned, thanks to DORA, and carols in the church and village institute had been poor substitutes for the yearly gathering on Bankside.

Caroline felt a deep sense of homecoming as she took her place in the pew. She vividly remembered Easter, and for some reason the petty row over the Communion cloth stuck in her mind. Were the Mutters and the Thorns still quarrelling or had war brought about a truce? A new Church year had begun since Easter. What would the rest of it bring? Looking around her, she could see so many people she was fond of, so many she loved – only Reggie was missing. No, she would try to think of happy things this evening, though he was forever in her prayers and dreams.

There was Philip Ryde, looking delighted to see her. Unable to volunteer because of his limp, he was a special constable, her mother told her, so far with precious little to do. Dr Jennings had now gone, but Janie was sitting with her parents. She was working with her father now, having done basic nursing training. They were expecting a temporary replacement doctor in the New Year, Janie's older brother Timothy was away at the front. Dr Cuss was still here, probably because he was the only vet in the village. The traditional Thorn pews were still crowded, as were the Mutters', and even dear Nanny had come this evening, sitting with her old enemy Mrs Dibble. All so dear and familiar, yet all so strange now. She was sitting between Isabel and Mother. Isabel was also looking round, as if she too were renewing acquaintance with the St Nicholas congregation. When she turned back, her cheeks were oddly flushed, and glancing round curiously Caroline saw several pews behind them was that strange hop-farm manager at Swinford-Browne's farm, Mr Eliot. He was staring straight at her, so she turned away quickly, flustered though she couldn't think why. Without thinking, Caroline looked round at the Hunney pew. She had avoided doing so, fearing that what she saw would fill her again with sadness, when she had decided to revel in her good fortune at coming home at all.

No Reggie. Of course not. Had she still been hoping? If so, it had been foolish to do so. No Daniel. No wonder, poor boy. Lady Hunney, carefully not seeing her. Sir John, who bowed his head in acknowledgement, and Eleanor who waved vigorously – another sign of changing times. She would never have dared do that a few months ago.

And now this service was beginning, the organ playing, her father already in the chancel with the servers to bless the incense. Slowly the procession began, headed by Samuel Thorn the verger, Harold Bertram, Timothy Farthing and the other churchwarden, the clerk bearing the cross, the candlebearers, the thurifer with the boat-bearer, her father in his cope and then the choir, and Charles Pickering the curate. While they waited for her father to reappear in his chasuble, Caroline let herself enjoy this special time of Christmas Eve. When she was too young to attend

Midnight Mass, she would lie in bed to listen for the angels' beating wings. It seemed to her the busy old world always paused for just a moment on Christmas evening, as if it could hear some silent music to tell it something important was happening; there was a stillness in which the faint beat of an angel's wings could be heard if one listened hard enough, the angel bringing the Christ Child to earth.

She slept soundly that night, tucked up in her own bed for the first time in nearly three months, feeling safe within the old brick walls. No bombs here; Dover was far away.

When she awoke it was light and she'd missed early service. Never mind, she told herself, she'd go to Evensong and God would pardon her, she hoped. She wondered what had awakened her, for little light crept under the blinds. But – had she imagined it? Surely there was a noise at the window. To her transfixed horror a hand was visible grasping the bottom of the blind and hauling it up, and pushing the sash down with the weight of his body. *His?* Whoever the *his* belonged to, he was climbing in.

Her first instinct was to scream, then she realised how stupid she was. It was George, of course. Trust him to play a prank like this.

'Go away, Father Christmas,' she shouted. 'You're supposed to be in the chimney.'

'Not nearly so handy as this.'

A huge shape half rolled and half fell over the sash even as she registered in her half-awakened state that this was not George's voice.

She flew out of bed, as he hauled himself painfully to his feet, and into his arms. 'Reggie!'

His face was buried in her hair, her breasts through the Viyella nightgown tight against his uniform. His lips were on her cheek, her eyes, her mouth, and then she could say no more, even had she wanted to.

'Remember I said I'd be back down the chimney at Christmas, like Santa Claus?' he half laughed, half cried at last. 'I couldn't quite manage that, this is the best I could do.'

'Oh, don't let me go. Kiss me again.' And a few minutes later: 'And again.' And a long time after that: 'Now I believe it's really you. *You're* Father Christmas.'

'And a deuced painful job it is. No wonder Shakespeare didn't bother to spout poetry about Romeo shinning on to Juliet's balcony.'

'What am I to do with you? Take you down to breakfast? When did you get here? How long are you staying? Do you have to go back?'

'Not down that ivy, I don't.'

'All right. Breakfast it is,' she said, greatly daring, wondering what on earth her father would say.

'It's all right,' he laughed, reading her thoughts. 'I asked your father's permission. He won't disown you.'

'Did you?' It struck her momentarily as odd that, in a life when all his rules were changed, Reggie still abided by convention. Then she rejoiced that he thought so much for her.

'Your mother wasn't too pleased.'

'She probably remembered I had the patched nightgown on. Hardly very beautiful, is it?'

He looked at her, not the nightgown. The starry eyes, the

curly hair, and the shape of the warm body he had just held close to his. He could say nothing: he had thought of her for nearly five months and now he was here he had nothing to say. He wanted to take her again into his arms, run his hands closely over her body, tear off that nightgown and forget all about breakfast, forget about war, forget all about his guilt at the fateful toss of the coin that had pitchforked Daniel into catastrophe and himself into at least temporary safety, forget about everything save himself and Caroline. But he couldn't. Dreams were far behind, and Ashden was here. Life in a trench concentrated the mind wonderfully, usually on mere survival, for he tried not to think of the past or future because it was too painful, but on some nights, when the men were singing ribald songs of women, then unbidden he'd think of her, dream of her, taking her like a French whore, until full of horror at himself he'd force himself to stop such thoughts. Now here in Ashden she seemed as far out of his reach as she had been to him in the trenches. Yet he was back with her, she loved him still, and he loved her. That was all that mattered, wasn't it, for one day soon the war would end and they would be married. Not now, for how could he marry, having seen the truth of war?

'There's a soldier outside the perimeter, Emily.' Miss Charlotte, torn between shock and excitement, peered out of their bedroom window over to the barbed wire.

'He has doubtless come to announce the arrival of the Germans, Charlotte. It is typical of the Kaiser to arrive on Christmas Day. An insult to Our Lord. I shall ring for

Johnson to admit this soldier.' She drew back her head from where it was leaning out next to her sister's.

As the drawbridge dropped, Jamie Thorn nearly jumped out of his skin. With all this barbed wire the place looked like a training camp. What on earth was his Agnes doing here of all places, with these two witches? Were they imprisoning her? He rapped thunderously on the door. He was a soldier of the King now, and wasn't going to take no for an answer – from anybody.

'I've come for Miss Pilbeam.'

'To take her away?' Johnson's face beamed in hope and he cautiously lowered the bayonet.

'Not yet.'

'Then you can't see her; she's cooking the goose.'

'I'll cook yours if you don't let me see her.' Talking tough was the only way to get things done.

Johnson looked him up and down in astonishment and sniffed. 'I know you. You're Jamie Thorn.'

Agnes, attracted from the primitive kitchen into the living room she'd insisted on decorating with garlands made out of old newspapers, stood still.

'Jamie.' Her voice was flat.

'Happy Christmas, Agnes.'

'What are you doing here? You never wrote.'

'Nor did you.' He disregarded the unwarm welcome and looked meaningfully at the swell of her stomach; it didn't show very much, but Agnes wasn't to know that. She flushed, and folded her hands over it.

'What do you want?' She sounded more belligerent than she had intended.

'You, Agnes, that's what. I got a forty-eight-hour pass, one of them special licence things, and a valiant longing to make you my wife.'

She stiffened. 'No, Jamie, I don't know how you heard, but the answer's no.'

'I'm not asking, I'm telling. Now is that or is that not my baby in there?'

'Jamie Thorn!'

'No need to look shocked. If I'm its father, and I know I am, knowing you, Aggie, you're going to be my wife.'

'That I won't.'

'When are they coming?' Miss Charlotte hobbled agitatedly into the living room, her stick clacking imperiously.

'Who?' asked Jamie.

'The Germans, young man.'

Jamie began to laugh.

'It's the invasion, isn't it?' Miss Emily followed her sister. 'That's what you've been sent to tell us.'

Jamie stopped laughing, for he saw his chance. 'It is, ma'am, and I've been sent to protect you ladies,' he told them gravely. 'I'm staying here tonight because they're coming tomorrow morning, see? Though I don't see how I rightly can, you all being unwed ladies. You'd better order Agnes to marry me. I can't stay here without. It wouldn't be proper. I'll make an honest woman of her early in the morning.'

'On your honour, young man?'

'I won't!' Agnes screeched.

'With this licence,' Jamie promised, waving it aloft.

471

'I think you'd better, dear,' Miss Emily said firmly. 'The Germans do terrible things to young girls. Worse than Napoleon. We do need a gentleman to protect us, if the Germans are coming tomorrow. Johnson isn't very strong now, and a soldier would be very useful. Young man, swear on the Bible to marry her, if you please.'

'I won't marry him!' Agnes shouted.

'Swear.' Everyone ignored her.

'I swear to marry Agnes Pilbeam tomorrow morning. Hereto I plight thee my troth, Aggie.' Jamie couldn't hold back his grins now.

'There now, you may kiss the bride, young man.' Miss Emily clapped her hands, a little muddled.

Jamie took Agnes firmly in his arms, as she struggled to break away.

'Aggie Pilbeam, you're a stiff-necked young witch, but I love you.'

Her face changed. 'Do you, Jamie?' She looked quite surprised.

'Wait till tonight – tomorrow night,' he amended hastily.

'Say what you like, there's nothing so nice as a good turkey.' Mrs Dibble was minded to break into 'Now Thank We all our God', but changed her mind. After all, it was Christmas and the Lord had heard enough singing this day, surely. Instead she rested her feet, watching Lizzie and Muriel wash up the Christmas dishes.

'Had the turkey stored away, did you, ma?' Lizzie asked, grinning.

Percy laughed. He'd never have the courage to do that

normally, but today was different. It was Christmas.

Margaret Dibble looked round her family; Fred scoffing an apple, Muriel, Lizzie, a chip off the old block, the little one, as they still called little Freddie, for all he was two now, and even Percy wasn't so bad. 'None of your cheek, young man. If you must know I sold my body to old man Sharpe.'

Fred took no notice, Lizzie and Joe and Percy gaped. Mrs Dibble's lips, long out of practice, slowly curved into a grin. After all, it was Christmas.

Caroline's excitement was still growing. This was the best day ever. The geese had been carried in in procession with traditional pomp, headed by Father, singing the Boar's Head Carol which seemed appropriate, even if it wasn't a boar but two fat geese.

The pudding too had disappeared into satisfied stomachs now, with all the silver threepenny pieces being found. Some years one or two mysteriously went missing, which never failed to alarm Elizabeth. Reggie had taken Christmas luncheon with his parents, but would be back any moment now with Eleanor for the event which more than anything else spelled Christmas at the Rectory: the playing of the game Family Coach, narrated by father. The door had been left on the latch since the two maids had gone home to their families, and the Dibbles' time was now their own. They were all talking so loudly in order to be heard over Phoebe's strumming of 'Alexander's Ragtime Band' on the piano that none of them heard the Hunneys' arrival. Only the opening of the drawing room door drew

Caroline's attention to it, as it was thrown wide with a crash, and the bugle call from Reggie instantly drowned the pianist.

'What is it?' Caroline laughed, hands over her ears.

'*Oh!*' It wasn't her, but Felicia who suddenly dived for the door to welcome the new arrivals, Reggie, Eleanor – and, in his invalid chair, Daniel, a faintly defiant air about him, but grinning nevertheless. He was hardly installed between Eleanor and Felicia before Father entered in his now traditional garb for the narrator, as Santa Claus with a long red cloak, i.e. his old dressing gown with white silk tacked round it, and partly as the Lord of Misrule with a jester's cap on his head (i.e. Grandpa Overton's nightcap with some tin bells sewn on, the latter always used to telling effect).

The Rector surveyed his family, and greeted his guests. 'And now,' he began, ringing the bells with a toss of his head, 'The Family Coach.'

What would it be this year, Caroline wondered, her hand clasped in Reggie's. Last year the Family Coach was going round the zoo, the year before travelling through the Forest. That hat came round and she drew her piece of paper. 'I'm a poor old clergyman,' she cried in delight, hobbling a few paces.

'And I'm the bride's mother.' Reggie studied his. 'I'd rather be the bridegroom.'

Isabel drew the bride's father, Tilly the coachman, Nanny Oates the bride ('Me at my time of life. At last, me dream's come true'). Elizabeth was the luggage, Felicia the doors, George the wheels (his favourite role), Eleanor the bridesmaid.

'And me?' Daniel asked. There was no paper for him.

Caroline held her breath, but her father was equal to it. 'You're the little cocker spaniel Mutt. Instead of leaping up and turning around like the rest of us, you can wave your arms,' her father told him matter-of-factly. 'And no cheating.'

Daniel grimaced. 'I wouldn't dare,' he said with some effort.

'There once was a wicked villain called Tom.' They hissed. 'And a handsome fellow called Marmaduke.' They cheered. 'And a beautiful lass called Appledora.'

'There's no such name,' objected Elizabeth, supremely happy. She had come into her own kingdom again, and now knew she had the strength to rule it.

'There is now. No more interruptions. Tom wanted Appledora for himself, but she and Marmaduke were greatly in love.' They 'aah'd'. 'Tom had prepared a grisly death for Marmaduke, and Appledora had just three hours to seek him out and marry him to put her out of Tom's clutches for ever. So what did she do?'

'Sewed a wedding dress.' 'Found a clergyman.' 'Paid her bills.' 'Wrote a long letter to her best friend,' were some of the offerings.

'No, she gathered together her father—'

Caroline nudged Isabel. 'You're the father.'

'I forgot,' screamed Isabel, leaping up and twisting round.

'We'll call that a dummy run. It's a forfeit next time, though.' Father continued, 'Her mother—'

Caroline dug Reggie in the ribs and he leaped up with a howl.

'Her bridesmaid,' (Eleanor leaped up) 'a poor old clergyman,' (Caroline was already on her feet) 'and a thin little cocker spaniel called Mutt.' Self-consciously, Daniel awkwardly swung his arms. 'The bride,' (Nanny squawked and started to clamber to her feet. 'Sit down like Daniel,' Elizabeth advised. 'All agreed?')

'Pushed them all into the family coach,' Laurence announced loudly as they all leaped up and twisted. 'And the doors slammed.' (Felicia jumped up) 'and the coachman' (Tilly's turn) 'shook the horses' reins,' (Phoebe) 'the luggage shivered,' (Elizabeth) 'and the wheels' (George jumped up) 'turned faster and faster and faster still . . . And up behind the family coach' (everyone) 'came the villain.' Hiss.

And they were off. From now, the story grew faster and faster, with doors falling open, luggage falling out, wheels spinning off, wedding cakes falling on the bride, the coachman drinking too much, and spirited deeds as they made their reckless journey towards Marmaduke and happiness.

Caroline was breathless with the constant jumping up and down and laughing, yet a small part of her was quite detached. This year they were all together. Next year, where would they be? Next month, even? Aunt Tilly was going abroad; she had a strong suspicion that Felicia would be moving away too, since clearly something had happened between her and Daniel. Isabel would be back at The Towers, perhaps with a baby if Robert came home on leave. Phoebe was, she agreed with her mother, growing restless, so was George. Eleanor had whispered her news that she was going to help Martin Cuss since she'd always wanted to be a vet (but she hadn't told her mother!), Patricia had become a policewoman, and Penelope was in Serbia. And Reggie and herself? The thought tore at her, she lost her turn, and promptly had to pay a forfeit (one of Mrs Dibble's prized home-made chocolates). Reggie would be back at war – and herself? Not here for sure, and not, she thought, at Dover much longer. Where then? Reggie had pleaded with her again not to go abroad; he wanted her here, knowing she was safe. She did not remind him that England could not be counted as safe any longer. How to reconcile his wishes with her own? She turned to him suddenly, and he smiled at her, seizing her heart so completely with his love that all was well again.

'And so,' (well over an hour later) 'the old family coach arrived, and the bride leaped out, followed by her mother, her father, bridesmaid, the poor old clergyman, the coachman, the luggage, and the little cocker spaniel Mutt. Exhausted, the wheels fell off and the doors flapped and the old family coach quietly expired.'

'*Until next year*,' was the traditional unison finale, as they all twirled round.

The jester paused, and Laurence looked at his family. 'And so may all the powers of darkness be overcome, as we rattle in our Rectory coach towards the light. O Lord, as we rush headlong forward into the unknown, give us Thy guidance and Thy love.'

And Caroline, feeling Reggie's hand in hers, thought she could know no greater happiness.

Late that night, the magic of the day over, a deep peace

filled Caroline. Tomorrow she would see Reggie again, tomorrow her father had agreed to solemnise Aggie and Jamie's marriage, tomorrow she would lunch with her family before leaving once more. She no longer feared the separation. Today they had been together, and that strength would carry them forward over the threshold of the New Year and whatever it may hold for them all. Like that tree outside, where the blackbird had sung confidently till autumn had come, God would decide when life would return, and the winter be over.

She opened the window to the chill night air, and thought of how she had done so when the tree had been coming into leaf. So much had changed, so much would change. But not her love for Reggie, nor the Rectory, for its family harvest was safely gathered in against the storms.

Acknowledgements

My thanks are due above all to my editor Jane Wood from whom the idea for this book stemmed, and to both her and my agent, Dorothy Lumley of the Dorian Literary Agency, for their continuous encouragement.

In addition, I have prized the help that I have received from Alan Bignell, Ned Binks, The Church of England Record Centre, my uncle Albert Hudson, Martin Kender, Audrey Kimber, Mary Lewis and Sheelagh Taylor. To all of them my deep gratitude.